The Chinese Magus

The Chinese Magus

Richard Yeo

Winchester, UK
Washington, USA

First published by Top Hat Books, 2016
Top Hat Books is an imprint of John Hunt Publishing Ltd., Laurel House, Station Approach,
Alresford, Hants, SO24 9JH, UK
office1@jhpbooks.net
www.johnhuntpublishing.com
www.tophat-books.com

For distributor details and how to order please visit the 'Ordering' section on our website.

ISBN: 978 1 78535 239 3
Library of Congress Control Number: 2015946048

A CIP catalogue record for this book is available from the British Library.

Design: Stuart Davies

Printed in the USA by Edwards Brothers Malloy

With grateful thanks to Louise Martin
for the whimsical map illustrations

To Pat and Alex
sometime fellow Magi

Prologue

Bagrash Kol: the Black Lake, in the Common Language. 'Black' because they say that it does not reflect starlight and, indeed, tonight it lies dark, profound, within the mountains' embrace. The arc of the heavens is lit with stars of a brilliance almost baleful, for this is the high plateau of Xinjiang Province where the atmosphere is thin. To the south marches peak beyond snowy peak.

Closer at hand is the dark bulk of the Governor's palace. No light shows for this is the second hour beyond midnight and the sentinels guard their night vision. No light, that is, save one: a red glow from high up on the western battlements. That is the turret room where the Magus keeps his watch.

Men call it a turret but, in truth, it is an octagonal room built on the palace roof. Starlight reveals a hemispherical cupola for it is, among other things, an observatory. It is here that the Magus works his rituals and seeks truth.

Come now. Light spills from an open shutter. See, within. He sits at a table, peering into a water-filled globe, lit by a red lamp. This is the Gōng (that is 'Lord' in the vernacular) Xiang Li, Mandarin of the Ruby Hat Pin, Governor of Xinjiang Province, arbiter of life and death to a million subjects.

Sigils and symbols adorn his robe. His hat, shaped like a pill box and tasselled, is encrusted with jewels. He is very old, sunken in upon himself, childlike. Yet once he went upon a long journey and it changed him, it changed him.

He nods now, close to sleep, and as he nods he murmurs, "Birth or death; was it birth or death?"

The red lamp flares. The globe pulsates. A picture is forming. It expands to fill the turret room. Look. The world is younger and Xiang Li is ordering matters of state.

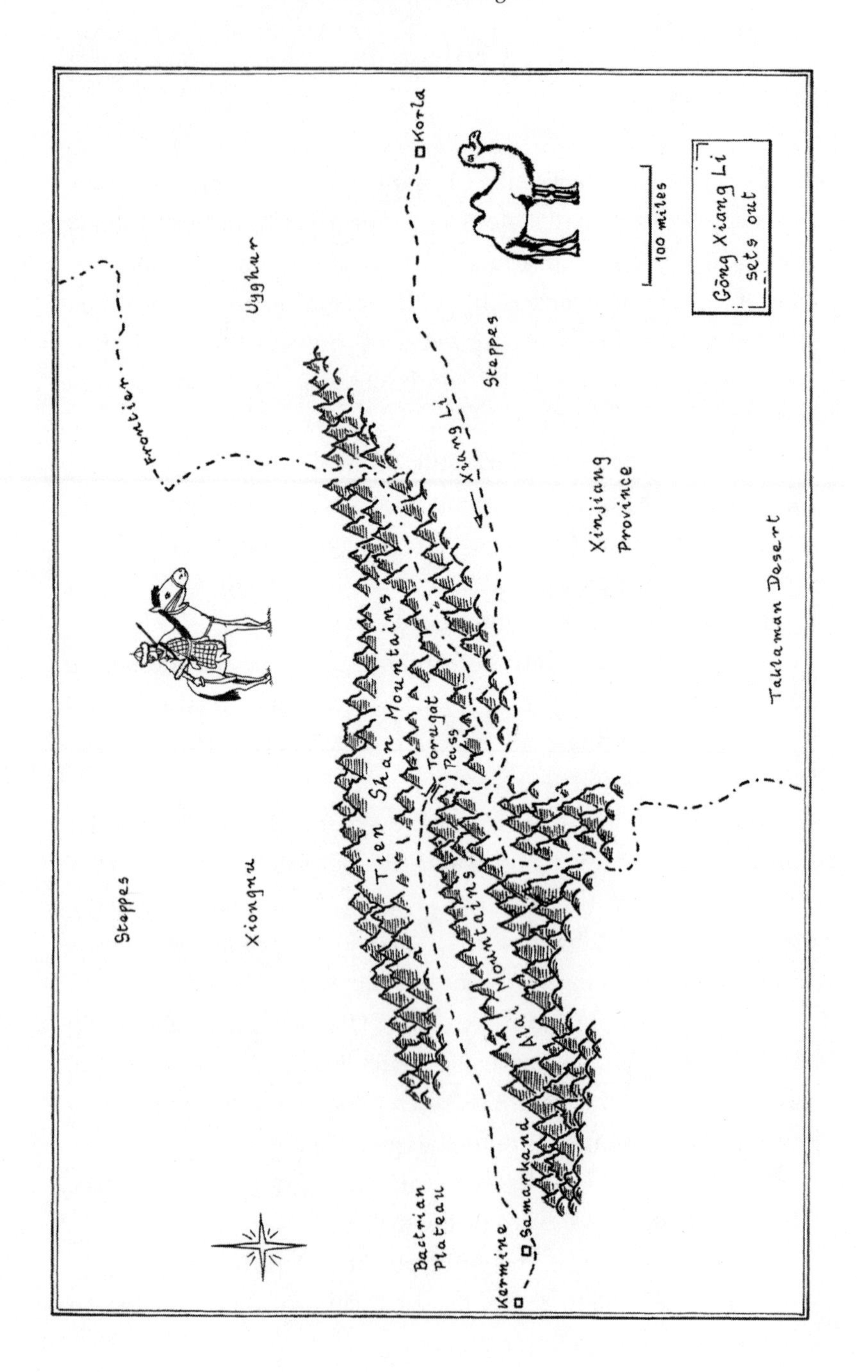
Gōng Xiang Li
sets out
100 miles
Korla
Uyghur
Frontier
Steppes
Xiang Li
Xinjiang
Province
Taklaman Desert
Tien Shan Mountains
Torugat
Pass
Alai Mountains
Xiongnu
Steppes
Bactrian
Plateau
Samarkand
Kermine

Part One

"A cold coming we had of it,
Just the worst time of year
For a journey, and such a journey:"

T S Eliot
The Journey of the Magi

Chapter One

Korla

"Every tenth adult male. All troublemakers to be included. One of every twenty male children under ten. The population to watch. Huts of the executed to be burned."

"Xiang Gōng."

The eunuch bowed his head, making notes.

"Did you hear that?"

Chief Eunuch Ping looked up. The Governor was gazing out of the window.

"Hear what, Gōng?"

Xiang Li turned.

"I thought I heard a child crying."

He shook his head.

"No matter. Who will you send?"

The eunuch consulted a list.

"Major Huan would seem most suited, Gōng," he replied.

Xiang Li considered.

"Make it so, but warn him not to exceed his instructions. There will be no repetition of Sugun. Leave him in no doubt that his head is at risk. Tax collectors to accompany the troops. Arrange the details. Next."

His gaze strayed to the window. Ping recognised the signs. His stylus slid to the bottom of the list.

"Xiang Gōng, the Xiongnu embassy awaits in the audience chamber."

Xiang Li closed his eyes, tapping his chin with one long fingernail.

"Is the porcelain ready?"

"Yes, Gōng. The merchants have arranged the viewing in the Saffron Room."

"The Xiongnu grow presumptuous. They need to understand their place. Have the merchants remove as much porcelain as they can safely hold and carry it through the audience chamber, then back to the Saffron Room, making sure that the embassy see them. Then have it whispered to the Xiongnu – an indiscreet servant would be ideal – that I am viewing porcelain. Later, I will receive them."

Ping bowed, collected his bamboo slips and backed silently out of the room.

Xiang Li turned back to the window.

There were hints of autumn in the air, the first cold breaths from the mountains, and yet here, in the Tarim Basin, summer lingered. Peasants laboured in distant orchards: *apricots,* Li rather thought. He could see three of the windmills, developed to his design, which raised water from the river for irrigation, and he allowed himself a brief glow of satisfaction.

Much done but so much more to do. Out here on the frontier he must be governor, general, diplomat, engineer ... so much to do. If there were unlimited time what might he not achieve.

He sighed. But time was limited.

No, not today. He would not allow his thoughts to stray down that path. He frowned, briefly then relaxed as he thought of the morrow.

In the morning he would set out with his retinue to the palace beside Bagrash Kol, the last visit to the summer palace before autumn slipped into winter. And although the cadre of eunuchs would follow and harry him with affairs of state, there would be time for his scrolls and bamboo slips; time for study and thought.

He raised his eyes to the distant mountains, stark against the sky. A ghost of yearning brushed his mind, not yearning for anything in particular, more an intimation of vast, unfulfilled need.

As the world counted these things, he was at the height of his power, Governor of Xingiang, one of the elite scholar-administrators of the Empire, yet at what a cost. He who wielded life and death in the name of the Emperor knew himself to be a façade; a façade which, if dropped, would shatter like porcelain. That was the cost of power.

The child running the banks of the Tuajiang River, laughing for joy, where was he? The young boy riding his father's wagons, feeding the oxen, rolling down a grassy bank ... all had been subordinated to this. And of course it was right and proper. Legalism and Confucianism combined in a rigid yet subtle framework without which anarchy would rule. What greater purpose could there be in this life than to use one's intellect to maintain the rule of law in this vast land?

The gates of the palace creaked open. An ox cart lumbered into the courtyard. The leather covers were loosed. Xiang Li leant his elbows on the window ledge. *Ah yes. Spears from the new supplier.* It was to be hoped that the ash shafts would be straight and without blemish, unlike those provided by Kao Jianyu. The sutler now hung in an iron cage outside the East Gate. Li made a mental note to ask Eunuch Ping whether he yet lived. Two weeks, he seemed to remember, was the sentence. Well, Kao had had enough fat on him to start with, so perhaps he had survived.

Xiang Li was not an unduly cruel man yet neither was he compassionate. His function was to administer the laws and the instruments of government, neither more nor less. Moral considerations were not part of his remit. The Empire ploughed onwards across all its dusty miles. And yet, and yet...

"Husband."

Xiang Li turned. Mei Su wore her blue silk gown today. A blush touched her cheeks. Her eyes sparkled. Li found himself smiling. Su pleased him.

"Wife," he said, offering his arm.

A last brief dimpling from Su then, masked by polite indifference, Lord and Lady paced from the room.

Chapter Two

To the Summer Palace

Governor Xiang Li held a pouch of aromatic herbs to his nose. When necessary, when, for instance, he found himself directing men and animals in civil engineering works, he would suffer the stench of faeces and sweat, but he would much rather not. In an ideal world he would have journeyed alone on a fleet horse to the summer palace on the Bagrash Kol, but this was not, alas, an ideal world.

As the representative of the Son of Heaven, Ruler of the World, he recognised the need for pomp. Hence this heavy, gilded wagon with its superstructure of rare woods and silk draperies, its unsprung weight lurching over the ruts. Hence also the six oxen plodding, defecating and stalling as they dragged the dead-weight eastwards, stirring up clouds of dust to add to that of the mounted escort, the wagons of the eunuchs and the baggage train.

Xiang Li glanced behind him to the cushioned interior where Mei Su lay amongst her handmaidens, prostrate with travel nausea. Xiang Li could only sympathize. He had never seen the ocean, let alone travelled upon it, yet he imagined that the combination of sickness and depression currently poisoning his being bore similarities with the marine illness about which he had read. The wagon lurched. The odours of animal and man hung around the procession and he held himself erect and prayed for the end of the journey.

His discomfort was compounded by the fact that this was a diversion from the main route and, unlike the trunk road, the surface was ungraded. The diversion had been necessitated by repairs to a bridge, weakened by floods. This was wearisome since the train of animals and wagons would now have to cross the river at a ford with all the concomitant delays.

To his right a group of peasants, harvesting maize, hurried to prostrate themselves as a cavalryman wielding a whip, cantered, shouting, towards them. Peasants prostrated themselves before the Emperor's representative because if they did not, then a small fissure would form in the edifice within which their lives were held.

He thought of the village of Zong-gu, even now the subject of Major Huan's attentions. It was regrettable. They had conspired to keep a quantity of livestock hidden in a remote canyon, safe, they had thought, from the eyes of the provincial tax assessor. It had been foolish and naïve of them. Everyone knew about the government's system of spies. Had they really thought that word would not get out? Now they would be decimated. Li deplored the necessity. Blood, in any quantity, appalled him yet only thus could the system of government be assured in this harsh land.

Taxes paid for the army without which the Xiongnu would pour across the border followed, in turn, by yet more barbaric peoples. Peace, stability and the commerce which provided gold for the Imperial coffers were what he sought and if that involved the early release from a miserable existence of a handful of peasants, then so be it. The position of Governor represented the continuing victory of order over chaos. It was a position to which Xiang Li had been born, not through privilege but through aptitude and intelligence.

At the age of thirteen he had been among sixteen boys from his province, selected to go forward for preliminary examinations. His mother had wept. His father, a respected merchant of Sichuan, had hidden his pride that his son might find a place among the scholar-administrators of the Empire. Xiang Li had done well, writing poetry of captivating beauty, as he had been instructed by his tutor, speaking with authority to the board of three ancients about the intricacies of Confucian philosophy and ancestor worship. He had earned the coral hat pin before the age of fifteen. Today, aged thirty-three, his rounded hat carried the ruby pin of a provincial governor.

Ahead, now, the train began fording the small but rapidly-flowing river. Mounted guards herded groups of peasants into position on drag ropes to assist the first wagon down into the water and up the steep slope at the other side. Much to his relief, Xiang Li's wagon ground to a stop. He beckoned to the captain of his bodyguard.

"I shall dismount," he said.

"At your orders, Xiang Gōng," replied the officer, bowing.

He turned and shouted at the close escort. Four troopers dismounted and approached the governor as he climbed down from the wagon.

Xiang Li closed his eyes, relishing the stability of the earth and the release from nausea. Then he set off for the ford, the four troopers, tall in their bamboo armour and crested helmets, forming around him. Sunlight filtered between the trees which bordered the road. Xiang Li was minded to look at the possibility of building a bridge here to circumvent this tiresome ford. Financially, it would probably not be viable but he put this thought to one side, intent on enjoying the mental exercise of overcoming a natural obstacle.

The slope to the ford was steep and the wagon heavy. Xiang Li noted the straining of the forty or so peasants on the two drag ropes, trying by main strength to manage the dead-weight. Why had someone not thought to put the ropes around the tree trunks as a simple purchase? Xiang Li despaired at the lack of intelligence – or was it imagination – exhibited by others.

As he drew nearer and was able to look down the slope to the water he saw that a smaller group of peasants was trying to control the progress of the wagon by jamming poles under one wheel and then the other. The six oxen stood motionless, water swirling around their legs. The wagon master, balancing on the driving seat, screamed at the peasants, confusing them. Xiang Li strode forward, opening his mouth to take control when the wagon slipped forwards, jerking the drag rope teams off their feet.

Simultaneously a scream arose from near the water's edge. Xiang Li saw that the off-side wheel had pinned one of the peasants. Holding his robes clear of the mud, he made his way down the slope.

"You," he said to the wagon master without raising his voice, "get the weight of the wagon on the drag ropes now!" The wagon master turned and bellowed up the slope.

The peasant under the wheel was thrashing and screaming. Blood stained the water. The other peasants stood around, gazing helplessly. Xiang Li looked down at the injured man, judging the situation.

"You: silence," he said.

The man tried to obey

Xiang Li took in the deformation of the lower trunk, the whiteness of the pelvic bones, the diminishing pump of blood. Hopeless.

He clicked his fingers at one of his escort and pointed downwards at the casualty then turned back up the slope. Abruptly the screams stopped.

To one of the mounted overseers he said, "Block the wheels." The man began shouting. *Why, why must everyone shout?*

As Xiang Li passed the wagon master, without raising his eyes he pointed and said, "Go."

The man went.

Xiang Li approached the left-hand drag rope. He judged the angle to the nearest tree. Without raising his voice he addressed the twenty peasants who strained against the weight.

"When I say, but not before, you will all move slowly sideways, following the direction of my arm."

They looked back with dull eyes.

He raised his arm, paralleling the line of the rope.

"Move."

Slowly he moved his arm away from the team towards the tree. Less than half of the peasants moved. One of the mounted guards, quicker than his fellows, nudged his mare towards the peasants, uncoiling his whip.

"No." Xiang Li's glance was enough. The guard backed off.

Now a few more of the team were moving.

"Move sideways. Follow my arm."

The whole team was now plodding raggedly sideways.

"Stop. Stay there." Li lowered his arm.

"You." He pointed at one of his escort. "Take the end of the rope round the trunk of that tree and bring it back to me. The guard saluted and set off, his bamboo armour creaking.

Fifteen minutes later, both drag ropes were bent round tree trunks, the drag teams repositioned to take advantage of the friction provided and the wagon was being lowered steadily into the stream. Unnoticed, the body of the fallen peasant floated free and, spinning gently, disappeared downstream.

Chapter Three

Mei Su and Te Zhu

It was the day after their arrival. Her husband was currently immersed in the never-ending affairs of the province so Mei Su was free to indulge herself. She knew how jealous Xiang Li was of his time here at the Summer Palace and that, as soon as he could shake free from the Cadre of Eunuchs, he would shut himself away in his turret room where only his body servant was allowed. She might not see him for two days or more and, whilst she loved her husband, she too valued time to herself.

She made her way down passages and staircases towards the south side of the palace. Here she passed through quiet cloisters and out into the peace of an extensive walled garden. Closing her eyes, she raised her face towards the autumn sunlight, reflected and enhanced by the honey-coloured walls. A gentle breeze, scented with late blossom, lifted a wing of her hair. Birdsong, complex and sweet, drifted down from the fruit trees near the further wall. *Bliss*, she thought.

Opening her eyes she looked around. Three gardeners were in sight but not the one whom she sought.

"Mistress?"

Mei Su turned. Te Zhu had approached, as ever, silent and unseen. Mei Su wondered again how she did it. The relationship between Mistress and servant was complex. Indeed Mei Su was unclear about the status of Te Zhu. Servant? Companion? Teacher? Yes, Teacher was probably the nearest and yet Te Zhu was a humble woman who spent her life in this garden where the other gardeners treated her with a kind of reverence, based upon her ability to coax life from the meanest of cuttings. Indeed, it was not unknown for them to bow to Te Zhu, just as Te Zhu was now bowing to her.

"Welcome, Mistress."

The little woman held her hands palm together at her breast and smiled, her slightly crooked teeth only adding to the overall effect of warmth. Mei Su placed her hands together and smiled back. With slight difficulty she managed to refrain from bowing. There was a time and a place for that but not here in the open garden.

"How good to see you, Te Zhu. How are you and how is your garden?"

"As to myself, the damp pain in my fingers causes me increasing discomfort but not as long as the sun shines. As to the garden, come, look."

Te Zhu turned, sweeping her arm across the panorama of trees, shrubs and plants.

"Let me show you the apricots, Mistress. I think you will be pleased."

The two followed a stone path to a point against the wall of the palace where six espaliered apricot plants spread their branches. Mei Su had planted them herself under Te Zhu's tutelage, two seasons ago, and had since learnt the intricacies of pruning the branches and attaching them to the slender bamboo trellises. Now the plants stood nearly three feet tall and here and there golden fruit peeped from beneath the leaves.

Te Zhu leaned forward, plucked one of the fruit and offered it to Mei Su. She took it and bit into it, closing her eyes, savouring the sun-warmed flesh.

"Beautiful," she murmured.

They turned and wandered further along the path, Te Zhu pointing out new plants and features. Gardeners bowed deeply but so engrossed were the two women in their talk that they might as well have been alone. Time stood still.

Eventually they sat on the coping of a small pool where water lilies floated in the gentle tumble of a small fountain. Mei Su trailed her hand in the water, enjoying the coolness and the stroking of plant tendrils. There was silence yet it was companionable. Competent and self-contained, Te Zhu sat in stillness. Mei Su often thought that this was the Teacher's chief characteristic. Even when she was in motion, she seemed surrounded by stillness. It was a comfortable stillness and it encouraged sharing should one be so moved.

"There is, as you see, still no child."

Te Zhu nodded gently, her eyes apparently following the slow passage from bloom to bloom of a Yellow Swallowtail. Continuing silence sought filling.

"It isn't as if we have not tried."

Xiang Li, although a most fastidious man, could be an ardent lover when the mood took him. He wished greatly for an heir. Indeed, he had proved his potency with the young women who made up a part of the household. There were four or five babies and toddlers who could call him father. Yet, although he never discussed it directly, Mei Su knew that he yearned to have a son with her, a child whom he could name as their own.

Not that he would inherit the province. The Land was largely a meritocracy under the Emperor but if Xiang Li acknowledged a son, he would be free to lavish upon him the training and attention which, given a modicum of talent, would ensure his future as a scholar-administrator.

For Mei Su it was a more fundamental urge. She loved her austere, sometimes forbidding, husband from the bottom of her heart. She felt she would give her life for him and that her life would only be complete when she and he had fashioned a child.

Te Zhu ceased nodding and raised her eyes to the roof line of the palace where a skein of rooks moved black against the sky. At length she spoke.

"There are many paths, child, many."

For a few heart beats she was again silent, nodding gently as if acknowledging a truth.

"We have our desires and they pull us this way and that. We

have our needs and mostly we ignore them."

She turned her face towards Mei Su, her eyes grave, and laid a hand upon her sleeve.

"Child, something is coming. I feel it. As yet I understand little but I sense that it will shake all of us to our roots."

She paused. Her eyes became unfocussed.

At length she spoke with accents of wonder, as if testing a thought.

"Xiang Li, the Governor, your husband. Yes."

Her voice trailed into silence. Mei Su felt the little woman's gaze pass right through her to somewhere achingly remote. Then Te Zhu shook her head. She looked puzzled.

"What did I say, child?"

"You said something about my husband."

Te Zhu narrowed her eyes and shook her head again, as if trying to clear it.

"No. It is gone."

Briskly she rose from the coping, brushing down her homespun robe.

"Tonight, Mistress."

She bowed deeply then turned and set off towards the further corner of the garden.

Chapter Four

Dorba Tembay

Dorba Tembay, sometime caravan master and sole survivor of the attempted crossing of the Taklaman Desert, was a questioning soul. He questioned, for instance, how much blood was contained in the human body and why it was so sticky. Its sticky nature was a considerable preoccupation at the moment as it was hampering his grip upon the handle of his scimitar, a long, ugly weapon, with a notched blade. Equally, he questioned what he might have done and why he couldn't remember.

The evidence that he had done something was, if circumstantial, strong. Firstly his massive, hairy body was rank with drying blood and, in the absence of obvious wounds, he did not think it was his own. Secondly, this had happened before and on those occasions, discrete enquiries had disclosed that someone, generally a professional sex worker, had been butchered in harrowing circumstances. Thirdly, and this to his mind was the clincher, at least half a dozen City Guards were in hot pursuit.

As Tembay loped along the dark streets he turned matters over in his mind. His memory went as far as the start of this chase but then met a wall of Crimson. This resonated. He knew a bit about the Crimson. He knew, for instance, that the Voices lived there.

Tembay had few friends. This did not worry him overly. He knew himself to be an intimidating person and was happy enough with the thought. It was what made him a consummate caravan master. Yet more and more, especially since the Taklaman Incident, men were loath to serve under him. So he was much alone and, being only human, felt occasionally lonely. At such times and, it seemed, more frequently these days, he was pleased when the Crimson arose and the Voices spoke to him.

He paused at a corner, breathing heavily, leaning on the stonework and looked back. The clatter of studded boots came closer. He bent and washed the handle of the scimitar in a puddle then stood, calculating. He was reasonably certain that he could damage this group of guards enough to send them packing but this would incite comment among their colleagues who would hound him mercilessly and the city gates would not re-open until dawn.

No, he thought, *best to hide.*

A cat's-paw of movement caused him to whirl.

The guard who had sidled out of an alleyway gave a startled "Ha", expressing surprise and fear but mostly regret. Despite youthful intimations of immortality, he wondered if he had time to run. Discarding the notion as unworthy, he held his sword uncertainly towards the huge, unkempt figure before him.

Tembay leapt. The guard had a confused impression of violence, intense pain and then he was on the cobbles, his life's pulse spilling through his severed arm. When, moments later, the sergeant of guards bent to him, he was able to point in the direction that his killer had run before he died.

* * *

All else being equal, Sergeant Zhao of the City Guards would have been happy to pursue the chase to an inconclusive end and retire to the guardhouse. Had they overtaken the fugitive, they would have killed him, thus saving the expense and complexity of taking him into custody. However, now he had killed young Bao and, although he, Zhao, had no particular brief for the foolish probationer, he had been a City Guard. Killing now became a secondary aim. Capture and lingering torment had become the preferred objective.

Corporal Chau, who had been bending over the corpse with his torch, shouted. He pointed to the ground. Zhao bent also. *Yes.*

The runner had stepped in the spreading pool of Bao's blood and red prints disappeared up the street. He signalled his men to gather round him and whispered his instructions, then they moved off at a walking pace. The road bent to the right and then became a dead end at the sheer city wall. Abutting the wall, on the right, was a house under repair, heaps of ashlars lying about in front of it. The footprints disappeared inside.

Sergeant Zhao signalled to Corporal Chau who took three of the guards ahead where, with much cursing and noise, they began quartering the ground in front of the house. Zhao, meanwhile, accompanied by the massive Private Soong, slipped silently into an alley.

* * *

Tembay crouches in the dark, staring between timbers at the torchlight.

Guards! he thinks sardonically. *Couldn't find their combined arses with a map!*

Two of them are standing at the foot of the city wall, pointing up into the gloom, gesticulating. One is trying to overturn a heavy stone. The other is sitting on a saw horse, examining the sole of his boot.

Tembay shifts his weight and waits. *Soon,* he thinks. *Soon they'll give up.*

But now the one who had been examining his foot gives a cry, stands up, points at something near the threshold of the building. The others gather around. Tembay grasps the handle of his scimitar more firmly. He has no fear. If they come in, they won't be going out again.

And then … nothing…

* * *

"Well done, Soong," said the Sergeant, gazing down at their handiwork. The ashlar lay to one side of its victim, blood and matted hair witness to its impact. Zhao's brother-in-law, the builder, had shown the Sergeant round the site only last week. He had been particularly impressed by the large stones lined up on the scaffolding, ready to be built into the higher courses. Couldn't have lifted one himself, of course, but Soong...

"Bastard's still alive," said Corporal Chau as he wrenched the rope tighter around Tembay's wrists.

And so Tembay made his unconscious journey through the darkened streets to the city jail and if his head collided with the occasional step and when the naked blade of his scimitar became entangled with his legs, well, there was no one to notice but the guardsmen and they were preoccupied by thoughts of the boiling kettle of chickpeas back in the guardroom.

Chapter Five

The Turret Room

Kwon Ru carefully added charcoal to the stove. Then, taking a broom and a dustpan, each with a long handle to save his ancient back, he swept up a small amount of dust. Each stove stood in an alcove with a flue, one in each semi-quarter of the compass. It was a broad, octagonal chamber with a floor of polished cedar. In the centre, stairs rose through a rectangular hole guarded on three sides by carved bannisters. Eight free-standing oil lamps gave a warm background illumination. Four oil-burners scented the air with rare essences from the Southern Provinces.

Kwon Ru looked around him. This was his kingdom when the Master was away and he guarded every detail jealously. But only when the Master was here did the place come to life and Ru then was content. He made his way to the small furnace in the South and, taking a pair of tongs, opened the door to the fire bed. The banked charcoal glowed red through grey. He closed the door and held a hand above the heating plate. Just so. The temperature must be exact for who could say which of his arcane skills the Master would wish to exercise on his arrival?

Sometimes he would heat mutable elements in an alembic as soon as he arrived and, in that case, all that would be needed was a small amount of added fuel and the opening of two vents. Or it could be the stars. Yes, it was a warm, still evening. Ru glanced up at the eight split-bamboos louvres which, through a system of pulleys, could be opened to the night sky. The cords had been renewed and the wheels lubricated by artificers in the last week and Ru himself had checked their operation.

Satisfied that all was ready, the old man took station in the West, facing the staircase, folded his hands and prepared to wait patiently.

* * *

"Veterinary officers to report the extent. All affected animals to be slaughtered. Diseased portions to be excised and the carcases given to the military commissary."

Eunuch Ping made a note and bowed. "Xiang Gōng."

"Is there anything else which cannot wait, Ping?"

There was but, as ever, Ping could read the signs.

"Nothing, Xiang Gōng."

"Then I shall be in the Turret Room. I am not to be disturbed unless a Category One situation arises, is that clear?"

"Xiang Gōng," said Ping, bowing and retiring, counting the fourteen steps which would take him backwards across the threshold. As the guards closed the doors behind him he straightened, turned and set off briskly for a man of his bulk, towards his quarters, there to divide up and delegate the remaining business among his staff. In truth there was no decision beyond the competence of the Cadre of Eunuchs but protocol, not to mention the guarding of backs, required that the most contentious issues be decided by the Governor.

Ping allowed himself a small smile. Not for all the treasures of the Empire would he want the responsibilities of the Gōng. For him life was a delight of machinations mixed with intellectual challenge and he was happy. However, he was under no illusions that it was within the protection of Xiang Li's rule that he was able to exercise his talents to the full. He knew his position to be one of great power where his patronage was recognised by soldiers and merchants, scholars and holy men. With one stroke of his pen and the right word in the ear of the Gōng, he could make or break anyone in the province.

But he had every respect for the Gōng's intellect and political acumen. In another place and another time he would have made a worthy opponent and Ping was by no means sure who would triumph. Yet, to Ping's mind, the Gōng had two faults. The first was his austerity. It would be easy to suppose that he had no feeling, not a scintilla of sentimentality. Ping's spies told him that the wall of reticence was occasionally removed when he was with Mei Su, his wife. But apart from that there was never a sign of emotion and in Ping's opinion, the failure to employ emotions detracted from the ability to rule. For what was the point of the exercise of absolute power unless one could enjoy the prosecution of hate and anger to their logical conclusion.

Ping sighed as he entered his chamber.

The second of the Master's faults, he thought, *was his infernal pursuit of arcane arts.* To Ping, who believed in little beyond what he could touch, such endeavours were a pointless waste of time. *Elixirs to extend life indefinitely? Scrying the future?* Ping could not avoid a click of disgust as he placed the bundle of bamboo slips on his desk. *Pointless rubbish.*

Still, he brightened. As long as the Gōng was immured in his turret, he, Ping, was in total effective charge of Xinjiang province but with none of the responsibility. A smile wreathed his fleshy jowls as he beckoned forward the first of his scribes.

"To Dang Yaochuan. Greeting. Your veterinary officers are to report the extent of the outbreak. All affected animals are to be slaughtered. Diseased portions will be excised and the carcases given to the military commissary."

Yes, he thought. *Power without ultimate responsibility. Now that was an elixir worth having.*

* * *

At the top of the long, spiral staircase, Xiang Li came out onto a landing. Before him was the polished door of sandalwood which led to his inner kingdom. This moment had been a long time coming. Not since high summer had he had the luxury, the peace, of communing with that other Xiang Li. As he reached for the latch, he felt the cares of state ease from his shoulders.

Leaving his slippers at the threshold, he opened the door, passed through and then closed it silently on its cushioned frame. He paused in the semi-darkness, breathing in the faint scent of roses then started up the carpeted steps. As his head rose above floor level, Kwon Ru bowed deeply. "Welcome, Gōng," he said.

Xiang Li gained the last step and looked around him, taking in the orderliness of the room, studying every detail.

"It is well, Kwon Ru," he said. "Tonight I shall study the stars. Bring me food and drink for the night and then you may retire."

"Your will, Gōng."

Ru bowed again then made his slow way down the stairs. Xiang Li knew that Ru would go no further that night than a straw-filled mattress in the room at the bottom of the stairs but it was part of the ritual between lord and servant that he should be given permission to leave the turret. Xiang Li knew full well that Ru had no existence other than tending him and, in truth, he also knew that at some stage in the early morning he would have need of a warm drink and would expect Ru to be near at hand.

Putting such thoughts out of his mind he moved to the work table where Ru had set in order his charts of the star mansions. Soon he was deeply absorbed and hardly noticed when Ru returned with a tray of food and drink. Ru set everything out on a table in the South-West. He turned, smiled benevolently at his master's back then made his silent way back down the stairs.

Xiang Li checked measurements and angles on the charts and compared them with the position of the Moon in the Mansions. *White Tiger of the East,* he thought. *The Mansion of Autumn.* He rather thought that the anomaly which had first caught his attention earlier in the year was somewhere between the Mansions 'Stomach' and 'Hairy Head.' This was born out by a bamboo slip sent to him by Ching Rong, a polymath of note, with whom he corresponded regularly. Having satisfied himself of the exact azimuth and altitude, he made his way to the West and hauled on the cord which governed the bamboo louvre in that quarter.

He noted with satisfaction that the mechanism worked freely. He had devised the system of pulleys himself but was aware that it was Ru who had implemented the regular lubrication without which it would soon cease to operate properly. Such things were balm to Xiang Li's soul. Why would anyone do anything less than perfectly?

With the western night sky exposed, he went to the south easterly corner of the room where a frame carrying a large, glass sphere stood. The frame was mounted upon castors and, again, he was pleased to find that, heavy as it was, he was able to move it with ease to the West. In the last year he had become fascinated by the ability of water globes to magnify and had begun experimenting with them in his searches of the heavens.

Checking his calculations, he positioned the frame as carefully as he could then made a round of the room, extinguishing the oil lamps one by one. When the room was in darkness save for starlight and the faint backwash of a newly-risen crescent moon he pulled a low stool across to the globe frame and settled down to await his night vision. Then, with great care, he began to search that area of the sky suggested by his calculations.

He searched for perhaps half an hour, minutely quartering the sky and occasionally making tiny adjustments to the position of the globe. So engrossed was he that, in fact, he nearly missed it. There was something fleetingly seen from the corner of his eye. He moved his head back, slightly to the left and there it was, a smear of white light which, with the naked eye, would have seemed but an ordinary star.

His eye began to water. Without moving his head he fumbled for a piece of cloth in his pocket and wiped away the tears.

Ah! Yes! Now he could see it more clearly, not circular. More elongated, perhaps like the flame of a candle. *What could it be?* Perhaps one of the wandering stars which occasionally crossed the sky. But he didn't think so. Those were well documented, predictable visitors and, although he would check the almanacs, he was unaware that one was due now. In any case, although he was barely willing to admit it to himself, this tiny flake of light was engendering a feeling of awe within him, quite different from anything he had felt from any of the other astronomical phenomena he had studied.

After another half hour during which he noted the exact co-ordinates of the light and made several attempts at sketches, he realized that he was shivering from the cold night air. Reluctantly, but aware that he had done all he could for the moment, he closed the louvre, re-lit one of the oil lamps then went to huddle over a stove.

What could it be? Ching Rong had not expressed an opinion but, then, he was interested only in the dry calculations involved and rarely committed himself about the nature of actual phenomena. Xiang Li turned over the possibilities in his mind. Opinion among astronomers varied about the cosmos. The main theories claimed it to be either a hemisphere or a sphere – he had an open mind either way – but nearly all agreed that it was a predictable device which ran on laws which, if not yet fully understood, was still orderly and seldom provided surprises.

Rubbing his chin, he looked around the turret room, noting the equipment with which he pursued his work. His eye fell upon the scrying globe, water-filled as the large one with which he viewed the stars yet smaller. Yes ... yes he would start there. A period of scrying would allow him to view the matter on a higher plane. Collecting the globe he carefully set it in place on the desk in the East, selected a tall, red candle and placed it behind the globe. Then, having lit it, he extinguished the remaining oil lamp and settled into the tall padded chair behind his desk. Feet planted evenly on the floor, he closed his eyes and concentrated on his breath. He rested a hand on each thigh, thumbs touching middle fingers with just enough pressure that, had they held between them a grain of rice, it would not have fallen. His pulse slowed with his breathing. He waited a little longer then opened his eyes.

Chapter Six

Goddess Mysteries

The High Priestess of the Goddess returned through the labyrinth, marked out by candles on the sandy floor of the grotto. Mei Su watched through half-closed eyes as the commanding figure in the tall head-dress made her stately way through the flickering lights, robes a-rustle. The warmth and the incense-heavy air made her feel dreamy, her thoughts coming and going.

Now the High Priestess stood before the altar and raised her arms. Mei Su rose to her feet with the others and, as the High Priestess intoned the first note of Joyful Thanks, she joined her voice to the paean, circling slowly counter-sun-wise. After three revolutions, the circle stopped and the women faced the altar. The High Priestess lowered her arms and there was silence. Now she began the Ritual of Closure, her hands following the time-honoured patterns without which the Sacred Time would remain open and unsealed. The Words of Power were spoken. She turned, executed the brief Ritual of Dismissal then left the grotto through the exit to her robing chamber.

One by one, in order of seniority, the other women departed through the larger aperture that led into their communal room. The silence continued for a while longer then one stretched her back with a groan and a crack which could be heard round the chamber. A chuckle arose and after that conversation started and grew. The women removed their robes – simple shifts for the lower degrees, elaborate robes for the Officers – and began to dress in their ordinary clothes.

The heavy curtain over the entrance to the Temple was pushed aside and they were joined by the High Priestess, now clothed once again in her homespun smock yet still carrying authority.

"That was well done," said Te Zhu. "The Goddess is pleased."

She passed among the women patting a shoulder here, administering praise there. To Mei Su, who had held the office of Dark Root in the North, she said, "That was well. You anchored us with depth and strength." She touched Mei Su's arm, smiled sweetly then moved on. Mei Su felt uplifted as she always did when Te Zhu complimented her. She had only recently been chosen to fulfil the Root function in the Temple and she was aware that it had nothing to do with being the Governor's wife.

These were the Women's Mysteries and advancement was strictly by spiritual attainment. It might be years before she was deemed worthy of acting as Golden Branch, much less Fragrant Blossom and she had no illusions that she would ever become High Priestess. Such were born not promoted. No one knew where Te Zhu came from. In truth, as far as any of the women were aware, she pre-dated all of them in the palace. But there was never any doubt that, though she worked as a gardener by day, she was their spiritual leader by night.

Mei Su tried to imagine a young Te Zhu but, smiling, completely failed. She might have come fully-formed from somewhere else. Indeed she might...

Drinks were being poured and dishes of sweetmeats handed round. Te Zhu was suddenly at her shoulder, handing her a cup. "Come, child," she said, gesturing towards the curtain.

Mei Su followed her.

The small chamber was sparsely furnished with a chair, a stool and a low table. Te Zhu took the stool, gesturing Mei Su to the chair. Zhu took a sip from her cup then placed it on the table. Su held hers, turning it round and round in her hands. Zhu looked steadily at Su for some seconds.

"Did you feel ought, child?" she asked.

Su thought for a moment. There was never any point in dissembling with Zhu.

"No, Mother. I felt nothing. I seldom do. You know that. I wonder that you allow me to be Dark Root."

Zhu smiled a smile of surpassing sweetness.

"Nay, child. Your place is there in the North, holding us to the Earth while others fly. Were it not for you they would become giddy and fall. Trust me: you were chosen for qualities which are obvious to all but perhaps you."

The smile faded. Vertical lines between her brows deepened.

"This is not a test. Put that thought from you."

She paused, looked down and ran her fingers along the grain of the table, thinking.

"In the Seeing," she began slowly, "there was something."

She looked up, dark brown eyes vital, transfixing Su.

"Something is coming, child. I said as much in the garden, did I not?"

Su nodded.

"Did I also say that it concerned your husband?"

Again, Su nodded. "You did." She began to feel anxious.

Silence for a beat. Then, again, Zhu spoke, choosing her words.

"I know not what I saw. I have conducted the Seeing for many years and count myself proficient in understanding. This Seeing was of Light Limitless as if the Sun came to Earth. There was the most intense joy but balancing it great pain and fear."

Zhu was quiet again, eyes averted, completely still. When she spoke again her voice held awe.

"Nothing will ever be the same again, Su. Mountains will fall, empires perish. We too will be transformed or … or mayhap perish too."

She looked up, laid a hand on Su's sleeve. Her voice strengthened.

"Xiang Li is being called and it is the most wonderful and the bitterest Calling. Understand this, Su: he could in theory deny the Call but if he did he would be diminished and would know no rest for whatever time was left to him, for that which comes has need of witnesses and of them your husband is to be one."

"We speak here as women of the Mysteries, handmaidens of the Goddess, Guardians of the hearth, the home, the womb but I must charge you, Su, most solemnly, that when the time comes, you must not hold him back, even though it break your heart."

And Te Zhu fell silent and it was as if the echoes of her speaking reverberated, dying away, absorbed by the rock and a tear ran down Mei Su's cheek.

Chapter Seven

Stupor

Chen Tengfei, physician, hurried through the deserted corridors, his night shirt flapping against his skinny shins. Despite the urgency of the summons he had grabbed his elaborate headgear before leaving his chamber and now it listed drunkenly over his left ear. Tengfei knew he must look ludicrous. He could have taken time to remove the hat but there was no time. He was summoned by the Governor's body servant and, anyway, it was unthinkable that he should attend a patient improperly dressed.

He slowed to a walk on the spiral staircase, breathing heavily. *Too old for this kind of thing,* he thought. *Not to say too august.* At the landing, the door to the Gōng's quarters stood ajar. Tengfei paused, trying to get his breath under control and making an ineffectual attempt to straighten his headgear. He was quite sure that the star wasn't straight and two of the pendant moons were inextricably tangled. He sighed. It would have to do.

He set off up the staircase to the turret room, holding himself erect, aiming for an air of competent authority. He had never been here before and, as his head rose above floor level, he looked around with curiosity. He saw a wide room in half darkness. Tables and equipment occupied the shadows. The air was warm and scented. He gained the floor and turned, still unable to see anybody.

"Over here, Doctor."

Tengfei saw the body servant's face peering over a desk. He made his way round the bannisters and saw the dim form of the Gōng stretched out on the floor. Ru had placed a cushion under his head and covered him with a blanket. He knelt beside the fallen lord.

"Light the other lamps, old man. I must be able to see more

clearly."

Ru hurried to obey.

Tengfei placed his cheek close to the Gōng's mouth. *Yes, there was breath.* He placed his fingers on the neck and felt the steady beat of the life force. *Again, good.*

The light increased as Ru lit the lamps. Tengfei settled back on his heels and considered.

"Tell me how you came to find the Gōng like this."

Ru blew out the spill he had been using and came over to the doctor, looking anxious.

"It was nearing dawn so I came from below with a warming drink for the Gōng. I always do this. You see he spends all night working so hard and he doesn't take thought for food or drink. This time I made him a cordial of ginger and..."

"Yes, yes, old man," said the doctor testily. "Just tell me exactly how you found him."

Ru, frightened, took a few moments to collect himself.

"The Gōng had fallen across the desk. He had been scrying. His face was down on the top of the desk and he had one arm, his right one I think, stretched out before him as if he had been reaching for something. When he did not answer me I went to him and eased him down onto the floor. I tried to make him comfortable before I went for help. I hope I have not done wrong, Your Honour."

"No, no, you have done well, old man. Now I shall need a stretcher and four strong men in order to remove the Gōng to his quarters. See to it."

Ru bowed and left.

Tengfei bent to his examination. First he checked for bruising, fractures and dislocations but found nothing. He paid particular attention to the skull, feeling all over for depressions or areas of instability but, again, all was well. So far so good. He rested on his heels again, considering the destructive cycle of the Wu Xing, the Five Elements. The Gōng was in a stupor he believed rather than a full-blown coma. What interaction of the Elements could have caused such a traumatic collapse. Earth dams Water perhaps? Or maybe Fire melts Metal?

Heavy footsteps sounded on the staircase and five martial figures, huge in their armour, erupted into the room, swords in hand. Without orders four of the guardsmen deployed around the room while the fifth marched to where the Gōng lay and placed the tip of his sword below the doctor's chin.

Captain Fong, thought Tengfei: bully, sadist and fool. Captain of the Gōng's bodyguard.

"Stay still!" shouted the Captain.

Whilst not unmoved by the sharp point nicking his skin, Tengfei was not afraid of Fong. The two of them had clashed before and Tengfei was aware of a latent tendency towards drama on the part of the soldier.

"Fong," he said calmly, "I have no intention of moving as long as I am in danger of having my throat cut. Now kindly remove your sword from my neck and allow me to carry on with my examination."

There was a silence as Fong appeared to be mustering a response.

"You hurt Gōng, you die," he shouted, before sheathing his sword and looking around him.

He strode over to a cupboard and wrenched it open. Inside were rows of glass bottles. Fong seized one, opened its stopper and smelt the contents. Then he placed his finger in the bottle, and made to lick it when Ru, who had appeared in the wake of the soldiers, waved his hands feebly.

"No, Captain," he managed in his reedy voice.

Fong froze. With narrowed eyes he glared at the servant. "What you say?"

Ru, aware of his danger, managed to say, "You must not taste it, Captain. It is antimony. It is a poison."

Fong lunged at the servant, grasping him by the collar of his gown.

"What you say, poison!" he barked. "You poison Gōng? Ha!"

Tengfei rose to his feet, dusting off his gown. This had gone on long enough.

"Let the man go, Captain Fong. The Gōng has not been poisoned. He is merely unconscious but otherwise quite well."

Fong jerked his face around to the doctor then back to Ru. He let go of the servant's robe. Ru fell to the floor. Fong marched over to the doctor, still holding the flask.

"And if I were you, I would put that flask down and wash your hand. Antimony is a poison, as the old man said, and even with your rank and eminence, you are not immune to it."

Fong banged the flask down on the desk, spilling much of the powder. He looked at the red dust on his index finger, looked at the doctor, scowled, then without another word, marched off down the staircase.

Chapter Eight

Dream

There is light. It paints his closed eyelids scarlet. His mind is not just clear but needle-sharp. And deeply peaceful. He snuggles into warmth.

There is the rustling as of many feathers and behind that, music, although what instruments might make that arching melody, he does not know. And the perfume … sweeter than the most costly incense yet plangent...

"Child?"

Something brushes the nape of his neck. A feather, perhaps.

"It is time to open your eyes, Xiang Li."

He raises a hand to ward against the light then opens his eyes. At first he can see only dazzle then a figure of green and blue. It seems to be the source of the light, at once emanating and absorbing great lobes of radiance. Swarms of smaller lights weave in and out of the aura around the figure, dipping and wheeling, transmitting evocations of joy.

There is no scale here. Is the figure vast and distant or tiny and close? It was a nightmare which haunted his early childhood dreams. He feels the seeds of panic and closes his eyes tight shut.

Again, the light touch to his neck, soothing, calming.

"Peace, child. You may open your eyes again."

The figure, clear-edged now, seen through a curtain of falling water, is clothed in a robe of green and blue iridescence, the colours shifting and running. It sits on a high-backed chair, in its hand a lily, at its brow a diadem shaped as a slim, silver crescent surmounted by a star. Small, winged figures pass to and fro, tiny points of light which cluster above the head of the seated figure.

Xiang Li feels the force of its gaze upon him, inspecting him. The figure smiles and it is a piercing smile.

"Xiang Li, you have travelled far but now I ask you, will you travel further? Will you answer the Call of Love? Will you be a Witness? For know that nothing is done by compulsion but only by the exercise of free will."

Xiang Li is lost, humbled. He bows his head.

"Mighty One, I know not what you ask of me so how may I answer?"

The figure smiles and nods its head. It is silent for a moment, considering.

"Xiang Li, despite your power and wealth, you find life empty, do you not?"

Xiang Li thinks of his eventual death and the futility of his greatest designs. He starts to cry. Unable to speak, he nods his head. The admission is an enormous relief.

Again, there is the touch, as of a feather upon his neck and his tears cease.

He stands with bowed head, empty.

And across the emptiness swoops an eagle, wings extended. He hears the fluting of the wind in its flight feathers, feels the lift and heft of unseen air currents. He feels the play of the bird's muscles and the fell focus of its intent.

And now he stands on the edge of a rice paddy, the grain in full, vivid life, ready for the harvest. Wind moves through the green stalks in waves. It lifts his hair and he feels glad. It is morning and everything is possible.

And now he moves within Mei Su at the moment of supreme felicity. He is lost, subsumed in time and space, made one with all…

"You are not alone, little one. Nor need you die. You are in life. A role has been reserved for you. If you will take it, the way may be bitter but you will live for ever and know that everything you do, henceforth, is charged with purpose."

Xiang Li feels his heart beating, hears the plash of falling water and knows that he wishes, more than he can express, to live outside the narrow constraints that life has shown him. He raises his head.

"I will do what you ask, Mighty One, although I do not understand what it is and I will need help."

The figure of green and blue nods once and smiles again then stands. And in standing becomes infinite. And there is a mighty crashing of waves and a thunder of boulders. The tiny winged ones flare and whirl in vortex, stretching to the heights and the depths.

And in the chaos, Xiang Li is Called.

Chapter Nine

Mei Su

"But, husband, why must you go?"

Xiang Li lay propped by pillows in his bed. Mei Su was at a loss. In all the years of their marriage she had become used to the exigencies of her husband's career, with his absences on official business, but this was evidently different. Xiang Li had merely told her that he was going 'to the West' for an uncertain period of time on an unspecified quest.

"Su…"Xiang Li struggled to order his thoughts.

"Su, something happened last night."

Mei Su quite understood this. She had sat by his bed, worrying, holding his hand until he had awoken apparently none the worse yet, to her eyes, subtly changed. Doctor Chen had told her that he could find nothing physically wrong with the Governor, spoke merely of an imbalance of the Elements; possibly, in his learned opinion, Fire melts Metal.

Yet Mei Su felt sure that if such an imbalance had been coming she would have known about it. Xiang Li was an austere man commanded by the Confucian Code. He was, above all, stable, dependable, even though her intuition told her that deep within him lay an unassuaged melancholy.

"Tell me then, husband, what was it that happened?"

Su longed to understand. She felt herself to be on the edge of something vast and powerful, something which lay beyond her comprehension.

"I … I do not remember properly, Su. There was light and water and someone who spoke. They spoke so clearly but not as you and I speak. I remember great sadness and calmness and … and..."

"And..." prompted Mei Su.

"And I cannot explain it but I think I was offered a task, a calling, which will make sense of my life."

"But, husband," said Mei Su, "what more sense need you make of your life? You are Governor, you have power and a beautiful home … and I love you."

Xiang Li turned his face to the pillow. How could he tell her of the great yearning that had always beset his soul, of his fear of the darkness that must claim even the most powerful. It was not seemly to utter these things, especially to one's wife. And yet he was aware at a deep level that he had been offered something besides which these fears scattered like dreams upon wakening. How could he explain?

He turned and took Mei Su's hand. He brought it to his lips and kissed it, surprised to discover that he was crying. He had never before cried in his adult life. He held his wife's tiny hand against his cheek.

"Su," he said. "Wife, I … I have been Called."

Then he burst into sobs and Mei Su was suddenly very afraid.

* * *

She found Te Zhu in the garden, robe kilted above her knees, watering seedlings from a clay ewer. The old woman turned and studied her mistress, taking in the red eyes and the strands of hair escaped from her head dress. She put down the ewer, brushed down her robe and sat on a stone parapet, patting the place beside her.

"Sit, Mistress," she said.

Mei Su sat. She took a square of silk from her sleeve and dabbed at her eyes then scrunched it tightly in her fist.

Te Zhu gazed at the shrubs in the central bed, noting the fall of a red azalea petal, savouring the gentle hint of autumn on the breeze. *She would miss all this*, she thought. Yet she had enjoyed it for many years more than her due and a life of service was just that. And beyond all, to her mild surprise, she recognised the desire for an adventure, something that would tax her once more. She smiled ruefully, wondering what an adventure would be like in the company of the damp pain.

"Te Zhu, he is going."

Te Zhu turned and regarded her Mistress. She placed an arm around Mei Su's shoulder and held her as she cried. And when the crying ceased she said, "Tell me, child," even though she already knew. And Mei Su poured out the events of last night and this morning and her love for her husband and her fears and her wish that none of this was happening.

"For it is as you foresaw, isn't it, Te Zhu? You said that something was coming and that it involved the Governor but Te Zhu, you didn't say that he would go away and I love him and how am I to live without him…?" and she cried as if her heart would break as, indeed, it would.

Te Zhu rocked her again for many minutes and towards the end Mei Su buried her face in the warmth of Zhu's robe and Zhu held her until the crying was finished. Then, gently, she raised Su's face and, taking the square of silk from her fist, wiped her Mistress's eyes and cheeks as a mother would a child. Then she tucked back the errant strands of hair and smoothed down her dress.

"Walk with me," she said and helped Mei Su to her feet. And the two women walked the paved paths of that peaceful place amidst the scents and the birdsong. Small white clouds passed above the garden on a brisk southerly breeze and sunlight warmed the stones. After some minutes they came to the edge of the lily pond and looked out across the pads to where a lone heron stood.

"Mistress," said Te Zhu, "this," she gestured with her arm to the trees and shrubs, the walls and the birds, "is all there is and yet it is also not. I know that you understand this with part of your mind. What we see is but a backdrop, a piece of painted scenery, if you will. Sometimes we catch it flapping in a breeze from somewhere distant and know that it is just scenery. But mostly we get on with our daily lives and assume that what we see and touch is the only reality. We should not blame ourselves for this. For our simple minds to live in the full glare of universal reality would be unbearable."

She turned to Mei Su and placed her hands on her shoulders. She looked deeply into the other's eyes.

"You may say either that we are very blessed or cursed because the scenery has become very thin in our time and in this place, so thin that your husband has seen what is beyond. He is aware of that greater reality now and it is awful for him because there is no turning back. He could try to pick up the threads of his daily life but it would be entirely without savour. He would never know contentment again."

Zhu took Su's hand and, turning, walked again. Two Plain Tiger butterflies danced ahead of them.

"But what can I do, Te Zhu?" asked Su.

"Child, if you love him, as I know you do, you can only support him now. He has been Called and he must follow his destiny even though it break your heart."

"But Te Zhu..!"

"Hush, child. All is not lost for I shall accompany him."

Mei Su looked at the old woman with big eyes.

"Have you been Called too, Zhu?"

Te Zhu laughed.

"Nay, Child. Such things do not happen to humble gardeners but I fancy a journey. There is much of the world that I have not yet seen and if this journey is to be organised by men, well, they will have need of some genuine wisdom."

Te Zhu turned and smiled at Mei Su and, despite herself, Su laughed.

Chapter Ten

Preparations

"And I will need a caravan master, one who knows the ways in winter."

Eunuch Ping made no attempt to note down the Gōng's requirements.

"But Xiang Gōng..." Ping found himself gobbling. *This was wrong!*

He tried again.

"Xiang Gōng, what of the taxes from Kumul? What of the Mongolian ambassador? The Imperial Bureau were most insistent..."

"Then see to it, Ping. You are eminently equipped to do so. See to it but I shall not be here. I have a journey to make. And that is all."

Ping knew that he was very close to a dangerous limit but for once in his life he was faced with something outside the bounds of the pragmatic cynicism within which he operated. Worse, he now realized that the Gōng had moved beyond those bounds too. He struggled for a more placatory tone.

"Xiang Gōng, might it not be as well to consult the seers, perhaps sacrifice a bull. The times may not be propitious and, indeed, from a practical standpoint, this is no time of the year to be making a journey."

He paused. The Gōng slowly raised his stylus and pointed it at him.

In a low but emphatic voice Xiang Li said, "If I need entrails to read then I imagine that your belly contains more than enough for the purpose. Now, unless you wish to see proof of their abundance, follow my instructions to the letter … and Ping..."

Ping, finding no words, nodded…

"...do not ever, *ever* attempt to thwart me again. Is that understood?"

Ping nodded again and, bowing, backed from the room.

* * *

Back in his own room, Ping threw down his bamboo slips and slumped behind his desk, staring at the wall, his mind in a state of shock.

This could not be happening. This *must* not be allowed to happen. The whole edifice which Ping had spent years constructing depended upon the existence of a state-appointed governor. Such a governor did not need to be competent – although that was a matter of debate among senior eunuchs. Ping inclined to the view that a competent governor made his job easier and more interesting. It required a greater degree of subtlety to manage a competent governor but the rewards were much greater.

Ping had no desire for the power which accrued to a Mandarin. Indeed, he would never be considered for such a position. His future had been decided when, at the age of nine, he had come to the notice of a minor official in Shaanxi Province who, impressed by his precocious intelligence, had put him forward for the regional civil service examination. Ping had excelled at every test. When the results were collated, he came top of his cohort but, it was noted with regret, that his family was low-caste, too low to countenance him joining the ranks of proto-Mandarins.

Instead, and without consultation, Ping's testicles and penis were removed with a maximum of efficiency and a minimum of sentiment by a government surgeon. Ping hadn't understood, then, what had happened, just knew that it hurt – how it hurt! Three other boys died but Ping abided and, although in time the physical wound healed, he retained a deep, bitter cynicism which grew with the years. Many administrations had found Ping's keen intellect indispensable. A few suspected the cynicism and wondered whether Ping worked a hidden agenda of his own but, since he never allowed it to affect his work, he was never challenged.

Ping bowed his head into his hands and thought of the networks of patronage and intrigue which were his life's work. These, though no-one but he knew it, would be his monument, his revenge upon the world. With no children to follow him, these would be his bid for immortality. And now they were threatened because the Gōng had apparently gone mad. Put simply, without the unifying power of the Provincial Governor, Xinjiang would fall apart and all that he had worked for would be swept away.

It must not be allowed to happen. But how to stop it?

Ping's mind began to work. He reached for a bamboo slip and stylus. After a few minutes a slow smile creased his lips. Yes, it might be done. He began writing. Yes, it might. And if this worked, it could prove to be yet another adornment to his career.

Zhiqiang Qiu would be part of the solution.

"Weng Liang," he called.

Weng, Ping's confidential secretary, entered the office. He was a small, rat-like man with a bald head and protruding teeth. Ping had selected him from the Cadre, noting in him an aptitude for intrigue. Ping would use him until the burden of shared secrets became too dangerous and then Weng would disappear. Weng understood this and had no intention of disappearing but that was a matter for the future and one of subtle judgement. For now, alert subservience was Weng's protection.

"Gōng," he said, bowing. Ping handed him a sealed message.

"See that this is delivered by confidential courier to the Imperial Inspector for the North-west Quadrant in ArAqmi. Then I shall have need of a caravan master, one who, shall we say, is not too … fastidious. Use your contacts."

Weng bowed and left.

Later he returned.

"Gōng," he said. "On the matter of the caravan master, such a one was taken by the City Watch two days ago. But..." He hesitated.

"Yes, Weng," said Ping. He knew that Weng would try for more information and had no intention of indulging him.

"The person in question may be, perhaps, a little too ... *extreme* for your purposes. Gōng, if I could know a little more of your requirements then maybe..."

"Where is he?"

"Gōng, he is in the city jail but he is reported to be violent and possessed of evil spirits."

"Then arrange for me to interview him," said Ping.

"Gōng," said Weng, bowing and quietly cursing.

* * *

Redemption was not an aim of the judicial system of the Empire, a fact emphasised by the interior of the city jail. Its subterranean walls ran with moisture and the smell was appalling. Nor was there any daylight. None of these things bothered Ping unduly. He had been here before. Ping had inspected every corner of Korla at one time or another in his quest for information. One never knew when it would come in useful.

"He's dangerous, Gōng," said the turnkey who lumbered ahead of the eunuch, carrying a pitch-pine torch. "If I was you, I'd speak to him through the bars."

"Well, I am not you, thank the stars. He is chained, is he not?"

The turnkey nodded.

"He's chained but you don't want ter get too close."

He scratched his head.

"He spits, he does – an'..." he muttered darkly, "...other fings."

They continued until the turnkey stopped outside a studded door. He selected a key and opened it with a screech of rusty hinges. He made to enter but Ping held up his hand.

"I will see him alone."

The turnkey protested but Ping took the torch and waved him away.

"Lock me in then remove yourself to the end of the corridor and await my call."

Ping ducked, entered the cell and held up the torch. The door slammed, the key turned and the turnkey's footsteps retreated.

To say that Ping was physically brave would be untrue but he held an abiding belief in his own invulnerability because of who he was and the power that he wielded. He did, however, feel a prickling at the nape of his neck as he straightened up and took in the scene before him.

The cell was small – perhaps eight feet by ten. Secured from the back wall by chains, so that its feet barely touched the floor, was a massive, naked figure, perhaps seven feet tall and with a girth to match; all of it, except for the face, covered with matted, black hair. It appeared to be unconscious, hanging limply by its wrists. By the light of the torch, Ping noted a long, crusted wound to one leg. Faeces lay heaped. The stench was overpowering yet Ping stood his ground and raised the torch.

The face was a hideous mess. One eye had disappeared in a livid black swelling. Mucus and blood hung in cords from a badly-broken nose while the interior of the slack mouth showed more gaps than teeth. It was evident that he had been badly beaten.

Placing a rag over his mouth, Ping took a breath and spoke.

"Dorba Tembay."

There was no response. He tried again, more loudly.

"Dorba Tembay."

The one remaining eye opened. It was yellow shot with blood and it fixed Ping with a look of such malevolence that he almost recoiled. For a moment he considered giving up but an innate stubbornness took hold.

"Tembay," he said, "you are going to die but before you do you will continue to suffer."

He paused to let his words sink in. Tembay ran his tongue along broken lips, gathered what saliva remained in his mouth and spat. The spittle ran down his beard.

Ping continued.

"You will die in agony, Tembay, unless..."

With infinite care Tembay took his weight upon his toes and straightened. He looked down at the bald, fat man in front of him with utter disdain then, quick as lightning, lunged forward to the extent of his chains, roaring. Ping fell backwards, hitting the wall behind him and falling on his bottom in the filth of the floor. The torch fell from his hand and guttered. He grabbed it before it could go out and raised it threateningly towards Tembay.

Footsteps sounded in the corridor.

"Are you alright, Gōng?"

"Yes ... yes. All is well. Go away. I will call you when I need you."

Ping floundered in the filthy straw until he could prop one shoulder against the wall and haul his prodigious weight upwards. Tembay, meanwhile, flung his head back and laughed, a mad, antic sound that beat on the walls of the cell.

"I made you shit yourself, Smooth-between-the-Legs. Admit it," he roared.

Ping looked at the wrecked man with undiluted venom. *When you have served your purpose, Filth,* he thought, *you are going to die most horribly for that.*

And yet the calculating part of his mind marvelled. Hanging a captive by his wrists was not just a mindless cruelty. Agony built up in the muscles from the hanging. The only relief was to take the weight on the toes but few could manage that for more than minutes and then the weight went back on the wrists and so on. Most could not last a full day under such conditions. Many would die. Yet this man had hung here for nearly three days. Not only did he still have control of his strength but his spirit had not been cowed.

Yes, Ping thought, *this was his man – as long as he could be controlled.*

He thrust the torch forward.

"Listen, Uyghur pig," he hissed. "I care not when or how you die but I have need of a caravan master. There are such in plenty within an hour's walk of this place so consider carefully the question I now ask you for it will not be repeated."

Tembay hung from his chains, the basilisk stare of his one eye focussed on the eunuch.

"*If* I have you released from here into my custody, will you obey me in everything, knowing that the least disobedience or attempt to escape will result in your death – a death which I will devise?"

For a long moment Tembay hung, considering. Whatever this castrated rabbit had in mind couldn't be worse than his present predicament. Trust didn't come into it. It would be something criminal and dangerous, without a doubt. Probably fatal. And yet, let him once get free from this jail and all bets were off. He hawked and spat.

"Yes, Smooth-between-the-Legs," he said. "I'll do what you want."

Then the humour of the situation hit him and he laughed and laughed. He couldn't have said what was so funny. Ping had the greatest difficulty in being heard by the guard.

* * *

"Prisoner to be thoroughly washed..." Ping sneezed. He hoped that he hadn't caught anything. Already he'd had to have his clothes burnt "...and given medical attention. He will be required in one week at which time prisoner to be handed to Captain Fong of the Household Guard. Memo to Fong: the prisoner is powerful, dangerous and possibly insane."

Weng scribbled away. Something was definitely going on, but what?

"A large escort and every precaution will be necessary. I will interview the prisoner in private – Fong to make arrangements for the interview, taking measures for my privacy and safety. See to it, Weng."

Yes, indeed, thought Weng.

"As you order, Gōng," said Weng.

* * *

Dorba Tembay and Captain Fong did not like each other. A cynic might say that they each saw themselves in the other and did not like what they saw. Fong, for one, knew himself to be a military genius who ruled his regiment with discipline tempered with fairness. Tembay, for his part, knew himself to be an indomitable freedom fighter and inspired leader of caravans. (In his view the Great Taklaman Disaster only added to his laurels).

Neither would have recognised the description 'mindless, blood-thirsty maniac.'

On this day Tembay, clean by the standards of the city jail, and somewhat recovered from his beatings, was being escorted in chains to the summer palace by six guardsmen and Fong. The latter, having been given no particular instructions on how the prisoner was to be treated, had just jabbed Tembay in the kidneys with his scabbard. Tembay had turned on Fong who had struck him in the mouth with the scabbard before the Uyghur was dragged to the ground by the guardsmen.

Tembay looked up at Fong.

"I rip your fucking balls off, soldier-boy," he spat.

Fong smiled lazily and kicked Tembay hard in the stomach.

"Get him on his feet," he shouted. Fong generally shouted.

The combined efforts of the guardsmen put Tembay upright. The Uyghur fought for breath. Crimson hovered around the edges of his mind. In the Crimson his Voices debated: *a violent, suicidal rage? That would be a fine release. But it would be a waste. So much more to do and wouldn't it be better to bide and watch and squash the little man when his guard was down? Yes, that was the way*. The Crimson receded and with it the Voices.

"Move the scum along!"

Tembay straightened and moved forward towards his destiny.

* * *

"You will proceed across the northern Tarim Basin and then take the mountain route through the Tien Shan towards Samarkhand."

Ping and Dorba Tembay sat in a small internal courtyard, the Uyghur chained to ring bolts in the wall, the eunuch at a distance of some feet in a cushioned chair.

Tembay spat. "The mountain route? At this time of year? Madness! Forty days to the passes and by then there will be snow. No. The Trade Road is the only way this time of year and even that will be difficult."

Ping selected a sugared date from the box on the table beside him. He considered it for a moment before popping it in his mouth. He chewed reflectively.

"Are your wounds healing satisfactorily?" he asked.

"Well enough."

Ping spat out the pit into a silk square.

"I imagine it would be exquisitely painful were they to be re-opened..."

Tembay glowered.

"...which is what will happen if you do not obey my orders. Is that understood?"

The last words were uttered in a low hiss.

"You are sending me to my death, then," said the Uyghur. "Why you not just say so?"

Ping closed his eyes and smiled.

"If you will just listen, pig, then you will understand that far from sending you to your death I am proposing to make you a rich man."

He selected another date. Tembay continued to glower, unconvinced.

"You will conduct the caravan conveying the Gōng to the mountain passes where you will find it impossible to proceed because of the snow. You will inform the Gōng of this and you will then conduct him back to the provincial capital. I will pay you handsomely for your services and you will be a free man. Is that clear enough for you?"

Clear enough, thought Tembay. *I return, you kill me. Yes, very clear.* His hairy face broke into a gap-toothed grin. It was not a pleasant sight.

"Well, Gōng, why you not say? Tembay your man, even unto death."

* * *

The following week was a busy one for Ping. A courier arrived from ArAqmi acknowledging his message and saying that Zhiqiang Qiu, the Imperial Inspector for the North-east Quadrant, was making his way to Korla with despatch.

Dorba Tembay, in the loose custody of household guards, toured the caravansaries and markets within a thirty mile radius, recruiting camel pullers and beasts. He explained to Ping that caravans were made up of strings of camels, numbering up to eighteen, each in the charge of a puller. Each puller, he said, should be allowed space to carry half a load of trade goods as an incentive. He also said that they would have to promise high wages to persuade them to take the mountain route in winter. (He made no mention of necessary incentives to sign on with the Taklaman Cannibal).

Ping had considered for a moment.

"No," he said. "Offer them whatever is usual but tell them that you are taking the Trade Road. Then, when you turn up into the mountains let it be known that you are doing so on the orders of the Gōng."

He said no more. Tembay puzzled for some seconds then a slow smile lit his features.

"So they will mutiny and go no further. Yes!"

He looked at the eunuch with growing respect.

"Exactly," said Ping. "Kill sufficient of them to make it impossible to go on but not enough to endanger the Gōng. Then return."

Ping also spent time putting together an extravagant train of servants to accompany the caravan. His aim was to make the venture so unwieldy that, with luck, it would collapse under its own weight. In several cases he used the opportunity to wreak revenge upon people he knew to be unsuited to the rigours of travel. He said nothing of this to Tembay considering, quite accurately, that the Uyghur would object.

In an effort to bring the Governor to his senses, Ping brought forward lists of matters requiring urgent decisions, many of them contrived in his fertile mind. This was, however, an unsuccessful ploy. The Gōng remained distracted, merely waving his hand and saying, "See to it, Ping."

Equally unsuccessful was his attempt to enlist Chen Tengfei, the Court Physician, in an attempt to diagnose a temporary imbalance in the Governor's powers of reasoning. Chen opined that there was nothing wrong with the Gōng's mind.

"Perhaps Earth damming Water but nothing a good purgative will not resolve," was his verdict.

Chen knew Ping of old and his plotting. He had no intention

of being drawn into a court intrigue on a matter evidently freighted with so much tension. Ping made a mental note to include Chen's name in the list of caravan followers.

As a last gambit, he sought audience with Mei Su.

"Tàitai," he began, once he had settled his bulk in Mei Su's quarters. "Madam, no-one has a greater respect than I for the mental processes of your husband, the Gōng, but I confess, and I say this with the greatest humility and in the strictest confidence, that I am deeply disturbed by his desire to make a journey at this time of year and one, may I say, which appears to have no rational aim."

He paused to see how Mei Su would receive his words. Ping, who was a subtle student of human beings, detected the tell-tale signs of stress in her face and posture but Mei Su merely nodded.

"Tàitai," he paused as if gathering his thoughts, "the Gōng stands high in the esteem of the Emperor and it is for this reason that he is entrusted with the governance of this most sensitive of provinces, here where the Uyghur hordes threaten, where the rule of law must be scrupulously administered."

He paused again, assuming his most unctuous face, radiating an air of the faithful servant placed in a most invidious position.

"I must tell you, Tàitai, and ask you to treat this information with utmost discretion, that I am informed through certain channels that even now, Gōng Zhiqiang Qiu, Imperial Inspector for the North-east Quadrant, is hastening to Korla. There can be little doubt as to the purpose of his visitation although how he has been informed so quickly of your husband's intent is a mystery, but if the Governor leaves his post at this most inauspicious moment, who can say where it may lead?"

He let the question hang in the air, certain that the Tàitai would fill the space with visions of disgrace, demotion, obscurity. There was still no reply although Mei Su shifted uneasily. However, after some seconds she cleared her throat and in a small voice asked, "What do you suggest, Eunuch Ping?"

Ping placed his hands, palms together before his lips to indicate wise thought and exquisitely fine judgement. He cast his eyes downwards and sighed.

"Tàitai, I have tried my poor best, with the greatest tact, having regard to my lowly position, to place before the Gōng the counter-arguments to his intended course of action but, alas, to no avail."

He raised his eyes and, with a hesitance becoming of one so humble, said, "Perhaps, Madam, if you were to say something to your husband..."

Mei Su looked away towards the window. Unconsciously she wrung her hands where they lay in her lap. What the Eunuch said made perfect sense and it chimed with her own fears. She felt she would do anything to keep Xiang Li by her side and the future, as laid before her by Ping, frightened her. The consequences of failure and shame in The Land were not to be countenanced.

And yet … and yet Te Zhu … Zhu seemed to be clear that the importance of what Li was about to do superseded any mundane concerns. At one level, at the level of the Mysteries, Su understood this. And yet her involvement in the Mysteries were relatively recent while her immersion in the Confucian Ideal – the cultivation of pragmatic virtue and the maintenance of ethics – was lifelong.

Su felt deep misery. Why had this come to her? How was she to make a balanced judgement of where her duty lay? Surely there could be no convergence between the rational and the numinous?

True, she had not promised Te Zhu anything. She turned back to the eunuch.

"Ping, I cannot give you an answer now. I must think."

Ping levered himself to his feet and bowed.

"Very good, Tàitai," he said. *Yes, very good.* If he was not mistaken the fish was hooked.

Chapter Eleven

Starting

A hint of dawn-light behind the autumn crests to the east. In the darkness, bustle. A caravan makes ready in the square above the lake, outside the palace gates. There is a hubbub of harness, animal noises and human shouts as well as a great stink of faeces.

"Xiang Gōng, this is madness."

Zhiqiang Qiu is careful to stand out of reach of the camel's teeth. Xiang Li, swathed in sheepskin, sits uneasily in the high saddle. It is evident to him that Ping has sent for Zhiqiang, hoping that he will dissuade him.

"It is late in the year, Li. The passes may easily be choked with snow within days if winter comes early."

The camel moans and shakes its head, scattering large drops of saliva. Zhiqiang steps back. He takes a square of silk from his sleeve and dabs at his robe, distracted. Xiang Li makes no effort to curb the camel. Indeed, he is quite unsure how to control it, a fact which serves only to increase his anxiety.

"And consider this: who will govern Xinjiang while you are...?"

"While I am what?"

Zhiqiang sighs. The growing light illuminates the red button in his hat.

"I merely note that the borders are insecure. The Xiongnu are known to be massing. Without a firm hand..."

Xiang Li leans forward, clinging to the cantle of the saddle.

"Qiu, I have left explicit orders covering that and every other eventuality. Ping and the Cadre of Eunuchs are quite capable of governing in my absence and the army knows what is required of it. I will not discuss this."

Zhiqiang pauses for a moment then moves close in to the camel's flank.

Peering up towards the Governor he whispers, "But why, Li? Why must you go? And if you must, why not the Trade Road? Why the mountains?"

Exasperated, Xiang Li looks to the west, as if seeking an answer. For a while he is silent then, with an impatient gesture of his hand he says, "I do not have an explanation which you would accept, Qiu, except to say that I must move swiftly. There is no time to lose, no time to take the Trade Road. You must trust me. I do not expect to be away for long," a lie, he knows, "and the Xiongnu will not move in winter. There is to be no more discussion."

Zhiqiang bows and steps back. A murmur, almost a low moan, passes through the ranks of courtiers and eunuchs.

Xiang Li looks towards the head of the line of beasts. The light is growing. Surely they must depart soon. He makes to hail the Caravan Master but as he opens his mouth, a figure darts out of the palace gate and throws itself to the ground in front of the camel. The beast baulks, raising its head in alarm, almost unseating him. A handler grasps the bridle and stills the animal.

Xiang Li looks down. It is Mei Su. Her hair is unbound. She is weeping.

"Su," he says, uncertainly. "Su, you must get up."

She raises a tear-blotched face to him; reaches out a hand. She tries to speak but can only hiccup.

Xiang Li is mortified by this unseemliness. He looks to the crowd of courtiers for help but none catches his eye.

"Su!" he hisses.

"Husband!" she finally manages. "Xiang Gōng, what is to become of me? How will I live…?"

Her voice ends in a quaver and renewed sobs.

Xiang Li looks at his wife of thirteen years, the shy, young girl, given to him to cement an alliance, who, against all expectations, had brought him love. For a moment his heart fails him. He reaches out a hand towards her. But then he closes his eyes and the Call is there, patient yet utterly demanding. His hand falls.

"You will be well looked after, wife. I will not be gone very long. I will return … if Fate allows."

His voice falls away into silence, her betrayal complete.

His last gambit failed, Ping gestures to two junior eunuchs who come forward and gently raise Mei Su. They half carry her back towards the gate. Her sobs gradually recede.

From the shadows, Dorba Tembay, the Caravan Master, a surly, simian figure clad in dirty hides, a great scimitar at his side, surveys the scene and spits. He considers the Gōng a fool. *The Tian Shan passes at this time of year? Stupidity!* But he cares not for snow or cold. He is being well-paid for this madness and, if push comes to shove, he will abandon the fool who has hired him. Impatiently now he lifts the horn of an auroch to his lips and blows a great blast. The camels moan and bellow.

Xiang Li grips the cantle of his saddle, almost unseated again, as his mount lurches into motion. The Journey has begun.

Chapter Twelve

The Plains

For the first four days, as the caravan passed through the cultivated uplands of western Xinjiang and up onto the open grasslands, progress was uneventful but slow. There were many reasons for the lack of speed. One was the sheer size of the train: two hundred and twenty-nine animals including camels, horses and yaks as well as goats and oxen to be slaughtered for their meat. Harnesses chaffed and snapped. Loads slipped and had to be readjusted. The overall discipline of the group had yet to be established.

Then there were the one hundred and eighty-four human travellers. Of these, seventy-six were handlers and herders under the command of Dorba Tembay, the Caravan Master, professionals, to a greater or lesser extent, of the caravan routes of Central Asia. These looked with quiet contempt upon the other one hundred and eight, the Governor's retinue.

Apart from a detachment of twelve mounted guardsmen of the Governor's bodyguard under the command of Captain Fong, there were cooks and handmaidens, scribes and stewards. There were three laundresses and a seamstress, all under the control of a bewildered chamberlain appointed by Eunuch Ping in revenge for some suspected slight. Te Zhu travelled with the retinue although on her own terms. She was, at her own whim, in charge of the disposal of night soil, a fact which caused her not a little amusement.

Few of the retinue had ever travelled further than the seventeen miles separating the provincial capital from the summer palace. Whilst Governor Xiang and the more senior members of his retinue rode camels, and an ox cart was provided for the handmaidens and concubines, most of the rest were expected to walk. No training had been given and by the end of the first day, many were limping.

Indeed, the less fit might well have been left behind already were it not for the frequent stops demanded by the requirements of the Governor. Three meals had to be prepared each day and whilst the first and last took place at the overnight camps, the midday meal required a stop of at least two hours while the ovens were unloaded and assembled and the dining tent erected.

The first time this happened, Dorba Tembay came storming from the head of the column, demanding to know what was going on. He was met by Captain Fong. The two faced each other. There was shouting. A whip was raised and a sword drawn. The chamberlain hurried, with raised hands, to remonstrate at the noise only to be barged by a horse and knocked to the ground. Although, in the end, no blows were exchanged, a message was passed. There would be a reckoning.

And if Tembay came to a seething acceptance of the meal stops, he was reduced to silent incandescence to discover that the caravan was required to stop every time the Governor felt a call of nature. For no Mandarin of Xiang Li's seniority could, apparently, be expected to piss down the side of his camel like ordinary mortals. No; the train had to stop while a blue and white striped silk privy was unloaded, erected and then packed up again, thus ensuring that no mortal eye should see the Governor exercising his bladder or bowels.

Tembay stood at a distance on a low mound as the privy was unloaded for the third time that day. His red-veined eyes took in the idling beasts and humans. Black bile filled his heart. He spat and turned his back. Far to the west rose the outliers of the mountains. *Yes,* he thought. *Yes, you pampered child. We'll see how you like* them. He chuckled. It was not a pleasant noise. Then he hitched the sling from which hung the great scimitar, and started back to the head of the train.

It was on the fifth day that the first members of the retinue began to fall by the wayside. One of the cooks, a vastly overweight man, had a heart attack and died. His body was hastily bundled into a shallow grave and the caravan proceeded. However it was soon clear that first one and then more were straggling hopelessly. Xiang Li, his mind elsewhere, failed to notice until the midday meal when the chamberlain, hands aflutter, apologised for the absence of one of the stewards who served his meals.

Xiang Li sent for Tembay and ordered him to round up the stragglers. Tembay stood his ground.

"On plains we wait for nobody. They can't keep up, they stay. They useless mouths. They endanger caravan."

He hawked and made to spit, then, looking at the silken carpet, swallowed, calculating that the time was not yet ripe for open insolence.

Xiang Li, seated in an ornate chair and surrounded by cushions, observed the large, hairy Uyghur. The man stank. In his mind he balanced his need for the man's skills against the danger of allowing his orders to be questioned. Of course he could call in Captain Fong and enforce his will but that would endanger the cohesion of the whole.

"You are suggesting that we let members of my household die?" he temporised.

Tembay relaxed his stance slightly.

"Gōng, this rule of caravans. Every journey, weak people die early. We carry useless mouths we run out of food. In mountains there no more food. Every man pull his weight or die. You thank me when we get to mountains."

Xiang Li tapped his teeth with one long finger nail.

"I hear what you say, Tembay, but humour me this once. We are yet many miles from the mountains and I would see what happens if we keep our stragglers with us. That is all."

Blood suffused the Uyghur's face. Then, abruptly, he turned away and strode from the tent, shouting orders.

Xiang Li sighed. It might prove to be a meaningless gesture but he wasn't ready to give up civilized principles just yet and there were, among the stragglers, some valuable servants.

* * *

And a meaningless gesture it proved to be. The half dozen stragglers soon became a dozen and then a score; old people, totally unsuited to the rigours of travel on foot, others with hidden weaknesses of heart, lung and joint. Xiang's suggestion that some of the camels carrying fodder be unloaded to allow them to ride, died, buried by logic. Every bit of the fodder would be needed once they started to traverse the mountains.

At Xiang Li's orders, some of the most infirm were squeezed into the cart holding the handmaidens and concubines, much to the disgust of the latter. It did little to help, however, and when, on the seventh day, one of the wheels of the cart split and it was discovered that no-one had thought to bring a spare, six young women joined the walking throng.

On the evening of the seventh day, Xiang Li held a meeting with Dorba Tembay, Captain Fong and the chamberlain. It was less than satisfactory. Fong and Tembay refused to address each other directly while the chamberlain, looking faint and drawn, seemed overborne by the problems surrounding them. Thus it was Xiang Li who made the decision to leave behind the sick and weak with what food they could spare as well as some shelters. The chamberlain roused himself sufficiently to beg to be left with the group and that was agreed.

And so, on the eighth day, the peaks of the far mountains outlined against a bruised and threatening sky, the caravan set out, leaving behind fifty-two exhausted travellers, huddled together against the cold, northerly wind and a bleak future.

That day the rain came and with it wind, fitful at first and then blowing with a raw intensity from the north-west. Xiang huddled miserably on the camel's back, the insides of his thighs rubbed raw against the saddle. He contemplated walking as a refuge from pain but conceded that he had neither the strength nor appropriate footwear. And so, hour by hour, he suffered, holding the two sides of a canvas sheet tight at his neck and feeling the steady dribble of cold water which eventually penetrated his inner clothes and lay dank against his flesh.

To compound his misery, when he alighted to ease his bladder, the silk privy blew away. Captain Fong despatched two guardsmen after it and, although they caught up with it, they rode over it twice ripping it beyond recognition. Peels of rough laughter rang out from the head of the column where Tembay stood and were taken up along the line by the herdsmen and handlers.

Te Zhu, taking pity on her master, put down the soil bucket, spread her cloak to hide him and turned her back so that he should have privacy. When he had finished, the Governor gave the woman a slight nod before remounting his camel. It is a fact that from that time he urinated down the hairy flank of his mount and no-one, least of all the camel, seemed to care.

Rain and wind continued that day and the evening camp was a sad affair. Despite many attempts, no fire could be lit so the evening meal consisted of strips of smoked meat and cold porridge. Xiang Li forced himself to eat. His pavilion flapped and shook in the wind. Water dripped from every seam. As he made his way to his damp couch, he was unaware that half his household were outside holding down the silken walls under the unrelenting glare of Captain Fong and the bodyguard.

It availed them little for, sometime after midnight the storm ramped up to an ear-splitting crescendo and the pavilion was gone. The screams of his two remaining concubines awoke Xiang from a haggard sleep to black, wet chaos. The two girls clung to him but then Captain Fong was there with three guardsmen. The concubines were cuffed away and Xiang Li lifted and carried off into the dark. Before Xiang Li could collect his wits, Fong was tearing aside the door curtain of a yurt.

"Out!" he was screaming. "Make way for the Governor!"

More guardsmen joined them and a stream of herdsmen and handlers, cursing and swearing, were evicted into the streaming darkness.

"Bring!" shouted Fong and Xiang Li was carried into the interior to be placed none too gently on a heap of smelly blankets. Fong, his duty done, strode out into the night with his guardsmen. The door curtain fell into place and Xiang Li was left in darkness. He lay stiff as a board, eyes wide, trying to make sense of the last minutes.

The wind screamed around the yurt yet, although it deformed here and there, it stood firm, witness to millennia of development in the inhospitable environment of the high steppes. Neither did it appear to leak. Xiang Li thanked his stars for these small mercies yet, so overpowering was the smell of unwashed humanity and bodily emissions that he would have left its shelter had he anywhere else to go.

So he stayed, confused and miserable, staring into the darkness.

Then he felt the tickle of tiny feet moving over his hand. He flapped the hand and the tickle vanished only to be replaced by another on his forearm, under the sleeve of his robe. He slapped at it, then realized that he was itching in a dozen places. He clambered to his feet, slapping at himself and stamping his feet. Wildly he staggered to where he thought the door curtain hung, colliding with the skin wall of the yurt. With no thought but to escape he lunged left and then right, finally finding the curtain and tearing at it, breaking several finger nails in the process.

Then he was outside, enveloped in a chaos of wind and water. In a moment he was drenched. Even here, on the lee-side of the yurt, the wind buffeted him and tore at his silk robe. He stared out into unremitting darkness and had never in his life felt so powerless and alone. Arbiter of life and death to one million subjects, ruler over mountain and steppe, wearer of the ruby hat-pin he turned and stumbled back into the foetid depths of the yurt.

Chapter Thirteen

Aftermath

The day brought with it a clear sky and gentle breezes. Te Zhu entered the yurt with a cup of steaming herbal infusion. Xiang Li raised himself, groggily, from his nest of infestation and grasped the cup, thankful for its warmth. When he had drunk he stood and stumbled to the doorway, eager to empty his bladder.

It was only when he had drawn aside the curtain and witnessed the devastation outside, that he remembered where he was. It was a defining moment for Xiang Li. A man of refinement, he nevertheless represented the virtues of courage and leadership nurtured in the meritocracy of The Land. He drew himself to his full height, strode out onto the sodden grass and, in full view of thirty camel pullers, urinated.

On completion he looked around him. Perhaps a dozen yurts stood in an irregular formation, covering an acre or so of the endless grassland. Scattered around were the remains of his pavilion and other tents that had not withstood the storm. Pullers were busy feeding the camels and other draught animals. Far out on the plains and on the flanks of the increasingly tall foothills to the north, handlers on horseback were herding knots of animals back towards the camp.

It slowly dawned on Xiang Li that, whilst he could see many camel pullers and animal handlers, there was no sign of his own retinue. Where, for instance, was the cook tent?

"Those that are left are helping to repair the storm damage and recover the animals."

Xiang started. How long had the night-soil woman been standing at his shoulder? She too gazed out at the scene. He would not normally have spoken to her but he supposed that things were not as they should be.

"You say 'those that are left'? Why? Did we lose people in the night?"

For answer Te Zhu gestured to the right where a pathetic row of bodies lay, covered by a mud-stained silk carpet.

"Three stewards, two guards, a cook and two handmaidens," she said. "I do not know how many are left. Captain Fong and twelve guards, certainly. Two are guarding the treasury yonder." She pointed towards a yurt.

Xiang Li shook his head in disbelief. He had been safe in a yurt, worrying about fleas, while his people had been dying. Admittedly, this was the way of the world but, for the first time in many years, he felt shame.

"Gōng!" The towering figure of Dorba Tembay approached. He appeared untouched by events, elemental in his solidity.

"So you yet live, Gōng."

Xiang Li was aware of the insolence implicit in the remark but chose to ignore it.

"What is the state of the caravan, Tembay?" he asked.

Tembay chuckled.

"Some weaklings dead, much useless baggage blown to the four winds. It will take a while to recover the stock animals but there is no serious damage. We stay here today, though. Put things right. Give animals rest."

Hoof beats sounded in the near distance and Captain Fong with four guards arrived in a flurry of dust. Fong threw himself from the saddle and marched to confront Tembay.

"You threaten the Gōng, pig?"

He drew his sword. Three of the guards joined him, surrounding the Caravan Master. Tembay stood unmoved, eye to eye with Fong. The air between them crackled.

"Captain Fong," said Xiang Li. "He was not threatening me. We were merely conversing."

Fong continued to lock eyes with Tembay for a moment, then turned.

"As captain of your bodyguard, Gōng, I must insist that you not be alone with this man. He is Uyghur pig. He is bad man, not to be trusted."

With terrible speed, Tembay pounced. Wrapping one arm around Fong's throat, he plucked the sword from the Captain's hand and flung it away. Then he tightened his grip. Fong began clawing at the Uyghur's arm.

"Tembay!" shouted Xiang Li, just as the three guards threw themselves upon the Caravan Master. He swatted away the first with ease but the others climbed upon his back, punching at his head with their mailed fists. Tembay stood firm. Fong began gurgling as his face suffused with blood.

"Stop it!" Xiang Li shouted, to no effect. The first guard regained his feet and, drawing his sword, rushed back to the fight. Pullers and stockmen converged, drawn by the noise and the hope of blood. The fourth guard loosed the horses he had been holding and he too drew his sword. The horses bolted into the gathering crowd, increasing the chaos.

"Cease."

Xiang Li heard the word within his head. It was spoken quietly and should have been drowned by the tumult.

"Cease."

It came again and Xiang Li felt himself relax. Tembay loosed his grip on Fong who fell to the ground, gasping. The two guards on his back loosed their grip and stood looking around them vacantly before wandering off. The other two guards stopped, the nearest in the middle of a scything attack which should have taken off Tembay's head. Both looked at their swords with bemusement before sheathing them. One shrugged his shoulders and set off after his mates. The other went to recover the horses.

Tembay turned to Xiang Li. "And we mend harness, balance loads. Perhaps, with your permission, some of your retinue could help with the animals, Gōng."

"Yes," said Xiang Li. "Yes, of course. Do what you think best."

Tembay saluted and lumbered off. Te Zhu cradled Captain Fong's head in her lap while she stroked his throat and crooned quietly. Fong's breathing had returned to normal as had his colour. He opened his eyes.

"Thank you, Mistress," he said then stood up, bowed, and went in search of his sword. Recovering it from the ground he sheathed it and strolled away. The crowd dispersed and Xiang Li was left alone with Te Zhu. Te Zhu rose to her feet, her hands upon the small of her back, groaning.

"I don't recommend growing old, Gōng," she remarked.

"No," said Xiang Li, then, "Woman, did you hear a voice just then?"

The old lady looked surprised.

"Me? A voice?" She shook her head. "What manner of voice, Gōng?"

"One that said, that said … one..."

Te Zhu smiled. She shook her head.

"Nay, there was no voice, Gōng."

Then she bowed and went about her business.

"No," murmured Xiang Li to her retreating back, "there was no voice."

Chapter Fourteen

Treachery

"The horses you may keep."

Tembay takes a deep draught of kumis, fermented mare's milk, and wipes a massive hand across his mouth. The interior of the yurt is dark and smoky, rank with the stench of unwashed bodies. Firelight plays upon swarthy features and hooked noses, a scene as old as time. Tembay belches. He is at home here. He is among Uyghurs, men of the steppes, cousins to whom the Taklaman Butcher is a hero.

A dish is offered. He scoops up the ewe's placenta, throws back his head and swallows it whole.

"Hazoor!" shouts the gathering.

The chief, a small, wizened man, unremarkable except for his ruthless cruelty, speaks.

"It will be as you say, Butcher. At the dried river. The two stunted thorn trees. We shall do our part, do you yours."

He thrusts out a hand. Tembay grasps it. They look deep into each other's eyes. A portal to evil opens.

* * *

The weather remained fair the following day and the caravan made an early start. Tembay watched as the animals passed, casting a critical eye over the loads and harness. He yawned. It had been a long night but worth it. Today he would be rid of Fong. His Voices had told him what to do. They had led him to the camp of the Uyghur brigands, hidden in a fold of the foothills.

The Voices had had nothing to say about the earlier events of yesterday. He was still puzzled why he hadn't killed Fong when he had the chance. He could remember the Crimson descending and the baying of the Voices. But then, nothing… When he came to himself, he had been berating a puller for allowing a gall to develop under a girth. Nevertheless, his blind hate of the captain of the bodyguard was undiminished.

Nor was it only blind hate. In as much as Tembay had a plan, it went no further than a refusal to return to the provincial capital, whatever happened. He felt that the situation could be turned more to his advantage but was not yet sure how. However, of one thing he was sure: as the only force capable of interfering with events, Fong and his guards would have to go.

He watched as the Gōng rode past on his camel, bodyguards to either side. The soft little fool rode well now, one leg cocked across the camel's back, his body giving with the motion. *Much good may it do him,* thought Tembay. If the man survived he doubted he would ever wish to ride a camel again. He chuckled.

Xiang Li was looking ahead. Distances were deceptive in the clear air but the plain seemed to be coming to an end. The foothills to his right were becoming taller and steeper with ribbons of scree running down their flanks. The track had begun to angle gently up into them. Ahead and slightly to the right the mountains formed a blue wall which imperceptibly grew taller as they approached.

Xiang's thoughts were interrupted by shouts from the head of the column.

He looked up. At first he couldn't make sense of the scene. A dozen horsemen were circling close in front of the caravan. There was shouting and, as he watched, a camel fell to its knees.

Captain Fong cantered up.

"Brigands!" he shouted.

He snapped orders to his guardsmen. Four of them peeled away and joined him as he set off at a full gallop. As the guards drew near, the circling horsemen broke off their attack and made towards the slopes. Fong followed them for a short distance but it was clear that his heavy mounts were no match for fleet-footed ponies. They turned and cantered back to the caravan.

Tembay stood conspicuously to one side of the beasts, hands on hips, smiling broadly.

"Too much for you were they, soldier boy?" he shouted. Then he spat.

Fong raged but rode on to make his report to the Governor. Tembay watched him go and laughed his deep, wicked laugh.

* * *

As the morning wore on, the brigands returned, each time to a different part of the caravan. Fong became more incensed at his inability to close with the enemy. He began drawing off more and more of his guardsmen as each attack developed until only the two guarding the Gōng and another pair with the camel carrying the treasury were left in place. On each occasion the result was the same although it was clear that the guardsmen were getting closer to their prey.

In a further attack, towards the height of the morning, one of the ponies stumbled as the brigands made their escape and its rider was thrown to the ground. He was on his feet in a moment, running. Another rider turned to his aid, scooping him across his saddle, just seconds before Fong could close with him. Even carrying two men, the pony outpaced the guards' heavy horses and so Fong returned, angrier than ever. Once again he came upon Tembay who smiled broadly and made an obscene gesture.

As the sun reached its zenith, the caravan came to a dried river bed with a straggle of low thorn trees marking its course. Tembay stood at the top of the shallow decline that led into the river bed. Seemingly out of nowhere, the brigands were on them like flies. This time they came closer than ever, firing arrows at the beasts although, strangely, with little apparent effect. Certainly one would have expected them to hit such an obvious target as the massive Caravan Master.

And then Fong was there, speeding down the length of the column at a full gallop, followed by eight of his guards. It was immediately obvious that the brigands had miscalculated. Distracted by their mischief they had failed to notice the guardsmen's approach. In any event, by the time they began to withdraw, it was clear that they were going to be caught.

At a panic cry from their leader, they began to stream away along the river bank with Fong and his men in a mass just a few horses' lengths behind them and gaining. The brigands headed between the first pair of gnarled, bent thorn trees. As Fong turned to follow, Tembay cried out, "You'll never catch them, you useless horse turd."

Fong glared his hate then raked back his spurs. His stallion leapt forward. He let out a war cry which was taken up by his men. As they passed between the two thorn trees Fong drew back his sword and began a murderous swing at the rearmost rider, just as his mount collapsed in a horror of hoofs, dust and breaking bones. Fong had no time to wonder what had happened before the life was crushed out of him by the falling weight of the following horse.

From his camel a quarter of a mile away, Xiang Li watched in horror. There was a boiling cloud of dust and a bedlam of screaming horses counterpointed by the screams of men. Through the dust he could just make out the brigands. They had slowed to a trot and were circling back, arrows nocked to their bows. Now some were dismounting, entering the dust cloud. Slowly the noise subsided. Now horses with the trappers of his household were being led away in pairs. But where was Fong? He should be here, reporting.

"Gōng?"

Instead here was Tembay looking up at him.

"Gōng, calamity. Guards all dead I think. Caravan in danger. You permit me to talk with evil bastards I maybe save us. Cost money. You permit?"

Xiang Li hesitated. "Will they not kill you too, Tembay?"

Tembay shrugged. "It possible but I go anyway."

"Then I will come with you," said Xiang Li. He didn't know why he said it and he was afraid.

Tembay made to protest but then he thought, *why not. The fool will only see what he expects to see.* He bowed.

"I honour your courage, Gōng, but no guards. They want kill us, they kill guards too."

Xiang Li waved away the protests of his remaining guards and urged his camel out of the line. Tembay strode beside him and, unnoticed, on the other side, walked Te Zhu.

As they neared the thorn trees, the full force of the disaster became clear. Amid a mound of dead horses could be seen the limbs of guardsmen, many of them bent at strange angles. Xiang Li watched as a small man wearing a filthy fleece drove his knife into the throat of one of the guards. The guard spasmed and kicked, then lay still. The small man wiped his blade on the guard's surcoat then began pulling off the corpse's boots.

Two men were attempting to coil up a rope which had evidently been strung between the trees. They were hampered in their efforts by the sheer weight of dead flesh lying on it. The air above the heap was distorted by rising heat. Xiang Li felt sick.

Tembay approached one of the brigands and spoke to him. The man gestured towards a small, erect figure who was examining the teeth of one of the late guards' horses. Tembay walked over to him and Xiang Li followed on the camel. The Caravan Master was in conversation with the brigand chief, gesticulating, now at him, Xiang Li, and now at the caravan. The chief appeared disinterested. Another horse was brought forward and he prised open its mouth.

Tembay turned and walked the few paces to Xiang Li.

"Chief say he not interested in caravan. He say you give him gold he leave us alone but he says no copper. He not like copper."

Xiang Li had made a pragmatic decision to carry bullion rather than the minted copper coins of the imperial currency. Obviously their utility diminished the further one moved from the centre.

"Ask him how much he wants," said Xiang Li.

Tembay walked back to the chief. They talked for a while as the chief picked up first one foreleg and then another, examining the hooves. Tembay came back.

"He say this much." Tembay made a shape with his hands, sufficient to maintain a moderate man in luxury for six lifetimes.

"Tell him half of that," said Xiang Li.

Without pausing in his examination the chief spoke over his shoulder.

"What did he say?"

"He say he don't mind but he done enough for one day and if he have to butcher you and the rest of caravan to get gold, he not be happy."

There seeming to be nothing more to say, Xiang Li turned his camel and, together with Tembay, made his way back to the caravan.

The brigand chieftain completed his inspection of the horse then, brushing his hands together, he turned and fixed Te Zhu with his liquid brown eyes. As he stared at her for a long moment, it was as if something shifted behind the eyes. It nodded the man's head, briefly.

"My Lady," it said. "Interfering again, I see."

Te Zhu smiled her sweet smile.

"I see you, Abaddon," she said. "May the Light shine upon you."

It twisted the man's lips in a sneer, stared for a further moment, then turning its back, gestured for the next horse.

Chapter Fifteen

Foothills

For the next three days the caravan wound its way slowly across the flanks of the foothills. The bones of the earth began to poke through the thin soil. What vegetation there was consisted of sear grasses and twisted thorn bushes.

Xiang Li looked to his left where the flanks of the hills fell away a thousand feet or more to the plain. He found the view vaguely depressing – endless rough grassland with no sign of habitation nor even human activity. The westering sun threw long shadows. He shivered. He felt very alone.

When a head count had been taken after the brigand attack, it became clear that his retinue had almost ceased to exist. Four guards remained as well as a steward and a surprisingly spry laundry woman who, her services no longer in great demand, had taken on the task of cooking for the Gōng. In addition Chen Tengfei, the court physician had so far survived all the vicissitudes of the journey, chiefly because he rode his own camel. And, of course, the night-soil woman still strode along, seemingly impervious to conditions. Xiang Li couldn't imagine what purpose she now served.

Not surprisingly, the ranks of the pullers and stock men had been barely thinned. These were tough men and women, well-adapted to the nomadic life of the steppes. All of them walked. Beasts of burden – oxen, mules as well as camels – were for carrying loads, either trade goods or fodder. Only the rich could command a seat on one of these.

Of course the purpose of this caravan was to carry the Governor where he wished but the habits of trade ran deep. Most of the pullers and herdsmen had full or half loads of trade goods, chosen with an eye to being portable and profitable in equal measure. The people didn't know the destination of the Gōng but certain items – silks, jewellery, spices – would find a ready market anywhere.

Xiang Li turned in his saddle and looked back to where the diminishing herds of stock animals stirred up a plume of dust, half a mile to the rear. As ever, when his mind had nothing else to do, he calculated. *How many remained and how long would they last as a source of food?* He rather thought that, given the greatly reduced population of the caravan, there would probably be fresh meat for a little less than a month.

Would that be enough? It was an open-ended question, given that he had no idea of his destination but surely it would see them through these first mountains and then, one supposed, it would be possible to purchase more.

His gaze shifted to the camel behind his, the one carrying the treasury chests. Corporal Hau, the senior surviving guard, had had it moved up and attached to the Gōng's camel so that both could be more easily guarded by the four remaining guards. On the matter of funds, Xiang was confident. Of the four small but heavy chests containing the gold, one had been almost emptied by their encounter with the brigands but the rest, surely, contained sufficient to see them to the ends of the known world if necessary.

He faced ahead again, surveying the track and the hillside across the rhythmic movement of his camel's head. Tembay was there striding along near the head of the column. The Uyghur had seemed to be in fine spirits since the attack which had killed Fong and his men. *Perhaps,* reflected Xiang Li, *he was one of those who thrive on adversity.* Certainly he seemed not to be as harsh as before in his dealings with his people. Xiang Li had witnessed Tembay slap one of the pullers on the back the previous evening and compliment him on some aspect of camel husbandry. The puller's smile could best be termed uneasy and he had made a sign with his fingers and thumb at the giant's retreating back.

Ahead, the mountains made a continuous wall from just left of their line of march round to the right where they disappeared behind the flank of the foothills. It was possible to make out details of the individual peaks. Xiang noted that there was snow to quite a low level. Again he shivered. A small, cold wind probed from the heights and his thoughts turned to the journey and its purpose.

He tried to bring his analytical faculties to bear on what he was doing but, as ever, they failed to penetrate what seemed to be a smooth layer of non-rationality. He knew that he had to head to the west and that it was necessary to pass through the Tien Shan Mountains, even though common sense told him that this was a dangerous course, given the imminence of winter. Why? Why the mountains and, even more pertinent, why was he doing any of this?

As to the first, if one allowed that there was a reason for what he felt compelled to do, perhaps the mountain route was the quickest. He had studied maps before leaving Korla and was fairly certain that the mountain route led directly to Samarkhand. Perhaps that was the justification but, if one accepted it, then it begged the bigger question of to what purpose?

Which brought him back to the second question: why did he feel compelled to do this? Because there was no other word for it than compulsion. On several occasions now he had toyed with the idea of simply turning back, returning to Korla and taking up his comfortable life again. There were projects to put in hand, the satisfaction of taking a leading part in the administration of The Land, the love of his wife to enjoy.

All of this … until old age led to impotence and finally death. For a few years he would be remembered perhaps as the gifted administrator who had built a few wind pumps and canals but then he would be forgotten, his body a diminishing food source for invertebrates and, in a little time more, his works too would crumble. It seemed to him that he had harboured these feeling of pointlessness for years, perhaps all his life. His personal belief system revolved around the pragmatic utilitarianism of Confucius which told him that his life had meaning through being a part of the system. He had never challenged this and yet, looking back, it was clear to him that he had harboured deep within, a growing despair.

The Call, when it came (and he could recall little of what had taken place except for water and light) had seemed to offer him a task of true meaning, perhaps an opportunity to serve some over-arching purpose. That feeling came back to him strongly now. He suspected he was approaching unimaginable dangers and privations and his heart quailed, but, if they represented meaning, he would face them rather than return to comfort and despair.

He squared his shoulders and made a promise, to who or what he knew not, that he would be true.

"Gōng!"

Here came Tembay, walking back down the line, a smile on his hairy face. "We stop, maybe four miles. There ruined caravanserai. We stay night."

He lowered his voice and leant in confidentially.

"There road head up into mountains."

"Thank you," said Xiang Li. Despite himself he could not feel comfortable with this new, helpful Tembay. It didn't feel authentic and that worried him.

Tembay winked and strode off down the line. The wink felt more worrying than all Xiang Li's fears about the passage of the mountains. What was going on in that patently deranged mind? Well, there was little he could do about it. He was dependent on the Uyghur's skill and knowledge. He took comfort in his four remaining guards.

* * *

When he had seen the beasts and the Gōng settled for the night, Tembay privily called to him the half dozen or so unofficial leaders of the caravan crew. They met around a fire in a secluded part of the ruins. Tembay handed round a flask of kumis. The conversation was general until the Uyghur considered that a reasonable level of inebriation had been reached. The rumble as he cleared his throat cut across the talk and there was silence.

"The Gōng has commanded that tomorrow we turn up into the mountains."

A confused babble broke out. Tembay let it run for a while then raised his hand.

"In this I support him. The Gōng paying us well and if he wishes to journey into Tien Shan in winter, then it not for us to question his wisdom."

He took a swig from the flask and let the talk run, waiting for the one who would act as spokesman.

The others, the pullers and herders, knew this game. Dorba Tembay was, at best, a dormant volcano. Stories abounded about his cruelty and no-one liked to think about how he had walked, fit and unharmed, out of the desert when fifty-four men and one hundred and fourteen beasts had not.

However, eventually emboldened by alcohol, one Husun, raised his voice.

"Master, it has long been the rule of the roads that all share in decision if destination is changed. Do we vote on plan to enter mountains?"

A cautious mutter of agreement met his words.

Tembay smiled his big, lazy smile and raised his hand again for silence.

"Husun make good point. Rule say we vote on change of where we go."

There were nods and sounds of approval.

"But, Husun, now, tell me, where do we go?"

Puller looked at herder. Stock man shrugged at slaughterer.

Husun, finding his lips strangely dry, licked them.

"We go … we go..." His voice faded.

"Yes, Husun?"

Tembay allowed the silence to grow.

"Gōng never say, Husun. *I* never say. You take money to join caravan to anywhere, Husun. You want argue now?"

Tembay looked round the circle of faces.

"Any of you?"

There was silence. None of them met his eye.

Just so, thought Tembay. *Let us see which of you breaks first.*

Aloud he said, "Then sleep now and tomorrow we leave early for mountain road."

He heaved his bulk to his feet and made his way into the night beyond the entrance of the ruined caravanserai.

* * *

Husun ties rags around his camel's hooves, a difficult task in the darkness but at last he straightens up. He clicks his tongue. Tabor and Nergűi materialise from the gloom, each leading a camel. Husun nods towards the entrance and they set off silently. The guard has been paid to look the other way but, even so, they are nervous. Starlight limns the broken door posts. Beyond is the track that will lead them back to the plain and safety. Angry as Tembay will be, they have little expectation that he will pursue them.

In the entrance, Husun pauses, his senses alert to the smallest sound or movement. Satisfied he steps from the darkness into the backwash of starlight. There is no transition. The sharp pain under his chin is simply there, as is the blast of foetid breath. He stops, rigid.

A familiar voice says, "I see only one traitor here. I ask myself, is he only one? I say to myself, shall I hunt around when I have finished with him and see if there are others."

In the silence that follows Husun hears the faint sound of turning camels and a susurrus of receding hoof beats. He sobs briefly.

"No," says Tembay, "there must only be one."

The Crimson laps his mind and his Voices chitter but he has them in hand. A noisy, messy interlude would be fun but he has plans for Husun which do not include waking the camp. Surprise and presentation are, in Tembay's opinion, everything.

* * *

The first beasts to leave the caravanserai baulked and bellowed as they smelled the blood. The eviscerated body had been placed on a ledge so that its intestines cascaded to the ground and part way across the track back to the plains. To the handlers who struggled to control the beasts, the message would have been clear, even had not word flown round the ruin in the pre-dawn darkness. And for any who lacked wit or sensitivity, the sight of Tembay's large bulk blocking the continuation of the low-level way, was enough. Men and beasts turned up slope between two rocky buttresses and so began the story which some would survive to tell to their grandchildren: how we crossed the Tien Shan Mountains in mid-winter.

Chapter Sixteen

Eunuch Ping (1)

Eunuch Ping tapped his teeth with his stylus. He calculated. Yes, if things had gone to plan, the Gōng should now be approaching the mountains. Which meant that he, Ping, had roughly another forty days left to exercise control of the province. He smiled to think that he had had doubts.

Zhiqiang Qiu had been most helpful, had provided backing and an official warrant giving Ping the legal power to act *in loco parentis* for the Governor. Ping had given the Inspector to understand that he felt strongly that the Governor's perambulation would end at the mountains and that he could be expected to have taken up the reins of government again before mid-winter.

Zhiqiang, who was wise in the ways of intrigue as exercised by The Land's bureaucrats, understood what he was being told. The Chief Eunuch, as a trusted servant of government, had taken steps. This was no more and no less than he would have expected of Ping. So, having cast an eye over actions being taken in respect of current issues, he returned to ArAqmi, leaving instructions that he was to be kept informed of events and summoned by fast courier in the event of an emergency.

Ping was enjoying the unbridled power granted him by the situation. Not that he had done anything outrageous. That was not his way. A little peculation here, a paying back of a suspected insult there. No, he understood the danger of becoming an object of interest to the powers in Xi'an, capital of The Land, and would hand back the reins of power in due time with a good grace and a degree of relief.

That there would be a term to the Gōng's travels, he had no doubt. Trusting not to the reliability of Dorba Tembay, he had given the redoubtable Captain Fong precise instructions as to his responsibility if the Uyghur did not turn at the mountains. Fong had agreed with commendable zeal. One way or another Tembay would receive his just deserts.

Yes, thought Ping, *life was very satisfactory.*

Chapter Seventeen

The Tien Shan

Had Ping possessed the wings and eyes of the eagle which circled above a deep cleft in the mountains, some two hundred leagues to the west, his satisfaction might have been short-lived. For the Uyghur strode at the head of the Gōng's caravan on a track heading just west of north, a course taking them deeper into the Tien Shan.

And Tembay was happy. In the three days since he had taken the caravan into the mountains, his Voices had become clearer and they too were happy. Although they did not use words, it was clear to him that They wished him to conduct the Gōng as far as possible into the mountains for purposes which were obscure and that he, Tembay, would be well-rewarded.

He had come this way once before, albeit in summer. In warm, stable weather it was a quick way to Samarkhand. And it was a well-marked route consisting of interconnecting valleys and a few high passes. Even so, Tembay had bad memories of the Torugart Pass where the air was thin and the cold winds strong enough to overturn a yak. Yes, fine in summer but in winter…

The track here followed a deep valley, winding along at the feet of successive peaks which rose to dizzy heights, directly from the valley floor. It was sheltered but cold. The Uyghur sniffed the air. *Snow*, he thought. *Not yet but soon*. The bulk of the mountain to the west cut out any view of the sky. But that was where the weather would come.

Tembay's was an interesting mind, containing within its depths a deeply professional attitude towards leading caravans and, at the same time, a reckless egotism which caused him to take insane risks. Thus, he was able, at the same time, to calculate courses of action best designed for the safety of his charges in the event of snow while relishing the probability of catastrophe for all except him. Because the disastrous Taklaman expedition had only confirmed him in the belief that he was indestructible.

A thought occurred to him and he laughed aloud, much to the discomfort of those nearest to him. He would come through this just as he had the Taklaman. He would walk out of the mountains alone, shaking the snow off his beard and people would marvel. Neither the heat of the desert nor the cold of the mountains could kill him, they would say. He was a Colossus. He was immortal!

His laughter echoed along the valley. The eagle sheered away and the caravan plodded onward.

* * *

Xiang Li too heard the laughter and was troubled. Had he trusted Ping's judgement too much in the selection of the Caravan Master? It was a worry. Certainly the Uyghur had proved himself effective in his job although Xiang Li did not approve his brutality. He recognised in his own work as Governor the need for brutality on occasion but when he used it, it was always with economy and he did not personally enjoy it. Tembay, on the other hand, showed every indication of enjoyment when he found cause to criticise or punish his people. And Xiang Li was far too subtle a leader himself not to notice the wary manner in which the pullers and herdsmen approached Tembay, nor the signs against evil they used behind his back.

There was, too, the matter of the cadaver, set on the rocks outside the ruined caravanserai. Tembay had dismissed it, saying it was the work of wolves and, certainly, wolves had howled in the surrounding hills that night. But no wolf would have set a victim upright on a rock and surely, it would have eaten the entrails, not left them spilling across the track. The truth was that Tembay had been daring him to pursue the matter and he, Xiang Li, weighing matters quickly, had declined.

He gazed around him. The landscape was awful in a real sense. The soaring peaks which surrounded the caravan made him feel tiny and the caravan's progress felt pitifully slow when measured against the seemingly unchanging backdrop of slope and scree. When he had questioned Tembay about the mountain route the Uyghur had been offhand, saying it was a well-used way with few difficult areas.

"You no worry, Gōng," had been his final word as he turned and strode away to curse a puller who had allowed his string of camels to become tangled.

And yet Xiang Li was no fool. One of the accepted principles of foreign policy in Xinjiang was that invading forces did not come through the Tien Shan, that the mountain border could, to a large extent, be left to its own devices. Put simply, the Tien Shan were impassable. Certainly the track they now followed was relatively easy, mostly following the course of mountain streams but what would happen when the snow came, as come it would?

Xiang Li looked upwards to where the snowline began. *Twelve hundred feet,* he estimated. *Well, it was clear that if they were to pass through the mountains they would have to go much higher than that.* He tried to imagine the path his camel currently trod, covered in snow. It would all depend, he supposed, on the ability of the Caravan Master to remember exactly where the path was. Any miscalculation could have beasts and people plunging into the torrent which thundered in its rocky bed below.

He thought for a wistful moment of the terraces above the Black Lake at Korla where he had soaked in the sun, waited on by handmaidens, fed sherbet mixed with ice brought by fast mule trains from the mountains. He wondered if he would ever be there again. Then he dismissed the thought, straightened his back and his camel plodded onwards.

* * *

As the caravan awoke in the bitter pre-dawn of their eighth day in the mountains, snow was falling, soft as thistledown *or perhaps,* thought Xiang Li, *like large white moths*. As yet it was just a steady lightness but it stayed, unmelted, on the rocks where it fell. The road they had been following had risen steadily and was now less than a hundred and fifty feet below the snowline. Xiang Li, who had a good grounding in weather science, looked to the west, the direction from whence the wind blew. Yet another precipitous slope blocked the view of the sky but what he could see of the clouds, boiling over the peaks, was not reassuring. He thought that a heavy fall was taking place on the windward slope and they were just experiencing the spill-over down here in the valley.

As the light grew, small groups could be seen talking anxiously and glancing up at the sky but they dispersed as Tembay called the train into line. Xiang Li mounted his camel and walked it over to the Caravan Master. He nodded at the sky. "Will this be a problem for us?" he asked.

Tembay shrugged. "Is small fall. No problem. Road easy from here."

He turned his back and began pushing a string of camels into line. Xiang Li followed him.

"What happens if it gets worse?"

The Uyghur turned again, barely suppressing his impatience. "It not get worse. Is small fall. We go on. You'll see."

And with that he raised to his lips the auroch's horn and sounded the 'Advance'.

Xiang Li walked his camel back to its place in the line where one of the guards attached the lead line of the treasury beast and then they were off.

At first it seemed that the Uyghur had spoken the truth. After a gentle rise they entered a sheltered U-shaped valley. The light snowfall merely served to muffle the footfall of the beasts and the going was good. However, they encountered their first taste of mountain weather around mid-morning as the gentle ascent of the valley brought them to a col just within the snowline. Suddenly the wind rose to a shriek, blowing large quantities of snow horizontally. Xiang's camel staggered then kept on. With great difficulty, the Governor wrapped a scarf around his head and hunkered down into his fleece. The snow flayed his exposed face. He could hardly bear to look into it and, when he did, he could not see the camel ahead.

But here came Tembay, marching out of the blizzard from the head of the line shouting, "Close up! Close up!" As he passed Xiang Li he cupped his hands round his mouth and shouted, "It not last long. Soon we go down into shelter."

Then he was gone, a massive, indefatigable figure, striding down the length of the caravan.

Xiang felt slightly reassured and, indeed, within half an hour the way descended and the rising wall of rock to windward gave a lee. Nevertheless he began to wonder how much worse conditions might become and how much of this the caravan could take. Looking around him, as men and beasts halted while the train closed up, he saw groups of pullers huddling together, casting worried looks at the snow which blasted over a rocky edge perhaps a hundred feet above their heads. Then Tembay was there and the groups dispersed.

That day they climbed above the snowline proper, which is to say, they passed the level where snow from last year had not melted. New snow was starting to build upon it; however, the way could not be called difficult and it was relatively sheltered. Indeed, they made good progress because the snow was hard and covered irregularities in the footing. There was evidence of previous caravans from earlier in the season. In the more sheltered spots there were hoof prints and dung and in one place the remains of several fires. Ominously, these traces were being steadily covered by the new snowfall.

Just before evening they passed through a deep gorge and

made camp where it debouched into a natural amphitheatre. When the yurts had been pitched and before the light failed, Te Zhu walked back to the entrance to the gorge and looked up at the cornices of snow which overhung the cliff top to windward. They made a spectacular sight, curved and sculpted by the wind and seemingly suspended in mid-air.

She gazed at them pensively for several minutes, tapping her lips with a finger. Then she shrugged, turned and walked back to the fire where the evening's food was being prepared.

Chapter Eighteen

Trapped

During the night, the snow began falling again to a depth of twelve inches. As a wan dawn light returned Xiang Li looked to the cliffs high above where a full, unbridled gale drove great snowflakes horizontally. The sight made him dizzy and he had to look down but still he could hear the shrieking of the wind.

It was clear from early on that there was a change in the mood of the caravan. Men went about their duties sullenly, casting many a covert look at one another and upwards at the blizzard. The animals seemed to sense the mood. Camels moaned and cattle lowed, adding to the atmosphere of unease.

Tembay was everywhere haranguing the people, cuffing them into line. Then an altercation broke out and Xiang Li saw the Uyghur floor one of the pullers with a massive fist. It was difficult to hear what was said above the noise of wind and animals but he saw Tembay place his hands on both hips and roar out a summons to the men and women. Xiang Li went forward with two of his guards.

When the caravan was gathered around him in a loose semicircle, Tembay addressed them, his voice rising easily above the hubbub.

"I hear you worms are frightened, frightened of a little snow. Well, Dorba Tembay not frightened and say we go on, say you signed on for caravan, took Gōng's money, now you make journey. Does anyone say different?"

There was silence. Tembay looked from under his shaggy brows, first to left and then to right. No-one would meet his eye but it was evident to Xiang Li from their body language, that the battle was not won.

"What, no-one?" said Tembay who was well-aware that a

crisis had come, one which he would surmount as he had all other crises.

"Then this is what we do. I sound bull's horn and all you worms who want to keep heads on your shoulders get into line and make ready, understood?"

There was no reply. No-one moved. Slowly, deliberately, the caravan master raised the auroch's horn to his lips, his red eyes roving over the people. One or two turned and started back to the animals but most stayed, their eyes following the horn, fascinated.

And then, when the suspense had become almost intolerable, Tembay blew a mighty blast and as he blew the Voices in his head shouted and screamed, urging him on and the Crimson arose and he blew again and again until the auroch's horn shattered into two parts, cleft through the middle.

The Voices hushed, the Crimson died. Tembay looked in bemusement at the shards in his hands then up at the crowd. Many had cowered away from the noise but now they were staring not at him but over his shoulder. Some were pointing, others beginning to turn and run. Puzzled, Tembay turned too and watched with a great glow of satisfied awe as the cornices of snow and ice above the gorge slid majestically forward and down, plunging into the depths in a mælstrom of dirty grey.

Xiang's bodyguards grasped the Governor under his arms, lifted him bodily off his feet and began to run too. Almost immediately they were overtaken by a cloud of choking snow and ice particles which belched out of the gorge. The bodyguards continued to run and finally broke free of the cloud into the middle of the amphitheatre where the rest of the train was gathering.

The guards placed Xiang Li on his feet and he turned and looked back. The gorge was filled from side to side and almost to its top with slabs of ice and heaps of snow. A huge cloud of ice particles, hanging on the near side, began to subside. Of Tembay there was no sign.

The people gazed in wonder then broke out in excited noise. Xiang Li sensed that hysteria was near. He tried to work out what he could do to take command of the situation and was just about to turn to Corporal Hua when a groan went up from the crowd. He turned. Tembay, covered from head to foot in white, had emerged from the ice cloud. He strode towards the throng, some of whom began to back away.

At ten paces he stopped and shook himself, emerging from his white coating with a sardonic grin on his lips. He threw aside the shards of horn, tossed back his head and laughed a great laugh which gripped him so much that he doubled up, his hands on his knees. When, after nearly a minute he was reduced to hiccupping and gurgling, he rose again to his full height, wiped a hand across his face and wheezed, "Now … now you *have* to go on." And he laughed some more and the pullers and stock men looking at one another, turned and went to salvage what they could.

And Te Zhu, sitting at a distance on a rock, nodded.

Chapter Nineteen

Journey

Xiang Li straightens in his saddle. He notes that the imagined weight of the slate-grey sky has caused him to cower. Clouds boil around the peaks at his level and lower. Sleet stings the small part of his face which remains exposed, caking his eyebrows. Now sure of his seat after nearly two months on the road, nevertheless he clings tightly to the cantle. The camel's motion, as it forces its way through two feet of snow, is enough to induce nausea. The raw areas where his inner thigh and rump rub against the saddle offer a continuous, miserable counterpoint to his other bodily ills.

Aware that a species of torpor is overcoming him, he tries to take an interest in his surroundings. The slope the caravan is crossing seems perilous and vast. To the left it curves up to vertical crags. To the right it steepens rapidly to end in a cloud-choked abyss.

Ahead of him are a dozen beasts. Tembay is using two yoked yaks to break a way through the snow. He strides along at the head of the column, seemingly tireless. Much as he dislikes the man, Xiang Li trusts him to know where the unseen path lies. He must.

Behind the yaks come camels and a few of the more powerful horses. He cranes round, as far as he can, and sees the longer part of the caravan following. Tembay has ordered that the beasts be tied one to the other, in a continuous string, for mutual support. Xiang Li wonders, idly, how much support would be offered on this treacherous slope; whether if one went, the others would follow.

The slope steepens. The wind rises to a shriek carrying sheets of snow and sleet before it and, with a dreamlike inevitability, his question is answered. The camel ahead of him, straying a little too far to the right, loses its footing. Its rear end goes down and slithers to the right. Xiang Li's mount baulks and braces its legs as the weight comes on the rope.

One of the pullers, risking his life, dives past flailing hooves and grabs the sliding camel's bridle. He braces himself, shouting for others to join him. Suddenly the Caravan Master is there, loping with giant strides from the head of the column, his scimitar in his hand. Hurling the handler to one side he sweeps the blade, once, twice, cutting free the beast now threatening the rest of the train.

The camel begins to slide, bellowing piteously, further, faster until it disappears into the abyss and is seen no more. Xiang Li sits stunned at the awful suddenness.

Tembay, meanwhile, has turned, snarling, and is belabouring the fallen man with the flat of his scimitar.

"You miserable worm! So you would threaten train's safety with your stupidity? Ha? You think you can support fucking camel with your puny arms? Ha?"

The man tries to shuffle away on his back, one arm raised but Tembay follows him. Already blood soaks the man's furs where a careless blow has cut flesh.

"No!"

Xiang Li suddenly finds his voice, appalled, but it barely carries. He coughs, takes a deep breath.

"No, Tembay. Leave him. I forbid it."

The Master snarls and turns bloodshot eyes on the Governor but he stops his beating. The snarl turns into a sardonic grin. For a long moment he locks eyes with the Governor, nodding and smiling cruelly. Bending for a handful of snow, he cleans his blade then returns it to its scabbard.

Then he nods and turns away. His time will come. For the moment they must go forward but his time will come. *Oh yes.*

* * *

The journey through the mountains lasted thirty-two days, an average progress of less than ten miles a day. It cost the lives of twenty-three men and women, mainly through frost bite and hypothermia although three were lost through falls and one was gored to death by a yak. Three of the dead were from Xiang Li's entourage, the steward, one guard and the redoubtable physician, Chen Tengfei. The doctor had self-diagnosed a minor heart attack and, rather than hold back the caravan, had stepped to his death into thin air over a thousand foot drop.

Of the surviving travellers, few were unscathed. Seven had frostbite, eleven showed the first signs of scurvy and four, with fractures and sprains, were being carried on pack camels. All were emaciated and a few seemed to have lost their wits.

Forty-three pack and draught animals had perished. All the horses were gone and a number of the older and weaker camels. The yaks plodded stolidly onward. The last of the stock animals had been butchered before the ascent to the Torugart Pass, in a planned move to speed up the journey and to give the people several good meals before the time of maximum exertion.

In the event the Torugart, although taxing and phenomenally cold, had been nowhere near as daunting as Xiang Li had imagined which was fortunate, he thought, because it could have been the end for all of them. He had felt unwell as they reached the snow-clad col at the top of the pass but an experienced puller told him that this was nothing new, that many of them suffered similarly at height.

Xiang Li was intimately aware that he neared the limit of his reserves and could only marvel at the endurance of the pullers and stockmen who had walked every mile. He noted that although, with the expenditure of fodder and fuel, there were now many camels free of loads, none of the regular caravan personnel would ride. Xiang Li could not make up his mind whether he was seeing a new aspect of caravan lore or if they were afraid of stirring up Tembay.

Yes, he thought, *Tembay.* The man was patently mad and getting worse but without him they would all have undoubtedly perished. He drove his people through fear, if necessary at the point of his scimitar and yet, perhaps without knowing it, he led by example, always being at hand when calamity threatened, ever trudging backwards and forwards along the line. It was his mood swings that were the most alarming. At one moment he could be seen with his arm around a stockman, sharing a joke and a flask of kumis and, at the next, shouting and punching at some perceived insult. No wonder the people feared and tried to avoid him.

The end of the mountains was a gradual transition to the bitter plains of Bactria, a dreary succession of high level steppes where the north-east wind blew unabated, carrying sleet when it did not carry snow. Conditions were only better relative to the worst aspects of the mountains. There were a few dirty, flea-bitten villages where surly peasants could be persuaded to part with small amounts of fodder for three times its value. Tembay wanted to take it without paying but, to his disgust, Xiang Li forbade it.

Their target now was the city of Samarkhand where they would rest and recoup their supplies and energies. Xiang Li also intended paying off Tembay and finding a more congenial replacement, *not,* he thought, *that that would be difficult.* But as they travelled westwards, they encountered rumours. The word was that there was plague in Samarkhand. Tembay laughed contemptuously. These sheep-shagging fools knew nothing, didn't even travel as far as the next village. What would they know?

But it was true. On the thirteenth day after leaving the Tien Shan, the caravan breasted a low rise and looked down upon black plague flags flying from every wall and bastion of the Golden City.

Chapter Twenty

Eunuch Ping (2)

Chief Eunuch Ping stood on the battlements above the gatehouse of the provincial capital and watched as the afternoon sun winked on the spear points of the escort of the Imperial Inspector of the North-west Quadrant. They were yet distant, coming into view around a bend in the North Road. From the lesser eunuchs and clerks around him there arose chatter but Ping remained silent, deep in thought. This could be a difficult interview.

He had been warned by a fast messenger of this visitation four days since. It was not unexpected. By his own calculations the Gōng should have returned two weeks ago. Scouts sent out to give him early warning of the Governor's return had seen nothing even though they had ventured as far as the entrance to the mountain road. There was a report of freshly scattered human bones at the turning into the mountains but, given his instructions to Dorba Tembay, this did not alarm Ping.

The Uyghur was evidently acting according to form but by now Captain Fong should have taken charge of the situation, butchered Tembay, and turned the caravan for home. It was all most perplexing.

Scouting parties had discovered the surviving remnant of the courtiers left to fend for themselves. These had been shepherded back to the capital where Ping had questioned them but he had learned nothing except that the caravan had been heading west when last seen and that Captain Fong and Tembay were acting in character when last seen.

So now came the reckoning. Ping knew the Inspector, Zhiqiang Qiu, to be a close friend of Xiang Li and that it was for this reason that he had been willing to allow the Governor some leeway rather than reporting his dereliction to Xi'an. Could such a report now be made?

Ping clicked his fingers and turned to make his laborious way down the stone steps to the main gate. His retinue followed, twittering excitedly.

The great wooden and bronze gates stood open and a commendably burnished honour guard was being pushed into place by the sergeants. *Fifteen minutes,* thought Ping. Another click of his fingers produced a chair placed in the shade of the walls. Ping lowered his bulk onto the silk cushions with a groan of pleasure.

Yes, he thought, *would the Inspector feel obliged to make a report of the Gōng's absence?* If he did, it could have repercussions for both of them and although Ping felt fairly confident that he could deflect blame onto the Inspector, he could not hope to escape altogether without damage.

A servant offered him a dish of sweetmeats. Ping selected a handful and waved the woman away. He popped a morsel into his mouth and chewed reflectively.

He didn't wish to be damaged and, then again, if he was honest, he had thoroughly enjoyed the last three months, wielding power without responsibility. Of course he couldn't expect it to go on for ever – didn't really want it to – but could there be a way of persuading the Inspector to agree to a further delay?

"Weng."

The little rat-faced man scuttled to his side.

"Gōng?"

"What do we know of the Imperial Inspector's … procliv-ities?"

Weng licked his ratty lips and smirked.

"Well, Gōng…"

Chapter Twenty-one

Tembay Strikes

"You must eat, Gōng."

Te Zhu did not wheedle. She spoke with the voice of maternal authority.

Xiang Li flicked a dismissive wrist. "Go, woman," he commanded then slumped back into gloom.

What had brought him to this? Months of mud and damp and ice, of lice and fleas and bodily smells and he no longer knew what it was all for. He had not realised how much he had been depending upon Samarkhand. For weeks he hadn't thought beyond it.

Samarkhand! He had seen how the eyes of the old herdsmen and pullers lit up at mention of the Queen of Cities. They remembered the exploits of their youth when the world was new and they were invincible and always their most wonderful memories circled around the fleshpots of Samarkhand.

Compared to theirs, his ambitions had been small: a bath, new clothes, a few nights in a bed. He had only wanted to regain his essence as a cultivated man. For he knew that he was not a man of action. For him, being infested with insects was a horror. He, Xiang Li who used to paint and write poetry, covered in bites!

And now all the comforts of which he had dreamed had been taken from him.

He noted that the woman – he could never remember her name – was still there.

"Did I not tell you to go?" he snarled.

"You did, Gōng," replied Te Zhu pleasantly. "And I will leave when you have eaten. Thus, to avoid further vexation, please eat."

She held out the dish of steaming camel stew.

"Choy Liqiu bought some herbs at that last village and edible tubers of a kind I have not seen before but they are very palatable."

Choy Liqiu, the laundry woman turned chef, had been preparing Xiang's meals now for three weeks, a fact of which he was completely oblivious. Nor did he recognise her name. However, at that moment, he caught a waft of rich sauce and knew himself ravenous.

"Put it there, woman." He pointed at a low table. "Then go."

The woman stood her ground.

"When you have eaten, Gōng."

Her intransigence piqued Xiang Li's apathy.

"Do you know what happens to people who disobey my orders, old woman?"

He sat upright on the mouldy heap of cushions upon which he had been reclining.

"I imagine you have them disembowelled and their heads put upon poles, Gōng. At least that is what you would do when you have the requisite number of guards and torturers to hand. As things stand, however, it will be necessary for you to disembowel me yourself and I would suggest that a good nourishing meal would only assist in this by strengthening you. Now please eat."

Not since the days of early childhood had Xiang Li been spoken to thus. For a further moment he considered ways of enforcing his authority but then an errant air current brought the smell of sauce to his nostrils again.

"Do you have chopsticks?" he asked.

Ten minutes later, the dish licked clean (and *that* was not something a cultured man would do) Xiang Li reclined again on the cushions. He felt somehow less depressed.

"May I suggest, Gōng, a walk in the fresh air? It would do you good. Also, the people are very low in spirit and I believe it would do them good to see that you are not downhearted."

"Woman," he said, "you presume too far. I am your Master. You do not give me orders."

Te Zhu bowed, humbly. "Gōng, I apologise but may I speak plainly?"

Xiang Li considered. He supposed he could order her to be silent and enforce it using his three remaining guards but it was a dull, dreary day with scant chance of entertainment so he nodded.

"Gōng, the people are very unhappy. Fear of Dorba Tembay and the thought of Samarkhand carried them through the mountains. Now all they have is Tembay and his devils are driving him to madness."

Zhu picked up the dish and dusted the table with a rag. When she looked up, Xiang Li noticed that her eyes were dark and penetrating. Her voice, previously soft and lilting, now took on an edge.

"If your quest is to go forward, Gōng, you will need these people. You will need to win their willing support for the time of Dorba Tembay draws to a close. They must see you, Gōng, this day. Trust me in this."

Te Zhu turned away, silhouetted in the doorway.

"What do you know of my quest, woman?" asked Xiang Li.

The woman turned back and he saw that she was frail and bent.

"I?" said Zhu. "I am but an old woman. I know very little." And her voice trembled with age.

* * *

Dorba Tembay sat on a crag, brooding. Below him spread the caravan's bedraggled camp; in the distance loomed Samarkhand with its blight of black flags. He too had been drawn by the promise of the city and the opportunities it offered for indulging his unusual needs. The authorities turned a blind eye to the spilling of blood. Indeed, slaves could be purchased for that very purpose.

No, Tembay thought, *this was bad*. Also he was bored with the caravan and especially the priggish attitudes of the bastard Gōng. Sooner or later, if he stayed, there would be a reckoning and his rational mind saw that the murder of a high official from The Land, even in such a distant place, could lead to consequences.

There was a deal of satisfaction to be had, though, from his outwitting of the fat Eunuch, not to mention the odious Captain Fong but here he was, safe on the far side of the Tien Shan and it was time for a new start. But what?

Below him he noticed a stir among the listless groups clustered around their damp, smoky fires. What was happening? Bored with the caravan he may have been, but he still felt an unhealthy sense of ownership which expressed itself in a need to know exactly what was going on.

He narrowed his eyes. Surely … yes, it was the Gōng. What was he doing? Was he *talking* to the people? He was! He had never done this before. He had no right! The Crimson hovered at the edge of his vision. Voices chittered distantly. And who was that, walking at his heel? It could only be the little woman, the one who hung around the Gōng's yurt. Tembay had marked her down as a probable casualty of the mountains but, annoyingly, she was still here.

The chittering increased. This was *his* caravan. These were *his* people. He was *angry*.

Tembay started to rise as the Crimson lapped his vision. His great hands balled into fists. His muscles tensed, ready to bound down the slope and wreak death.

But for once he was not unleashed for his Voices whispered beguiling words in his ear. This was not the time. There was a greater future awaiting him. Others had need of his many and great talents. And the Butcher of the Desert Way listened and, listening, sat again upon the crag where he rocked and crooned and dribbled for a time.

* * *

Tabor and ten other pullers sat around a fire of dried camel dung. To call it a fire was to tamper with the truth. So damp was the air and so old the dung that it did little more than smoulder. In truth, they had only lit it because that's what you did when you camped. From time to time one or other would poke it listlessly but to no obvious effect.

Conversation was desultory. There was little left to say. Tough though they were, poor diet and the privations of the winter journey had reduced them. The thought of Samarkhand had kept them going with visions of drink and women, food and soft lying. Most had assumed they would sell their trade goods here then wait out the bad weather and return home. Most would admit that without Dorba Tembay they could not have survived the mountains but the Uyghur was patently slipping into a madness which saw him endlessly patrolling the camp, muttering to himself.

Only yesterday he had broken the jaw of a stockman and then kicked the fallen man into a coma from which he had not recovered. Many of the men would have deserted had there been anywhere to go. It would have been easy to blend into the population of Samarkhand and, anyway, the accepted assumption had been that this was where the caravan would end. It had occurred to none of them to question the Gōng's objective. He was far too remote and august a person and, anyway, Samarkhand was where caravans started and finished. Everyone knew that.

"May I join you?"

Tabor looked up then began to struggle to his feet. The other did the same.

"No, no," said the Gōng, "stay where you are." And he sank

onto a camel blanket and held his hands out to the smouldering dung, as if he expected to be warmed by it.

There was an uneasy silence. None of the men had ever been this close to a Gōng before, unless it was making a back to allow a Gōng to mount a horse.

"The Gōng would like some kumis."

Tabor heard the words very clearly inside his head and without thinking fumbled for the flask of fermented mare's milk. He hesitantly offered it to Xiang Li.

"May it please you, Gōng, to share our drink. I fear it is a rough brew but..."

At which point he ran out of words.

"It would be good to accept the flask, drink deeply and compliment the man."

Xiang Li, who had been looking suspiciously at the dirty flask with its unknown contents, heard the words and, instead of saying that he was not thirsty, reached forward with a courteous bow, took the flask, raised it to his lips and drank deeply.

The paroxysm of coughing which followed horrified the men around the fire. They dwelt in the shadow of violence and humble men had died for less. Eyes searched for the Gōng's bodyguards or the Caravan Master.

"It..." Xiang Li wheezed then coughed. He tried again. "It is a … noble brew." His voice came out high and breathless but the men seemed to understand. Emboldened he said, "I have never drunk a better … kumis? What is the recipe?"

Muttered conversations took place round the circle and an elderly greybeard was pushed forward.

"May it please you, Mighty One, it is first necessary to milk a mare. This is a dangerous business and one must proceed very carefully in the following manner..."

Te Zhu smiled and nodded. *Just so.* She turned and walked away, confident that the men could be left to spin the thread.

In later years, Xiang Li had only hazy memories of that day.

He could recall, with reasonable clarity, the greybeard demonstrating milking, using a stockman as the lactating mare and another as the foal (which had to suckle but then be pulled from the teat but kept in contact with the mare's flank, do you see, Gōng?) That was when the laughter began and when men from other fires drifted over to see what was happening.

As darkness began to fall, flames leaped up. A stack of thorn branches had been discovered, hidden in a gully, and dragged to the fire by willing hands. More kumis was found. From where she sat on a distant rock, Te Zhu heard the thin, plangent music of the steppes start as long-hidden instruments were brought out. She smiled.

The circle round the fire broadened as the heat increased. A young herdsman, emboldened by alcohol, demonstrated some dance steps in front of the Gōng. He was joined by others and suddenly, the fears and pain of the mountain journey, the joys of survival, poured forth in whirling limbs and shouts. One of Xiang Li's last clear memories was of offering a prize of gold to the best dancer as judged by acclamation.

From his rocky crag, Dorba Tembay glowered at the figures silhouetted by the flames. He heard the music and the clapping and a small part of him, feeling lost and alone, longed to join in. All his life he had been on the outside, denied a place at the fireside. Could he not, even now, walk down the hillside, sit by the fire and revel in good fellowship?

For a long moment his loneliness battled with the deep well of anger and hurt which filled his soul. But then his Voices crooned. He was greater than these miserable beings. He was born for mightier things. Not for him the fellowship of lesser men. He was a hero and the path set before him was the lonely path of destiny. A tear ran down his hairy face but Tembay dashed it away. *Bastard scum. Dance your little dances. Sing your pathetic songs but you will know me and weep!*

* * *

Some time after midnight, the party broke up with many an expression of mutual esteem. Xiang Li, singing a phrase from an Uyghur folk song, was helped to his tent by Corporal Hua, followed by a round of applause. Slowly the last voices were stilled and the camp descended into deep silence.

A young herdsman named Ogele had been deputed to guard the animal lines while the celebrations took place. A flask of kumis had seemed fair recompense and now, in the small hours, he nodded, half dozing by his small fire. He was hardly aware of the hairy hand which clamped over his mouth and even less of the vicious torsion which dislocated his neck.

Tembay lowered the limp form to the ground and went in search of Sweet Breath, the fastest and worst-natured camel in the caravan. Grasping her halter, he whispered soft words to her. Sweet Breath bared her filthy teeth at him but, when he tugged the halter, she came docilely enough.

Guardsman Mu, unlike the unfortunate Ogele, was wide awake. Nothing that had happened so far on this journey had damped his military ardour. Indeed, with the loss of a large proportion of the escort had come hopes of promotion. Corporal Hua (whom Mu regarded as an undistinguished plodder) had let it be known that he expected to be promoted to Sergeant at any moment. That would leave a vacancy for Corporal and whilst Mu had every respect for Guardsman Jiao (the balance of the force), he, Mu, was quite clearly the candidate of choice.

Thus, as he marched up and down outside the small yurt which housed the treasury chests, he practised his sword drill with many a muttered 'ha' and 'yo!' Sadly it was this laudable excess of military diligence which led to his downfall for, just as he finished executing a particularly difficult and technically perfect parry in tierce which had taken all his concentration, a hairy hand clamped over his mouth, his sword was plucked from his hand, reversed and slid up between his fourth and fifth rib. It was as peaceful a death as a guardsman could hope for.

As Tembay lowered to the ground his second corpse of the night he had difficulty suppressing a loud snigger. He was sorely tempted to rampage through the camp, maiming and slaughtering but his Voices were quite clear that this was not acceptable. So, looking left and right, he bent and cut the lacings of the treasury yurt. Inside he fumbled in the darkness. He found three small but heavy chests and one lighter one. Each lay within a web of straps which allowed it to be hung from the carrying harness of a camel.

Tembay was tempted to make off with all four chests but, again, his Voices counselled caution. Given his own bulk, the weight of the gold and the fact the camel would need to carry him far and fast, one chest would have to suffice. So he cackled to himself, picked up one of the heavier chests and left the yurt in search of Sweet Breath and a new life of idleness and pleasure.

Chapter Twenty-two

A Change of Command

It was Corporal Hua who woke Xiang Li the following morning. The Gōng had to struggle through layers of a vile dream involving extreme thirst, pain and filth. Returning consciousness brought little relief.

"Gōng, Your Honour, please to awake," shouted the NCO. Hua lay prostrate, his forehead in the dirt.

The Governor waved a feeble hand at the guardsman and croaked, "Quiet," but it did no good.

"Gōng, Guardsman Mu is dead and the treasure is taken and I prostrate myself before you as a miserable worm and plead that you will merely flog me and not take my worthless life."

The pounding in his head made rational thought almost impossible but, had he had the means to hand, he would indeed have executed Corporal Hua there and then, simply to keep him quiet.

Fortunately, at this point Te Zhu entered the yurt and placed a cup of steaming liquid in Li's hands. She then knelt beside the recumbent solider, place a hand on his neck and whispered in his ear. Hua stood, a look of quiet bemusement on his face, bowed to the Gōng and left the tent.

Xiang Li looked at the cup and considered being violently sick, then, at Te Zhu's instruction took a sip. Within moments the roiling in his gut calmed. He drank deeply. The liquid had a sharp, aromatic taste which spoke to his nervous system of peace and stability. For want of anything else he said, "What is this, woman?"

"It is Rosy Dawn, Gōng, a remedy known to the women of my people. Now it is time that you were up and abroad. Much has happened in the night and the people have need of your guiding hand."

Xiang Li gulped down the remainder of the liquid, arose and stretched but when he looked around for the woman in order to chide her, she had gone.

Outside, in the dawn, there was much confusion. The body of Ogele had been found by the herdsman who was to relieve him. He had reported to an older man who had raised the alarm. Then a similar discovery had been made by Guardsman Jiao who had reported to his Corporal. There was much running about and shouting. Knots of people coalesced and fragmented.

Xiang Li had an innate dislike of chaos and disorder. However it went against his culture to usurp a chain of command. Tembay should be dealing with this but evidently he was not. So he looked around for Corporal Hua, gestured him to his side and made his way to the centre of the camp where a fire blazed.

"Call them," he said to Hua.

The Corporal raised his hands to his lips and bellowed, "Be quiet! Come here!"

Faces turned. The Corporal bellowed again and the pullers and stockmen began to drift towards the fire.

"Find me something to stand on," said Xiang Li.

Hua cast around and came back with a wooden crate. He helped the Gōng up onto it as the last of the people straggled in to form a semi-circle around the fire. They looked at the Gōng, some expectantly, others fearful.

Xiang Li cleared his throat. "What has happened?" he asked in his best commanding voice.

Immediately fifty voices replied so that his voice was drowned out. He gestured to Hua who roared "Quiet!" again.

Silence fell. "One of you is to tell me what has happened. The rest of you, remain silent."

The instruction was well-received. More than anything these men craved someone to take charge. There was a shuffling and muttering and then a man was thrust forward. Xiang Li recognised the elderly greybeard who had explained the making of kumis, the night before.

"What is your name?" asked Xiang Li.

"May it please you, Gōng, it is Chimbai Dargan."

"Then, Chimbai Dargan, tell me, what is the meaning of this uproar and where is the Caravan Master?"

Chimbai raised his arms and shrugged. "As to Dorba Tembay, Gōng, he has flown with the night. The camel Sweet Breath is missing and Ogele, who guarded the animals, is dead. His neck has been broken."

Xiang Li turned to Corporal Hua.

"What of the guardsman and the treasure?"

"May it please you, Gōng," said Hua, clearly operating under a weight of fear, "Guardsman Mu has been murdered with his own sword and one of the treasury chests is gone."

Xiang Li raised his voice again.

"When was Dorba Tembay last seen?"

Remembering the Gōng's last order, the crowd remained silent.

"You may speak," said Xiang Li.

The crowd turned in consultation. Chimbai Dargan walked back to the men and asked questions. Then he returned to stand before the Gōng.

"May it please you, Gōng, he was seen late yesterday afternoon, sitting on yonder crag." He gestured up the slope.

Xiang Li considered.

"You are all to break your fast. Then you are to appoint three leaders, acceptable to yourselves, men of sagacity and experience. In one hour, they are to come to me at my yurt. That is all."

With Hua's aid he climbed down from the crate and made his way back to his yurt. Te Zhu bowed as he entered. She was pleased to have her confidence in the Gōng confirmed but said nothing, merely began to serve the morning stew.

* * *

An hour later, three men presented themselves at the yurt. Each was nervous, believing that one false word could see them executed. That the Gōng's strength was reduced to two guardsmen while the caravan yet numbered near fifty counted for nothing.

Corporal Hua announced their presence and they were shown into the yurt. The Gōng sat upon cushions. He gestured to the three to be seated on a carpet. Unasked, Te Zhu handed round cups of tea before retiring into the shadows. Xiang Li cast a critical eye over the three. The men shifted uncomfortably.

"Chimbai Dargan, you I know. Introduce the others."

"May it please you, Gōng, this," he indicated a swarthy, hook-nosed man of middle height who sported an abundant black beard, whiskers and a turban, "is Devet Berdi, a senior camel puller with great experience of the Bactrian plateau."

Devet Berdi placed his hands together and bowed.

"And this," Chimbai Dargan pointed to a large, muscular young man with blond hair, "is Jochi Khasan who was chosen by the stockmen."

Khasan nodded his head in a manner which perhaps showed a lack of deference. *Good,* thought Xiang Li. *He has a mind of his own.* He paused as he gathered his thoughts.

"I have called you here," he said, "because Dorba Tembay has deserted his post. Thus the caravan lacks a leader. It is my intention to take over that leadership. I shall make decisions but I will need your professional guidance. I shall also expect you to implement my decisions and carry out the day to day administration of the caravan. For this you will be paid well in gold. If you feel unwilling or unable to accept this situation, it would be well that you say so now. You will then be replaced."

The three men sat transfixed. Some of the Gōng's formal wording had been beyond them but they understood the gist of what he had said. Emotions warred in their breasts. On the one hand gold was being offered. On the other was the threat of 'replacement' which could mean anything, not excluding death.

"Are you willing to serve?"

Berdi and Dargan nodded, although with no obvious enthusiasm. This did not perturb Xiang Li. He looked at Khasan. The stockman stared back. After a pause lasting seconds, he briefly inclined his head.

"Then I shall tell you my requirement and you will advise me on how it is to be achieved. It is my intention to travel towards the west for an unknown period of time."

He stopped and looked at each of the three men. There was a long pause and then, diffidently, Dargan said, "Is there no destination, Gōng?"

"No," said Xiang Li. "I travel..." He paused. "I travel towards an event. I know the direction but as yet not the destination. You must therefore advise me what is required to sustain this caravan for an unknown length of time."

Dargan and Berdi looked nonplussed, but Khasan spoke.

"Caravan not go on. Lack food, fodder, stock animals. Carrying beasts in poor conditions. People, worse. Many sick. They hoped rest Samarkhand. Tembay gone. He mad but he leader. Need rest, buy provisions. No rest, caravan die."

The stockman continued to look the governor in the eye, apparently unafraid.

"Thank you for your assessment, Khasan," he said. "Please would you use my honorific when speaking to me?" Although he did not raise his voice there was, for those who cared to hear, a thin filament of steel in his tone.

The young man continued to gaze for a moment then nodded. "Gōng," he said.

Xiang Li went on.

"Self-evidently we cannot rest here. Samarkhand is of no use to us." He turned to Berdi. "Where then is the nearest place which can supply our requirements?"

The swarthy man cleared his throat. "May it please you, Gōng, Bukhara lies less than fifty leagues to the west. There we would find all that we need." He turned to the others. "But that would take us ten more days and I know not if that is too long."

Dargan looked at Khasan who pursed his lips then shook his head.

"Summer, perhaps. Winter, no."

"Is there somewhere nearer?" Dargan asked Berdi.

Berdi mused. "There is Kermine," he said slowly. "That is only thirty leagues. The road is good. Maybe we take seven days?" He appealed to Khasan.

Again Khasan pursed his lips. He tipped his hand to and fro. "Seven days, maybe." He smiled and his dour face was transformed. "Anyway, stay here, we die."

"Then," said Xiang Li, "we shall proceed to Kermine."

And thus Xiang Li, Imperial Mandarin of the Ruby Button and Governor of Xinjiang Province, made his first decision as a caravan master.

Part Two

Then at dawn we came down to a temperate valley,
Wet, below the snow line, smelling of vegetation;
With a running stream and a water-mill beating
the darkness,
And three trees on the low sky,
And an old white horse galloped away in the meadow.

T S Eliot
The Journey of the Magi

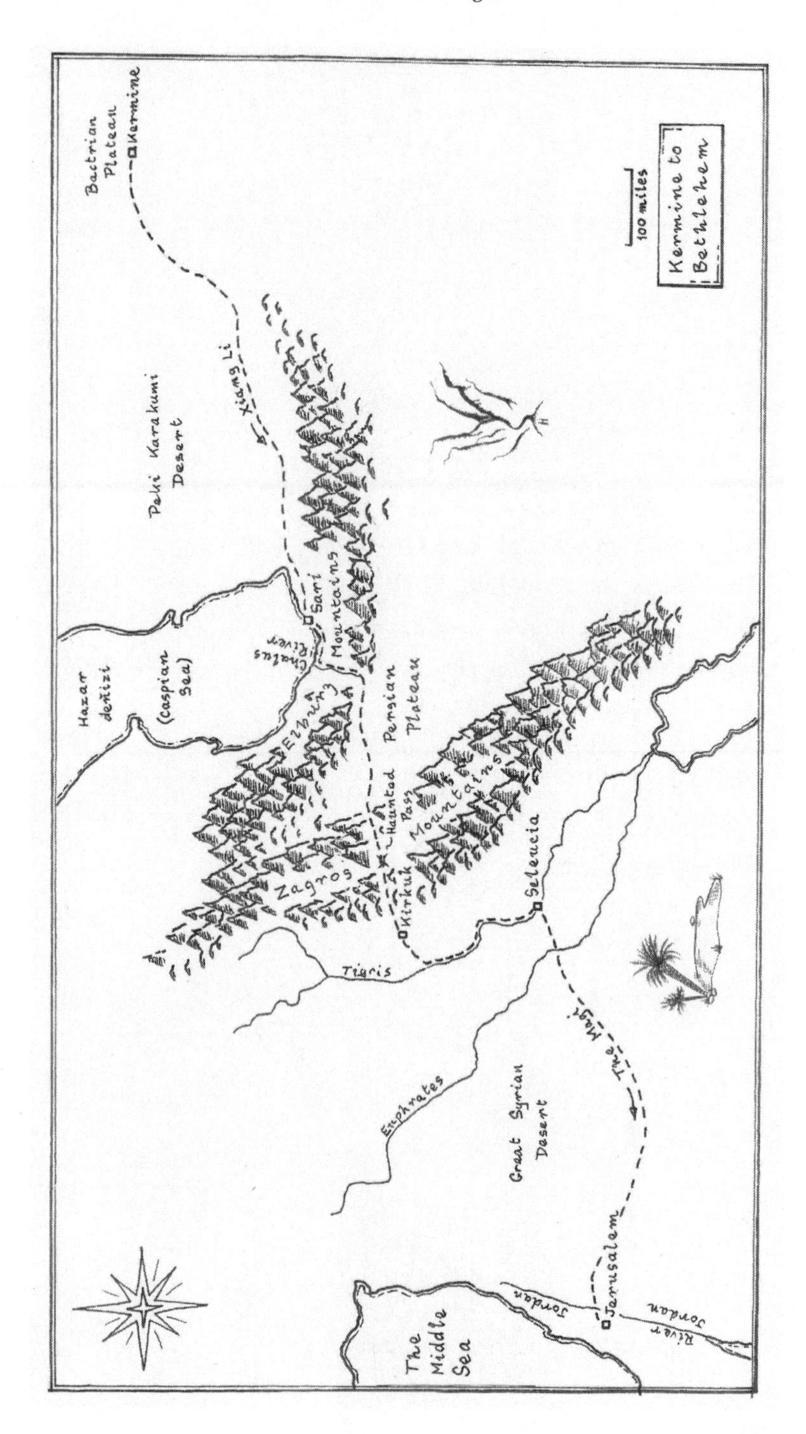
Kermine to Bethlehem
100 miles
Bactrian Plateau
Kermine
Paki Karakumi Desert
Xiang Li
Sari
Mountains
Chalus River
Hazar denizi
(Caspian Sea)
Elburz
Persian Plateau
Haunted Pass
Zagros
Mountains
Kirkuk
Seleucia
Tigris
Euphrates
Great Syrian Desert
The Magi
Jerusalem
Jordan
River Jordan
The Middle Sea

Chapter Twenty-three

The Bactrian Plateau

Kermine had proved an inhospitable town. It was clear of plague and intended to remain so. However, there was a caravanserai half a mile to the west. It was basic – just four walls and a straggle of leaking buildings – but to the exhausted people it was Paradise. The skeleton staff who maintained it left quickly.

Arrangements were made to leave goats in a pen two hundred yards from the gate in exchange for gold. At Xiang Li's insistence, nets of vegetables – mostly root crops – were also left and he used his authority to ensure that the people ate them. A widely read man, he had long understood the correlation between lack of vegetables and the imbalance of the elements called Water drowns Fire, known in the vernacular as the Bruising Sickness.

There was plenty of fodder stored in the caravanserai, albeit somewhat old and dusty and, as time went on and it was evident to the townspeople that no-one in the caravan was dying of plague, more was brought in from outlying villages. With rest and plentiful food, the animals soon began to put on body mass.

The three men appointed to run the caravan had found their feet during the journey from Samarkhand and formed a good team. Xiang Li marked out Jochi Khasan as a natural leader. He was tempted to promote him to caravan master but bided his time, not wanting to offend any unwritten norms of the road. After all, Khasan was a mere stockman while Dargan and Berdi were camel pullers.

He consulted with all three regularly and received good advice.

"For the first hundred leagues we follow a road along the foot of the high ground, at the edge of the desert plain they call Peki

Karakumi," said Berdi. "The way will be easy as long as there is no snow. There are towns and villages every few leagues. Then we will come to a great body of water, the Hazar deňizi, and there my knowledge finishes. Whichever direction we take from there, we will need to cross mountains."

Xiang Li pondered the map Berdi had drawn in the dust. He had rather hoped that, in travelling, his destination would become clearer but this had not happened. Certainly, the road to the sea went roughly west. Perhaps by its end he would receive some kind of insight.

"So," said Xiang Li, "we will plan the journey stage by stage. First we will proceed to this sea. Berdi, what is your assessment of the availability of fodder and food along the way?"

"Gōng," said Berdi, "there will be both because caravans use this route throughout the year but, since it is winter, it will cost much and will perhaps not be of the best quality."

Xiang Li nodded.

"Dargan, do we have enough beasts?"

Dargan took his time answering. At length he said, "May it please you, Gōng, I am thinking that we have fifteen strings of camels and eighteen yaks. If we were to travel only as far as the sea, I would tell you we had more than we required since we do not need many beasts to carry fodder. But I am also thinking that you will travel beyond into mountains."

He paused and looked at the governor. Xiang Li followed his line of thought.

"So we would arrive at the sea with enough beasts to make the passage of the mountains. Yes," he mused, "but equally we could sell some of the beasts here then buy more before the passage of the mountains."

Khasan said, "May I speak, Gōng?"

Xiang Li inclined his head.

"There is matter of people. Some sick. Others not wish go forward. They worry. Not know where you go. Want return home. Many never travel this far."

Khasan tried to gauge how his words were being received. He was a confident young man and had come to have some trust in this austere autocrat. All the same, he knew that he might be trespassing on dangerous ground.

Xiang Li gestured for him to continue.

"Gōng, we not know where you go. We not able tell them."

There was silence in the yurt. Dargan and Berdi tensed, wondering if Khasan had gone too far.

Xiang Li sat and thought. These were practical men of the camel routes. How could he tell them that an idea had seized hold of him, that he could find no rest unless he followed his destiny. Also he was a private man and rational. Even he had difficulty in his waking moments believing in the enormity of what he had embarked upon. Telling these men, these ... peasants (for he had no other word in his vocabulary for them) would make him vulnerable. Perhaps they would laugh at him.

"Tell them, Xiang Li. Take them into your confidence for they are men just like you. Without their trust the Quest cannot go forward."

Xiang Li heard the words very clearly within the confines of his head. He rather thought that the voice was female, possibly that of an older person. It was authoritative yet calm. A small part of his mind resented the intrusion but he was aware that it had restored clarity to his mind.

Te Zhu appeared as if from nowhere with cups and a flask of kumis. She handed round the cups, poured the liquor then retired again to the shadows. Without thinking Xiang Li raised his cup in a toast and the others responded. He drank deeply, grateful for the warmth on this raw day, then placed his cup upon the ground.

"I am, to some small degree, a seer," he began. "I study the stars."

"Ahhh," said Dargan and Berdi. Khasan nodded approval. This they understood. Men of the high steppes could not but be aware of the stars. A deep, superstitious awe was inculcated in them from an early age as they saw the march of Great Lights across the vast skies of Central Asia.

Encouraged, Xiang Li continued.

"Some months ago, I saw something that should not have been there. It was not, I believe, a star and yet it filled me with a great..."

He gestured helplessly with his hand.

"Fear?" suggested Berdi. The three men now leant towards the Gōng, deeply engaged in his words.

"Something like that, perhaps," said Xiang Li. "But it was not frightening. It was much warmer than that. And there was a great longing and desire."

He shook his head, ruefully.

"I would have studied it more closely. There are means. But then I do not know what happened. There was a … a vision or mayhap it was a visitation. The details are lost to me. For a while I swooned but when I awoke it was with an urge to travel to the west."

He looked up, fearful that he would see incredulity or worse, pity but the three men were completely caught up in the story. The words now tumbled from his lips.

"Know this, men of the steppes and trade routes, something comes, something wonderful. I cannot tell you what it is but it is my destiny to bear witness. I can do nothing other than follow my Calling. I will go on, on my own if necessary, even to my death. I cannot command you to support me nor will I try but it is clear that I will need help to reach my goal. I therefore ask you humbly, as free men, to come with me if you will and to use what influence you have to bring along a caravan suitable to my needs … whatever they may be."

For five seconds or so there was silence in the yurt, then Dargan spoke.

"Gōng, I speak only for myself. I am an old man. I have seen much and travelled far and yet, always, there has been a longing in me to fulfil some worthwhile task ere death. There is a light upon your brow, Gōng. If you will take me, I am your sworn man."

Dargan leaned forward presenting his hands, palms together and Xiang Li instinctively placed his hands around them although he had never done such a thing before.

Then Berdi spoke. "Gōng," he said, "my life is one of commerce. I have a home, a wife and children. Yet everything is known. There are no great challenges. I too would journey with you for surely there is a story here which shall be told around the fires as long as men roam the steppes. I too would be your man if you will have me."

Again, the hand-fasting.

No-one looked at Khasan but he sat, shaking his head and one would have believed that he wanted nothing to do with this foolery. And one would have been wrong for with a loud guffaw he slapped his thigh.

"Gōng," he said, "You great man, ruler of many yet you die quick without help. Khasan let Gōng wander into mountains, die in snow, then Khasan not man. I come too. And who know, maybe I see this thing that come to pass."

And there was laughter and a raising of cups as Khasan placed his hands between those of the Xiang Li. And unnoticed, Te Zhu slipped from the yurt.

Chapter Twenty-four

Eunuch Ping (3)

The arrival at dawn of the Imperial Inspector for the North-east Quadrant was noted by few and anticipated by fewer. Of the latter, Eunuch Weng Liang was the least surprised. It was ten days since he had sent the message.

Despite his rodential appearance, Weng was a subtle man, well able to sense an approaching crisis in his relationship with Chief Eunuch Ping. Both men had long known (whilst hiding their knowledge from the other) that a day would come when Weng's usefulness to Ping would be outweighed by the burden of secrets he carried. In the months since the departure of the Gōng Xiang Li, Ping had embarked upon a campaign of peculation and fraud of noble proportions, assisted in detail by Weng.

It was clear to both of them, and yet, again, not acknowledged, when Ping's experiment went beyond the bounds of what would be overlooked by the Imperial administration. To Weng, the Chief Eunuch had the air of a gambler, unable to control his addiction. As a party to a growing weight of fraud and blackmail, Weng had become uneasy.

There were signs. Ping had begun to cultivate a clever, junior eunuch named Ngai Jinjing. Weng would come upon them deep in discussions which ceased when he appeared. Then there were bamboo slips which either disappeared from his desk or never arrived. Weng was not a blind horse and well able to interpret nods and winks. His time as Confidential Secretary to the Chief Eunuch, he felt, was swiftly approaching a bloody end. Best to get his defence in first.

And so a fast rider had carried a message north to ArAqmi, detailing Ping's worst excesses and supplying supporting evidence. Zhiqiang Qiu, he knew, was still smarting from the blackmail performed upon him by Ping. (Had Weng himself not supplied the damning material?) Revenge, he felt, would not be long delayed and here, indeed, as the grey light of late winter brushed the stones of Korla's gatehouse, was the Imperial Inspector himself, at the head of a squadron of cavalry.

"Open the gate," said Weng and the gate swung open.

"Gōng Zhiqiang," he said, bowing deeply.

The Imperial Inspector reined in his horse opposite the bowing man. The horse snorted, its breath pluming in the cold air.

"You are Eunuch Weng?"

Zhiqiang had seen Weng on many occasions but one eunuch more or less made little difference to the mandarin.

"May it please you, Gōng, I am."

"Then take me to the miscreant."

Weng bowed again and set off towards the palace. Half the cavalry peeled off at the gate. The remainder followed the Inspector.

The first Ping knew of the matter was Ngai Jinjing shaking his arm. Slowly he had awoken. First he noted the look of horror upon the face of the junior clerk as he tried to cover his nakedness. Then his gaze took in the smirking guardsmen ranged along the wall of his chamber. Lastly, with a sinking feeling, he turned to the cruel smile of Zhiqiang Qiu.

"Out!"

The Imperial Inspector gestured to Ngai. The young man leapt from the bed and ran from the chamber.

"Chief Eunuch Ping Quon, I have here a warrant for your arrest on numerous charges of theft, blackmail and intimidation. You have five minutes in which to get dressed."

Zhiqiang Qiu turned his back, nodding to the captain of the guard to take over.

History would record that it took Chief Eunuch Ping a whole five minutes to roll to the side of the bed and lever himself upright. He was thus naked when he was taken to his deep, cold cell.

Weng, he thought, as he lowered his bulk onto the damp straw. *So he had underestimated the little rat*. He felt a brief spurt of admiration, quickly suppressed, for his Confidential Secretary. A flea landed on his thigh. It bit him. He slapped it, leaving a red smear. The game was not over. It was merely suspended. Weng would suffer for this.

Chapter Twenty-five

The Yellow City

Te Zhu sat on a net of straw and watched, with interest, as Xiang Li held court. A camel puller had accused a stockman of stealing a decorative camel blanket, a charge which the accused vehemently denied. Normally such a disagreement would have been solved quickly and effectively by knife but the Gōng had let it be known that such resorts were unacceptable to him and that, in future, he would arbitrate disputes.

Te Zhu rather thought that had the Gōng been challenged on his motives, he would have said that he could ill-afford the loss of any more of the caravan's limited manpower. She rather thought, however, that trial by knife offended the Gōng's fastidious nature. Now he sat on a rock, flanked by his two guardsmen, chin in hand, as he listened to the two men trade claim and counter-claim.

If Te Zhu had one defining characteristic it was her fascination with everything around her. She awoke each day with a sense of wonder at life in general. Now her attention was fixed on her dour, æsthetic master. The Governor who had once dressed in silks and bathed daily wore a filthy fleece and a disreputable woollen cap. Where once he had distantly made decisions affecting the lives or deaths of millions, he now focussed his considerable intellect on the fate of a camel blanket.

There were several reasons to wonder at the scene unfolding before her. Firstly, that the Gōng was actually interested in the matter at all. Once upon a time such matters would have been settled far from his sight and, had they come to his attention, they would merely have annoyed him. Secondly, he would, she knew, deliver exact justice as he saw it, without fear or favour. But the third reason for wonder was that these rough, hardened, violent men of the steppes, accepted his right to disperse justice and therefore to lead the caravan at all.

This was a matter of great wonder to Te Zhu herself. She thought that this was, perhaps, the best-run caravan at present traversing the Trade Road and she was pleased for her master; pleased that he was immersing himself in the brute matter of everyday life; that he was becoming earthed. She pondered the strange ways of men, how they yearned for a leader and would gladly hand over part or all of their freedom to him.

Thus they had allowed Dorba Tembay to rule their lives, even though they knew him to be a violent man who had not their interests at heart. And now they let a physically weak but highly intelligent foreigner dictate to them. But the atmosphere of the caravan, despite the filthy conditions of the journey, was so much lighter. Men now smiled and there was music most nights around the camp fires.

Te Zhu pondered. The Gōng was discovering love and this was good, even though he might never acknowledge it and, innately, the people felt its power. Yes, it was good. The game was in play. The Gōng had a long way to go both in miles and growth but the preparation was well in hand.

* * *

Xiang Li stood on the shore. It was sunset. He had never before seen such a large body of water and noted that it awoke in him deep feelings which he could not name. Small waves broke on the sand at his feet. The sun drifted behind a low bank of cloud on the horizon, sending up a halo of rays. Delicate purple, deepening by the moment, washed the sky. After weeks of rain and sleet he felt his spirits lift.

He turned and trudged up the beach towards the Yellow City that some named Sari – 'yellow', he had been told, because of the citrus groves which surrounded it although now, in the pit of winter, there was precious little colour of any kind. He shivered.

The caravanserai was a substantial affair, built of limestone, quarried from the Elburz Mountains which marched on the southern horizon. The mountains. Yes. Still he was no clearer about where he should go next but, inevitably, it would involve mountains. Sari was at a crossing point of trade routes and it was possible to travel from here towards each of the cardinal points and in each direction there were mountains.

He entered the carved gateway of the caravanserai, saw his men and beasts settling down in the arcade to the left. He felt preoccupied. Surely by now there should have been another sign? His only certainty seemed to be that time was limited, that he must make his best effort to move forward. In the absence of any other course, he would call a council of his three advisers this evening.

But here came Dargan, running across the sand, a broad smile on his face.

"A messenger, Gōng," he panted, "a messenger for you."

From out of the shadows of the arcades emerged a small, hook-nosed man, wearing a dark robe and a skull cap. He stopped in front of Xiang and, placing his hands together, bowed deeply.

"Effendi," he said, "my master has sent me to bring you to him."

"How is this?" said Xiang. "I know no-one in the Yellow City and nobody knows me."

"Effendi, my master is dying. When he heard that your caravan had arrived this morning he became agitated. He said that he must speak to the leader. He sent me to bring you to him. Please, Effendi, it is not far."

The clouds cleared from his mind.

"Corporal Hua," he shouted.

Hua appeared from the arcade.

"Collect your spear and attend on me in one minute."

Hua saluted.

"Dargan." He turned to the old camel puller. "Find Berdi and Khasan. Begin to make everything ready for our departure. Hire a guide if you can find one. I wish to be ready to leave as soon as possible."

Dargan bowed, turned and made off towards the arcade, calling out for his colleagues. Meanwhile, Corporal Hua arrived, hefting his spear. Xiang turned to the small man.

"What is your name?"

"If it please you, Effendi, I am called Sendi."

"Then Sendi, lead on."

* * *

They arrived at an archway in a wall, down a narrow alley. Sendi opened a wicket gate and held it open for the others. Within was a courtyard. Once upon a time it would have been a pleasant oasis but whoever had cared for it no longer did. In the middle was a dry, cracked fountain, choked with climbing weeds. Around it, brambles held sway. A few of summer's lingering roses still bloomed but they were sick and sere. Sendi hurried across the broken paving to another archway. He beckoned them within and along a dark passageway.

In the gloom Xiang Li made out indications of past opulence – dingy tapestries and pieces of porcelain. Once he would have wanted to explore further, to indulge his fascination for fine things, but now he followed Sendi's hurrying footsteps deeper into the house and up a broad stairway. On the landing at the top stood tall double doors, their brass bindings dull with verdigris, the lacquer peeling off the cedar facings.

"Effendi, may your guard remain here?" said Sendi.

Xiang Li nodded to Hua who executed a smart turn and grounded the haft of his spear with a thump. Sendi grasped the left-hand handle and pushed open the door. It squealed. Xiang entered the large chamber within with an air of recognition. This, if he was not mistaken, was the work room of a savant but, whereas his work room in Korla was tidy and clean, this one was not.

Equipment cluttered every horizontal surface. It was equipment he knew. He identified two types of retort and three alembics but instead of the clean lines to which he was used, these were decorated with finials, signs and sigils. They offended his sense of rightness. Against one wall stood a furnace but it was designed as a lion, the opening to its firebox being its mouth. *Unnecessary*, he thought. An acidic smell pervaded the room as well as a faint odour of corruption.

Drunkenly suspended overhead – one of its supporting wires had evidently snapped – was a large reptile. He had to duck under its belly in order to join Sendi at a door in the far wall. Sendi knocked and opened the door. He stood back to allow Xiang Li to enter. It was a smaller room and slightly cleaner than the work room. It was rank with the smell of sickness. A narrow bed stood beside the further wall and on it, raised on pillows and covered with quilts, lay the skeletal figure of a very old man.

On a stool beside the bed sat a woman, swathed in a black robe and veil. She looked round then, picking up a dish, rose and hurried out past Xiang Li. Sendi closed the door, leaving Xiang Li with the man on the bed. He moved a step or two closer, noting the hectic yellow tinge of the man's skin. *Jaundice*, thought Xiang Li. *Dying*.

A hand fluttered. "Come here," breathed the man. "Sit."

Xiang Li moved the stool nearer to the bed and sat. The smell of corruption was stronger here. The man licked his lips.

"I am dying, you know." He paused. "I am frightened. Please will you hold my hand?"

A large tear rolled down one wizened cheek. With some distaste Xiang Li reached for the nearer hand. It was cold and felt like a small bundle of twigs. The man gathered himself.

"I am – I was – a seer. I have spent my life trying to isolate the Life Force." He laughed bitterly, the laughter turning into a cough which racked his spare frame.

"Water," he croaked when the coughing subsided.

Xiang Li found a cup on the floor and, with a gentleness he did not recognize, placed a hand behind the man's head and raised the cup to his lips. The man took two sips then nodded. Xiang Li lay the emaciated head back on the pillows and placed the cup on the floor. He paused, momentarily, then resumed his grip of the claw-like hand.

"Now that I need the Life Force," the dying man continued in a dry whisper, "it is deserting me and I have nothing to show for my life."

He turned his head slightly, looking at Xiang Li. The whites of his eyes were yellow and blood-shot.

"I thought that when it came I would be brave but I am not. And yet something happened, something which seems to indicate that this is not all there is. I had a … a visitation or mayhap a dream but it foretold your coming and gave me a message for you. You are hurting my hand."

Xiang Li released his grip.

"Tell me, then; what is the message?"

The man swallowed.

"I was visited by a Great Spirit, one of the Guardians. Its colours were blue and green. By these and the water and by the diadem on its brow shaped like a crescent moon, I took it to be Gabriel whom some know as God-is-My-Strength or Haurvatat. He told me of your coming and told me that … that I should not die. Do you think that is true?" he asked.

Without thinking Xiang Li nodded. "It is true," he said with all the sincerity at his command. *After all*, he thought, *there is no harm*. The dying man closed his eyes and smiled slightly, nodding his head.

"What was the message?" prompted Xiang Li.

With infinite care the old man levered himself up onto one elbow. When he spoke his voice took on cadence and power.

"Thou shalt go by the mountain road toward the setting sun. Thou shalt go now and thou shalt go with speed. At times thou wilt travel by night. Study the western sky for there shalt thou see thy salvation. Keep the faith. There is a light upon thy brow."

With that he fell back upon his pillows, pale, sweating and breathing heavily. Xiang Li felt a faint tug upon his hand. The dying man wished him to come nearer. He leaned over the bed, placing his ear near to the ravaged mouth.

"I ... did ... well ... did I not?" breathed the dying man.

"You did very well," replied Xiang Li.

"And ... will I ... live?"

"Yes," said Xiang Li. "Yes, you will live for ever."

The old man smiled and, smiling, died.

Xiang Li placed the limp hand on the bed. He found to his surprise that he was crying.

After a while he rose and quietly left the room. A small figure stepped from the shadows and stood by the bed. Te Zhu carefully crossed the frail hands on the thin chest and placed within their grasp a faded yellow rose. She closed the old man's eyes then bent and kissed the cooling brow.

"Go well, brother," she said.

Chapter Twenty-six

The Elburz Mountains

They find a guide, a Mede named Aktas Selcuk. A citizen of Rhaga beyond the mountains, he wishes to return home and is happy to guide the caravan as far as the Persian Plateau. At his behest they travel westwards for seven days along the shores of the sea to the mouth of the Chalus river, where it empties into the sea. There they turn southwards, into the mountains, following a well-defined road beside the river which races down a boulder-strewn trench to their right.

The northern face of the Elburz is covered in tall, moss-draped trees, oaks, elms and beech, which shelter the travellers from the wicked north winds. However, the rain seldom stops and as they push higher, it turns to sleet and then wet snow. At Aktas's suggestion, they travel at night under a three-quarter moon, when the snow is crisper, making easier footing for the animals.

After six days, the Chalus, now a small stream chuckling by their path, they strike out through the snow for a col. Beyond it, they follow another stream downwards and find that there is less snow. Within days they are at the bottom of a broad valley and the weather, although cold and overcast, is almost dry.

On the fourth day beyond the col, they reach a cross-roads. Aktas Selcuk points them to the road heading west along the valley floor and with many protestations of goodwill, they part and the caravan sets out across the dreary winter fastness of the Persian Plateau. Aktas stands and watches until the last camel disappears beyond a low rise.

He thinks of the austere foreigner whose will binds together this group of people and animals. He wonders where they are going and why, for, being a courteous man, he had never asked and they had never volunteered. He believes that for a while he has been within reach of a great mystery. Then he shrugs, smiles ruefully and turns his face to the east, towards Rhaga and home.

Chapter Twenty-seven

The Persian Plateau

Of the crossing of the Persian Plateau little need be said. Day followed day in dreary cold, laced with rain and sleet. Snow lay on the higher points and all around on the peaks. At night the howling of wolves echoed around the valleys. The people, fifty souls or so, were the hardiest of that puissant expedition which had left Korla three months before. Or perhaps it would be truer to say that they were individuals whose attitude did not admit of failure. Thus they did not regard the privations of the journey as great.

Yes, they were filthy and infested. True, they were often wet and cold but there was always a track of some sort, following the lower ground between the peaks. And there were villages and the occasional town although all were deep in wintry torpor and inclined to resent being roused by indigent travellers. Fuel and fodder were, if not plentiful, at least occasionally available at usurious rates.

Twice they were attacked by bandits and on both occasions the attacks were beaten off by a determined defence, organised by Khasan. Indeed, although the triumvirate of Dargan, Berdi and Khasan continued to administer the caravan, it was more and more to Khasan that herders and pullers turned for day-to-day leadership and the other two were happy to step back a little. Xiang Li was happy too since Khasan made a clear distinction between tactical and strategic decisions. There was never any doubt that it was Xiang Li's vision that drew the travellers onward, that bound them together and Khasan would always refer to Xiang any decision concerning their course.

On a twilight, camped in a high pass, Xiang Li stood outside his yurt and gazed into the clear sky to the west. Te Zhu stood near him, to one side and slightly behind. Xiang Li was aware of her presence. Once, a long time ago, it seemed, it had irritated him beyond measure but, since none of his efforts to dislodge her had had any effect, he simply ignored her.

As he waited now for the evening meal to be prepared, he watched the slow emergence of the stars he knew so well on this, the first clear night they had experienced in weeks. There, to the south-west, Biē Yī began to twinkle and to the right, higher up the celestial arc, there was the cold, blue spark of Lóusù Zēng Liù. Judging the height above the horizon with his closed fist, he looked for Wĕi Sù Yī, one of his favourites when he noticed an anomaly. He wiped his eyes then used the old trick of peering slightly to the right, so that the sensitive edges of his eyes would focus on what he thought he'd seen.

A small cloud passed across his field of vision. As it moved away on the wind, its trailing edge uncovered a distinct luminous patch. With growing excitement, Xiang Li realized that he was seeing, with his unaided eyes, the anomaly he had first noted back in Korla. It was unmistakable – elongated, shaped like a candle flame, lying on its side. *But it must be so much brighter than when he had first seen it,* he thought. He checked the angles subtended with other stars and the distances. *Yes, there was no doubt.* Suddenly his body was covered in goose pimples. The awe he had felt on first seeing it returned but much stronger now, out here on this barren mountainside.

"It comes."

Xiang glanced down, saw the small woman now standing close by his side. Her face reflected a faint, silvery light. She looked up at him.

"You have your sign, Gōng," she said.

Not for the first time, Xiang Li sought a devastating riposte which would put this old peasant woman in her place. What was she doing on this journey anyway? He had never discovered. Since the long-ago loss of his privy, she appeared to fulfil no obvious function. But there was something about the direct manner in which she looked into his eyes... He sighed.

"Yes, old woman. I have my sign."

* * *

On, then, and on; the land rising, the villages fewer and fewer, the weather colder, the snow deeper. High in the foothills, the headman of a village, sharing a flask of ardent spirits with Khasan asked where they were going. Khasan simply gestured to the west where white peaks marched.

"Zagros! In winter!" The man looked at Khasan askance.

"No-one travel Zagros in winter!"

"Yet," said Khasan, "that where master wish go. Is a road?"

The headman looked away and spat. When he looked back, Khasan saw fear in his eyes. The headman took a long pull at the flask then wiped his lips.

"There is road," he said. "It called Ghost Road or Haunted Pass."

Khasan waited for more. When it did not come he asked, "Is good road?"

"Don't know," said the man. "Once it trading route, many caravans. Then good road but now ... for many years now, it haunt of djinns." He spat through his fingers.

Khasan was not frightened by weather or bandits but he was a man of the high steppes where reality was stretched thin, where entities and powers from the other side often broke through. Nevertheless, he continued to probe, knowing that the master would need details.

"How I know road?"

The man shook his head, looked at Khasan now in exasperation.

"You mad?" he asked.

When Khasan did not answer, he pointed at a distant cleft

between two peaks.

"There," he said. "There ruined caravanserai at mouth of gorge. Stop there, friend. Listen to voices of djinns calling in night. Turn round, come back."

Again he took a long pull at the flask. Khasan continued to look towards the cleft in the mountains.

* * *

Startled birds clattered from the ruins of the caravanserai as they arrived. Xiang Li surveyed the broken walls and fallen timbers. It had a dismal air and by common consent the travellers did not enter. While camp was being made, he went forward with Khasan and Dargan as far as the mouth of the gorge. The cliffs on either side were tall and steep, the gorge itself no more than a hundred feet wide. Although it was only mid-afternoon it was dark inside and somehow malignant. A cold wind gusted from its depths, carrying with it an odour of rot.

"You will note," said Xiang Li, eventually, "that the going is generally level, easy footing for the beasts. What do you think?"

He turned to the others. They remained silent and avoided his eye.

"Khasan, what say you?"

Khasan continued to look into the gorge, his lips pursed.

"I think it bad place, Gōng. You say we go there, we go but..."

He lapsed into silence.

"Dargan?"

"It is as Khasan says, Gōng. I am an old man. I am frightened."

Xiang Li looked at the two men and then back into the gorge.

"And I tell you that there is nothing in there that can hurt us. Certainly it feels intimidating but then it is dark and dank. The worst that can lie within is bandits or wild animals, both of which we can deal with. I promise you that we will pass though it as quickly as possible and then we shall be clear of the mountains."

He turned and walked back towards the camp. Khasan and Dargan exchanged a long glance then both shook their heads and followed him.

Te Zhu, who had been standing, unremarked, to one side, went forward and stood within the shadow of the entrance. She raised her head, her eyes closed, scenting the air. Powerful? *Yes,* she thought. Certainly powerful, but moronic. A manifestation of evil, of course, but not complex. Probably the result of a massacre; that was how most of them found fertile awfulness in which to root.

From the depths of the gorge came a deep, rumbling moan.

Te Zhu laughed. She raised her arms. "I hear you, my dear," she called.

An affronted silence fell.

* * *

Back in the camp, preparations were made. Khasan sent men out before dark to collect firewood. Te Zhu took from her baggage a quantity of cleansing herbs – sage and asphodel among them – which she had begged from the women of the village, the night before. She set a number of the people who were skilled with needle and thread to making small pouches with strings to allow them to be hung round necks. These were stuffed with herbs and then blessed by Te Zhu in an impressive if *ad hoc* ritual, watched by the entire crew.

Te Zhu then went to bed early. She doubted she would get much sleep in the next few days.

* * *

In the morning the train made ready but with many a doubtful glance at the louring entrance to the gorge. Xiang Li noted the lack of conversation and a degree of fumbling with familiar harness. The beasts were clearly unhappy too. Camels moaned and from the stock animals came lowing and bleating.

"Call the people together," he said to Khasan. "I will talk to them."

He climbed onto a rock.

"Men and women," he said, when they were gathered, "it is my intention to transit the pass ahead of us because it is the quickest way to the lands beyond. If there are robbers or wild beasts within, we will deal with them, for you are hardy, brave people of the steppes. There is nothing else within which can hurt you. To prove this, I shall walk ahead of the caravan until we reach the other side."

He paused to allow muttered conversations to take place.

"Even so," he continued, "if anyone is unwilling to make the passage, they will be paid and may leave with no hard feelings but I hope that you will all come with me because you are all equally important to the success of this enterprise."

He climbed down from the rock, hefted his staff and set off towards the gorge. Te Zhu passed among the people handing out pouches of herbs and blessings. The people were nervous but nobody made to turn back.

Khasan raised his voice and ordered the Advance. The caravan set forth and Te Zhu took up position a few paces behind the Gōng. It was dank and cold in the pass which narrowed, in places, to less than thirty feet. No sunlight penetrated here and there was the steady drip of water. Sick-looking fungi covered many of the rocks. Apart from that there was no plant life.

Around camp fires, in later years, the story of the Haunted Pass would be told and embellished. In truth, during the first day there was little worse than distant moanings and unexplained rock falls. The people relaxed slightly and so did the beasts. Men and women fingered the guardian herbs hanging round their necks and took comfort. They took comfort too from the figure of Xiang Li, striding ahead of them. For his part, product of the rational, pragmatic culture of The Land, he admitted of nothing spiritual and was unaffected. And Te Zhu? Te Zhu appeared to be enjoying a stroll in the countryside.

That night they built fires around a tight camp and men fed them throughout the dark hours. Xiang Li slept but, at first, few others. Wind arose and howled in the rocks. On it was snow, bitter and wet. Shapes, half-seen, prowled the edge of the firelight. There was moaning and rumbling and a miasma of low-level fear. The people looked to the Gōng, wrapped in his blanket and were reassured. Then they looked at Te Zhu, sitting on a tall rock in the middle of the camp site, her eyes closed. Before her burned a small fire of aromatic herbs. She crooned quietly, and those who heard, yawned and many turned away and slept.

The going became worse on the second day. Spiteful squalls hurled snow and hail against them. The temperature fell and it was as if an invisible force opposed their passage. Booming laughter echoed around the peaks and the pullers were hard put to keep the beasts under control. Hearts began to quail yet there was now no return. The Gōng still led them and Te Zhu, sometimes barely glimpsed through the blizzard conditions. Xiang Li called for two yoked oxen to take the lead, as Dorba Tembay had once done, to break a way through the deepening snow.

A camel went down, its leg broken. It screamed until its throat was cut. Pullers quickly removed its load and distributed it to other beasts. A yak bellowed and ran amok, injuring two stockmen before it was brought under control. People shivered through fear and cold, struggling under a great weight of oppression.

Night came early and it was a shaken, fearful group that gathered to make camp in a bleak place. Fires were lit with great difficulty. Xiang Li and Te Zhu passed among them offering their own kinds of reassurance. None slept that night although Xiang Li made a performance of wrapping himself in his blanket and lying as still as he could. Te Zhu sat in the midst of the camp again and although there were strange noises as well as half-seen shambling shapes, nothing broached the perimeter fires.

As a cheerless day dawned, the shrieking wind rose to a full gale which caused man and beast to stagger. Xiang Li and Khasan took stock, leaning close and shouting to be heard.

"How much further do you think?" asked Xiang Li.

"I don't know, Gōng. We not move fast but headman at village say two days, maybe three."

"How are the people?"

"They not take much more. Frightened, some frostbite. Also we nearly finish fire wood. Not last another night."

"We had better move, then. Sound the Advance."

And Xiang Li, bent almost double, clasped his cloak at the neck and forged on westward.

Chapter Twenty-eight

The Mountains End

Many miles to the east of Karkha d' Beth Slokh, in the District of Sulaymaniyah, Nouri leans on his crook, surveying the upland slope before him. It is early to be this high but Nouri understands the need to survey the pasture early in the year. Soon there will be decisions to be made, flocks to move. Still, it is a killing cold this high and he will not stay long at the edge of the snows.

The wind howls around the crags. Pulling the fleece tighter around his body, he raises his eyes to the sheer black cliff and shudders. About half a mile away, a great ravine splits the rock from top to bottom. As a lad, Nouri had ventured as far as the entrance but no further. Men said it had once been a trading route to who knew where but now it was the haunt of djinns. The boy had been sure that he heard their voices, although there was no wind that day, and had run all the way back to the hut in the valley bottom.

He watches now as an icy gust blasts out of the ravine, picking up clouds of snow, bowling them down the slope. He thinks that nothing would make him venture in there then amends the thought: maybe if a ewe had wandered in he would go as far as the entrance and perhaps a little further but, hardened mountain man that he is, he is not a fool.

Even now he starts to hear voices in the vast bass of the wind. *Time to go,* he thinks, then catches movement at the edge of his vision. He shades his eyes and focuses on the mouth of the ravine. Yes, there is no doubt, something is moving. Fear enters his gut. He prepares to run but curiosity makes him take one last look, to try to understand what he is seeing.

Surely ... yes, it is a camel. And, if he is not mistaken it is being led. It cannot be. *Nothing* comes out of the Zagros at this time of year except the killing winds of winter and yet he must believe the evidence of his eyes. There – another and a yak and a camel which falls and then struggles to its feet. Can these be real? His keen eye, even at this distance, takes in the gaunt frames of the animals and he wonders if they may yet be ghosts.

The ragged line of misery emerges from the ravine, staggering down the steep slope, through the snow patches and on into the poor grass that winter has left clinging here. The men, if men they be, are screeching to one another. One tries to run down the slope. He falls and is helped to his feet by another. The animals stagger and weave. Nouri sees the raw patches on their flanks.

* * *

Xiang Li gazed with disbelief. Rock suddenly gave place to smooth, wet snow sloping downwards into a broad valley, enclosed by rounded hills. Lower down were patches of green. Off to the west he caught glimpses through the cloud of a wide plain, quite clear of snow.

Suddenly dizzy with relief, he closed his eyes and clung to his staff, the ash branch he had carried from somewhere near Samarkhand. He felt the need to give thanks but, as yet, his tired mind refused to encompass the task. Yet he knew, deep in his inner core, that he had not been found wanting. He had been faithful to the Call.

A violent gust from the ravine at his back nearly overturned him and he stumbled forward down the slope and then, because it seemed logical, kept walking. Around him, spreading out across the snowy turf, the animals and men staggered along. One or two knelt, giving thanks to their gods. A small knot of four danced drunkenly around in a circle, their reedy voices lost in the wind.

Xiang Li felt joy too. It grew as a bubble from his central

being, infusing his blood vessels, making his heart race until he recognised near hysteria and clamped down. There would be decisions to make. Men and animals could yet die. He must stay alert. He looked around at the gaunt, ragged figures. There would be need for rest, for food and warmth.

From the corner of his eye he saw the small, compact figure of Te Zhu. She stood, gazing back into the pass, her hands raised. Xiang Li wondered why then dismissed her from his mind.

Off to his left, stood an old man clad in fleeces, leaning on a crook. Xiang Li raised his hand. In a trance, the old man raised his in return, then shook his head, as if in disbelief, turned and began to trudge down the hill with the remains of the caravan. Quickly he overtook the shambling group before passing out of sight as the path dipped into a fold of the hillside.

The air became warmer as they moved downwards, the snow less and the grass more. There was now a rough path. It became slippery and more than one fell and did not begrudge the falling. There was even weak laughter. Here was a crude wall, boulder upon boulder, and behind it a rough lean-to of the kind where shepherds spent the summer. There was an amazing comfort in the knowledge that these had been built by man; that people carried on some sort of life even at this height.

Another mile and Xiang Li heard a regular beating noise, a clacking. Around a sharp bend, the path passed over a small stone bridge, spanning what was clearly an artificial water course, just such a leat as he had caused to be constructed to water the stone fruit of his distant province. And beyond the bridge, a small stone water mill.

He paused, leaning on his staff and mused. *A mill? Here? Why? Not for grain, surely? There would be no arable farming at this altitude. What aspect of sheep herding had need of a water mill?* Here was a mystery to challenge the mind of the practical governor. *Perhaps something to do with processing fleeces? Yes; that was a possibility.* He would have to ask.

In the meantime, why the clacking? Well-run water mills were silent in his experience but for the sounds of flowing water. He bent down, peering beneath the under-shot wheel. *Ah; there it was.* One of the paddles had come loose. That would need fixing which meant stopping the wheel.

A brake? No. Too crude a structure. So, there must be a means of shutting off the leat upstream. Then a fairly simple repair although using hardwood, for it must be elm or something similar to avoid rot. That would come at an expensive premium up here where no trees grew. So there would be expense and there must be a community around here technologically advanced enough and therefore rich enough to have built the mill in the first place.

Fascinating, thought Xiang Li, straightening, unaware of the healing caused by the simple exercise of his rational mind. But elm wood; he had seen elms that grew in the Hyrcanian Forest on the northern slopes of the Elborz Mountains, facing the Hazar deňizi, but that was many miles from here. He turned and nearly fell. On the skyline across the valley at a distance of perhaps two miles, stood three gaunt trees, black, silhouetted against the yellow sky. They seemed very close, threatening. He shuddered, his soul assailed by an awful oppression.

"Wych elms," he mumbled then, pulling his fleece around him, set off down the path, his face averted.

Te Zhu watched all this from a little distance. She noted the bowed shoulders of her master then switched her gaze to the skyline, nodding to herself.

Slowly, she extended her right index finger. She made the Sign of Banishment, speaking the Word of Power, adding emphasis on the gutturals. The trees swayed for a moment then faded to black dots which streamed upwards and were born away on the wind. A faint sigh swept up the valley and was gone. Te Zhu smiled briefly then turned and plodded after her master.

Xiang Li felt a lightening of his soul but kept his eyes on the ground at his feet until he was sure that the contours of the land had hidden the trees from sight. Then, looking around he noted the long line of animals and people following, churning the path to mud. There was an air of hope but also of stress. They would need shelter soon and as much rest as he could give them. Somewhere soon there would be a village and he devoutly hoped that it would be friendly.

The path took a turn to the right and the valley opened out as the slope lessened. Here was a network of meadows bounded by stone walls with byres and in the distance smoke rising from unseen chimneys. Sheep grazed and one or two oxen and here – he stopped in his tracks – here was a white mare, ears up, eyes bright, gazing over the wall at him. Gently he held out his hand to stroke her muzzle but the mare would have none of it. She snorted and threw up her head, turned on her hindquarters and bucking, set off at a canter across the hillside.

Xiang Li smiled; the first smile he had managed, it seemed, for weeks. His heart went with the galloping mare and it seemed that a weight fell from his shoulders. He was a good judge of horse flesh and, although this mare was old, he liked her spirit.

Te Zhu smiled.

Chapter Twenty-nine

Kirkűk

Washed, shaved and dressed once more in silks, Xiang Li selected a date then lay back on the deep cushions. His recent transformation from lice-ridden, filthy traveller was still fresh enough in his mind to be a source of great joy. He looked around the room with satisfaction – cool white walls with pierced windows picked out in a motif of subtle blues, plants with broad, shiny leaves in earthenware urns, delicate pottery on polished, hardwood stands. For the moment, his heart felt as light as a butterfly.

The arrival of the caravan from the depths of the Zagros had been a nine-day wonder in the district of Karkha d' Beth Slokh. Xiang Li had been happy enough to bed down with his people in a well-found caravanserai, to drink in the signs of advancing spring here in the Warm Country and to sleep, deep and long. Here, after all their privations, were fodder for the animals and fresh food for the people. Of most immediate importance to Xiang Li, here were hot baths and a barber. For the pullers and herders there were also strong liquor and women and Xiang Li was happy for them.

People from the town came to look at the strange travellers who had arrived in their midst and to wonder at their scarecrow appearance. However, interest had waned by the third day when the wanderers began to look little different from them.

In consultation with his three deputies, Xiang Li had reluctantly conceded that it would take at least a week for the animals to recover sufficient condition to continue the journey. Indeed, so rapid had been their translation from marginal survival to warmth and plenty, that he was not clear how to proceed. The plains that stretched before them to the horizon seemed to offer soft living and rapid travel and while the anomaly still hung in the night sky a few degrees to the south of west, it was by no means clear how he was to approach it with most speed.

It was at this point that an expensively-dressed servant sought him out with an invitation from his master.

"The Gōng Yin Xianliang would esteem your presence at his table this evening, if it may please you, Gōng," he said.

The Gōng! Xiang Li had known that The Land discretely sent ambassadors and agents out along the Trade Road in order to facilitate commerce and to act in the interests of distressed subjects. It was his luck that one apparently resided here in Karkha d' Beth Slokh. That was his first thought. His second was how he might be received as the runaway Governor of Xinjiang Province. Logic, however, dictated that if it had taken him nearly five months to make the journey in the depths of winter, it was unlikely that an imperial messenger would yet have arrived this side of the mountains, let alone in a relative backwater like Karkha d' Beth Slokh.

"Tell the Gōng Yin Xianliang that I am indeed honoured by his kind invitation and am delighted to accept. It will take me an hour to prepare. Perhaps you would return then and conduct me to your master's residence?"

The servant bowed and left. Xiang Li looked around him. Te Zhu was idling nearby. (When was she ever not?)

"Woman," he said. "Have my wardrobe brought to my quarters. It is in the black leather pannier carried by Great Mother."

There: that should put her in her place. Te Zhu hurried off.

Later, as she brushed the Mandarin's hat with the ruby button she played the 'Garrulous Good-wife', a role she enjoyed but seldom indulged.

"Another Gōng! Well fancy that! And us so far from The Land. I expect he'll be able to tell you where to go next, Gōng, him knowing the whereabouts and all. And perhaps you'll tell him that you are on a secret embassy to a new king in a land far to the west? Won't that amaze him? And he'll never need to know who you are."

Xiang Li, who had been concentrating on fitting a badly bent slipper onto a swollen foot had heard not a word, just the annoying babble. With the slipper finally in place, he turned impatiently.

"Be silent, woman!"

"Yes, Gōng," said Te Zhu. "I'm sorry, Gōng. Sometimes my tongue just runs away with me."

A pause, then:

"And I expect he'll be able to tell you where you can find the other Gōngs who are going to the same place."

Xiang Li gave her a furious look as he snatched the hat from her hands and marched out into the sunlight. Te Zhu bent to pick up various items of clothing.

"Well, that went rather well," she said, when she was sure the Gōng was out of earshot.

* * *

Yin Xianliang bustled back into the room.

"My apologies, Gōng Li. An urgent matter concerning a consignment of pomegranates. Or, more to the point, a matter which should have been settled by underlings who lack any obvious sign of wit."

The Gōng Yin Xianliang was a fat, slightly pompous man, currently sweating profusely despite the gentle warmth of early spring. He eased himself onto the heap of silk cushions across the table from Xiang Li and poured from a filigreed, bronze jug, misted with condensation.

"Sharbat," he said, handing a cup to Xiang Li. "Specifically Ghoore, a confection of rose water, hibiscus and lemon."

Xiang Li took a sip. It was so cold that several of his teeth hurt.

"And the ice?" he asked.

"Brought by fast courier from the Zagros," said Xianliang, and then smoothly, "but you would know more about ice and the Zagros than I."

The pause hung in the air.

"Certainly," replied Xiang Li, "the mountains contain ice in abundance but I never thought to see it cooling a drink on the plains."

Another pause.

"And may I humbly ask why you were crossing the Zagros so early in the year, a journey, I may add, that all the local experts claim to be highly dangerous, if not impossible?"

Xiang Li placed his cup on the table, picked a date from the dish and considered it, taking his time.

"Gōng Xianliang," he said at last, fixing the man with an inscrutable gaze, "I am on a mission of the utmost secrecy for our Imperial Master. I am ordered to travel with greatest despatch and that has necessitated taking great risks. More than half of my original party has died on the journey."

Xianliang returned his gaze with equal inscrutability. In the game of imperial politics, it did not do to accept first impressions. Xiang Li knew this. He was a great exponent of the game. His gaze did not waver as he calculated his next lie.

"I was told that I was to seek out Karkha d' Beth Slokh and the Gōng Yin Xianliang, a name, I might add, spoken of with favour at the Imperial Court."

Xianliang bowed slightly to acknowledge, but not necessarily accept, the gambit.

"May I suggest that we refer to the city as Kirkűk, the name used by the inhabitants?" said Xianliang.

He broke eye contact in order to select a date. He bit into it, deftly removed the stone.

"And what assistance may I humbly afford you, brother?" he

asked.

Xiang Li replied, "I am sent as an ambassador to a king in a country far to the west." For a moment the face before him swam out of focus and he was standing on the seashore outside the Yellow City. "It is a land which lies beside a vast sea."

Xianliang pursed his lips, considering.

"There is a land," he said slowly. "But brother, if it were possible to travel directly there, which it is not, on a fleet camel, the journey would not take less than six weeks. Since there is no direct route, your journey will be much longer."

He paused again.

"It would help me greatly if you could name this king or his realm."

The next lie came easily.

"Gōng Xianliang, I may tell you, but in the strictest confidence, that the Imperial Soothsayers have given notice of a royal birth, one of the utmost felicity and importance. It has yet to happen but our Imperial Master wishes me to witness it."

Where, thought Xiang Li, *had that come from?*

Again Xianliang paused then lifted a small bell from the table and rang it three times. A clerk appeared from an inner door.

"Fetch me the map covering the trade routes to the Middle Sea," he said. The clerk bowed and left.

"If I am not mistaken, the country you seek is under the domination of a barbarian empire which lies far to the west, beyond the sea. It is an imperial power called Rome, uncouth but not to be toyed with."

The clerk returned with a roll of parchment. At Xianliang's direction, he cleared the table and unrolled the map, weighting its corners with dishes and cups. Xianliang took up a chopstick.

"Here," he pointed with the stick, "is Kirkűk, here the Zagros."

Xiang made out the wavering line of the mountains.

"Here," Xianliang pointed to the left, where a blue line

indicated the edge of a sea, "is Judaea of which I know little except that it is occupied by a contentious and rebellious people under the domination of Rome."

Xiang Li ran his finger to the west of Kirkűk, the direction in which he proposed to travel. Save for a few marks, resembling palm trees, the map was blank.

"Yes," said Xianliang, "you see where the desert lies. This whole area," he swept his hand from the mountains towards the sea, "was, until recent history, the fiefdom of another barbarian empire. It was called Seleucid. But even though that empire has died in squabbling and death, the Romans have not sought to absorb it."

He shrugged.

"The area simply isn't worth anything. A few nomads live there, eking out a miserable existence, but there are no trade routes, no visible tracks. However," he traced southwards with the chopstick, "note these two rivers and the area between them. This we call the Blessed Arc for here there is water aplenty, crops and wealth. And here," he pointed to a red dot, "is the heart of it all, Seleucia."

He took a draught of sharbat and settled back on his cushions.

"Seleucia," he said reflectively. "I have visited it and whilst it does not rival our Imperial City in grandeur, it is, nevertheless, a mighty centre of trade and learning. It was founded by the barbarian Seleucids and has changed hands many times over the years. At the moment it is in the hands of the Parthians but the Romans would dearly love to have it back."

Xiang Li studied the map. He loved maps. He traced the trade routes that converged on Seleucia.

Without thinking he said, "If one were to seek other ambassadors, bent on being at the birth of a king, perhaps Seleucia would be the place to find them for it seems to me that all must pass through there, whatever their starting place."

Had he looked up, he would have caught an expression of

calculation crossing the other's face.

"But yes," said Xianliang. "If that is what you wish, then it can only be Seleucia."

He leaned forward again, pointing with the chopstick. "For see, if they came over the mountains from the east, that is where the road crosses the Tigris River. From the south, ships come to the mouth of the Tigris and her sister river. There, cargo is broken and carried to Seleucia on river craft."

He placed the chopstick on Kirkűk. "And for those, such as yourself, brother, who would approach from the north, the obvious route is by raft down the Tigris."

* * *

Later, when his guest had departed, Yin Xianliang sat deep in thought, tapping his teeth. After a while he stirred on his cushions and rang the small hand bell. The clerk appeared.

"When do we expect the first caravan to depart to the east?" he asked.

"Gōng," said the clerk, "the word is that the lower passes will be clear in ten days and the first caravans are already assembling. Five days would be my guess."

"Very well," said the Mandarin. "I shall dictate a message."

When the clerk returned with his parchment and stylus, Yin Xianliang began.

"To the Most Noble Gōng Zhiqiang Qiu, Imperial Inspector of the North-west Sector. Concerning the Gōng Xiang Li, Governor of Xinjiang Province..."

Chapter Thirty

To Seleucia

"Dargan, how many beasts have we?"

The old man consulted his tally stick.

"May it please you, Gōng, ten full strings of camels and eight yaks."

"And of those, how many do I own?"

Dargan consulted with Khasan and Berdi.

At length he said, "Twenty-three individual camels and all the yaks are yours, Gōng. The rest belong to pullers."

He could see from their expressions that the three men were ill at ease, wondering why they were being asked these questions. Shyness overcame him. He had not given thought to the handling of this situation and now that it had come he lapsed into didactic mode.

"Following advice it is my intention to proceed south by river to the city of Seleucia. I shall therefore no longer need your services, nor the use of the caravan. You will sell such beasts as belong to me, obtaining the best prices you can. You will distribute one half of the surplus arising among the people. You three will be paid in gold as previously agreed. Are there any questions?"

The three men sat looking at their master in silence. It made Xiang Li feel very uncomfortable. Curse these peasants, the old man with his soft voice and wisdom, the fat, little merchant with his ready smile, the rock-solid, dependable stockman. What right had they to any consideration from him? Was he not their master? Was he not on a mission?

They are your sworn men, Xiang Li. You cannot put them off so easily. They understand your quest. Each must be allowed to make his decision.

The words were there in his head as clearly as if someone had spoken out loud. Te Zhu came silently from the shadows, placed a dish of fresh-baked bread on the ground in the circle of the men then retired.

It was Khasan who broke the silence.

"Where you go after city, Gōng?"

"Well ... I expect to travel west."

"The river going west?" asked the stockman.

"I ... I think not."

"Then you need camels. You have camels. You need men. We your men. We swear with hand-fast, you remember? You tell Khasan 'Go', Khasan go but not take gold."

He folded his arms and glared at Xiang Li. Dargan squeezed the stockman's arm. He turned to Xiang Li.

"Forgive Khasan, Gōng. He speaks as he finds but he speaks true. You are now my lord. If you tell me to go, I will go but I hope you will not for I wish to see what you will see even though, in my heart, I think I shall not long survive the seeing."

Silence again. No-one looked at Berdi. After a while he sighed.

"Gōng, Dargan and Khasan speak true but, Gōng, the passes will soon be open again and my heart yearns for my home, my wife, my children." Tears coursed down his cheeks. "We have travelled a great journey together, Gōng, but I would ask that you set me free from my oath so that I may return home."

Xiang Li looked from one face to another. Tears were very close. Only with an effort did he hold them back. What was happening to him? He felt humbled and unworthy and he wished to feel neither.

"Khasan is right. I had not looked that far ahead. I will need men. I will need advice. I will need ... friends. Berdi, you are free to go with my gratitude. You have been a true friend and I owe you more than gold. Dargan, Khasan," he looked at each in turn, "if you will come with me, it would make me very glad."

And so it was arranged. Ten of the remaining fifty pullers and stockmen volunteered to follow Gōng Xiang Li. The rest were royally paid off with the profits from the sale of the Gōng's beasts. They would sell their trade goods, buy more and then, when the passes cleared, join an east-bound caravan and resume the steady rhythm of their lives.

In addition there were the remaining members of his retinue. Choy Liqiu, who had cooked for him since the loss of his chef in the Tien Shan, was now pregnant from a stockman named Ng Shilin who came along with her.

On the day before departure, Xiang Li called to him Corporal Hua and Guardsman Jiao. They crashed to attention in front of him, both red-faced and sweating in their bamboo armour.

"Corporal Hua," said Xiang, "I travel now as an ambassador and have need of an enhanced escort. You have done well. You are promoted to Sergeant."

Hua beamed at attention.

"Guardsman Jiao, I have been impressed by your attention to duty. There is a vacancy in my escort for a Corporal. You are thus promoted."

"Th-thank you, Gōng," stuttered Jiao.

"Silence when you speak to the Gōng," bawled Sergeant Hua. *Things were going to change around here now he was a Sergeant,* thought Hua.

"That will be all," said Xiang LI

Both guards grounded the butts of their spears, saluted and crashed off.

Xiang Li rather thought he was developing a headache.

* * *

Apart from flying insects, the trip down the Tigris was a delightful interlude for the travellers. The raft was long, heavy and narrow, manned by a steersman and four labourers with poles who kept it from grounding on sandbanks or colliding with rocks in the frequent rapids. It was equipped with an awning and a small cabin although the latter was so stuffy that Xiang Li declined to use it.

The countryside was at first dry with bare hills close at hand but, as they progressed, palm trees appeared on the banks and then fields being prepared for planting. The river broadened and became more placid on the second day. It was edged with reeds amongst which waded the sacred ibis.

They stopped each night – rapids and narrows made night navigation too dangerous – but Xiang Li estimated that they made nearly fifty miles a day, simply drifting along on the current. Occasionally they would pass other rafts being hauled upstream by teams of oxen and the crew would shout good-natured abuse at their colleagues. As night fell, they would moor at riverside villages where there was accommodation for the Gōng and good food for all.

And over all, in the west, for those with eyes to see it, the luminous anomaly shone.

On the fourth day the steersman pointed across a wide loop in the river.

"Seleucia," he said.

Xiang Li shaded his eyes and peered into the morning glare. Behind a low mist he made out the walls and towers of the distant town. They seemed to waver in his sight. *Heat rising from the ground?* he thought. Then a violent shiver racked his frame, making his teeth chatter. Te Zhu, suddenly alert, rose swiftly from her nest among the cargo and, leaping the intervening fifteen feet with an athletic grace at odds with her years, was just in time to cushion Xiang Li's head, as his body folded under him.

"Khasan!" she shouted.

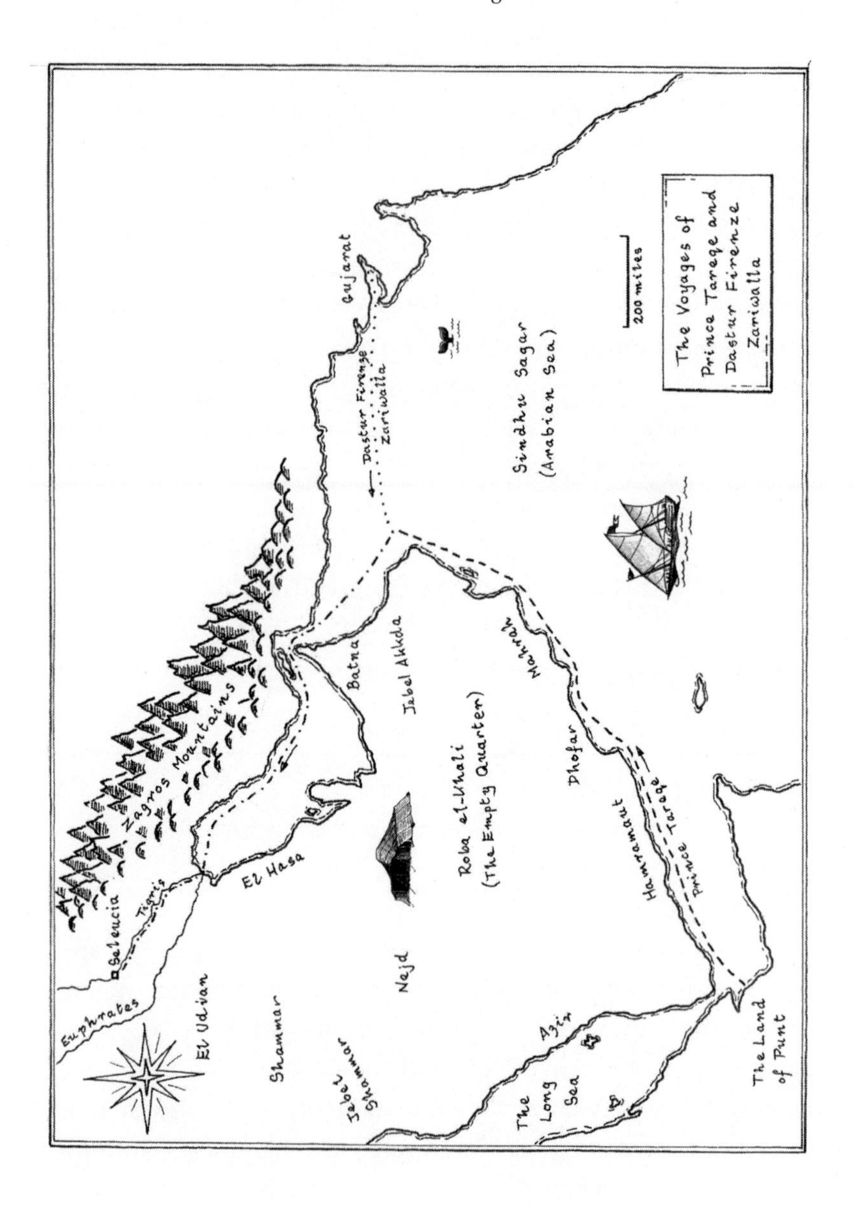
The Voyages of
Prince Tareqe and
Dastur Firenze
Zariwalla
200 miles
Gujarat
Dastur Firenze
Zariwalla
Sindhu Sagar
(Arabian Sea)
Zagros Mountains
Seleucia
Tigris
Euphrates
El Udvian
Shammar
Jebel Shammar
Nejd
El Hasa
Batna
Jebel Akhda
Roba el-Khali
(The Empty Quarter)
Mahrah
Dhofar
Hamramaut
Prince Tareqe
Azir
The Long Sea
The Land of Punt

Chapter Thirty-one

Prince Tareqe

Prince Tareqe squats motionless in the shade of a rock. His face is towards the ocean, sightless. He is deep within. He hears the footfall of an ant, the dry rustling of a dead leaf, half a mile away. He has squatted here since dawn, his breath almost stilled, his pulse barely perceptible.

He raises his head questing unseen currents then, in one graceful movement, rises. He stretches, runs his hands through his greying curls then calls, "Negasi."

A youth rises from the shade of a bush and lopes along the beach, his ebony skin gleaming in the setting sun. He bows. "Prince," he says, placing a gourd into the other's hands.

Prince Tareqe drinks deep from the gourd before handing it back.

"It will be tonight," he says, "at moonrise. Run now and tell the elders."

Negasi touches his brow, turns and speeds off through the dunes.

Pulling his light cotton stole around him, the Prince makes his way down the beach to his boat. It is an elegant craft, worthy of a prince, created of juniper planking from the hinterland. Its prow is high and built into it is a covered area. The tall mast carries a dipping lug sail of stout cotton, currently stowed in the hull.

He leans over the gunwale and checks once more the water gourds and food stowed in the bows. He doesn't know how far he will travel but is confident that more supplies will be provided as necessary. He checks the lashings on the steering oar and the paddles stowed under the thwarts.

The sun is slipping behind the dunes now. Prince Tareqe turns towards the ocean and shades his eyes, looking to the north-east. The Gebanite coast lies there beyond the haze. He thinks that he will head towards it at first. He half expects that it will then be the Long Sea to the north-west, the seaway to Egypt, but he keeps an open mind.

A harmony of bass voices swells over the dunes and he turns, watches the elders come to him in two files, bearing gifts. Negasi dances along beside them. They form a semi-circle around their Prince, beating time with their feet. Fsha raises his voice in a brief ululation. At its abrupt finish, the men still.

Prince Tareqe casts his gaze slowly over them from left to right; his friends and sometime opponents but always loved. They understand what he must do and none will stay him. Even if he goes to his death, they are glad for him.

"Fsha, stand with me," he commands.

Fsha comes forward, turns and stands beside him.

"Fsha is your leader," he says in a clear voice. "Obey him in all things."

"Wa!" say the elders, stamping their approval.

The Prince turns and kisses Fsha.

"Go well, my brother," says Fsha. He hands the Prince a package wrapped in leaves.

"It is the myrrh resin, as you asked."

Prince Tareqe takes the package, thanks his brother, turns to stow it deep under the covered bow.

One by one the others come forward with their gifts for the voyage – gifts of food, water and practical items like knives. Each is approved of then stowed. Then the men stand looking towards the east in silence. The sun has set behind the dunes and the eastern horizon is limned with a silvery radiance which grows by the minute.

Prince Tareqe and Negasi take their places in the boat. The elders gather round the gunwales. The radiance grows until, suddenly, a sliver of silver breaks clear of the horizon.

As one the elders shout again, "Wa!" They stamp into the sand, chanting, push the boat down towards the gentle breakers. On and on they go, reluctant to lose their last contact with their Prince, until they stand shoulder-deep. The Prince commands Negasi to hoist the sail. It catches the wind as the young man sheets it home and the boat picks up speed.

Prince Tareqe turns and raises his hand in farewell. The elders raise theirs in return. There are no more words. The Prince sails outward along the moon path.

Chapter Thirty-two

Dastur Firenze Zariwalla

Dastur Firenze Zariwalla, High Priest of Zarathustra, Arthravan and Magoi, weeps. He is an old man with a long, snowy beard who has tended the sacred fire and dispensed justice through the dadgah court for many years. He wishes to die here in the fire house above the beach, at the end of the harbour. He does not wish to travel. Gujarat is his home.

For months now, since he has completed his analysis of the prophecies to be found in the fragments of the Avestan belonging to this Parsi community, he has resisted the Call, telling himself that he is self-deluded, wishing upon himself a status which is not his.

But now the star has come. He is conversant with the stars and their wanderings. At first he had taken it to be the Seed Star, Sothis, glowing brighter, a remarkable phenomenon in itself. But now he knows it is something else, something awesome, awful – something which confirms his studies. The end time is coming when evil be will be wiped from the face of the Earth and the molten metal from all the Earth shall pour into Hell and it shall be no more.

He should be joyful that he is alive to see it – indeed to be a Witness. But, instead, he weeps.

Where will he find the energy? Who will tend the sacred fire? What will become of Pavaani, his wife? He rocks to and fro, tears falling on his white robes.

"Father." It is Haarith, his son. He places his hand on the old man's shoulder.

"The ship is ready, Father. The shipmaster says he must sail with the tide. Come, now."

He helps his father to his feet. The old man dries his eyes on the sleeve of his robe. Haarith watches with pride as his father masters himself. His back straightens and his eyes take on the look of command, the gaze of a Dastur. He places his hands on his son's shoulders, looks deep into his eyes.

"I shall not return, son."

Haarith makes to protest but Firenze shakes his head impatiently.

"No time for that, my son. Wherever it is I am called to go, this old body will not bring me home. You are now Dastur. You have done well. You deserve this honour. I am proud of you."

Haarith bows his head. The tears are now his. Firenze places his hands on his son's head and murmurs a blessing, calling on the mighty angel Mithras to guide the way of his feet. He kisses his son, bends with a groan and picks up his bundle.

"You will tell your mother when the ship has sailed. Look after her, my son."

With that, he pats his son on the arm and makes his way on stiff legs out of the atash gah, down the beach to the waiting ship.

Chapter Thirty-three

First Meeting

Prince Tareqe and Negasi sail for many days. Their way lies not up the Long Sea to Egypt since, before they reached the Gebanite Coast, the wind has turned foul from the north-west. So the Prince bears away to the north-east on a broad reach and Negasi trims the sail. They parallel the Gebanite Coast, keeping an offing of some three miles to avoid shoals.

Mostly they sail all night, guided by the moon and stars. Negasi catches fish with a long line and they eat well. They put ashore from time to time, at the mouths of rivers, to replenish their water but they avoid the occasional coastal villages and small ports for this is an un-chancy coast where thieves and pirates are not unknown.

The Prince owns deep knowledge of the sea-lore of his forebears so he is unsurprised when, on the sixteenth day, the land which has hitherto trended to the north-east, falls away around a mighty headland. He debates whether to follow it round to the north-west but at first the wind is foul then it falls away altogether.

Night falls and the boat rides uneasily on a low swell, the halliards rattling against the mast. Prince Tareqe sits serenely, awaiting that which will happen.

* * *

Firenze Zariwalla is awakened by shouts and the sound of running feet. It has been an easy voyage so far although the Dastur is not a natural sailor. For much of the time he has remained in bed or, when the weather is fine, on a charpoy which the master has arranged for him near the steering platform.

Firenze is alarmed. He struggles from his bed and notices that the door to his cabin is outlined in flickering orange. He feels panic but fights it down. It will do him no good. He stops and thinks then gropes around first for his belt which contains his small supply of gold. He straps it round his waist then puts on his robe, his turban and his slippers. Then, grasping his bundle, he gingerly opens the door.

The scene on deck is terrifying. Flames belch from the hold, stark against the night. The master and his four crewmen are silhouetted against the fire. They are hauling buckets of water from the sea and throwing it on the flames but to no effect. A detached part of his brain thinks *cooking oil*. Yes, that's what the master said was the major part of the cargo. It was bound for Oman, he remembers.

As he watches, the hair of one of the crew catches light. The man screams and throws himself overboard. Firenze staggers as the swell lifts the hull. He shields his eyes with his hand and gropes his way to the side of the ship where he grasps the rigging. Part of the deck between him and the mouth of the hold now collapses and a gout of flames seers his face. He can no longer see the crew.

He turns to the side of the ship, looks down at the dark waters, wondering if death by drowning would be preferable to burning. There is a grinding noise and something – a pole perhaps – passes his face. He wonders if he is losing his mind. Then there are hands, beckoning and voices speaking a strange language. As if in a dream he passes his bundle to the hands then struggles to climb the bulwark.

It is soon evident that his strength is too little. A lithe figure leaps to his side, slings him over its shoulder, as if he were a child, and climbs back down into the boat. He is laid gently on the bottom boards then there are more strange words and the boat stands off from the burning ship.

* * *

Prince Tareqe and Negasi paddle the boat to a safe distance then heave-to. While Negasi watches for survivors, the Prince gently wraps the old man in blankets and places a roll of sailcloth under his head. The old man is shivering now, deep in shock. Prince Tareqe places his fingers on the man's head and his thumbs on his temples then closes his eyes and is silent. After a time the old man relaxes into a deep sleep.

The Prince makes his way back to the steering oar and between them he and Negasi quarter the dark waters, seeking any sign of life. After half an hour the ship is burnt to its waterline. It turns turtle and the fire is quenched. The two men take paddles and slowly navigate through the wreckage, calling out from time to time but there are no replies. They stay until the dawning sun reveals a field of devastation. They see two bodies. One is being jerked from below in a parody of life. The big fish are at work. There is nothing more to be done.

With the dawn comes a fair breeze from the south. Negasi hoists the sail and, as it begins to draw, the Prince puts over the helm until they are running before the wind. Small waves chuckle under the prow and a small school of dolphins comes and leaps ahead of them.

At the steering oar, the Prince is content. This, then, is the way. In two to three days they will pass through a narrow gap between two great headlands into an inland sea. Then they will see. He wonders briefly what part the old man will play. Then Negasi comes aft with biscuit, fish and water for his breakfast.

Thus it is that the Prince Tareqe of the Land of Punt and Dastur Firenze Zariwalla, High Priest of Zarathustra, meet and sail together into the Gulf.

Chapter Thirty-four

The Magi Gather

Te Zhu sat on a bollard on the Great Wharf that fronted the River Tigris. She could not have said why she sat there at this time on this day but she looked around her with great satisfaction. The port was busy with purposeful activity. Here were rafts, poling down from the hinterland, there a sea-going dhow, nosing in towards the wharf on the last breaths of the morning breeze. Around her slaves carried bales and boxes from a barge tied up alongside.

She raised her face towards the morning sun and closed her eyes. Yes, this was a place where a sufferer from the damp disease could be happy. She flexed her fingers. No, not a twinge. But then she smiled ruefully. It did not seem likely that she would be allowed to stay and, anyway, she had not yet had her fill of adventure.

Opening her eyes she looked downstream and there, weaving among the river traffic, was an elegant sailing boat, also ghosting in towards the wharf on the dying wind. She stood and took the few steps to the edge of the wharf so that she could follow its approach. She noted that two of the crew were slim, black men. Although she had never seen black people before her arrival in the Land of the Rivers, she was so open to wonders that she took their appearance in her stride. She imagined that somewhere in this world there might even be white people, if only one travelled far enough.

The tall youth in the bows of the boat let the sail fall and began coiling a rope attached to the bows. He looked at Te Zhu and held up the coil, nodding in the universal language of sailors which she took to mean "If I throw this to you, can I trust you to catch it and not do something silly with it?" She nodded back.

The young man threw the rope; Te Zhu caught it, whipped it round the bollard and took in the slack as the boat touched the pilings ten feet below her. The young man made a revolving gesture with his hands. Te Zhu took in the last of the slack and made fast with a knot learnt from the camel pullers.

Moments later a face split by a large grin arrived at the top of the ladder and said something to her in a strange language which she took to be thanks. She said, "Not at all," and held out her hand to help the youth onto the wharf. He went aft and took another rope from down below, making it fast to another bollard, then came back to the ladder, lay on his stomach and reached downward. There followed a period of muffled words, heaving and straining before a very old man wearing a very crooked turban came into sight.

With Te Zhu's assistance the very old man was brought onto the wharf where he stood swaying, supported by the young man. Almost immediately another face appeared over the edge of the wharf. Te Zhu was transfixed by its nobility and serenity, also the grace of the tall body as it stepped from the ladder. *This,* she thought, *is Such a One*. For a long moment the two gazed deep into each other's eyes then, as one, they bowed.

In her best coast-wise, trading patois, learnt from the bargemen, she said, "Take-see master. Come along me."

And Prince Tareqe of the Land of Punt touched his breast and said, in the same language, "Much thank you."

* * *

Xiang Li relaxed on a couch under an awning on the roof. Simon ben Zephaniah, his Jewish host, stood to one side as the Greek physician completed his examination.

"Laudable," was his verdict, as he began repacking his bag. "Rest and nutrition have worked their inevitable cure. Light activity is indicated in order to improve muscle tone. Other than that, given a sensible regimen coupled with regular purging, your cure is complete, an outcome for which I can take very little credit."

Xiang Li thanked the physician and handed him a small, heavy bag. With expressions of mutual esteem, the Greek took his leave and Simon ben Zephaniah resumed his seat at Xiang Li's side.

"So, my friend," he said. "You will soon be able to resume your journey."

Xiang Li was hazy about how he came to be a guest of the Jewish seer and alchemist. Nor was Te Zhu ever likely to explain how it came about. Simon, on the other hand, a compassionate man of learning, had been delighted to facilitate the recuperation of such a great seer and savant from beyond the mountains, once the little, yellow woman with the penetrating eyes had explained his importance.

"Yes, dear colleague," said Xiang Li. "The desire for speed is strong and yet there is that in my mind which tells me to pause here awhile. Not," he turned to his host, "that I would trespass on your hospitality."

"As to that," said Simon, raising his hands, "you are welcome to stay here as long as you wish. It is not often that I am granted the chance to speak at length with one of such cultivation and knowledge."

As he had recovered from the physical collapse brought on by the journey ("Perfectly understandable although culpable in one not suited to the rigours of winter travel" as the Greek physician had put it) Xiang Li had delighted in discovering the depth of knowledge displayed by his host. Techniques in astronomy and astrology were exchanged, details of scrying methods discussed. Simon showed Xiang Li the secrets of his alchemical workshop and it had seemed natural to share with him the reasons for his journey.

What he had not shared with the Jew was a further visitation by the Being of Power at some stage after he fell into stupor. The memory of what had been said was not clear but it seemed to him that he had been told that he was not to proceed alone. For this reason, although the pull to move westwards was strong and the stellar anomaly grew nightly in intensity, he tarried here, waiting.

A bell rang in the courtyard. There was the sound of footsteps and a door being opened then a small commotion. Both men stood and went to the parapet. Below them Xiang Li saw Dargan, Khasan and the servant woman together with a tall, black man and two porters carrying a litter upon which lay an old man with a white beard. Simon turned to the stairs and Xiang Li followed.

Chapter Thirty-five

Counsel

"It is the Sun behind the Sun," said Firenze.

"Tiphareth, the Martyred God of Qabbala," said Simon.

"An astronomical anomaly," opined Xiang Li.

Prince Tareqe held his counsel.

The four men stood on the roof of Simon's house, taking turns to view the burgeoning light in the sky through a water-filled sphere. Each spoke using the common language of trade and, if their words were not quite as exact as given, they were each understood by the other.

"The question is, what does it mean?" said Xiang Li, looking at the others. "Would it be true to say that each of you have felt the Call?"

Firenze nodded. "I felt the Call from hidden meanings in my religion's texts. I fought it. I wished to die at home, but when the Light came, I could deny it no more. I believe I shall die on this journey but that is not the point. My witness is needed."

They turned to the Prince.

"I felt the Call through the earth and the wind. It bade me wait so I provisioned my boat and waited. When the moment came, it was very clear. We launched our boat and put ourselves in the hands of wind and current."

"And I shall ever be grateful that you waited, my Prince," said Firenze, crossing his hands on his breast and bowing. He turned to Xiang Li. "And what of you, Gōng Xiang Li?"

Xiang Li said, "I am a rational man and perhaps I needed a more specific Calling than either of you, my friends. I fell into a stupor and a Being of Power spoke to me. Simon tells me, by my description, that it was an Archangel called Gabriel." He hesitated. "The same Being came to me in my recent illness and told me to await two companions before I journeyed on."

The three were silent. Simon raised his hands.

"To be honest, although I have studied the Star and wondered, I have felt no Call, only curiosity. And having heard your words, Xiang Li, it is clear to me that these are your companions. I shall be happy to do all I can to support you in your onward journey but my place is here."

Silence fell again for a moment. Then Xiang Li said, "It is well, Simon. You are a true friend and we are grateful for your help. Now, my friends, hear my words and give me your wisdom. I have followed the – shall we call it 'Star' – for many months. Always it has stood just to the south of west and that has been the direction of my travel. I have formed the opinion, although based upon very little, that we are Called to the birth of a king in a land called Judaea."

"Ah, Judaea!" said Simon. "Home of my people. But Judaea has a king, King Herod Antipater. If an heir were due word would surely have spread along the trade routes by now."

He paused, looking thoughtful.

"Unless ... unless..."

"Yes?" prompted Xiang Li.

"We Jews had a prophet, that is a seer, one who foretells the future, called Isaiah," began Simon, slowly. "He told us that a king would come, one who would lead Israel, that being our foremost tribe, out of captivity. This king we name 'The Messiah'. We long for his coming. Our holy book, the Torah, reports Isaiah as saying, "The people that walked in darkness have seen a great light; they that dwell in the land of the shadow of death, upon them hath the light shined."

He turned his face up towards the Star and his features were bathed in a dim, silvery light.

"And I ask myself, could this be the coming of the Messiah?"

Chapter Thirty-six

Onward

And so it was decided that the Three who had been Called should travel on, as quickly as possible, to Judaea and preparations were made.

Khasan was consulted. He had already sought diligently for details of the onward journey.

"Ways are good. Many caravanserais. We no need fodder, travel light. Buy good camel, we maybe take less than two month."

So Sergeant Hua was summoned to bring the one remaining treasury chest. Xiang Li lifted the lid. Although it was nearly full, the latest outgoings would make quite a hole in it. For the first time he wondered how he would finance his return journey. *Well, there was no help for it,* he thought. No doubt with a strict budget it could be managed somehow.

The health of Firenze Zariwalla posed a problem. Although rest and good food had brought him back from extreme frailty, he was not a well man. Nor, as it transpired, had he ever ridden a camel. The advice of the Greek physician was sought.

"Out of the question!" had been his response. "Here," indicating Firenze, who lay on a couch, stripped to the waist, looking apprehensive, "we see a case of a heart weakened by years of poor exercise and fatty foods. You will note the breathlessness, the fatigue and the swelling of the ankles. Riding astride a camel takes reserves of energy and a muscle tone that this man patently does not possess. Should you be foolish enough to disregard my advice, I can take no responsibility, no responsibility *whatsoever* for the outcome."

Again, Khasan provided the solution.

"Camel litter," he said. "Couch one side of hump. Load

balance it other side. Priest ride lying down. Very comfortable."

Prince Tareqe's boat was hoisted out of the water and stowed in a corner of a warehouse.

The pregnancy of Choy Liqiu, Xiang's cook, was so far advanced that she could travel no further. She was desperately unhappy to be parted from the remaining group of those who had set out so long ago from Korla. Xiang gave her and Ng Shilin sufficient funds to cover the period of the confinement and more, as well as the promise that they would rejoin the caravan on the return journey.

Xiang Li pondered his reduced retinue – Sergeant Hua, Corporal Jiao and that woman. Well, the guardsmen could not be expected to minister to his needs. He thought he really should speak to that woman, explain her new duties but somehow there was so much to do that, in the end, he didn't.

There had been much discussion as to where they should aim. Judaea was such a large target. On the final evening, Simon brought out a scroll from his copy of the Torah.

"My friends," he began, "to my great sorrow I am not as great an authority on our Holy Book as I would wish, but something has been nagging at my mind. So I sought the advice of Rabbi Sharrett. He directed me to a prophecy by another of our prophets named Micah."

He unrolled the scroll, found his place. "This is what the prophet says: 'But thou, Beth-lehem Ephrathah, which art little to be among the thousands of Judah, out of thee shall one come forth unto Me that is to be ruler in Israel; whose goings forth are from of old, from ancient of days'."

He looked up, expectantly. They others looked back at him blankly. Simon realized that he would have to explain.

"You see, the prophet is saying that a king shall be born in Bethlehem in the district of Ephrathah, which has long been sacred to my people. He will be a leader of the tribe of Judah which is the largest tribe in Judaea that we also know as Israel."

There was a pause then Xiang cleared his throat and said, "Simon, I would not wish to give offence but, look around. We come from the furthest corners of the world. While we may be very happy for your people that a king is to be born to you, why have we been Called to witness?"

Crestfallen, Simon said, "I ... I cannot say."

Then Firenze spoke. "My friend, you say that this has been nagging at your mind: can you explain that further?"

Simon brightened. "It was two nights ago. I had been restless and awoke in the middle of the night. The name 'Micah' was in my mind."

He looked around. "Trust me, my friends, the name is known to me only through the readings at the synagogue. I am not aware that I have thought of it at all otherwise. But when I awoke it was still there. It gave me no rest until I sought out the Rabbi."

Firenze nodded, thoughtfully. "Do you see, my friends? This has much in common with our own experiences. We have little idea where we are going or why so if the name of this town has been vouchsafed us through our good friend Simon, we should not be quick to ignore it."

Prince Tareqe said, "You speak well, brother. We cannot deny the Call. Neither can we deny the Star. Signs and portents abound. We walk in strange paths, not of this world. We must be open to every new sign, open as children. We cannot say how important this birth is to all of us or how far its ripples will spread."

So it was agreed that Bethlehem should be their eventual goal but discussion continued about whether they should go straight there.

"My advice," said Simon, "is that you avoid drawing the attention of the Roman authorities. From all I know of them, they are pragmatic, wanting only to collect tolls from ordinary travellers. But once raise their suspicions and they are notably officious. If you come to their attention they will meddle."

Firenze felt that, if only as a matter of protocol, they should first call upon Herod Antipater, the ruler of Judaea.

"For we represent our own lands and it could be seen as a snub if, after travelling so far, we do not pay him obeisance. Besides, he is most likely to have knowledge of an important birth and will be able to speed us on our way."

As a ruling prince, Tareqe was inclined to agree but Xiang had doubts.

"It seems to me that the birth of a non-dynastic king would threaten this Herod. Successions are chancy things. Many a legitimate heir has been done away with and many a pretender too. I have reservations about walking into the middle of such a situation. What if Herod knows nothing about this birth and we are the ones who bring him the news? Might we not find ourselves accessory to murder?"

The discussion continued well into the night with no firm decision taken. In the end it was shelved until nearer their arrival.

Chapter Thirty-seven

The Desert Way

And so the day of departure dawned. Xiang Li could not but compare it with the departure from Korla, with all its fear and chaos. No Dorba Tembay bullied and shouted. Khasan could shout when he needed to but he seldom did. Ordered strings of camels waited in the main caravanserai outside the city, most of them led by his own, trusted pullers. He, Xiang Li, was now competent to control his own mount, an aristocratic beast, named, in the vernacular, Aneesa the Witch.

Chimbai Dargan supervised the loading of Firenze Zariwalla into his litter with commendable solicitude. The old men had struck up a friendship in the last week. Dargan, sensing the other's fear of the coming journey, had set out to dispel his worries and ensure that it would be as smooth as possible.

Khasan made his way towards Xiang Li. "All is ready, Gōng," he said.

Xiang Li turned to Simon. "Thank you for everything, brother," he said. "If Fate allows we will pass this way again and tell you what happened."

They embraced. "Go well, brother," said Simon. "Whatever happens, I am glad to have been a part of it."

To the Camel Master, Xiang Li said, "Let us go, Jochi Khasan." Then he mounted Aneesa who groaned wickedly and rose to her feet.

"Forward!" shouted Khasan, and, in a moaning, tinkling cloud of dust, the caravan lurched off.

* * *

Their route lay at first to the south west through fields of wheat and vegetables to the River Euphrates. They crossed easily in an hour on a large raft then, again, through fields irrigated by river water for several days. Gradually arable farming gave way to high, steppe-like plains where herds of animals grazed. They headed south-west for some weeks, their aim being to pass to the south of the Great Syrian Desert and then to join the major trade route which came out of the Hot Lands to the south and so onwards towards the sea.

The caravan quickly shook down into its daily routine. They ate before first light then made as many miles as they could before the main heat of the day. While the sun passed through its zenith, they rested in what shade they could find before going on in late afternoon and early evening. Xiang Li calculated that they covered perhaps a third again as much as had been managed on the steppes of Xinjiang since they were a smaller group, mounted on first-class beasts and unencumbered by stock animals.

At night they would sometimes stop at caravanserais or, as the country became drier, oases. At other times they would simply sleep under the stars and Xiang Li came to love such nights, gazing up at the heavens. The further they travelled, the brighter became the Star. It began to outshine the new moon. He was aware that it lay somewhat to the right of their line of march and he became impatient for the moment when they could turn towards it.

Other than that, he was content, indeed, he sometimes thought, happier than he had ever been. The heat agreed with him. He had adopted the light clothing of the desert traveller including a head dress which he could wrap around his face when the wind whipped up the dust. If there was one blot on the horizon, it had been in the culinary department.

Although she hadn't been asked, Te Zhu cheerfully took over duty as the Gōng's cook and, by extension, that of Dastur Firenze Zariwalla and Prince Tareqe. If Te Zhu had a fault, it was a belief in her own ability. Generally speaking this was justified but, in the matter of fine cooking, it was not. The situation had worsened by a fine collection of herbs and spices which Choy Liqiu had pressed upon her.

Prince Tareqe was the first to absent himself from the evening meal on the second day into the journey. This was after the previous evening's highly unusual chicken dish. On the third evening Firenze did not appear in the Gōng's yurt and therefore missed an excursion into marinated yak. Xiang Li chewed grimly on. Despite all the privations of the journey, the provision of a private cook continued to seem a necessity for a man of his status.

On the fourth evening, as he chewed his way through a ragout of goat, his teeth crunched upon something. Removing it from his mouth he found part of the beast's jawbone including an array of discoloured molars. He gave Te Zhu a look which, in Xianjiang Province might have killed, placed the jawbone on his plate and left.

His arrival at the puller's fireside went largely unremarked. He sat between the Prince and Firenze. Nothing was said as he scooped a share of stew from the communal pot and began to eat. And it is a matter of history that for as long as he stayed with the caravan thereafter, he ate with the pullers and never regretted it.

Prince Tareqe and Negasi chose not to ride and Xiang marvelled to watch them stride on mile after mile apparently without effort. Even Firenze, his fears forgotten, seemed to bloom. Many of his aches and pains dissipated in the hot, dry air and Dargan marched beside him conversing, as old men will, of times gone by when the world was a better, more beautiful place.

Khasan had hired the services of an experienced guide, Dara Sukhaara, one who knew the trade routes intimately. Soon he began earning his keep as the way climbed up onto an arid, sandstone massif. What water existed up here was contained in oases and a knowledge of their whereabouts was essential to the management of the beasts and their watering. Yet the road was well marked.

Xiang Li sensed that they were travelling a route which had existed since antiquity. In the barer areas, where the sandstone poked through the thin soil, it was often worn smooth by the passage of endless hooves. And then there were the oases – Tayma, Dedan, Duma, Jawf, Sakakah and more – each with their ancient temples and cisterns, mute, timeless.

They passed caravans heading the other way and at times arrived at oases, already occupied. Then there was singing and dancing into the night. They were figures of curiosity, coming as they did from so far away. The pullers of this trade route travelled thousands of miles every year through the Hot Lands but they could not get enough of Khasan's and Dargan's tales of the High Steppes beyond the mountains.

And night after night, the Star grew in size and brilliance and all men looked at it and wondered. There came a dawn when the sun had not yet risen, when Xiang Li, speaking with Khasan about the day's march, realized that the caravan master's face was glowing faintly silver. He turned and saw that the Star was yet visible, even against the growing blue of the sky. And then the sun rose above the horizon and the Star was gone.

On the twenty-ninth day after leaving Seleucia, they joined another great trade road and turned to the north-west. They entered a wide valley. Dara Sukhaara said it was the Wadi Sirhan which would carry them all the way to the frontier of Judaea. Sandstone heights stood on either side but gradually became more distant as they travelled.

The land was more arid and the heat intense. Flies were everywhere and Xiang Li took to wearing gauze across his face. The way became a wide, straggling weave of tracks. Oases were fewer and more widely spaced – Isawiya, Tarfeiya, Ghutti, Nebk. Their water came from deep wells. At the end of a hot day, it was a joy to gulp down a cupful, even if it was warm and tasted of minerals. Dara Sukhaara schooled them in the way of the desert – to avoid drinking water in the heat of the day but, rather, to suck a pebble.

One night Xiang Li stood alone, away from the campfires, gazing at the stars. He held his fist before him at arm's length. Prince Tareqe came and stood beside him. After a while he spoke.

"What is it you do, brother?"

Xiang Li lowered his arm and turned.

"You will have noticed that the Star grows ever brighter as we travel?"

The Prince nodded.

"Well, I have just realized that it is also rising in altitude."

The Prince looked blank. Xiang Li beckoned him to his side.

"See," he said, "when I first saw it, months ago, many miles to the east, it stood beside Sothis, the Seed Star."

He pointed to a bright, bluey-white star. Prince Tareqe knew it as The Hound.

"Three months ago," Xiang Li continued, "I noted that it stood just below the yellowish star we call Wěi Sù Yī." He pointed.

"It is Head-of-the-Lizard in my country," said the Prince.

"But now," said Xiang Li, "look. It stands before Lóusù Zēng Liù."

He turned to Prince Tareqe.

"As we travel west, the Star is moving up the sky, towards the zenith."

They were silent for a moment, considering.

"Then it must stand above a point somewhere ahead of us," said the Prince, slowly.

"Yes," agreed Xiang Li and the two men turned again and gazed at the light in the sky.

Chapter Thirty-eight

Chief Eunuch Ping (4)

The insurrection, when it came, was not unexpected. Whilst he was possessed of a subtle mind, Weng Liang lacked almost every other quality of leadership necessary to rule a numerous and contentious people. Indeed, he was probably the first to realize that he had made a mistake in displacing Chief Eunuch Ping.

When the Xiongu made one of their periodic incursions in strength, Weng insisted on deploying the Dragon Regiment in an untenable position, resulting in its massacre. The generals were furious and thereafter thwarted him at every turn.

His peculations, particularly in the field of tax collection, lacked the elegance and finesses that had characterised Ping's. Nor was he consistent in his punishments and praise. It became unsafe for him to walk the streets so he remained in the palace, gnawing his nails.

Then a large part of the crops failed which would not have mattered but he'd sold all the surpluses. There was hunger that winter and on the heels of hunger, rioting. The generals refused to intervene and, in the end, Weng was dragged from the palace and hanged from the battlements above the northern gate.

Zhiqiang Qiu, Imperial Inspector of the North-western Quadrant, being made aware of events, rode to Korla at the head of a strong force and put down the rioting with characteristic savagery. Sitting in the palace in the aftermath, it quickly became clear to him that there was no-one suitable to take over the running of the city until his enquiries revealed that Chief Eunuch Ping yet lived in his dungeon.

Ping was released, roughly washed and brought before him. The eunuch made a sorry sight. His hair was gone and his skin was covered in sores. Worst of all, the enormous stomach of which Ping had been inordinately proud, hung slack and empty, nearly all the way to his knees. Yet his eyes still burned with intelligence. *Something,* thought the Imperial Inspector of the North-western Quadrant, *might be salvaged.*

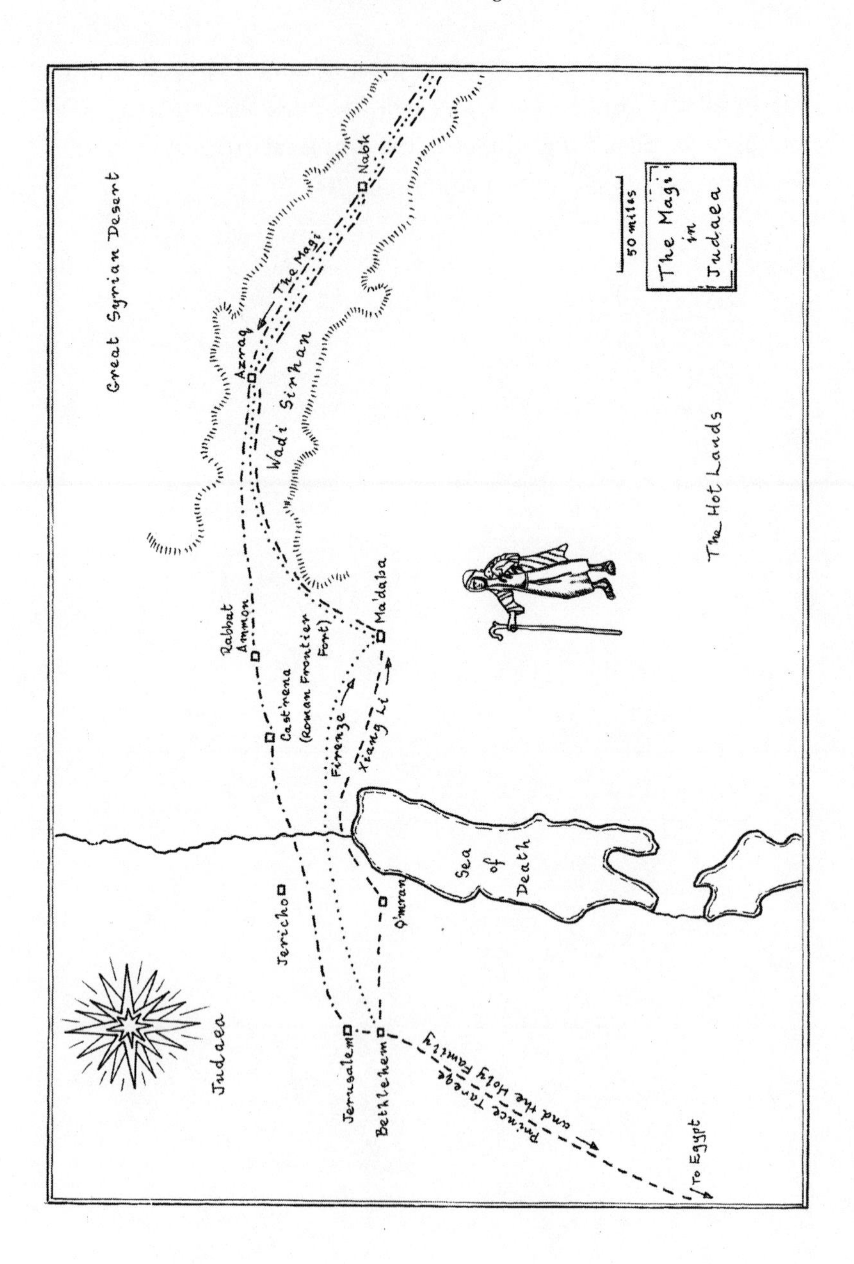
The Magi
in
Judaea
50 miles
Great Syrian Desert
Nabk
The Magi
Azraq
Wadi Sirhan
The Hot Lands
Rabbat
Ammon
Madaba
Cast'nena
(Roman Frontier
Fort)
Firenze
Xiang Li
Sea
of
Death
Jericho
Q'mran
Jerusalem
Bethlehem
Judaea
Prince Tareqe
and the Holy Family
To Egypt

Chapter Thirty-nine

Enter the Romans

By the forty-third day of the journey, it felt as if they had travelled the desert for ever. The trade route now wove between isolated, conical hills, trending towards the western side of the wadi, nearer to the steepening slope of the sandstone massif. Towards evening, the massif began to fall away and they camped that night among date palms, at Azraq, an oasis where a road from the north joined theirs. On the morrow their route, said Dara Sukhaara, lay to the west, to the Nabataean town, Rabbaṯ ʿammôn.

"Normally we would turn south there to Petra, the capital," he said. "That is a great centre for the trading of incense, myrrh and frankincense mostly."

"Tell us of these Nabataeans," said Firenze.

"Lord, they are an ancient race, fallen upon hard times. There was a time when they ruled all the land from Sinai to the mountains." Sukhaara swept his hand in a wide arc. "They fought battles and were victorious more often than not. But then," he paused, sighing dramatically, "they fought the Romans."

He paused awaiting the inevitable question.

"And what of these Romans?" asked Tareqe.

Sukhaara's face became bleak.

"Ah the Romans. The Romans wish to conquer all the world. They are not as other people. They rule in straight lines and without mercy. When they fight they are like..." He waved his hand as if seeking inspiration. "...like a steel tortoise. They defeated the Nabataeans but instead of taking over their lands, they allow a king to rule in Petra but one chosen by them. And the Nabataeans pay them tribute each year."

"But you will see the Romans soon as you travel on to Judaea. You will see whether Sukhaara speaks true. But this I counsel you," he said, holding up a finger, "if you come to their notice, always seek to be submissive."

There was silence while the others took in his words. At last Xiang Li spoke.

"And what of our onward journey?"

"From Rabbaṯ ʿammôn. we will travel straight on for two days. After one day we will cross the border into Judaea and there you will be levied tax by the Romans. The next day we will cross a river called the Jordan. We turn south on the far bank and it is then but a further day's journey to Jerusalem."

* * *

At Sukhaara's suggestion, the three men took counsel and agreed that, to the Romans, they would present themselves as emissaries to King Herod. Xiang Li was still not convinced that they should seek audience with the king but accepted that their status as emissaries would facilitate their entrance into Judaea.

"We shall call ourselves Magi," said Firenze, gently joking. And when they asked him want this meant he explained that Magi were the high-priests of his religion.

"It is they who are the sacred fire-keepers, the wisest of wise men under Ahura Mazda, the One God. And you see," he said, gesturing to the heavens, "we are led by the fire and are we not wise?"

"The Three Wise Magi," said Prince Tareqe, tasting the name on his tongue. He laughed. Yet amongst them the name stuck, partly as a shorthand and partly as an ironic joke.

And so it was that on the forty-ninth day of their journey, in mid-morning, they came in sight of a squat, sandstone fort, lying to the north of the track. As they approached, the gates of the fort opened and a section of Roman cavalry rode forth. Xiang Li observed them with the critical eye of one used to military formations.

They rode in two files, the leader of the left-hand carrying a lance with a pennon, that on the right bearing a white plume on his helmet, marking him as the leader. The mounts, stocky ponies of no great height, were evidently out for the first time this day. They shook their manes and snorted but Xiang Li noted that their riders had them well in hand. The formation was tight. The files crossed their line of march then curved tightly round and halted, blocking their way. No orders had been given.

Xiang Li and Prince Tareqe went forward with Sukhaara as interpreter. The Roman decurion, resplendent in chain mail and a burnished helmet, walked his horse a short way towards them. Sukhaara spoke, indicating the two men and the caravan. The Roman replied in clipped tones. Sukhaara turned to Xiang Li.

"They wish to inspect the caravan. It would be wise to let them."

The inspection took half an hour, during which time a clerk had ridden out from the fort. The decurion announced that the tariff would be one sescuncia of gold in respect of the trade goods belonging to the pullers and a further uncia as entry fee for the caravan to the Province of Judaea. Sergeant Hua was called forward with the treasury chest. His uniform excited a degree of ribaldry from the Roman ranks, quickly silenced by a sharp order. Ingots were weighed and shavings made into the clerk's scales.

As the transaction was completed, another officer appeared on foot, with an escort of four spearmen. A broad, muscled man, he cut an impressive figure in his red tunic and metal-inlayed, leather half armour. The red plume on his helmet nodded in the faint desert breeze. The decurion dismounted, saluted by bringing his clenched right fist to his breast and made his report.

"This is centurion," said Sukhaara discretely to Xiang Li and Tareqe. "He command fort."

Just then the guide was called forward. The centurion questioned him. Sukhaara indicated the two men several times and then the centurion beckoned them forward.

"Centurion wish to know where you from. You speak slowly, I tell him in his language."

Xiang cleared his throat. "I am Gōng Xiang Li. I come from The Land. It lies many miles to the east," he waved his hand, "beyond the mountains. I come as ambassador from my emperor to the court of King Herod Antipater."

The centurion looked at him long and hard, then turned his attention to the Prince.

"I am Prince Tareqe of the Land of Punt which lies many miles to the south, beyond the sea. I too am an ambassador to King Herod."

At the urging of Firenze, Dargan now brought forward the camel upon which his litter lay.

"And I," he said in a reedy voice, "am Dastur Firenze Zariwalla, High Priest of Zarathustra from the Land of Gujarat, far beyond the eastern sea."

The centurion looked at them each in turn then spoke. Sukhaara translated.

"Centurion say, how is it that you all come from so far away but arrive together?"

Xiang Li, keeping an impassive face thought quickly.

Tell him you have all had a dream.

The voice was very clear in his mind. He was sure he had heard it somewhere before. He looked around but, apart from his comrades, there was only that woman, standing half way between them and the caravan. He turned back to the centurion.

"Each of us, Commander, had a similar dream, telling us to come here. We met at Seleucia and now we travel together to Judaea."

The centurion shook his head. He spoke briefly.

"Centurion not believe. Want truth."

Tell him of the Star, said the voice.

"The dream told us to follow the Star." Without thought, Xiang pointed upward to where he knew the Star showed itself at night. The centurion looked up, following the finger. Just at that moment the sun went behind a small cloud. Xiang Li heard the centurion gasp. Then there was an outbreak of surprised comment from the cavalrymen. Xiang Li too looked up.

There, ghostly but clear in the blue sky, stood the Star. A moment later the cloud passed and, as full sunlight returned, the Star disappeared. But a change had come over the company.

What the Magi did not know and perhaps Sukhaara too, was that rational, hardened fighting men though the Romans were, beneath the steely exterior lurked a healthy respect for the gods and their signs. Xiang Li saw fear in the eyes of the cavalrymen. The centurion was more successful in keeping his feelings to himself but Xiang Li noted dilated nostrils and a distant look in the man's eyes. The officer spoke.

"Centurion say, stay here."

The officer turned, barked some orders at the decurion, then set off back to the fort. The decurion redeployed his men in a wide half circle ahead of the caravan. Camels lay down and pullers found what shade they could along their flanks. After a while, a detachment of half a dozen cavalry left the fort and set off at a canter towards the west. Shortly afterwards the centurion returned. The Magi, with Sukhaara, went to meet him. The guide listened attentively as the centurion spoke then turned.

"Centurion say he send message to headquarters in Jerusalem. He say we go straight there now, report to Præfect at Antonia Fortress. He send messenger ahead. He say, we go but escort follow, join us in one hour. He say, don't even think of going anywhere else."

Taking it upon himself to act as spokesman, Xiang Li bowed and said, "Tell the centurion we are flattered by his care for our welfare, that we shall do as he commands without demur and that we wish him a long life and many children."

When Sukhaara finished translating, the centurion snorted, gave Xiang Li a long, hard gaze, seeking signs of sarcasm, then turned on his heel and, followed by his men, set off back to the fort.

Chapter Forty

Into Judaea

As the caravan and its escort headed west, the land became steadily more fertile, at first just in the wadi bottoms but increasingly on the higher land. The Roman escort kept to themselves. Everyone began casting eyes towards the zenith. When the sun occasionally went behind a cloud, a rustle of comment swept through caravan and escort alike. With the sun occluded, the Star stood forth with the radiance of a waning moon by day.

"It moves to our left."

Prince Tareqe had come to walk beside Xiang Li's camel. He pointed.

"See, as it rises, it moves more and more this way." Tareqe moved his arm to the south.

"Yes," said Xiang. "It is as you say. It is as if it stands over a point somewhere to our left and not very distant."

"Jerusalem?" hazarded Tareqe.

"Bethlehem?" suggested Xiang Li.

They camped that night on the east bank of the River Jordan, the Star high above them, vying with the moon, lighting up the surrounding vineyards and olive groves. Xiang Li had expected a deep, bold river, but here it was more a wide, placid stream. At the camp-fire, Sukhaara spoke of its significance.

Pointing across the river he said, "Jewish tribes call this Promised Land. It promised them by their God. Many years back, Jews held captive in Egypt." He pointed to the south.

"They escape, wander many years then come to river. They think crossing river give them freedom and it true. They free to fight each other many years until," he lowered his voice, "Romans come. They also call it Land of Milk and Honey." He paused reflectively. "More like Grape and Olive but you see tomorrow. It good place."

And he was right. They forded the Jordan soon after dawn and the desert was forgotten. True, there were still outcrops of arid sandstone, but in the wide valley bottoms, irrigation and farming were intense. They turned just south of west. Xiang Li noted that the Star, almost at the zenith, still stood a whisker to the left of their track. *Perhaps not Jerusalem,* he thought. But then all other thoughts were swept away as they breasted a rise and the Holy City came into view.

Xiang Li took in the tall, honey-coloured walls. He marked the fortified gates and the many towers. *A place of defence,* he thought, *but to man those long walls ... It would take many thousands of warriors. Even from a distance it emanated, what? – power, antiquity, reverence? All of these,* he thought. Perhaps it was simply the fact that he was finally here after so many miles and hazards. Perhaps it was this that brought a sense of wonder to his mind and a moistness to his eyes.

Two of the escort detached and cantered ahead towards the city. The decurion fell back to ride beside Xiang Li. Sukhaara closed in to interpret.

"Caravan will stop there." He pointed towards a huddle of buildings outside the wall. "You, Gōng and other Lords go with him to Antonia." He pointed towards a crenelated gate. "Præfect see you when he ready."

The decurion kicked his horse into a trot and rode back to the head of the column.

* * *

A mighty fortification, thought Xiang, as they passed through the huge, crenelated gatehouse in the city wall. But fortifications are only as good as those defending them and he was not impressed by the gate guards. Several were obese. Uniforms were shabby and stained. In one case he saw a spear leant against a wall while its owner gnawed on a bone.

"High priest's men," muttered Sukhaara, noting the direction of the Gōng's gaze. "They not Romans. Bandits more like." He made to spit then thought better of it.

They came out of the shadow of the gate. A large, blocky building with a tower at each corner stood before them, white in the glare of the sun.

"Antonia Tower." Sukhaara's voice held an edge of fear. "Romans control city from there."

He indicated the wall of a vast building beyond.

"Jews' Temple. Romans sit in Antonia looking over wall, waiting for trouble."

This, thought Xiang, *was more like it,* a compact fort with high walls commanded by towers.

The decurion led them towards a tunnel-like gate. Roman guards stood tall in spotless uniforms on either side, their spears vertical. Others patrolled their sentry beats with measured tread. Xiang Li was impressed. More, he felt at home. This was a well-organised, military headquarters. To Firenze and the Prince he said, "Will you be happy if I do the talking on our behalf? This is the kind of environment in which I used to live." Both nodded.

Outside the gate they paused while Firenze was helped from his litter. An optio emerged from the gate and the decurion made his report. He beckoned them forward. It had been agreed that each of the Magi should be accompanied, to make a retinue. Thus Dargan supported Firenze, Negasi followed the Prince and Xiang Li led Sergeant Hua and Sukhaara. At the last moment, as they entered the gate, Xiang saw from the corner of his eye, the compact figure of that woman, who had apparently attached herself to the group. He was furious but it was too late to order her away.

Along corridors they were led, through a courtyard and up a flight of stairs. Having stopped impatiently several times, the optio finally slowed his pace to accommodate Firenze's laboured progress. They entered a small anteroom. The optio spoke.

"He say wait here," said Sukhaara. Dargan and Negasi helped Firenze onto a bench. Xiang Li moved to a window. He found himself looking down into the Temple, a vast complex of arcades, and tiled roofs. It was dominated by a huge, square building with marble pillars and golden finials. Not for the first time the pragmatic mandarin pondered the amount of energy and money people were willing to expend on their gods. *A clean water supply and proper drainage would be more to the point in this heat,* he thought.

A door opened and a young officer beckoned. They stood and made their way into the room beyond. It was a cool, elegant chamber with doors leading to a balcony. Standing looking out of the doors with his back to them was a tall, grey-haired man, his loose robe billowing slightly in the breeze. *Just as I would have stood,* thought Xiang Li, *and now he will turn.*

The man turned. First impressions were of a hooked nose and a commanding eye. He opened his arms and spoke. Before Sukhaara could translate, a clerk spoke in the common tongue of the trade roads. "Julianus Secundinius Publius, Præfect of Judaea, Samaria and Idumea bids you welcome."

Xiang bowed. "We are grateful to the noble Julianus Secundinius Publius. May I present Prince Tareqe of the Land of Punt and Dastur Firenze Zariwalla, High Priest of Zarathustra from Gujarat. I am Gōng Xiang Li, from The Land, Governor of Xinjiang Province, Mandarin of the First Level."

The clerk struggled a little with the translation. The Præfect spoke again.

"I see that one, at least, of your company is fatigued by your journey. Please be seated and take some refreshment."

They sat on couches and servants placed before them cakes and cups of cool liquid. While their needs were attended to, the Præfect took up a clay tablet.

"My commander at Castr'ena tells me that you are emissaries

to King Herod, come to Judaea as a result of a shared dream. He further states that you believe there to be some link between the dream and the phenomenon in the sky which has been turning the night to day for months past."

He looked up, his keen eye taking in each of the Magi. "It is clear that the worthy Centurion Cornelius does not believe this story. Perhaps you would care to convince me."

There was a pause while Xiang Li marshalled his thoughts, then speaking slowly so that the clerk had time for translation, he began.

"If I may, I will start with a question, Lord Præfect."

Secundinius nodded.

"You have seen the Star. Would you agree that it is an actual, objective phenomenon?"

"I know what I see," he replied, carefully. "What it is and whether it is a sign from the gods, I do not know."

"Tell me," said Xiang, "when did you first see it?"

Secundinius turned and exchanged some words with an aide who stood in the shadows.

"It was first noticed some six months ago. I am told that those who study the sky failed to notice it at first because it is so near the zenith. Also, at first, it was very faint. Since then it has become steadily brighter. I may say that it is causing some disturbance among the populace who fear that it is a portent."

Xiang Li closed his eyes and calculated. Then, "Præfect, I first saw this phenomenon very faintly nine months ago, so far to the east that it has taken me eight months to travel here. It was very faint, at an altitude of perhaps twenty degrees and almost due west. As I have travelled it has slowly risen in the sky and become brighter."

Secundinius was impressed. Clearly this was not one of the god-crazed fools that wandered out of the desert from time to time.

"And what of the dream?"

"Lord Præfect, mine is a pragmatic culture. We do not believe greatly in gods. Neither do we disbelieve. Whether 'dream' is the right word, I do not know. I fell into a stupor whilst studying the Star and it seemed – forgive me – that a Being of Power spoke to me. It told me to travel towards the Star because I was needed as a witness. I have no explanation of this but, when I revived, nothing would do but I took to the road. It was a compulsion."

Secundinius studied the dry, aesthetic man before him. He had heard travellers' tales of an empire, far beyond the mountains, where people had yellow skins and strange eyes. It was where the silk, so coveted by Roman society, came from. The matter of the Star had lain heavy on his mind for some months. He was of the opinion that it was a portent. But of what? He turned to Firenze.

"And what of you, Dastur Firenze Zariwalla? If you will forgive me, I think this journey has taken a toll of your strength. Why, then, do you travel?"

Firenze, already much recovered, placed his hands together and bowed to the Roman.

"May it please you, Lord Præfect, my Call came not from a dream but, rather from my studies of the Sacred Texts of my religion. It became quite clear to me that the End Time is upon us and, with that realization came the Star. I wished to die at home in my own fire-house but, like my noble friend, there was no gainsaying the Call. I set sail and later was rescued by Prince Tareqe. Together we sailed to the city of Seleucia where we met the Gōng Xiang Li and joined him in journeying here."

Secundinius nodded. "Thank you." He turned to the Prince, who had sat throughout, straight-backed and serene.

"And what of you, Prince Tareqe?"

Fixing the Roman with a steady gaze, he spoke slowly and clearly.

"I study the sea. I listen to the land, Lord Præfect. I scent the breeze. I gaze long into the fire at night. They tell me that something comes, that I must witness. At the full of the moon, I launched my boat. Wind and current brought me here. Often in my life I am called but never like this. Never so strong. I come."

Secundinius sat for a moment transfixed. Then he blinked. He turned again to Xiang Li.

"So," he said, "you have each explained what brought you here. Why do you say that you are emissaries to King Herod? And if emissaries, whom do you represent?"

Tell him of the birth. Once more the voice invaded his mind. This time he resisted. He was not going to do its bidding – certainly not tell this Roman about the possibility of a royal birth.

"We believe we are summoned to a royal birth and it is for this reason that we seek audience with King Herod."

Years of diplomatic training prevented Xiang Li from jerking round towards Firenze. *We agreed we wouldn't mention that,* he wanted to say. *We agreed that I would speak for all of us.*

"A royal birth? I know nothing of a royal birth. What exactly have you heard?" asked the Præfect.

Firenze, ashen-faced, looked towards Xiang Li, beseeching him to answer.

"We know nothing for certain, Lord Præfect," said Xiang Li, smoothly. "One might say it is more an intuition. The Star stands above Jerusalem and, if a portent, it must portend something important. It seemed natural to seek audience with King Herod to ask him if he could unravel this mystery for us."

Secundinius rose abruptly and strode to the window, tapping his lips with the clay tablet. He stood for a while, looking down into the courtyard. Then he turned.

"You should know, all of you, that Judaea is a turbulent province and that the royal succession has seldom been bloodless." His voice, previously smooth and diplomatic, had taken on a commanding edge. "King Herod is a client of Rome, maintained on his throne by Roman arms. Factions abound. The balance is extremely fine. The Jewish people seek any justification for insurrection. If a rival for the throne has been born, I need to know about it."

He turned to his aide and issued a string of orders which were not translated. The aide left the chamber.

"I have sent a messenger to the King's court requesting an early audience for you. In the manner of these things 'early' probably means tomorrow, if not later. For now, I suggest that you return to your caravan and await a summons. You will be escorted to the King by my representative and an honour guard."

And so they were dismissed. In the ante-chamber Firenze turned to Xiang Li.

"Brother, I am so ashamed but it was as if I lost command of my voice. I have no idea where the words came from."

So clearly agitated was the old man that Xiang Li could not be angry.

"Firenze, my friend, the same thing has happened to me on several occasions since I started my journey. It was not your fault. I know not from whence comes this voice but if I find out, there will be a reckoning."

He looked searchingly around his retinue. In the background a small figure humbly bowed.

Chapter Forty-one

Waiting

Back at the caravanserai, Khasan was called and they took counsel.

"We seem to find ourselves in the middle of a political crisis," said Xiang Li. "The Roman Præfect holds military power and King Herod is his puppet. However, the peace here can be very quickly compromised by the advent of a pretender to the throne. I have made no secret of my doubts about involving the king in our quest but now we are committed to speaking with him and in front of the Romans. How, then, are we to complete the task before us, that of witnessing a royal birth, without bringing disaster in our wake?"

There was silence. Then Prince Tareqe spoke.

"Brothers, we forget in our anxiety, that we have been Called here by powers beyond our understanding. Think for a moment. We came from three corners of the world, unknown to each other. I met Firenze in the moment of his greatest danger in the middle of the ocean. We came together at Seleucia. All had been Called. All had seen the Star."

"Ask yourselves now, have we seen the roads thronged with others following the Star?"

The company looked one at another. There was a low mumble of conversation then a shaking of heads.

"No," said Tareqe. "Even though everyone can see the Star and wonder what it means, only we appear to have followed it."

He raised a finger.

"I say this to you: have faith in the Power which has guided us here. Worry not about tomorrow. For now, eat, sleep and be ready, for of this you can be sure: we will see our part when the moment comes and we must be ready."

* * *

And so they go, each to their own place but few to sleep.

Xiang Li opens the last treasury chest and counts its dwindling contents. He sighs and then, not knowing why, he removes one golden ingot and places it in his money belt. He closes the chest and replaces it, then sits, and, despite the Prince's words, worries about what the morrow will bring.

Firenze tosses and turns unable to sleep, ashamed and humiliated by his outburst in front of the Præfect. He feels that he is a useless old man; that his mind and body are betraying him. In the end he rises and gathers sticks and dried camel dung into a pile. He goes to the remains of the campfire and, selecting a burning stick, sets light to his small fire. He squats before it and begins the prayer of supplication to Ahura Mazda. Later he will find rest.

Dargan and Khasan go round the people of the caravan, speaking to them in low voices, answering their questions, sensing their temper. They check harnesses and discuss the beasts and their loads. They finish at the door of the caravanserai, looking out into the night. Khasan, whose eyes are sharp, points out several figures, lurking in shadows and doorways. They are watched.

At the prompting of Sergeant Hua, he and Corporal Jiao look out their bamboo armour. It is battered but still serviceable. They start cleaning it. Conversation across military ranks is ever strained but after a while they relax and talk of Korla on the Black Lake, of Captain Fong and their lost comrades. Corporal Jiao produces a whet stone and late into the night they put an edge on every spear, sword and knife in their small armoury.

In the Antonia, lamps burn long into the night. Præfect Secundinius makes his military dispositions in preparation for an uprising. He curses the fact that they are in the middle of a census with all its turbulence. Tribunes and centurions are called from their beds and ordered to report their commands' operational status. Spies are called in and questioned. Others are sent out to watch and wait. Finally, he consults the soothsayers, to very little purpose, as it turns out. The general consensus is that Jupiter is angry. *Nothing new there then,* thinks the Præfect.

Te Zhu and Prince Tareqe meet briefly at the door of the caravanserai. Without words they acknowledge each other's presence then go each to opposite ends of the camp. There they take up their posts. Powers and Principalities are abroad tonight. For those with ears to hear there is the plangent music of the stars. Yet for others, there is the bestial howling of the Netherworld. Universes collide, possibilities arise and collapse in this tiny corner of the world tonight. Together the small Chinese woman and the Prince of the Land of Punt will protect those in their care.

Chapter Forty-two

King Herod

The day dawned overcast and sultry. The Magi rose and put on their best garments then sat together. Talk was desultory. The sun climbed. They wondered if the summons would come today at all. The first aroma of the communal lunch was wafting across the caravanserai, starting gastric juices, when a burnished guard of six legionaries headed by a tribune halted outside the entrance.

Removing his plumed helmet, the tribune entered, accompanied by a clerk.

Referring to a clay tablet the clerk said, "We seek Gōng Xiang Li, Prince Tareqe of the Land of Punt and Dastur Firenze Zariwalla."

The three men rose, Firenze assisted by Dargan and Negasi.

"We are they," said Xiang Li.

"Then will you please accompany Tribune Trebatius who will escort you to King Herod's court."

The Præfect had sent a litter and four stout slaves to carry Firenze. Xiang Li was impressed by this detail and more inclined to think kindly of the Romans. Their way lay through the crenelated gate, past the Antonia and through the narrow streets of the city. The heat was oppressive and flies rose in clouds at their passage.

They passed through a gate in an inner wall.

"The Gate of Ephraim," whispered Sukhaara.

There before them rose a confection of colonnades and beyond them a huge building. As an amateur architect of some experience, Xiang Li appreciated its elegant proportions and flowing lines. He wondered why his appreciation was spoilt by a sense of oppression.

In the long, sandy space between the stone walls of the city and the colonnades, stood perhaps fifty guards. They were smarter than the guards who manned the city gates but still compared unfavourably with the Roman legionaries. Xiang Li rather thought it was a matter of attitude. He imagined the Romans would cut a way through to the Nether-world if ordered but would do so without undue emotion whereas the King's guard had the look of fire-mountains preparing to erupt. Certainly the eyes following their progress across the sand expressed suspicion and disdain.

Tribune Trebatius led the party to a gate in the colonnades, guarded by two soldiers who barred their way with spears until a burly under-officer emerged from the gatehouse and cast his saturnine gaze over the company. He grunted and the spears were removed. Within were wide gardens. Here were fountains and trellises bearing grape vines. Peacocks strutted with mournful cries.

Now the looks which followed them were those of courtiers, or so it seemed to Xiang Li, although not of the kind he would have entertained in Korla. They drifted around the gardens, apparently aimlessly, communicating in low twitters and although every face was turned in the direction of the little cavalcade, each one seemed to bear the stamp of extreme disinterest and boredom.

A chamberlain bowed to the Tribune and ushered them towards a door in the massive palace building, guarded by some ten men. They exuded a sense of swagger and, again, looked on the newcomers with suspicion. The tribune spoke to the optio commanding the escort who ordered his men to halt. More words were exchanged.

"Officer say keep men out of trouble. Stay clear of palace guards," whispered Sukhaara to Xiang Li. "This not nice place," he finished.

The tribune turned and spoke to the party. His clerk translated.

"We are about to enter the palace of King Herod. You may each be accompanied by one servant. You will now be searched for weapons."

"May we be permitted our translator, in addition to our servants?" asked Xiang Li.

The tribune spoke to the chamberlain who shook his head.

"You have no need of a translator," said the clerk.

Sukhaara, shrugged, a look of relief flooding his face. He went to join the legionaries.

Each was now subject to an expert, invasive search. Xiang Li exchanged a look with Prince Tareqe. Both understood this as a ritual of humiliation. They would not allow themselves to be humiliated. For Firenze, who stood, supported by Dargan, it was not so easy. In Gujarat his person was inviolate and he was a very old man of great dignity. By the end of the search he was glassy-eyed and sweating profusely. Xiang Li and the Prince went and stood by him.

"Courage, my friend," said Xiang Li. "They want to intimidate us. Do not let them."

For his part, the Prince simply placed his hand on the back of the old man's neck for some seconds. Firenze closed his eyes and relaxed a little.

The chamberlain gestured them forward. Dargan held the arm of Firenze. Negasi took up station behind the Prince. Xiang Li realized that, forbidden his translator, he had no servant to follow him. Looking around, he caught the eye of that woman. What on earth was she doing here? She smiled demurely at him. The others were entering the door. Angrily, Xiang Li snapped his fingers at Te Zhu and, thus supported, he entered the place of King Herod Antipater.

* * *

Xiang Li dislikes Herod on sight, a soft, oily man, with the eyes of a cobra. His sumptuous tunic, designed to accentuate lost youth, cannot hide a protuberant belly. Nor can cosmetics remove the ravages of dissolution from his sensual face. And yet he is all affability, if one can ignore his failure to meet the eyes of his visitors.

"My friends," he lisps, "welcome to Our humble home."

The tribune has explained that it is usual to approach the throne on hands and knees although an exception could be made for the old men, indicating Firenze and Dargan. Xiang Li and Prince Tareqe choose not to understand. Negasi and Te Zhu follow their lead. Four guards step from behind pillars, hands upon hilts, but Herod waves negligently at them and they back away.

Introductions are made, gifts exchanged.

"My friends," the King says, "ambassadors from far lands. Our loyal Præfect Secundinius has told Us of your journeying from afar. Sit now. Eat. Drink. Tell Us of your quest."

Xiang Li makes to remain standing but is waved down. A cloying scent of incense burning on tall tripods distracts him. Courtiers drift closer in a sibilance of silk, their pale, moon faces soft with boredom. A voluptuous young woman glides from the shadows and sinks upon the steps of the dais, at the King's feet. He places a be-ringed hand upon her head, stroking and kneading. Her gaze strips the mandarin, promising him fleshly delights of unimaginable depravity.

"Your Greatness." Xiang Li finds his voice and struggles on. "We have travelled, as you say, from far lands, each in his own way Called. Latterly, we have journeyed towards the Star which hangs here almost overhead."

Xiang Li pauses, not sure how much of their quest to reveal. He awaits the intervention of the voice but nothing happens.

The King has turned away. A servant is offering a tray. Herod selects a plump grape and pops it into his moist mouth. He chews, his black beard, shot with grey, working in time with the motion of his jaw. He turns back to Xiang Li.

"And?" he says, gesturing for more with his free hand. "And?"

His voice is soft but carries an undertone of menace.

"And Lord, we do not know why we have been drawn here." He falters.

"But?" The smile resembles the snout of a jackal. "But?"

Xiang swallows. "But, Your Greatness, we think it may be because we are called to witness a royal birth."

"Good!" chortles King Herod. "Well done, my friend. See, that was not so difficult, was it?"

The courtiers titter and guffaw. The sound is not pleasant. Xiang Li wishes he was anywhere but here.

"You see," continues the King, and the laughter stops, "our good Præfect Secundinius has appraised Us of this fact and We declare it has intrigued Us no end. A royal birth! Would We not know of a royal birth in Our own kingdom? Mariamne," he cups the chin of the woman at his feet and raises her face, "have you forgotten to wash your passage with lemon juice again?"

Shrieks and gales of laughter ensue. Courtiers clasp each other in pantomimes of paroxysm. Xiang Li looks straight ahead in stony silence. He hopes that he is not blushing. Herod raises his hand. Silence.

"No, but it does not do to make game of our honoured guests, even so slightly. Friends, We will ask you to leave Our Presence for a while as We take counsel with Our wisest advisers. It may be that they can shed light upon this matter. Then We shall recall you and tell you of Our royal decision."

He waves his hand in dismissal, raises Mariamne's face and bestows upon her full lips a kiss both long and lingering. The Magi rise.

"One backs from the Royal Presence," whispers the tribune.

Xiang Li looks at Prince Tareqe. They nod. The party backs from the audience chamber. They have under-estimated the peril of this place.

As the cedar doors slam shut, King Herod stands, Mariamne clinging to his right leg. The King extends his arm. He sweeps one bitten index finger in a slow arc across the faces of the courtiers.

"Know this," he hisses. "The next King that occupies this throne will be an issue of *my* loins! Hm?"

He searches the jumble of faces, seeking fear. He finds it.

"And if any one of you," his finger moves back through its arc, this time stabbing at each female face, "who thinks to hide one of my by-blows from me, will scream for *death! Hm*?"

He turns, drags Mariamne to her feet by her hair.

"Advisers to me," he shouts and stomps from the room.

* * *

The Magi and their retinue stand in a pillared ante-chamber.

"What…?" begins Firenze but Xiang Li raises his hand.

"This chamber is very similar to one in my summer palace at Korla." He places his finger across his lips and looks into the eyes of each of his companions.

"Note the cornices and here, these carved pediments. But the greatest feature was the pierced walls."

He gestures towards the intricate piercing between two of the marble pillars.

"They are a wonderful device for keeping cool in summer." He forces a chuckle. He speaks slowly, with emphasis. "Sadly they also transmit sound exceedingly well and we could hear all the words of our waiting guests. It was sometimes very embarrassing."

He looks at the others once more. Suddenly Firenze's look of mystification clears. "Aaah," he says and winks at Xiang Li.

* * *

"Well, *advisers,*" sneers Herod. "It seems we are to be blessed with a royal birth. Why do I know nothing about this? Hm? Why have none of you thought *to inform me*?" His voice ends in a shout.

A Pharisee, a Sadducee, a Medean astrologer, a soothsayer from Persia, a small rabbi and a Qabbalist who wishes that he hadn't lied about his lack of occult knowledge, stand transfixed. There is conflict in the mind of the Qabbalist as to whether he is more transfixed by the threat implied by the King's words or the sight of Mariamne who is squirming upon the Royal middle finger, hidden under her dress.

The woman gasps. *"Silence, bitch!"* screams Herod, flinging her from him. She hits the floor then crawls off behind a curtain. A servant enters and offers a golden bowl to the King.

"You!" He nods at the soothsayer. "What said the entrails?"

Herod shakes his hands clear of water and wipes them on a linen towel. The servant withdraws.

"Greatness." The Persian's voice is grave, freighted with wisdom. "One kidney was marred by a growth. The left ventricle was occluded..."

"What did they say, fool?"

The Persian, who has made his reputation by surviving the wrath of kings, loses confidence for a moment.

"They ... there ... it seems that a royal birth is unlikely. Now..."

"Unlikely! Unlikely! Then why the fuck is there a fucking great star hanging over the palace and three otherwise sane men have travelled here from fuck knows where to see a fucking royal birth? Guards!"

Large men in armour emerge from the shadows. They pinion the Persian's arms. King Herod rises from his couch, takes a dagger from his sleeve and stabs the Persian in the stomach. The Persian makes mewing noises.

"Get him out of here before he stains the tiles." Herod waves the guards and the dying man away.

Herod hands the dagger to a servant who wipes it carefully

then offers it back, handle first. Herod replaces it in his sleeve. He turns, smiling, to the remaining petrified men.

"Sit, my friends, sit."

They sit. Herod resumes his couch. He receives a goblet of wine, drinks deeply.

He points to the little rabbi.

"What is that you carry, rabbi?"

The rabbi licks his lips. At first no voice emerges. He coughs.

"Greatness," he wheezes, "it is the Torah, oh Greatness."

"And what says the book of our fathers that is pertinent to this situation?"

"Well, Greatness..." The rabbi hurries to unroll the scroll. He drops one end. It rolls across the floor. None of his colleagues attempt to help. King Herod rises from his couch, picks up the errant parchment and places it in the rabbi's trembling hands.

"Take your time, rabbi, take your time," he says solicitously.

The rabbi takes a deep breath. He finds his place, marks it with a finger.

"Greatness, I have been thinking about the Star, that it appears to hang just above Jerusalem. I discussed it with my colleague." He indicates the Medean astrologer who tries to make himself very small.

"He pointed out to me that it is not exactly overhead but very slightly to the south and a little bit to the west."

King Herod nods, his wine for the moment forgotten.

"We pondered, if the Star was not overhead Jerusalem then what was it marking? We examined a map." The rabbi warms to his subject, gesticulating with his free hand.

"There are a number of small towns lying a little way to the south and west, mostly nondescript. But one caught my eye. It was Bethlehem. I knew I had heard it mentioned somewhere so I studied the Holy Books and I found it, Greatness, I found it in the Book of the Prophet Micah."

He raises the scroll close to his face and reads.

"But thou, Beth-lehem Ephrathah, which art little to be among the thousands of Judah, out of thee shall one come forth unto Me that is to be ruler in Israel; whose goings forth are from of old, from ancient of days."

Fearfully, his body draining of adrenaline, the little man raises his eyes towards his King.

"Yes," breathes Herod. "*Yes!*" he screams, flinging his goblet at the Pharisee who fails to duck.

Herod bounces to his feet, leaps the few paces to the quailing rabbi, grasps his right cheek in a vice-like grip and shakes him.

"*I fucking love you!*" he screams in the little man's face, then strides from the room.

The rabbi sobs, quietly. The Sadducee tries to staunch the flow of blood from the Pharisee's brow. The Medean astrologer vomits. The Qabbalist looks at his hands and thinks of the bakery his parents run, by the Sea of Galilee. It would be good to be baking bread again, he thinks.

* * *

The Magi and their retinue are summoned back into the royal presence. Herod sits kingly-straight on his throne although Xiang Li notices a tic in his left eye.

"Sit, my friends." The King gestures towards gilded chairs placed in a semi-circle around the dais. The Magi sit, their servants taking station behind them.

"We have taken deep council," says the King. "We have read the oracles and studied the holy books. Although nothing is clear, We are convinced that you three ... Wise Men ... have a vocation and that it is the will of He-That-We-Do-Not-Name that We assist you in your quest."

He stands.

"Hear then oh Judaea." His voice echoes about the audience chamber. "Thus says Herod Antipater, King of Judaea, Lord of

Galilee and Patriarch of Gaza. These, Our well-beloved Friends are made free of all Our lands, to roam at will and to seek diligently up and down for the King-That-Is-to-Be-Born."

He sits. The courtiers applaud.

"There," he says. He smiles wolfishly. "We will send out a proclamation that you are to be given every help in your search. Travel where you will. Call upon Our Treasury, by all means."

He pauses, as one in thought, finger on chin.

"Bethlehem. Yes, Bethlehem. Now why did that little place come into Our head? We wonder if it might be a sign. But your search could begin there as easily as anywhere. Yes, go to Bethlehem. Go tomorrow. It is a small town in the district of Ephrathah just a few miles from here."

He smiles again. The smile is marred by the tic which now involves all of the left side of his face. He points at his guests.

"But this." His voice changes and Xiang Li understands that the crisis approaches. "Yes, this: search diligently but with just this condition, just this: that when you find the royal babe (if babe there be) then hurry back to Our presence and tell Us so that We too may worship at the place of confinement."

The audience is at an end. The Magi stand, bow deeply and back out of the chamber. The doors slam to behind them. Firenze staggers. Dargan and Negasi catch him and lower him to a bench. Te Zhu goes behind him and massages his neck. Xiang Li looks at Prince Tareqe and they shake their heads.

"Come," says Tribune Trebatius, putting on his plumed helmet. He doesn't understand what he has just witnessed but will report it word-for-word to the Præfect.

Chapter Forty-three

Preparations

The Captain of the royal bodyguard stands to attention before the King, his helmet under his arm.

"They are to be followed. We wish this done covertly. Let them do the searching. None of your flat-footed military nonsense, this is a Matter Spiritual and beyond your poor comprehension. They will find a place, possibly in Bethlehem, possibly not. You will surround it. Let them leave then, when they are at a distance, kill them."

He licks his lips.

"Then kill whoever you find in the place you have surrounded."

The officer salutes, already selecting in his mind the best men for the job.

* * *

Tribune Trebatius makes his report. Præfect Julianus Secundinius Publius hears him out.

"Thank you, Tribune, that will be all."

Trebatius salutes and leaves. The Præfect rises, goes to the window, looks out at the dying day.

"Drusus."

His aide materialises at his side.

"Who are we using for assassinations these days?"

* * *

Back at the caravanserai, the travellers again take counsel.

"There is evil in the man," says Prince Tareqe. "He is awash with blood. He is not yet sure what we are going to find in Bethlehem so he will have us followed at a distance. Then he will try to destroy whatever is there."

"But surely," says Firenze, "the Powers of Light will protect the new King."

"You are a good man, Firenze Zariwalla, but this world is perhaps more complex than you deem," says the Prince. "The Powers of Light can only act through us. So we must plan and plan well."

"You are right, brother," says Xiang Li, the tactician. "We cannot afford to wait until tomorrow. We must leave quietly tonight."

"Gōng," says Khasan, "there problem. We are watched."

Dargan nods. "Spies surround us. Last night we counted four, at least, hiding in the shadows."

Xiang Li rubs his chin, thinking, then, "Sukhaara, which way lies Bethlehem?"

"Gōng, you follow the city wall that way," he points to the south, "and when you get to the corner there, you keep going. It's about six miles over the hills."

"Sergeant Hua."

"Gōng!"

"In an hour, I want you and Corporal Jiao to make your way, individually, to that corner and hide." He indicates the city wall that glimmers in the light of the Star and the point where it bends out of view. "Take with you your arms and armour but do not draw attention to yourselves. Use a disguise. When we pass you, be ready. Bar the way. Do not let anyone, anyone at all, follow us, is that clear?"

"Gōng!" says Sergeant Hua.

Khasan says, "Gōng, we can help. Pullers have knives..."

"No!" says Xiang Li, then more softly, "No, Jochi Khasan. Your responsibility is towards these people, now." He indicates the herders and pullers sitting round their fires. "We cannot know what will happen tonight but it is your duty to see these people to safety."

Khasan tries to protest but Xiang Li cuts him off.

"Khasan, you are my sworn man, yes?"

"Yes, Gōng," says Khasan.

"Then you will do my will. I am giving you the remaining treasury chest. You must use it wisely and see these people home to The Land, do you understand?"

Khasan gazes at his master for a beat then bows his head. "It shall be as you say, Gōng."

Prince Tareqe chuckles. "There is another service you may do us, Jochi Khasan. Tomorrow, there will be uproar and you will be questioned. We will need all the time you can make for us. How good are you at being an idiot?"

A big smile crosses Khasan's swarthy features. "Oh Prince, me biggest idiot in Judaea."

They all laugh, grateful for a break in the tension.

Xiang Li takes up the discussion.

"We cannot know the outcome of this night. We may be separated. We need a rendezvous. Sukhaara, is there an isolated oasis, perhaps three or four days march into the desert?"

The guide thinks for a moment, stroking his beard.

"Ma'daba," he says slowly. "Yes, Ma'daba would do. It is south of the main trade route and isolated."

"Then as soon as the caravan is free to leave, you will guide it there. Khasan, you will wait for seven days at Ma'daba. If we have not joined you by then, start the journey home."

Chapter Forty-four

Rearguard

Sergeant Hua and Corporal Jiao help each other strap on their bamboo armour. Jiao has carried it and their arms here on a mule while Hua played the part of a drunk, making his way home. Jiao hands the Sergeant his helmet. It is good to be dressed properly again. The mule is tethered to a tree, swords, spears and knives are distributed, then the two men settle down to wait.

The Magi with their servants gather in a dark recess of the caravanserai. Firenze is mounted on a mule with Dargan and Negasi supporting him. The ten pullers, stockmen and herders are gathered round them. They whisper words of farewell and blessing. More than one comes forward, self-consciously, to touch the hems of their garments.

Khasan, with tears in his eyes, speaks for them all. "It was long road, Gōng. Many dangers, many good times. You all good Gōngs. May Light shine on Path. We pray see you Ma'daba."

Firenze whispers a brief blessing on them. Xiang Li looks at Prince Tareqe. It is time. They take the lead, followed by Firenze on the mule. Te Zhu lingers behind for a moment. Khasan kneels before her. "Bless us Mother," he says. She places her hand on his head then, with a sweet smile to all her friends, she follows the others.

There is no point in pretence. Although it is the dark of the moon, the light of the Star shows everything in a silvery luminescence. Out of the corner of his eye, Xiang Li sees covert movement in a doorway. They move forward steadily, rounding the corner. He sees the two guards, tall in their helmets and nods as they pass.

The guards remain hidden until the first dark figure appears. Sergeant Hua steps out into its path, spear levelled. Corporal Jiao takes position to his right and to the rear. The figure stops but it is not alone. Jiao counts five more behind it. There is a moment's silence then one of the figures mutters in a language Jiao doesn't understand.

Instantly, the small crowd leaps forward, attempting to run round the two guards. Starlight glints on steel. The Sergeant stands his ground while Jiao steps away from the wall to block the path. He lunges at one of the men who, faster than the others, is almost past him. The spear takes him in the flank and he goes down. At the same time a second figure crashes into him, grappling, slashing at his armour. Jiao lets go of the spear, pulls his dagger from its sheath and drives it into his assailant's breast. With a bubbling groan he goes down.

Jiao turns. Sergeant Hua is slashing with his scimitar. Two bodies lie at his feet. The man in front of him is feinting with a cudgel. What Hua has not seen is a second man who has crept behind him. Jiao shouts a warning but too late. The man has slid a blade into the gap between the Sergeant's armour and his helmet. Despite this, Hua continues to slash with his blade.

Jiao draws his scimitar, screams in anger and falls on the man who has wounded his sergeant. The blade cuts into his head with a sickening clunk. Without thinking, Jiao places his boot on the man's chest before he has fallen and drags the blade from the cloven head. The one remaining assailant, unaware of his peril, is smashing at the sergeant's head with his cudgel. Hua is now down on one knee, supporting himself with his left hand while he tries to raise his scimitar.

Jiao steps to one side. Deliberately he brings his blade up to the man's neck. For a moment the man rests, panting, gathering his strength for the killing blow. Then he realizes he is not alone. Battle lust will do that for you. He drops the cudgel and starts to raise his hands. Jiao feels his lip curling with hate. The man never hears the word 'Die' because the blade has severed his spinal cord.

Jiao drops to his knee. He raises his sergeant's head and cradles it on his thigh. Gently he removes the helmet. There is blood everywhere. The sergeant breathes with great, shuddering gasps. Jiao's eyes fill with tears. This is his last comrade. A tear falls on the upturned face. Sergeant Hua opens his eyes. With a great effort he says, "Crying … Corporal … Jiao? … Soldiers … don't cry."

"No, Sergeant," sniffles Jiao.

The sergeant closes his eyes again and Jiao thinks he has gone but they open again. With one last supreme effort, the world going grey around him, Sergeant Hua says, "It's … up to you … now … lad … Make sure … they are not ... followed."

Then the dark takes him.

* * *

The travellers hear the sounds of battle and stop. Xiang Li turns but there is nothing to see. There is just the clatter of metal and the occasional shout.

"Come," he says. "We cannot help them. Our task is to reach Bethlehem before dawn."

They plod on down a track, into a broad valley. The countryside for miles around is lit up by silvery radiance. Xiang Li cranes his neck to the zenith. It is difficult to tell but it seems as though they are walking towards the Star. Night birds call. There is the occasional bark of a jackal. And so the Magi traverse the starlit Judaean Hills towards Bethlehem.

* * *

Jiao lays Sergeant Hua's head on the ground. He looks around. Bodies seem to be everywhere and the stench of blood. Without thinking, he walks over and pulls his spear from the side of his first victim. It makes an unpleasant sucking sound. Then he recovers the sergeant's spear. Carefully he wipes all the weapons. They are slippery with blood. All this he does automatically, not knowing what else to do. Then he remembers his military training – 'Follow the last order'. Well, that's clear enough. The sergeant had told him to make sure that the Gōngs are not followed. That means staying here. He relaxes.

Just then he hears the sound of marching feet coming from the north. He picks up both spears and takes cover behind the corner of the city wall. A squad of six Roman soldiers marches into sight. They stop at the scene of slaughter. The squad breaks up as legionaries turn over corpses, surreptitiously looking for loot.

"'ere decurion, ain't this one of them funny buggers they told us to watch out for?" shouts one of the men, trying to turn the body of Sergeant Hua over with his boot. Then he lets out a loud gurgle and grasps the haft of a spear which has become lodged in his stomach. One more man goes down before Corporal Jiao's frenzied attack before the others close ranks and hack him to pieces.

"Well, I never," says the decurion, wiping his brow, "it's another of them funny buggers."

They'll need to know this up the Antonia, he thinks. No point trying to follow the others now and anyway, one dead, one wounded, he needs to cover his back.

It is an interesting fact that most civilians imagine that the headquarters of a military unit represents a paragon of organisational efficiency. This is not so. In the hour taken for the squad to bind up wounds and carry their dead back to the Antonia, midnight has passed and with it the previous day's Duty Officer, a keen young man who had read all the latest bulletins including the one about a putative royal birth, who has been relieved by a negligent young man who is drunk.

Not only does he fail to read the bulletins, but he falls asleep almost immediately. In his subsequent evidence, the centurion who shook him awake will state that the tribune was befuddled and petulant. *No,* the tribune had said, he would not wake the

Præfect. *Put the decurion on a charge. Go away.*

The centurion, an old hand at this game, puts in a written report and tells the decurion to hop it. It is not until well after sunrise that the Præfect reads the report.

* * *

A shepherd of Ephrathah leans on his crook. He watches the small cavalcade, crossing the valley floor below him. There is a Light upon their brows. *These,* he thinks, *are the Ones Awaited.* They may be safely passed, unhindered. Ever since that night of frost and Starlight, when the Shining Ones came with their Song, the shepherds of Ephrathah have guarded the Child, awaiting the Witnesses.

He raises his voice in the time-hallowed language without words of the Judaean herders.

* * *

The Magi hear the melodious sound echoing across the hills. They understand instinctively that it offers them no threat but, rather, announces their coming.

* * *

Once the Roman patrol has gone, Khasan and a group of sturdy camel pullers creep out into the Star-riven night. At the corner they find the scene of carnage. Khasan whispers his orders. The bodies of Hua and Jiao are lifted with reverence and carried away into the scrub land to the east of the city walls. One of their number follows, brushing away all trace of foot prints and blood with a branch.

Well before sunrise the guardsmen have been buried and all sign of them obliterated.

Chapter Forty-five

Bethlehem

Bethlehem lies on a rise, backed by a range of arid hills. The Magi arrive at the outskirts around the first hour. Although it is a small place, Xiang Li wonders how they are to find that which they seek. Then Prince Tareqe touches his elbow and points. In all the slumbering village, there is but one light. They make their way towards it.

As they near the light, they see that it is a lantern, visible between the shutters of a window. Xiang Li feels a reluctance to go closer. The mule, however, breaks into a trot with a hideous braying squeak so that Dargan and Negasi have to run to keep up.

A man steps from the shadows and grasps the mule's bridle, bringing it to a halt. There are others, perhaps a small crowd. They are gathered in front of large, double doors. Remaining behind his companions, Xiang Li tenses, ready for trouble. But Prince Tareqe raises his hand in the sign of peace. "Shalom," says the man holding the mule's bridle.

One of the double doors is pulled open. Firenze is helped from the mule, much shaken by its brief canter. They are beckoned within. In the dim light of the lantern, they see a carpenter's workshop, rich with the smell of cedar. It is very tidy. The floor and the work bench have both been swept. Tools hang neatly on the walls – a buck saw, a set square, a rack of chisels. Xiang Li approves. Workshops, in his opinion, should always be tidied at the end of the day. The man is leading them to a staircase at the end of the workshop. Dargan and Negasi start to help Firenze up the stairs.

Seeing him hold back, Prince Tareqe offers his hand to Xiang Li. The Prince takes him by the elbow and gently urges him ahead. Xiang Li feels panic building. He doesn't know why. Te Zhu steps forward and touches the Prince's arm. They look at each other. A smile is exchanged. The Prince nods and moves ahead, up the stairs.

Te Zhu takes the Gōng's hand. *Come child, all shall be well.* Xiang Li hears the voice. He is once again in the cherry orchard in Sichuan with his mother. He allows himself to be drawn forward, up the stairs, up to the Light which is spilling through a door at the top. He pauses at the threshold. Here is a simple chamber, candle-lit, with a table and chairs and a bed. On the floor, on a cushion, sits a young woman wearing a blue gown. Standing beside her, his hand on her shoulder, is a bearded man in a homespun robe.

It is a boy child, perhaps eight months old, wearing a simple linen shift that rivets his attention. The woman is holding him upright against her knee. Xiang Li does not like young children but there is no feeling of impatience here but rather awe. The scene swims out of focus and Xiang Li sways, on the edge of fainting. Te Zhu squeezes his hand and he becomes steady again. Prince Tareqe and Firenze Zariwalla stand before the family, looking down at the child with rapt attention. Dargan and Negasi each keep hold of the priest's elbows.

Now the Prince turns to Negasi who hands him a leaf-wrapped package. Prince Tareqe of the Land of Punt takes it and, stepping forward, kneels before the Child. With head bowed, he offers up the package. "Myrrh, My Lord," he murmurs. The Child reaches out one chubby hand and touches the offering. Prince Tareqe looks up and is transfixed by two brown eyes imbued with infinite wisdom.

They grow and he is swept into their depths. He becomes one with the Dance, then is whirled into Chaos for an aeon. In sweet elegance he is strained through the Veils to coalesce with the Ancient of Days, brooding over the Void. He is born again with the Duality of Force, swept into Form and riven by the grief of the Dark Mother for her children. He experiences the enigma of the Empty Room Without a Door and glimpses multiple Universes, other Creations.

For an age as the Great King in Peace he dispenses Justice then is transformed into the King at War, mercilessly trimming misplaced energy. And finally he comes to the centre where the King and the Child are one and all is Equilibrium. And the King is the Sacrifice and the myrrh will one day embalm the flesh of the small body before him and he knows that his gift is acceptable. The visions fade and he is again a mortal man kneeling before a little child who studies him with guileless interest. He touches his brow, mouth and breast, looks at the Mother and bows, then stands and retreats to the shadows near the door.

Dastur Firenze Zariwalla, High Priest of Zarathustra is helped forward by Chimbai Dargan and Negasi. It is clear that the old man is near the end of his strength. With great difficulty he is lowered to his knees. The others kneel with him, continuing their support. Firenze knows that this will be the last act of a long life, one which he hopes will redeem all his faults and failings. He fumbles in his bag and extracts the casket which he has carried all these long miles. He opens the lid and holds it forward, head bowed. "Frankincense, Lord," he whispers. "Deity is owed nothing less."

There is silence. Greatly daring, he raises his head and all at once knows that he is loved. The Child's eyes radiate Love, not of the earthly kind but of the all-consuming Entity which binds together Everything That Is. Firenze closes his eyes and for an endless moment bathes in the warmth of being One. *Now,* he thinks, *now I can die whole.*

Then he opens his eyes again and the Child is holding out his hand, not to the frankincense but to Firenze. The old man has grandchildren and without thinking he offers one old, arthritic finger. The Child grasps it. There is a pulse of pure energy.

Firenze's rheumy old eyes fly wide and suddenly all is colour and clarity. He hears the braying of the mule from the street below and the tiny scuffles of a mouse in the thatch. He gasps, looks at the Mother who is smiling.

Forgetting himself and the formality to which his life has been subordinated, he leaps to his feet, turns to the others, his mouth agape. Then he remembers himself, turns back and bows more deeply than he has been able to for thirty years. He goes and stands by the Prince.

Negasi and Dargan remain kneeling, not knowing what to do. The Mother beckons them to come and kneel close to the Child who looks for a long moment into the eyes of each of them. They rise together and bow then turn with looks of wonder on their faces.

Xiang Li is trembling. There is no-one between him and the Child now, just an endless space of floor. He cannot move. *Come, child.* Te Zhu takes his hand and leads him forward. *Kneel, child.* He kneels, his head hung low for he knows that he should not be here. None of this is meant for a rational man. *Offer your gift.* But he doesn't have a gift! No-one told him that he had to bring a gift!

Then he remembers the single ingot of gold in his money belt, the last remaining vestige of his riches, the gold which was to fund his journey home ... Barely aware of what he does, he reaches into his tunic, unlatches the money belt and takes out the gleaming rectangle. Hesitantly he holds it forward. "This is all I have," he says, miserably. "I forgot to bring a proper gift. But perhaps you will need help with your journey and, anyway, a King needs gold for his crown."

There is silence. He looks up. The Child is mesmerised by the shining metal. Xiang Li moves it so that the candle flames strike lights from its facets. The Child gurgles happily then transfers Its gaze to the kneeling man.

In later years all Xiang Li will remember is that the look was deeply curious as if the Child had never encountered anything like this before (as, of course, it would not, having only recently been born). Also, he felt his soul (in which he does not believe) held up and scrutinized. And perhaps a message was passed, although without words (for, after all, a babe cannot form words). He never tries to put the message into words. Indeed, he forgets all that happens that night for many nights afterwards.

Stand, child. Bow.

Xiang Li stands, bows.

Go, stand by the Prince.

He turns and goes to stand beside Prince Tareqe.

Te Zhu kneels before the Child. She bows her head. When she raises it again, Child and woman gaze into each other's eyes. Then the Child chuckles and so does Te Zhu. She rises, bows as deeply as her aching back will allow, smiles at the Mother and the Father then turns and joins the others.

The Child yawns hugely. The Mother lifts him tenderly to her breast, rises and takes him to his crib. She lowers him gently and tucks his blankets around him. The Child places His thumb in His mouth, chews happily and closes His eyes.

Chapter Forty-six

Dispositions

A man seeks entry to Herod's palace. He is nearly spent, having run for more than a mile. He leans, one hand against the wall, trying to catch his breath. Between gasps he says, "… got to … see …Yedidyah. … 's urgent … let ... me in."

It's been a long watch and the guard hasn't had any entertainment.

"Let you in? You gotter be jokin'. An' who are you, anyways?"

He lounges, taking his weight on his spear.

The other has straightened up and almost gained his breath.

"You know me. I'm Mordechai, one of his watchers. You know: we're the ones who hang about and watch."

"That's as maybe," says the guard, "but at this time of night, you need proper identification."

He looks to the east, sees the first slight greying of dawn. Ought to be able to string this out almost to the end of the watch.

While the guard is distracted, Mordechai attempts to scuttle past but, despite his apparent indolence, the guard is too fast for him. He thrusts forward his spear haft, striking the other on his temple. The man goes down.

"Sarge!"

The Sergeant of the Guard pokes his head out of the guardhouse, wiping goose fat from his chin.

When he finally regains consciousness, the watcher is manacled in a cell and it is a further hour before Yedidyah, head of King Herod's intelligence service, is summoned and told of the death of six of his watchers.

* * *

The father is Joseph ben Judah, the mother Mary of Nazareth. They sit round the table with Prince Tareqe and Te Zhu. Firenze has gone out into the street with Dargan and is telling anyone who will listen that he can see and hear properly for the first time in twenty years and that his arthritis has disappeared. Xiang Li sits quietly in a corner, his head resting on his knees.

"You must leave before dawn," says the Prince. "Evil is abroad. Regrettably, our coming has brought it focus, but it could not have been otherwise. It will now try to kill the human form of the Christed One."

Joseph is a serious, sober man.

"Where then shall we go?" he asks.

"Tonight it would be as well to make as much distance away from Jerusalem as possible which means heading south," says Tareqe. "It is in my mind that Egypt lies in that direction. It is a land with very different gods where you may hide until the time is right to return."

Joseph looks at Mary.

"It was so comfortable here," she says. "The people are so friendly but, if it is as you say, then we must go for the Child's sake."

She takes her husband's hand.

"There will be work for a skilled carpenter wherever we go, Joseph."

"Well, we have the means for the journey thanks to your colleague," says Joseph, nodding at Xiang Li. "But who will show us the way? We have never travelled so far."

Te Zhu and the Prince exchange a look.

"The Prince will accompany you, will you not?" she says.

"If you will allow," he says, "for Negasi and I may as easily return to our land on an Egyptian trading ship as retrace our steps. And there is this: if it should happen that Egypt is not the safe haven that I think, you would be welcome to accompany us to my Land of Punt."

And so it is settled. Within the hour a donkey is found and loaded with the Family's meagre possessions. Mary takes the Child from his crib, wraps him warmly and fits him into a sling under her cloak. Joseph packs his best carpentry tools in a bag and hangs it over his shoulder.

The Magi meet together for the last time.

"Firenze, you will make your way to Ma'daba, will you not?" says the Prince.

"Yes," says the priest. He cannot stay still but hops from foot to foot. "Dargan knows the way. And you will come with us, brother?" he asks Xiang Li.

Xiang Li seems confused by the question. He struggles to answer, then falls silent.

"The Gong will not be coming with you," says Te Zhu. "There are things he must do. But when you see Khasan, tell him that, on his return to Korla, he is to seek audience with Mei Su, the Gong's wife, and tell her that her husband is well and will return in the fullness of time."

Firenze looks at Xiang Li but finds only a troubled passivity there. He opens his mouth to speak and then closes it.

"And now, brothers and sister, the dawn approaches and we must be gone," says the Prince. Hugs are exchanged, words of farewell muttered. At last, Prince Tareqe of the Land of Punt, turns to Te Zhu, gardener, and kneels.

"Please give me your blessing, Lady," he says.

Te Zhu places her hands on his head for a long moment then kisses him on the brow.

"May peace mark your going, my son," she says, raising him to his feet.

* * *

And so the Magi part for the last time, never to meet again in this life. Tareqe and Negasi conduct the Holy Family to Egypt and it is as if a cloak of invisibility covers their path. With the family settled, Prince and servant take ship from Port Tewfiq and arrive safely in the Land of Punt. As a reward for his service, Negasi and his younger brother are sent by trading ship to Seleucia where they recover Prince Tareqe's boat and sail it home.

Firenze Zariwalla and Dargan arrive at Ma'daba just as Khasan is preparing to leave. They travel together to Seleucia where, with a deal of emotion, goodbyes are said and Firenze takes ship to Gujarat. There he lives well past his allotted span. When he dies, he is mourned as a man of love.

Khasan and Dargan guide the caravan back to Xingjiang by the Trade Road, crossing the mountains just before winter closes the passes once more. Khasan gives Te Zhu's message to Mei Su who thanks and rewards him. When he has gone she goes up onto the battlements, looks to the west and cries bitterly.

Xiang Li goes home by a different road.

Part Three

We returned to our places, these kingdoms,
But no longer at ease here, in the old dispensation,
With an alien people clutching their gods.
I should be glad of another death.

T S Eliot

The Journey of the Magi

Chapter Forty-seven

Qmran

The young goat bleats piteously. It is difficult to see what it is standing on or what is preventing it plunging to its death down the sandstone precipice. But Xiang Li has become wise in the ways of goats. Yes, it had followed a faint goat track out along the face of the cliff and certainly, it gives every evidence of being trapped twenty feet out and unable to turn. However, Xiang Li is not fooled. So he sits in the shade of a large rock, holding out a small bunch of green leaves and makes noises calculated to sooth and encourage.

The sun rises higher, flaying the dun-coloured hills, sucking moisture from the ground. Xiang Li shades his eyes and looks to the east where the Sea of Death shimmers in the distance. Part of his mind is curious about it – the fact that a man can apparently float upon its surface as on a mattress. He even ponders the link between this and its evident salinity but arrived at no conclusions before his mind wanders away.

He croons, the goat bleats and the sun rises higher.

"No, little goat," he says out loud, "I am not going to come and get you. You must come to me and, if you do, I will give you these green leaves to eat."

The goat considers. It makes up its mind. Apparently defying gravity, it turns back towards the man with the leaves, pebbles and rocks cascading from under its hooves. It ambles over, regarding the man sardonically for a moment before dipping its head and snatching the food. Xiang Li pats its bony head. He continues to croon but it is a croon of thanksgiving.

* * *

"He has ordered the slaughter of all male children under the age of two years," said Rabbi Isaac.

Te Zhu closed her eyes and sighed deeply. She wondered if there was more they could have done, perhaps a different approach. But no. They were in the hands of something vast and complex and she must just trust that whatever happened was meant for some greater good.

"It is as our prophet Jeremiah said: 'A voice was heard in Ramah, lamentation, weeping, and great mourning, Rachel weeping for her children, refusing to be comforted, because they are no more,'" said the Rabbi.

Te Zhu pondered the tendency of the Rabbi and his community to select an apposite quotation from their holy books to cover every occasion, often a quotation which engendered a passive acceptance of fate. She understood that it suited them and perhaps also suited this arid land with its mysterious vistas of sand and broken hills. It didn't suit her. Te Zhu's guiding philosophy involved the exercise of will to a degree just short of meddling. However, she was a guest here so she murmured a non-committal response.

"And tell me," said the Rabbi, "how does your protégé come along?"

Te Zhu shifted her seat on the sandstone bench in the shade of the portico.

"Still very much within himself, Rabbi. It will take time for his mind to re-adjust from the shock. It cannot be rushed. But I appreciate that we are a burden upon your hospitality and I continue to be in debt to your compassion."

The Rabbi waved his hand dismissively.

"It is, to some extent, why we are here. Certainly our community is dedicated to study and contemplation but it is the very peace thus engendered which draws people to us. Some come to study, others for sanctuary. We would not have turned you away."

Te Zhu thought back to that evening, nearly a month ago, when she had stumbled upon this complex of buildings, hidden, apparently hewn out of the Judaean hills. She had led the Gōng for two days and nights towards the east, away from the impending dread she had felt growing behind them. She had no clear understanding of why they must head east but her instincts had not let her down. The Gōng had been just short of stuporous, able to walk, but having to be fed. It had not been an easy journey.

But when they arrived, footsore and weary, they had been taken in without question, given food and bedded down. A physician tended to their cuts and bruises. When he was physically recovered, Xiang Li had been assessed and, since he was not speaking but appeared sentient, he was put in charge of the goat flock. His duties were not onerous – take fifteen goats out in the morning and return with the same number in the evening – and he had performed them perfectly.

Te Zhu, meanwhile, apart from keeping an eye on the Gōng, had performed such domestic chores as appealed to her and spent much time in deep conversation with saintly old Rabbi Isaac who led the community. In him she found an evolved soul with whom she could speak more or less freely. Together they had tried to piece together recent events and put them into historical context.

"Whether or not the Babe is in fact the longed-for Messiah is by no means clear but everything that has happened – the birth at Bethlehem and the slaughter of the first-born, fits with our prophecies."

The Rabbi smiled a twinkling smile at the small woman.

"I think, perhaps, you are impatient with our preoccupation with ancient writings but you must understand that we are living history. Our God is very real to us and all around," he waved a hand in a semi-circle, "are places where He has made Himself known to us. To us, history is a living journey and our prophets have laid down way-marks for us which, if we interpret them correctly, will show us how to proceed."

Te Zhu smiled back. She liked the Rabbi, especially his self-deprecation.

"Rabbi," she said, "this is your land and your God. I cannot listen to Him as you can. I would be a fool if I wandered here without giving heed to one such as you, steeped in the wisdom of this place."

The Rabbi waved away the compliment. They were silent for a while, looking out across the vegetable gardens, carefully tended and irrigated with water drawn from deep cisterns in the rock.

"How do you conceive of the way ahead for you and your Lord?" asked the Rabbi, at length.

Te Zhu considered.

"He will go home, for he is now a Witness, but when and how must be decided by him. He will know when that time comes and I must not interfere. What I can do – what we can both do – is to watch for signs of returning competence."

She paused, sipping from a cup of water.

"You see, in his own land, the Gōng is a supremely powerful figure. He is also an intelligent and practical man. But the philosophy of the ruling classes of The Land is one of rational pragmatism. This allows for the exact management of a complex empire yet it acknowledges nothing of the spirit. For what reason he was Called, we can only speculate but it has resulted in him suddenly confronting a spiritual reality for which many lifetimes would scarce be preparation."

The Rabbi nodded.

"It is a wonder that his mind was not overborne entirely," he said. "Obviously he is a soul of great strength. As to why he was Called, perhaps your Land needs the seed which now germinates within him. Certainly, my dear, we will watch for signs of his mental healing and when it is time for you to depart, we will do everything in our power to help you on your way."

* * *

It was towards evening, some weeks later. The goats had been returned to their pen and the heat was going out of the day. Xiang Li sat on a rock some distance from the vegetable beds. A small part of his mind noted 'that woman' carefully packing mulch round the stems of seedlings. The rest of his consciousness floated somewhere high above among the pink-tinged cirrus clouds. It was pleasant there, warm and cocooned.

And yet he felt a prick of irritation pulling his mind away from its peaceful dozing. He tried to ignore it but found he couldn't. It had to do with 'that woman'. Now there was a surprise. What was she doing?

Te Zhu, having packed the last of the seedlings with mulch was now laboriously hauling a bucket of water out of the nearest cistern. It was an awkward lift and the bucket was heavy. When she finally landed the bucket on the rim of the stone opening, some of the precious water slopped out, to be lost in the sandy soil. Te Zhu placed her hands in the small of her back and gave a small groan.

Xiang Li silently tutted. *Inefficient,* he thought. A large part of his mind set out for the clouds again but found itself anchored. Another small but intense piece of his brain, which had not been heard from for some time, was calculating.

Te Zhu was too far away to hear the Gōng murmuring but, had she been closer she would have heard: "Timber – yes. But what quality. Palm wood? Is that viable? And rope. Lots of rope. The barrel, now. Hmmm. Palm wood again? Elm? But where from? Iron struts? Too much to hope for."

So the little Chinese woman laboured away happily and, when she finally stood up, was not surprised to see that the Gōng had disappeared.

* * *

Ahmed was a cheerful little man. He had secured his niche in the community as a general handyman. On this particular morning he was sitting in the large room set aside as his workshop, sipping a warm, herbal concoction while considering which of the small tasks before him he might tackle.

Suddenly the door opened and in strode the tall stranger who had been staying with the community for the past few months. In his hand he carried a cured goatskin. With no preamble the man cleared a space on Ahmed's work bench and spread out the skin, anchoring its corners with tools and pieces of wood. Ahmed put down his cup, arose and went to look over the man's shoulder. He saw a plan, marked out neatly in charcoal with arrows and dimensions.

"Pump." The man's voice was creaky from disuse and, anyway, he spoke in a language foreign to Ahmed. However the little man understood from the diagram and the man's hand gestures, something of what he was seeing.

"Timber?" The man placed his hand on a rough plank of date palm timber and nodded. Ahmed nodded back, cautiously.

"Yes," he said, "we can get plenty of that."

"Rope?" The man made gestures again. After a moment Ahmed thought he understood. He went to the back of the room, rummaged around, and came up with a coil of grass rope.

"Yes," said the man with unmistakable triumph. The two men beamed at each other.

Te Zhu, who had followed the Gōng and peered in through the door, nodded, smiled and went to let the goats out.

* * *

The building of the wind pump became a source of intense interest to the community. The tower, with its web of struts, went up first. Palm wood was very coarse-grained timber and the finished result was not as elegant as Xiang Li would have liked. Likewise, the twelve-bladed vane was scarcely a thing of beauty but it worked. When the first puff of a morning breeze turned the blades cries of 'Alleluia' rose from the assembled crowd.

As a mark of confidence in the project, Rabbi Isaac set aside a sum of money from the community's funds and Xiang Li and Ahmed walked to Jericho with a mule and brought back scarce hardwoods. With these, Ahmed proved adept at creating the gear wheels, necessary to transfer the rotation of the vane to the shaft.

The barrel of the pump proved a problem. Xiang Li thought that it could be built up from sections of hardwood bored through the middle however it was soon clear that the result would be vastly heavy and unwieldy. They talked, still largely in gestures and through the medium of diagrams, about possible solutions. Finally, Ahmed made it known to Xiang Li that he thought he had the answer and would be away with the mule again, this time on his own.

For two days, Xiang Li strode to and fro impatiently, making small adjustments to the structure but also climbing frequently to the brow of the hill over which the road to the west disappeared. It was on the third morning that Ahmed returned, dusty but ecstatic. Strapped to either side of the long-suffering mule were sections of pipe made of a dull grey metal which Xiang Li recognised as lead.

He made signs of enquiry to the little Jew. Ahmed ran his hand through the air above his head, evidently stroking something. Xiang Li shook his head. Ahmed thought for a moment then marched up and down, swinging his arms. At once Xiang Li understood: Romans! He took his charcoal and sketched a Roman soldier, his helmet adorned with a horse hair plume. Ahmed shouted "Yes, yes!" and the two men laughed. In the excitement, Xiang Li never asked Ahmed whether the pipes were bought or stolen and Ahmed didn't say.

Three days later the community gathered by the cistern at dawn. With the coming of the sun there was usually a breeze flowing down from the hills towards the Sea of Death and Ahmed had let it be known that this was the day when it would finally be harnessed. In the half dark, Xiang Li and Ahmed made their final adjustments then stood back. There was an expectant hush. Several minutes went by. The upper limb of the sun appeared above the horizon beyond the sea and with it the first, faint puff. Nothing happened. Then another, stronger breath of air and with a loud creak, the vane began to turn. There was a cheer.

Xiang Li peered down the hole while Ahmed painted goat fat onto the wooden bearings carrying the shaft to the water screw. Faster turned the vane. The tower creaked and swayed slightly. Xiang Li stood up and beckoned Ahmed to look into the cistern. Ahmed looked then turned to the crowd and called them over. They arrived just as the first dollop of water came out of the pipe and into the start of an irrigation channel.

There was cheering and stamping of feet and dancing despite the early hour. Greatly daring, Ahmed patted the strange foreigner on the arm. He was rewarded with a wintry smile. Then Xiang Li walked through the crowd. He went to the goat pen, let the beasts out and followed them to his shady spot overlooking the sea.

Te Zhu turned to Rabbi Isaac. "It will be soon," she said.

Chapter Forty-eight

Homeward

"The goats have not been let out."

Te Zhu jerked out of a reverie. Rabbi Isaac leant on his staff before her.

"No one has seen him since last night. I think he is gone."

Te Zhu rose to her feet.

"Is everything ready?" she asked.

"The mule is being loaded and the boys are out along the roads. I doubt he is gone far and they will be back soon to tell us his direction."

Considerable thought had gone into this moment. The Rabbi had promised her the mule with supplies and water containers as well as various bits of equipment. The older boys had each been given a road to watch and had been instructed, when the word was given, to run out along it for two hours. This, Te Zhu and the Rabbi reckoned, should be enough distance either to find the Gōng or at least news of him.

Te Zhu set off to collect her meagre belongings. She was carrying them to the mule when a small, tousle-haired boy rushed into the compound. He came to a stop before the Rabbi in a cloud of dust, heaved a couple of theatrical breaths then pointed to the north and gabbled some words. The Rabbi turned to Te Zhu.

"He is an hour's walking journey to the north. It is as you thought. He will need to round the top of the Sea before he can turn to the east."

"Then Father," said Te Zhu, pushing her small bundle into a pannier, "I must be gone. Will you please bless me?"

The old man twinkled at her.

"If you will bless me," he replied.

Blessings were given and received, a long hug exchanged, then Te Zhu mounted the mule, gathered the reins and set off home.

* * *

She caught sight of the Gōng later that morning, his tall figure striding northwards in a swirl of dust. There was just the stony track with the Sea of Death off to the right and the occasional stunted olive tree. Te Zhu had given some thought to how she would manage the business of travelling with the Gōng whilst not interfering with his journey.

His mental state was still, in many ways, fragile and she doubted his ability to fend for himself successfully. At the same time, spiritually, he was now in the hands of that great Power which had summoned him here. The journey – pilgrimage, if you would – was an integral part of whatever the Gōng was to become. She saw her role as one of ensuring that he did not die in the process.

Te Zhu was quite aware that she was almost invisible to the Gōng, except as a source of occasional mild irritation. Thus she could be in his vicinity without having any great effect. The problem for her was to draw a line for herself where care became meddling and she knew this would be her biggest test. Thus, when she had closed the gap between herself and the man to one hundred yards, she dismounted and continued on foot, observing.

She noted, first of all, that he was well shod in stout sandals and that was a relief. However, he had no protection for his head against the pitiless sun and carried only a small satchel and water flask. Apart from that he was walking well. This was no surprise because the journey to Judaea had hardened him. Physical strength was not an issue. In the silence of the landscape she realised that he was singing to himself, something she had never before heard him do. Te Zhu dropped back another hundred yards and awaited events.

After nearly an hour the road dipped to a stream which ran off to lose itself in the Sea. At the point where the stream crossed the road, there was shade, afforded by a large rock and Te Zhu was pleased when Xiang Li stopped in the shade and sat down. She too stopped with the mule in the shade of an olive tree and watched as he ate lunch then lay down, evidently intending to doze through the heat of the day. This was encouraging. The Gōng was thinking rationally.

After eating and drinking, Te Zhu rummaged through the panniers on the mule. She put together a package of hard bread and goats' milk cheese then brought forth a battered sun hat, woven from palm leaves. She unhitched the mule and set off along the road, pausing only to lay the food and the hat by the sleeping man. She continued up the road for a further mile then turned aside into an olive grove where, with some difficulty, she removed the panniers from the mule and hobbled the beast before sinking down gratefully and slipping into a light sleep.

When Xiang Li awoke, he took a swig of water from his flask. He looked around and discovered the hat and the package of food. With a lack of curiosity he placed the one on his head and the other in his satchel. Then he filled his flask from the stream and set off up the road. Why this road and why this direction, he did not fully know. The mandarin with a passion for maps was buried deep within but had not gone away. He paid no attention to the mule and the sleeping woman as he passed the olive grove.

Te Zhu noted his passing. She waited a few minutes then yawned, stretched and arose. Loading the mule was a struggle, not because the beast misbehaved – Te Zhu had a way with animals – but because of the sheer weight involved and her lack of height. As she cinched the girth she realised that this was not something for which she wished to be responsible for the length of the journey.

Thus it was, after night had fallen and she was sure that the Gōng was asleep, she breathed silence into the mule's ears and led it close to the sleeping man. As quietly as she could, she removed the panniers and attached the bridle to them. Then she crept over and covered Xiang Li with a blanket before taking her own satchel and water flask off to a distance where she slept with the satisfaction of a responsibility well-shed.

The next morning, Xiang Li was woken by the mournful braying of the mule. He sat up and saw the beast which had knocked the panniers over so that they trapped the bridle, thus holding its head nearer the ground than was comfortable. Xiang Li had no memory of owning a mule but, then, he had little memory of anything much. Nor did he have any memory of owning a blanket but he folded it up then stood and went to the mule.

He released the bridle, tutting gently to the beast. It made straight for the small stream and drank before ambling to a patch of dry grass where it grazed contentedly. Xiang Li opened one of the panniers where, again, with a total lack of curiosity, he discovered bread and cheese. He ate it whilst gazing at the view. The seashore, as he had expected, was tending away to the east and the road followed it. Te Zhu, watching from her camp site, heard the Gōng whistle. The mule pricked up its ears and turned its head, finishing off a last mouthful of grass before trotting over to its new owner and standing obediently while he loaded and secured the panniers.

Bridle in hand, Xiang Li took to the road and the mule followed. Te Zhu rose, stretched and yawned. She picked up her satchel and flask, turned her face to the rising sun and gave thanks for the day's march.

Chapter Forty-nine

Eastwards

And so the rhythm of the journey was established. Xiang Li led the mule and Te Zhu followed at a distance. Every evening Xiang Li would make camp and when he was asleep, Te Zhu would remove from the panniers such food and water as she needed for the following day. Xiang Li was assiduous in looking after the mule, rather better, Te Zhu had to admit, than she would have been since the matter of finding grazing and pouring water down its throat when no other source was available, was an intricate and time-consuming business.

There were occasional villages. Xiang Li would march through them, often attracting small crowds of children who would follow for a while, mimicking his walk and shouting mild insults. Te Zhu would take the opportunity of trading some of the small reserve of coins given to her by Rabbi Isaac, for food. This she would secrete in the panniers later when the Gōng was asleep.

At one such village a mother came to her, carrying a babe whose eyes were closed with dried pus. The child grizzled. The mother held it out to Te Zhu, nodding hopefully. Te Zhu took the baby then followed the woman to her mean hut. There she boiled dried herbs from the supply she kept in her satchel and bathed the rheumy eyes. The child ceased crying. Te Zhu laid healing hands on its head and handed it back to its mother.

Turning to go, she found another woman ducking into the hut, carrying a small girl with an ulcerous leg. Altogether, she spent two hours ministering to cuts, bruises and infections and although she was rewarded well with food, she was exhausted when she finally caught up with the Gōng at his evening campsite. However, the incident did give her an idea.

The countryside became more arid as they progressed eastward. This was the start of the desert through which they had passed on their journey from Seleucia. After six days, they arrived at the oasis of Ma'daba and here Xiang Li stopped. Te Zhu was not certain why he had stopped but was glad that he had. Further progress to the east, with its widely-spaced oases, could well have spelled their deaths.

For three days they waited. Xiang Li sat in the shade of a clump of palm trees with the mule and gazed out to the west. Te Zhu spent the time replenishing her stock of herbs and nostrums. She was surprised at what was available in the oasis. Although it was not on a major trading route, it boasted, as well as a caravanserai, a number of small stores selling food, a harness maker and a carpenter's shop. One of the food stores had a jumbled section at the back displaying herbs, spices and charms.

Having nothing better to do, Te Zhu put them into order, badgering the owner into supplying a dozen earthenware pots in which to put things. Eventually the owner was grudgingly grateful and allowed her to take away quite large quantities for not very much money. On his part he was glad to be rid of stock which sold little. Te Zhu, on the other hand, recognised several rare and valuable items and chortled quietly to herself.

On the fourth day, towards dusk, a cry went up. Xiang Li came to his feet, shading his eyes against the setting sun. Te Zhu doused the fire upon which she had been decocting tinctures, and went outside. Snaking round a shoulder of land, two miles to the west, came a camel train, silhouetted by a plume of red-lit dust. Ten minutes later, the head of the train arrived in the oasis with a great jangling of harnesses, cries of command and welcome. Suddenly the sleepy place was alive.

Te Zhu watched Xiang Li, wondering what he would do. He sat back down in his shaded corner and calmly watched the hubbub. Slowly the noise and activity decreased. Strings of camels filed into the caravanserai where they lay down and were relieved of their loads. Goats and a few cattle were herded into pens. Cooking fires were lit and, as darkness fell, savoury cooking smells wafted round the oasis. Xiang Li waited perhaps two hours before he arose, buckled the panniers on the mule and set out for the caravanserai. Te Zhu followed.

He stopped at the gateway and she saw him look around then make his way to a group gathered at a fire. Rather than join the group, he led the mule into the shadows outside the firelight, unloaded the panniers and settled down. Moving closer, Te Zhu recognised the group by their garb and talk as herdsmen. She nodded.

Looking around she identified the fire of the caravan leader. The group at this fire was smaller, the clothes richer. Pulling herself to her full height and assuming an air of unquestioned authority, she made her way across to the fire and stopped in front of the large man with a bald head who seemed to be in charge. She bowed. The man finished speaking to his neighbour and turned to her.

"What can I do for you, Mother?" he asked, his tone neutral.

"Rabb," she said, using an honorific to which he certainly was not entitled, "I seek passage with your caravan. I am a healer of some experience both in the diseases of men and beasts. I shall happily deploy my skills at no charge for the opportunity of travelling with you."

Now it is a fact that the men of the trade routes did not treat their women very well at all, yet all of them lived in quiet awe of 'wise women'. Wise women were treated with wary respect since no man knew the full extent of their powers and none really wanted to find out. The figure standing before the caravan master seemed larger than it was and imbued with what might be termed a friendly menace. *Look at me,* it seemed to say. *I can make your life much easier. You would not want anything else, would you?*

For the sake of appearances, the caravan master made a pretence of considering the matter for a few moments before saying, "You are welcome, Mother. All I ask is that you keep up with the train. And your skills will be welcome."

In truth, Ihad Sayyid was a courteous man who held his position not by force but by the strength of his character as well as a proven record of wise decisions in the face of an unyielding environment. This pleased Te Zhu. Whilst she could have handled another Dorba Tembay, she would much rather not.

"Help yourself to food. You may bed down wherever is convenient. We leave at first light."

Te Zhu bowed, put down her satchel and helped herself from the communal cooking pot.

* * *

Amir Gabr scratches himself. It is one of the less pleasant aspects of being a stockman, even Chief Stockman, that one is subject to permanent insect bites. Today they are worse than usual and so is his temper. In the grey light before dawn he snarls at his men as they herd the beasts out of the pens and hold them in a milling throng, waiting for the strings of camels to emerge from the caravanserai. He strides round the group of beasts, cracking his stock whip, mainly for effect.

But what is this? A tall, gaunt man holding the bridle of a mule stands among the herdsmen. *What's he doing here? He wasn't here yesterday.* Amir Gabr barges through the crowd towards the stranger, opening his mouth ready for an excoriating confrontation when he hears a voice.

"This is an experienced stockman, very skilled with beasts. He will be an asset to your team."

He stops, his mouth hanging open. A struggle takes place in his mind. Certainly this is an experienced stockman but a mule, a mule as part of a camel train?

"The mule is essential to his joining the train. It will be no problem. He will be responsible for it."

Amir Gabr closes his mouth. He points at Xiang Li and raises his voice.

"This is an experienced stockman, very skilled with beasts. He will be an asset to the team. He will be responsible for the mule."

Stockmen and herdsmen look at him strangely, then at the tall man with the mule. For a moment Amir Gabr hovers uncertainly, wondering what has just happened. The new stockman stands quietly by, evidently awaiting the order to start so that he can prove himself an asset to the team. *That's an excellent piece of mule-flesh he has there,* Amir Gabr thinks. *I expect it is essential.* He turns on his heel, cracks his stock whip and scratches. *Looks like nice weather for travelling. Not too hot.*

Te Zhu smiles. She makes her way to the mule, opens a pannier and puts her satchel of medicaments inside. Xiang Li fails to notice her.

Chapter Fifty

The Desert

The caravan made its way south-east along the Wadi Sirhan. Te Zhu calculated that it was nearly four months since they had travelled this way and well over a year since they had left Korla. That meant that it must be nearing the middle of winter yet not like any winter she had known heretofore. Certainly it was cooler than when they had last been here. One certain difference was that twice, black clouds rolled out of the south-east and disgorged heavy rain.

When this happened the caravan stopped and, in a well-rehearsed routine, canvas funnels were spread to catch the rain in water skins. When every skin was filled, men stripped and cavorted like children. And afterwards the desert bloomed in an extravagant profusion of wild flowers for a day or two, wild meadows of purples, pinks and yellows where before had been just rock and sand.

Amir Gabr continued to treat Xiang Li with a wary respect but not so the other herdsmen. At first they neither understood nor welcomed his presence among them. The lead billy goat was a brute named Shaitan who did much as he wished since he was vicious. The only reason he was tolerated was that where he went, the nannies followed so, if he could be coerced to go in the right direction, all was well.

At dawn on the second day of the march, Shaitan stood a quarter of a mile away, chewing on a thorn bush. Before heading off to take counsel with the caravan master, Amir Gabr had given orders that Shaitan was to be caught and brought back, ready for the march. No one wanted the job since, at best, it would mean a fruitless scramble across sand and scree. At worst it could mean injury from horn or teeth. Then one herdsman suggested that the job could be advantageously given to the tall stranger so that he could demonstrate his skill with beasts. The idea was taken up with much sniggering.

"Effendi," said one to Xiang Li, "see you the poor stray goat on yonder hillside?"

Xiang Li nodded.

"Would you, of a kindness, go and bring it back here so that we may start the march?"

Xiang Li nodded again, tightened his belt, selected a handful of fodder and set off. The herdsmen followed him, still sniggering, intent on getting a better view of the disaster. For his part, Xiang Li seemed oblivious to their presence. He began to croon. Shaitan pretended to ignore the approaching man, concentrating instead on wrenching lumps out of the thorn bush. Wicked thoughts circulated in his small but intense brain.

But then he heard the crooning. It soothed him. More, it underlined the weariness of an existence which put him at variance with everything around him. He raised his head and contemplated the man who had stopped some feet away. He seemed a nice man. To Shaitan's hircine eyes the man appeared to be surrounded by a halo of shimmering light. Not only was he crooning in a most agreeable way but he was holding out something towards Shaitan.

He ambled over and sniffed at the offering. Fodder. *Garigue with overtones of asphodel,* he rather thought. Suddenly the whole idea of thorn bush as a food lost its appeal. He had only been eating it to be perverse anyway. He took a mouthful of fodder and chewed it reflectively. The man patted him on his horny head and Shaitan allowed it. He took the rest of the fodder, exhibiting uncharacteristic care not to bite the man's fingers. Now the man put his face close to Shaitan's and whispered in his ear. Shaitan understood not in words but at a much deeper level. Here was a human being who liked goats, who understood their problems and who wanted Shaitan to follow him.

The sniggering ceased, nudges were left un-nudged. The herdsmen looked on with disbelief as the tall stranger turned and started down the slope, his hand on the billy goat's muscle-bound neck. The pair came straight towards the crowd which parted. Whilst the episode did not immediately alter the herdsmen's attitude towards the tall stranger (not least because the rest of the beasts had wandered off while unattended, thus drawing upon them the wrath of Amir Gabr) a degree of respect was created. For his part, Shaitan sought the company of his new friend whenever his other duties allowed.

Ten days into the march, when the caravan halted at the oasis of Sakakah, a pregnant nanny goat went into labour in the middle of the night. It was a difficult presentation and, although two kids were delivered, the mother prolapsed and was killed. Xiang Li, who had helped with the delivery, asked what would become of the kids. The herdsmen prodded one of the small bodies with his toe.

"This one's dead. The other one'll be gone soon. We'll joint them and seethe their meat in their mother's milk." He smacked his lips. "Taste's lovely."

Xiang Li picked up the live kid. With his little finger he scooped muck out of its nostrils then breathed gently into them. The kid kicked feebly and bleated. Xiang Li stood, holding it to his chest.

"This one will live," he stated.

"Hey, what about my kid-seethed-in-milk?" said the other.

Xiang Li bestowed a wintry smile upon him.

"You may have the corpse," he said.

The herders were slightly scandalised by the stranger's actions. Beasts were beasts. You ate them. Many heavy jokes were made about a second helping of kid-seethed-in-milk when the other kid died. Xiang Li ignored them. He obtained milk from a lactating nanny, soaked a rag in it and encouraged the little goat to suck. On the march, he carried the kid around his neck. Despite all forecasts to the contrary, the kid began to put on weight. Soon it was walking for small parts of the day, skipping at Xiang Li's heel and butting his leg when it wanted to be carried.

Gradually the jokes ceased and Xiang Li's dedication to the kid became a minor source of pride to the hard-bitten men of the trade routes. The sight of the two of them lightened the mood on the long march. Slowly the eccentric stranger became a member of the team who was welcomed into the circle around the evening fire. Only Shaitan retained an objection to the man's new-found companion but Xiang Li whispered in his ear that he was still loved and he relaxed.

Te Zhu watched from afar and approved. She was making her own name as a wise woman and doctor. Every evening she held a clinic where she treated the cuts, bites and sores which were the common currency of desert travel. When the doctoring was finished she lingered and on most evenings, one or two men would sidle out of the darkness and consult her upon matters of love or fortune. Te Zhu seldom told them anything bad unless it was clear that they could do something about it. Thus she grew in stature and held a permanent place at the caravan master's fire.

On the twenty-first day, high on the sandstone plateau, a cry of 'Doctor' went up from halfway down the column. Te Zhu hurried from her place near the rear. A man was down, writhing in agony.

"It was a Devil Snake, a Blunt-nosed Viper," she was told. "He will die."

Without thinking she sent out a Call. *Come to me.*

Xiang Li appeared, loping across the sand.

"Hold him, calm him," said the gardener to the Governor.

Xiang Li knelt by the man's head, placed his hands under the base of his skull and closed his eyes. The man ceased to thrash quite so wildly although his pupils were wide with shock. Te Zhu asked for a knife. She found the bite just above the left ankle.

Already there was swelling and mottled blue colouring around the lips of the wound.

"Steady now," said Te Zhu to the man and to Xiang Li. Xiang Li pressed hard and concentrated. Swiftly, Te Zhu made two deep cuts just above the wound. The man cried out but managed to hold fairly steady. She dropped the knife, bent and sucked blood, spat and sucked again and again.

"Water," she said. She flushed her mouth. Then she poured some of the contents of the flask onto the wound, placed her hand on it and bore down hard.

"Fetch the mule," she ordered. Men ran to do her bidding. When it was brought, Te Zhu asked for her satchel to be lifted from the pannier. One-handed she sorted through its contents, found what she sought. She removed her hand from the wound and sprinkled some dried herbs into it then bandaged it loosely.

She sat back on her haunches.

"You may relax," she said to Xiang Li. The Gōng laid the man's head on the sand, sighed deeply and wiped the sweat from his brow.

"You did well," said Te Zhu.

Xiang Li nodded, stood and made his way back to the rear of the caravan where the stock animals waited.

* * *

Before long the high sandstone plateau began blending into the high steppe, covered in coarse grass. They encountered the first herds of hardy sheep. Swarthy, hooked-nose shepherds watched them pass. The grass became more abundant as they slowly went lower and then they came upon the first small fields of arable crops, mostly scrubby barley. A sense of expectation was evident in the caravan crew. They were entering the Blessed Arc, a land of abundance after the desert journey.

The caravan's destination was Babylon on the Euphrates.

Much as she would have liked to have seen the great city, Te Zhu kept a close eye on Xiang Li. In the absence of any other information it seemed likely that he might retrace the course of the outward journey. Her watchfulness was rewarded when, on a night, two days short of Babylon, Xiang Li, leading the mule and followed by his goat, quietly left the sleeping caravanserai and struck out towards the north. Te Zhu, her belongings already packed into one of the panniers, followed.

A short distance from the caravanserai, an awful howling bleat rent the air. There was a sound of banging and splintering. Te Zhu turned and was almost bowled over by a large, hairy figure, its head stuck through the remains of a hurdle. Xiang Li too had turned. Shaitan skidded to a halt in front of him and bleated piteously. Te Zhu watched as the Gōng knelt, removed the wreckage from the goat's neck and hugged him. He whispered for some seconds into the goat's ear. Shaitan bleated, as if in question. Xiang Li stood and placed his hand on the goat's head, then turned and set off up the track. Te Zhu followed. Shaitan paid her no attention as she passed him, simply continuing to stare up the track after his friend.

If this was a fictional tale then Shaitan's friendship with Xiang Li would have permanently changed his character for the better. Indeed, for several days he was very quiet. Had anyone troubled to understand, they would have known that he was in the depths of grief. Sadly no-one did and the herdsmen began taking liberties with him. On the third day a herdsman pushed him aside and was butted so severely that two of his ribs were broken. Indeed, but for the intervention of his mates he might have been killed.

Even grief has its season.

Chapter Fifty-one

Simon

Xiang Li and Te Zhu walked for three days. The climate, six weeks after the winter solstice, was cool and they made good progress. There were plenty of villages and Te Zhu was able to barter for or buy food. On the fourth day they came to the Euphrates ferry they had used on the outward journey. There was plenty of traffic, camels and mules as well as carts loaded with produce. Xiang Li led his mule and goat aboard and stood looking passively at the further bank.

When the ferryman came to collect his fee, Te Zhu intercepted him before he could reach Xiang Li. She pointed at the Gōng, then tapped her forehead and, crossing her eyes, handed the man a coin. The ferryman looked from the man to the woman, shook his head and laughed.

At evening on the fourth day, the walls and towers of Seleucia came into sight. Xiang Li stopped for the night. Te Zhu wondered what he intended. Judging by events, he would likely look to travel up the Tigris on a raft. If he did, she knew that their meagre resources would not cover the expense and she had to assume that the Gōng neither knew nor cared. She felt a strong urge to speak with their friend Simon ben Zephaniah.

Shortly after dawn Xiang Li set off and Te Zhu followed. As she had half expected, he made his way straight to the Great Wharf where he stopped and looked up and down the river. There were, for the moment, no rafts in sight. He removed the panniers from the mule then sat with his back against the wall of a warehouse. Te Zhu struggled briefly with her innate tendency to meddle before giving in.

Sit there, sleep, until I return.

Xiang Li gave no sign that he heard but his head began to

nod. His chin fell on his chest and he started to snore. Feeling only a little guilty, Te Zhu left the wharf and made her way into the town.

"I wish to speak to your master."

The steward who had opened the door looked down his nose at the travel-stained little woman before him.

"And what business might you have with my master, crone?" he said.

Te Zhu smiled at the man. The man felt slightly queasy.

"I *wish* to *speak* to your *master*," she repeated.

"Stay there," said the man, hastily closing the door.

Some minutes later the door re-opened and there stood Simon ben Zephaniah looking pleased and astonished.

"It *is* you," he said. "But where is your master?"

"There is much to tell and little time," said Te Zhu. "May I come in?"

"Of course. Of course," said Simon, standing aside.

It had been Te Zhu who had negotiated Xiang Li's convalescence in Simon's house half a year ago so he not only knew her but understood something of the relationship between master and servant. Also, Firenze had called on him before taking ship for home and told him much of what had taken place. He had hoped that he might see Xiang Li again although he had feared the worst. He saw Te Zhu settled in a chair with food and drink then sat himself and listened as she told him of their journey and its outcome.

When she had finished he said, "But your master must come and stay with me again. I'm sure he would benefit from some rest and I would value more time to speak with him."

Te Zhu shook her head. "The Gōng is a changed man, Simon. He has experienced a deep spiritual shock. Some might say he has been driven mad but that is not so. He has gone deep within and all he wants now is to return home. I believe that the journey is necessary for him, that deep changes will slowly take place within him as he travels."

"But by all means come and see him. He is at present sleeping on the Great Wharf. When he awakes he will seek passage upriver on a raft although in his present state he will not realize that it will cost money that he does not have."

"That can be easily remedied," said Simon. He rang a bell and, when his steward appeared, ordered him to bring money and a satchel of food. When it arrived, the two set out for the Wharf.

Simon was shocked by the appearance of his friend when he saw him sleeping in the weak winter sunlight. He was thin as a rake and his countenance was gaunt with deep lines incised on either side of his mouth.

Wake up.

Simon looked around, sure that someone had spoken but no-one was there.

Xiang Li stirred and stretched. He looked around then up at the man who was standing beside that woman.

"I know you," he said.

"Of course you do," said Simon gently. "It is me, Simon, Simon ben Zephaniah."

"Ah, the alchemist," said Xiang Li, before apparently losing interest and gazing around the Wharf.

Simon crouched down in front of him. "How are you, my friend?"

Xiang Li brought his gaze back to the man before him.

"I have been ill, you know," he said, then fell silent.

"And ... and did you find what you sought?"

The Gōng furrowed his brow.

"There was a babe," he said uncertainly. He looked up into Simon's eyes. "Yes, there was certainly a birth but there was also death." He sighed. "So much death. Death for all of us. I have died, you know? ... but..."

He shook his head and looked away. Simon saw that tears

were running down his face.

"But?" he prompted.

Suddenly Xiang Li was smiling through his tears.

"But there is Life too – for all of us – so *much* life..."

Simon found himself overawed. A deep well of happiness seemed to have been broached within him.

"Oh here it is at last," said Xiang Li, scrambling to his feet. A raft hauled by a team of oxen had come into view from down river and was making its way in towards the Wharf. Apparently dismissing Simon from his mind, he hefted the panniers and began strapping them onto the mule.

Simon stood and turned to Te Zhu. He too felt close to tears. Something immense seemed to have taken place and he wished – oh how he wished – that he had been part of it.

"But you have," said Te Zhu, as if he had spoken out loud. "You gave comfort to the Gōng when he was ill. It was under your roof that the three Magi came together. You told us where we were to go. The Star touched you as well, Simon. None of this would have happened without you."

Without thinking Simon knelt before the little woman. She laid her hands on his head. He felt their warmth.

"Go now. Lead a long and happy life. Tell all who have ears to hear what has happened. You too are a Witness."

She took his hands, raised him to his feet, stood on tip toes and kissed him on the cheek. Then she turned and followed Xiang Li, his mule and the goat to where the raft was making fast.

Chapter Fifty-two

The Water Mill

Since both Te Zhu and Xiang Li were together on the raft, it was the first opportunity she had had for some time to study him at close quarters and she was pleased to notice that he was able to interact with the other passengers and crew. True, he spent much of his time in silent contemplation of the passing scenery but then he would suddenly ask a question of a crew member on a practical matter – navigation of rapids or management of ox teams – and show a deep interest in the answer.

The crew made him welcome which, considering his slightly outlandish appearance, was not a given. Indeed, she was intrigued to notice the others casting glances at the Gōng, glances perhaps of puzzlement, as if they were seeing something out of the ordinary. Rafting up the Tigris was a physical, rough pastime, but after six days as they made their way into the landing place, a day's march from Kirkűk, there was a notably happy atmosphere among the raft's crew. They were quite clearly sorry to see the Gōng leave them.

Governor, mule, goat and gardener resumed their march from the landing stage through an increasingly wintry landscape as the land rose towards the mountains. However the weather if wet, was bearable in this, the start of the third month after the solstice. Every day the sun rose a little higher in its arc across the sky and the temperature became slightly greater. There was plenty of snow covering the hills but it was starting to melt.

They did not pause in Kirkűk, merely sheltering for the night in a corner of the caravanserai. Thus it was that the spies of the Gōng Yin Xianliang, consul to The Emperor in the District of Karkha d' Beth Slokh, failed to make anything of their arrival and he was not appraised of their presence. Indeed, to be fair to the spies, of whom the caravanserai keeper was one, they had been told to look out for a substantial caravan heading from the west towards the mountains not a ragged man with a mule and a goat or an old woman who might or might not have been with him.

Once more, Te Zhu wondered what Xiang Li intended as they followed the winding road through the Tasluja Hills, eastwards towards the Qaiwan Range behind Sulaymaniyah. Somewhere beyond were the real mountains, the Zagros, and the Haunted Pass. Whilst she was resigned to making that perilous passage once more, she hoped that the Gōng was not intending entering the high mountains until the lower levels were clear of snow.

She need not have worried. Xiang Li had a plan although, since he did not acknowledge her presence, he shared it only with his mule and occasionally, when it was willing to concentrate for long enough, the goat. Even then it would be difficult to say at which level the plan existed for Xiang Li's mind, although moving towards wholeness, was yet working in several sundered parts, a fact of which he was unaware.

"The water mill," he said to the mule. The goat stared at him uncomprehendingly with its alien eyes.

"It has a loose paddle, you see, and it is simply inefficient." The mule tossed its head in agreement. The goat delicately removed a small branch from a thorn bush and chewed it, reflectively.

"I may be wrong, I hope I am, but I doubt they have repaired it and I cannot leave it in that condition. They will have to see sense, however difficult it is for them to obtain hardwood, preferably elm."

The mule whickered encouragingly. The goat hiccupped. Whether or not it was an encouraging hiccup is difficult to say.

Six days beyond Kirkűk they passed through the large, muddy village of Sulaymaniyah. Te Zhu took the opportunity of buying as much in the way of fresh supplies as was available. Civilization, she knew, was about to run out and they would need to be able to live on their own resources for many days.

Xiang Li headed on up into the Qaiwan mountains. These were more like high hills than mountains but, even so, they had their first taste of real cold for more than a year. Forgetting her self-imposed exile, Te Zhu crept into the Gōng's camp at nightfall and snuggled into the warmth of the mule. Xiang Li appeared not to notice.

Beyond the Qaiwan was a wide valley and beyond that the daunting flanks of the Zagros Range. It was warmer here and Te Zhu felt the very first intimations of spring. Xiang Li led the way to the village of Marivān which stood on a sheltered platform, part way up the foothills of the Zagros. Te Zhu recognised it as the first place of safety they had found after the winter passage of the mountains. It was clear that the Gōng knew where he was because he led his mule straight to the house of the headman. Te Zhu closed the distance between them.

Xiang Li knocked on the door and after a pause it was opened by an old woman in a black robe.

"Water mill," said Xiang Li in the argot of the trade routes. "Mend water mill."

The woman, who knew no language other than the dialect of Kurdish used in her valley, looked from the tall stranger to the old woman standing slightly behind him. Te Zhu cast her eyes significantly towards her Lord and tapped her forehead.

"Aaah," said the old woman, raising her chin. "An idiot."

She beckoned them in then screeched as Xiang Li tried to follow her with the mule and goat. When order had been restored and the animals placed in a lean-to, Xiang Li and Te Zhu entered the headman's house. Sometime later Dilşad Şivan, the headman, returned. He was appraised of happenings by his wife. He peered closely at Xiang Li, then clapped his hands and beamed.

"It's the madman from the mountains!" he said to his wife. She too peered at the tall stranger but declared herself unconvinced. Disregarding her doubts he announced that there would be a feast. His wife asked if this would be one of those feasts where she did all the work while the menfolk would drink too much kumis and fall over. Dilşad Şivan ignored her and sent his sons to invite the elders of the village.

Te Zhu feared the effect of the fermented mare's milk upon her master but she need not have worried. Although he drank cup for cup with the others and although the elders became noisy and boastful, it seemed to have no effect on Xiang Li. Relentlessly, despite the noise and drunkenness, he pursued his mission, with the aid of sketches, gestures and what common language they shared, until the gathering understood that he proposed to repair the old water mill on the high pasture. This led to more silliness and many toasts until, one by one, the gathering fell asleep either on or under the table.

Early the next morning, Xiang Li was ready. The headman's wife took sadistic pleasure in waking her husband and reminding him of his promises of the night before. Dilşad Şivan stumbled outside, smiled blearily at Xiang Li then raised his voice and shouted, "Nouri!"

A wiry old man, wearing a fleece, emerged from a house further down the village street. Dilşad Şivan beckoned him over and explained that the tall madman wished to repair the old water mill on the high pasture and that he, Dilşad Şivan, was unable to conduct him thither owing to important meetings, so please would he, Nouri, act in his stead. Nouri gave his headman an old-fashioned look, tightened his belt, bowed to Xiang Li then led the way up the hillside.

The mill was still clacking mournfully and Xiang Li peered again into the gloom under the building to ascertain that the paddle was still loose. It was clear that nothing could be done until the mill leat was shut off so he forged off upstream trailed by Nouri and Te Zhu. At the mouth of the leat he discovered a sluice gate, broken and hanging askew. He tutted.

"Shoddy," was his verdict.

He stood, chin in hand, thinking for a while. Then he turned to Nouri.

"The gate will need to be repaired before we can progress. Tell me, do you have a carpenter and a stock of hardwood, preferably elm?" Xiang Li spoke slowly and loudly.

Nouri raised his hands and looked helpless. Trailed by his companions, Xiang Li returned to the village.

Listening to the subsequent discussions, conducted under severe constraints of language and culture, Te Zhu was able to piece together the fact that the mill had been built at the orders of a provincial governor with a view to allowing the local shepherds to wash and felt fleeces in situ. That the local shepherds had neither asked for nor wanted this facility became clear which was why the mill had fallen into disuse. However, the elders were perfectly happy for the mad stranger to repair it if it would entertain him.

Almost as an afterthought one of the elders said to the others, "Did not the mad governor leave some wood in the barn which is now ruined, in the field behind Awan's hovel?"

The meeting rose as one and conveyed Xiang Li and Te Zhu down the village street and up a muddy track to a dilapidated structure. The combined strength of four strong men opened one half of the doors and they went inside, Te Zhu keeping a wary eye on the sagging lintel. Sure enough, deep in the shadows, shrouded in dust and animal droppings, lay a stack of timber, each plank carefully separated from the others by laths.

Xiang Li was ecstatic. A plank was lifted from the top of the pile, taken outside and tipped to clear it of debris.

"Cedar!" he said and his joy was so infectious that the elders broke into a spontaneous round of applause.

The next two weeks were a whirlwind of activity such as the village had never known. Fortunately, since they were waiting for lambing and had nothing much else to do, the menfolk were happy to help. Ancient woodworking tools were found. Parts were prefabricated and taken up to the mill where a workbench was built. A team was set to damming the mouth of the leat while another made the parts for a new sluice.

Xiang Li was everywhere, supervising, measuring and demonstrating. The workforce initially regarded him with good-natured forbearance but this changed to respect as it became clear that, mad though he was, he also wielded a towering intellect and an incisive way with problems. Once the leat was dammed he waded through freezing mud underneath the mill to survey the wheel. He emerged carrying the broken paddle and announced that three others would need replacing.

By the end of the first week the new sluice gate was in position and work had begun on shaping the first paddle. Labour stopped briefly for a feast and its after-effects and then, in the second week, the shavings flew and the sound of hammering echoed down from the high pastures. There were scuffles about whose turn it was to use the plane. Finally the work was done. The day before Xiang Li had commanded that the earth damming the mouth of the leat be removed and now Dilşad Şivan grasped the handles and raised the sluice gate.

The assembled throng cheered as water poured through the gate and they ran, keeping pace with it, as far as the mill. The level rose until it touched the wheel and then rose some more. Then the wheel turned and it was almost silent in its operation. There was more cheering and hugging. An impromptu dance broke out. Dilşad Şivan made a speech which was largely drowned out by the celebrations.

Te Zhu noticed that Xiang Li had disappeared. She saw that the door to the mill was open so she looked within. There in the semi-darkness, the Gōng was running his hands over the complex wooden mechanism, talking quietly to himself.

"I see ... a ratchet then the double – no treble – reduction gearing and here a clutch. I wonder..."

He was fondling a large lever. As Te Zhu watched, he came to a decision, placed both hands on the lever and pulled. There was a groaning and creaking and then the whole building shook. Wheels began to turn and half seen shapes moved backwards and forwards. Xiang Li wandered among the movement lost in admiration, opening valves and pulling levers.

Just then the assembled villagers began to enter the mill. They stood in open-mouthed incomprehension of the scene before them. One man reached forward.

"Don't touch that!" shouted Xiang Li and the man jerked his hand back. Xiang Li grasped the clutch lever, heaved it upright and the movement stopped.

"What you have here," he began, "is a complex gearing mechanism designed to transfer the motion of the mill wheel through a triple reduction gearing to a washing action and a felting hammer. This valve allows..."

The men began to drift outside, speaking of a celebratory feast and the consumption of heroic amounts of kumis and what fine fellows they were to have repaired the mad governor's thing on the hillside. Left alone, Xiang Li sighed, took one last look around then left the mill, closing the door behind him.

He made one more attempt at the feast, that evening, to explain the entirely beneficial effect upon the local economy that would accrue if the mill were fully utilized for the washing and felting of fleeces but he made no headway. The men were too full of themselves and fermented mare's milk to understand and, anyway, they had always done things one particular way and there was great comfort in that. Te Zhu who had helped with the serving of the feast noted the look of resignation on his face. She went into the kitchen and said to the assembled women, "It will be tomorrow."

Dĩyar, the headman's wife, nodded. She turned to the other women and said, "Sisters, please bring your contributions here. We will pack the mule's panniers together tonight."

And thus it was that when he arose before dawn on the morrow and loaded the mule, Xiang Li found the panniers much heavier than they had been. He also found four nets of forage and hung them on the long-suffering animal. Then he whistled for the goat and set off, for the last time, up the path to the high pastures.

Dĩyar and the other women waited at a distance with Te Zhu.

"Will you not reconsider?" asked Dĩyar.

"Nay, it is my Gōng's decision and if he wishes to take the Haunted Pass, nothing I can say will stop him. Besides," she said, turning her smile upon them, "mayhap it is no longer haunted."

Dĩyar snorted.

"And my man is not a drunken sot," she said. "Then, if go you must, bless us Mother."

The women knelt and Te Zhu blessed them, calling down the Light upon them. Then she turned towards the greying dawn and set off after her Lord.

Chapter Fifty-three

The Haunted Pass

The high pastures were clear of snow. Te Zhu tramped up the path and watched as Xiang Li, the mule and goat, approached the dark ravine that split the dizzying flank of the mountains. She was not frightened of the Haunted Pass, just wary. Of course, on the outward journey, she had had to protect an entire caravan and that had necessitated days of vigilance interspersed by cat naps. It had been a wearying time. Now there was just her, the Gōng and the animals. The weather looked settled which would help.

As she thought this, the Gōng made to enter the chasm. The mule suddenly baulked and reared. Xiang Li played the bridle until the animal stood shivering but refusing to go forward. She watched as he smoothed its face then leant forward and whispered in its ear. There was more stroking then he tugged gently on the bridle and it moved ahead. The goat remained, rooted to the spot, bleating. As Te Zhu came level with it she placed her hand on its head and said, "Walk with me, little one. All will be well."

The goat looked at her as gratefully as a goat is able, nestled in towards her leg and set off into the Haunted Pass.

* * *

For the first hour they plodded forward, Xiang Li with the mule and fifty feet behind him, Te Zhu with the goat. She was aware of a steady build-up of extreme negative energy which she kept away from herself. The negative force would concentrate on what it perceived to be the most vulnerable individual and she knew that it remembered her. That meant that Xiang Li was most at risk. While she remained poised to protect him if necessary, she also wished to see how the Gōng would deal with it.

She did not have long to wait. Rounding a blind bend she became aware of an intense, dark cloud hovering some twenty feet above the floor of the ravine. She wondered if the Gōng saw it. If he did, he gave no sign, simply plodded on. But the mule sensed it and began to buck. Xiang Li stopped, put his arm around the animal's neck and stroked its face. When the mule had quieted, the Gōng turned his face upwards.

The cloud intensified. It began buzzing like a million flies and gave off a strong smell of faeces. With awful deliberation, a finger unrolled itself from the mass. It stretched and straightened, pointing directly at Xiang Li and descending upon him. For his part, Xiang Li remained quite still, his arm around the mule's neck. Te Zhu tensed, ready to intervene as the cloud swelled and loured over the Gōng.

And then a strange thing happened. Just before the finger of cloud reached the man, he raised his right hand and stretched out towards it, his own index finger pointing. There was a flash of white light accompanied by a loud bang. The cloud roiled, withdrawing its finger as if it had been burnt. A dreadful wailing echoed through the dank reaches of the pass and the cloud fell in upon itself, disappearing with a small pop.

In the silence that followed Te Zhu heard a strange sound. At first she could not place it. Then she realized that the Gōng was laughing. It was a rusty, creaky laugh. She tried to remember when she had last heard him laugh, but gave up. The pass was still a dank, dark place but it was now clear of spiritual oppression. And even though she remained awake and on guard that night, so it remained for the rest of the time it took them to reach the high plains on the further side.

On the second night after they had left the Haunted Pass, they stopped at the small village where Khasan had questioned the headman on their outward journey. The headman received them courteously and asked about their journey. When Xiang Li said, off-handedly, that they had come through the narrow pass over there, beyond the ruined caravanserai, the head man looked at him sharply to see if he was being made game of.

"And did you see aught of ghosts?" he asked.

Xiang Li shook his head.

"No."

Concluding that the stranger was either mad or lying, the headman changed the subject.

Te Zhu who had been sitting in the kitchen with the headman's wife, listening to the conversation, turned to her and said, "It is as my master says, although I think your husband does not believe him. It is possible that the Haunted Pass is no longer haunted although I would not bet my life on it. Perhaps when the moment is right, you might tell your husband this and perhaps some of your braver young men might wish to see for themselves."

And it is a fact that in the years to come, caravans made their way once more through that which had been known as the Haunted Pass because it was a quick and convenient route to the rich lands beyond. And it is a fact that the village prospered and that, before he died, the headman became, by the standards of the district, remarkably rich.

Chapter Fifty-four

Spring Comes

They continued their journey across the high, Persian plateau. As the spring advanced it was a wonderful place to be, so unlike the wintry face it had shown on their outward passage, that it might have been a different region entirely. Everywhere was new growth and greenery. There was enough warmth in the air to make sleeping out of doors a pleasure rather than a penance yet there were also plenty of villages and the occasional inn. Te Zhu supplemented their meagre funds by offering her healing services while Xiang Li, from time to time, spent a day or so repairing things that took his interest.

However, it was clear to Te Zhu that home was calling him. Often they covered thirty miles or more in a day, twice that attained by their caravan. At the end of two weeks they arrived at the crossroads where the road continued to Rhaga, the district capital. They turned north and followed the well-worn track up into the Elburz Mountains to the high col where the Chalus River was born. There was snow on the high peaks but none on their path. As they descended the northern slopes, there was birdsong in the tall, moss-hung trees and occasionally, through gaps between the tree trunks, they would glimpse distant views of the Sea.

In the caravanserai at Sari, the Yellow City, seemingly by accident, they became attached to a caravan, heading for Samarkhand. Te Zhu scolded herself for meddling but she fancied the company of others for a while. Walking behind the Gōng was all well and good, but she craved conversation, something for which the goat was ill-equipped. Thus, on hearing that the Head Herdsman was short of skilled help, she let it be known that the strange, tall man, talking to the mule, was a goat-whisperer of the highest order.

For herself, she took on the role of wise woman – doctor – confidante once more and for four weeks she thoroughly enjoyed herself. Xiang Li, she noted, came out of himself more readily with the other herdsmen than he had before. He intrigued them, especially when they found that he could drink heroic amounts of kumis with no apparent ill-effects. In his way he fulfilled a similar role among the herdsmen as Te Zhu occupied in the caravan at large for they found that he was knowledgeable on many subjects. One evening around the camp fire, a herder referred to him as the Magus and the name stuck.

Te Zhu had rather hoped that she might at last get to see Samarkhand but it was not to be. Towards evening, with the walls and towers of the Golden City before them, she saw a lone figure leading a mule, striking off up the rock strewn slope to the east. She sighed.

"Effendi," she said to the caravan master, "I must leave you."

He looked surprised.

"But Samarkhand..." He gestured towards the city.

"I am called to cross the Tien Shan, Effendi. Thank you for your hospitality."

"The Tien Shan, eh? Well, be aware, Mother, that with the spring and the opening of the passes come the brigands. I would say 'have a care' but something tells me that it is the brigands who should be warned."

They laughed together. He gave her a small bag of gold as a thanks offering for her treatment of his haemorrhoids and off she went, into the lengthening shadows, following her master.

Chapter Fifty-five

Dorba Tembay

Spring blended into summer. They crossed the Bactrian Plateau and climbed on into the mountains proper. In the high reaches of the Tien Shan it was cold at night but not the killing cold they had experienced before. After eight days they trudged through the Torugart Pass. Ever practical, Xiang Li timed his passage for the middle of the day, the period of greatest warmth. There was snow up here but it was hard-packed by the hooves of recent caravans so the going was easy, if slippery.

From time to time, Te Zhu became aware of distant figures, watching their progress from vantage points. These, she supposed, were brigands. She was curious to know why they did not attack so one day she made a detour and a hard climb, arriving noiselessly behind a large bearded man. She stood at his elbow, unnoticed, for a full minute, watching the Gōng and the mule, wending their way many feet below.

Then she said, conversationally, "Why don't you attack him?"

The man whirled, a knife ready in his hand.

"Peace, my son," said Te Zhu. "I am merely curious as to why you have not plundered him."

The whites of the man's eyes showed. He made the sign of the horns. Te Zhu encouraged him to answer.

"Why? Why?" the man spluttered. "Because he is touched by the gods, that's why. Anyone can see that."

"Oh," said Te Zhu. "Thank you. Goodbye."

The man never quite recovered from being accosted by the small, female djinn. Unwilling to speak to his colleagues about it, he slipped away and joined the Samarkhand City Guard where, over the course of twenty years' service, he rose to the rank of lance-constable.

Two days after this episode, with Te Zhu trailing Xiang Li across a vast stone field, an enormous, hairy figure carrying a rusty scimitar, stepped out from behind a large rock and planted itself in front of the Gōng.

* * *

The past year had not been not been kind to Dorba Tembay. His sudden access of wealth in the shape of the stolen treasury chest did little but raise his levels of fear and paranoia. Afraid of pursuit he had avoided Samarkhand and ridden Sweet Breath, the camel, hard to the north, into a barren land on the edge of a vast desert. There he made a lair in a remote cave and counted his gold over and over again.

His Voices told him to leave the money there and to support himself by raiding the wretched villages of the region. Word spread of a devil riding a camel which descended on villages in the night, killing and raping, apparently for the joy of it, and making off with food as well as anything else portable. A plea was sent to the local warlord who, piqued that anyone but he should prey upon his people, deployed men-at-arms.

Within a week the devil, galloping openly into a sleeping village, found himself confronted by ten armoured men who shot Sweet Breath from under him and then attempted to take him. The subsequent disorganised meleé, in the dark, resulted in the death or maiming of six of the men-at-arms. However, Dorba Tembay, although he escaped, was wounded in several places. By the time he dragged his pain-racked body within sight of his cave, he saw that it had been occupied by a force of men who had back-tracked along Sweet Breath's trail.

Thus was his treasure lost to him as were many of his remaining wits. A great darkness came upon him. His Voices deserted him. Without plan, his feet carried him south again. A muscle in one of his legs had been severed, leaving him lame. He subsisted on plants and such small animals as came within his reach. It was as if by accident that he wandered, once more, into the Tien Shan Mountains. He felt safe there.

In a moment of clarity, he sought out a brigand band and joined them. However his homicidal tendencies proved too much even for outlaws. In mad anger he hit the chieftain's son such a blow that his nose was driven into his brain and he died. Tembay was pursued for many days and nights, deeper into the mountains and now, desperate, hungry and ill he confronts a man leading a mule. He sways on his feet. For the moment the killing lust is not upon him. All he wishes is to take the mule and whatever it carries, just so long as it is food.

"Give me the mule, little man," he says, waving his scimitar.

The man stops and stares up at him with a puzzled frown.

"Dorba Tembay?" he says. "Yes, it is. Dorba Tembay as I live and breathe! But I am deeply sorry to see you in such reduced circumstances."

Tembay shakes his head. His vision is blurring. There is a buzzing in his head. His Voices have returned.

"Give me the mule. Now ... now … or I'll … split you in two." He raises the scimitar.

Yes, say the Voices. *Kill, Kill, KILL.*

"But you are hungry, Dorba Tembay, and unwell. You have a wound to your leg and, if I am not mistaken it is bleeding."

Kill him NOW, say the Voices. *KILL HIM, KILL HIM!*

The scimitar is high above his head. He totters forward two steps and begins to bring it down in a cut which will sunder the little man.

"Sit down here, Tembay, here on this rock and we will feed you then have a look at that leg."

The scimitar crashes down, missing Xiang Li by inches. Its blade shatters on a rock. Tembay looks at the hilt in his hand in disbelief. "My sword," he groans and breaks into great, sobbing tears. Disgusted by the weakness of their chosen vessel, the

Voices depart and never again return to Tembay in the brief time left to him.

Xiang Li puts an arm around him and helps him to a seat on the rock. He leaves the hapless brigand to sob out his grief while he opens the panniers and puts together a good meal of smoked meat, cheese, hard biscuit and a few wrinkled dates. These, with a water skin, he takes to the big man where he sits hunched over, sniffing, looking utterly dejected. Xiang Li sits beside him.

"Here, Tembay, eat. There is plenty. You must not neglect your diet in remote regions such as these. You must maintain your strength."

Dorba Tembay takes a bite from a hunk of smoked meat then, overcome by hunger, stuffs the whole piece in his mouth and reaches for cheese.

"Woman," calls Xiang Li.

Te Zhu steps out of the shadows from which she has been watching.

"See to Tembay's leg. It is bleeding."

Te Zhu comes forward and inspects the crusted wound. She tears apart the rotting material of his breeches then goes to the panniers, rummages and returns with an armful of herbs and ointments.

"This will hurt," she tells both men. "Gōng, will you still him, please?"

Xiang Li stands and makes to go behind Tembay. The man jerks to his feet.

"Nay, nay, Tembay, I mean you no harm," says Xiang Li. "Settle you and I will take away such pain as I may while the woman works."

Doubtfully, fearfully, Dorba Tembay sits down again and stuffs a handful of biscuit into his mouth. Xiang Li takes his position behind Tembay and places his hands on the man's head. He nods to Te Zhu who begins cleaning the wound. After a quarter of an hour, the wound is as clean as it is going to be. She packs it with healing herbs and bandages it then sits back on her heels and looks up. Tembay is half asleep. She nods at the Gōng who removes his hands. Tembay looks around him and yawns. Te Zhu returns to the shadows. Xiang Li sits beside Dorba Tembay. They are silent for a space then Xiang Li chuckles.

"We had some adventures, did we not, Tembay, when we came up through here last year?"

Dorba Tembay peers at the little man. For the first time in months, perhaps ever, his mind is clear. There are no Voices, no fears. Doubtful recognition dawns.

"Gōng?" he says.

"Yes, I was the Gōng. And you were my caravan master, were you not? And such a caravan master. I doubt that anyone else could have brought us through the mountains in winter."

"Yes," breathes Tembay. "Yes, Tien Shan in winter."

A troubled look comes to his hairy face.

"But Gōng, I leave you. Steal gold. I bad man."

Xiang Li places a hand on his arm.

"All that is forgotten. As far as I understand it, all our sins are forgiven. You see there has been a birth although the Babe will die. And we have all died because of him but are being reborn. The thing is that there is now hope. It is really quite wonderful. Do you see, Tembay?"

Dorba Tembay does not understand but feels a deep peace stealing through him, a peace such as he has never known. Words form in his mind and struggle to make their way to his lips. Finally, for the first time in his life Dorba Tembay says, "Sorry."

He cries a little and the tears make runnels down his filthy face.

"I sorry, Gōng. I bad man."

Xiang Li claps him on the arm.

"No you are not, Tembay. Not anymore. All is forgotten, all is forgiven."

They sit for a while in companionable silence, warmed by the thin afternoon sun. Then Xiang Li turns to Dorba Tembay.

"Will you not travel with me, back to Korla?"

Dorba Tembay considers this.

"No, Gōng. I done bad things. I go say 'sorry'. Then who knows."

He rises to his feet.

"Wait," says Xiang Li. "You will need food."

He rummages in the pannier and makes a rough parcel. He gives it to Dorba Tembay.

"Go well, Tembay."

A great smile breaks across the hairy face.

"You good man, Gōng. I not forget."

Then he turns, smiling, and dragging his wounded leg, sets off into the mountains.

* * *

He was still smiling when his pursuers sprung their ambush, twelve vicious, armed men, bent on revenge. Dorba Tembay turned to the chief and held out his hands.

"I sorry…" he began, but they hamstrung him and the smile died on his lips.

Poor Dorba Tembay, his death was long and cruel. At moments when the tide of pain ebbed a little, he was able to remember that the Gōng had forgiven him. It brought some comfort. At the very end he recalled that the Gōng had said that there was hope and, hoping, he died.

Chapter Fifty-six

The Steppes in Summer

On an evening, before they left the mountains, a large billy goat appeared on a high crag. It bleated. Their own goat stopped, raised its head and bleated back. Te Zhu had been aware for some time that it had entered puberty and was in heat. Now it looked from Xiang Li to Te Zhu and back to the male goat. It bleated plaintively once more.

Xiang Li knelt before it and took its chin in his hand.

"Go, little one," he said. "Have many kids. Be happy."

The goat licked Xiang Li's nose then, bleating happily, scampered off into the rocks. The male goat disappeared from its crag and after a few minutes there was a chorus of bleating followed by silence.

As the solstice arrived, Xiang Li and Te Zhu came out of the mountains at the ruined caravanserai and began the interminable trek across the steppes. Te Zhu gave up the pretence of travelling separately since there was nowhere to hide. She walked just behind the Gōng and shared his camps. For his part Xiang Li continued to ignore her.

It was not long before they came to the dried watercourse where Captain Fong and the guards had died. There, waiting for them on the farther bank, stood a group of Uyghurs, mounted on ponies. Their dress and manner marked them as brigands. Xiang Li led the mule into the bottom of the watercourse and up the further slope.

"Peace," he said, raising his hand as he came abreast of the group. "Have you any cheese or biscuit to trade?"

Cynical laughter met his words. The leader, a small, wizened man, kicked his pony forward a few paces and stopped. He spat. Ignoring Xiang Li he spoke to Te Zhu.

"So, the Holy Fool returns. You must be proud, Mother."

Te Zhu came to stand beside Xiang Li.

"Not proud, dear man. Just very grateful to be nearly home."

"Ha!" said the leader. "And what is to stop us hanging the Fool from yonder tree?"

"Nothing," said Te Zhu. "Nothing but an old woman."

For a long beat their eyes locked then the man sneered and made to turn his pony.

"Stay, Abaddon." Her voice was quiet.

The man kicked the pony viciously. It reared but would not turn. The cords stood out on the man's neck as he wrestled with the animal, but it would not budge. Finally he gave in and turned to face the old woman but the look on his face was deadly.

"Your time is coming to an end, Abaddon, your time and that of your legions. For there has been a birth and there will be a sacrifice and for that sacrifice, you will bay and slaver. Yet it will defeat you, Abaddon. This man is a Witness. As such he is under protection. Do not hazard yourself or your band by threatening him. Now go."

With that the pony turned, bucked once and broke into a gallop. The brigands looked at one another, then at the dust cloud which marked their leader's departure. As one, they turned and followed him. Te Zhu felt a dart of satisfaction followed by a pang of guilt. "Showing off again," she tutted.

"Ah well," said Xiang Li to the mule. "Perhaps they only had enough cheese and biscuits for their own needs."

The mule whickered and they continued their journey.

Chapter Fifty-seven

The Taxman

There were no towns or villages on the steppes but they came across the yurts of the nomadic herds-people from time to time. They were a proud but hospitable folk, living by cultural rules of their own. A place at the fire and a hot meal were always available to strangers and they could have stayed as long as they wanted, had the pull of home not been so strong on Xiang Li. Te Zhu returned the hospitality by doctoring when such was needed. She also picked up valuable gossip as they drew nearer to the populated end of the province.

"Ruled by those fat no-men they say. There have been battles between them. The whole place runs out of control."

The old Uyghur woman spun as she spoke, her hands working the spindle and distaff with unconscious dexterity.

"Me, I'm glad I'm Uyghur. We travel so we don't have to put up with much of the goings on. Mind you," she sniffed, "we suffer when they come out collecting taxes. It's usually some jumped-up little rat who we'd send packing were he not backed up by a section of cavalry. They levy whatever they want and no doubt keep much of it themselves."

"What say people of the governor?" asked Te Zhu.

"Gone travelling these last two years," said the woman. "Some say he's dead, others, mad. Myself I wish he would come back but I doubt he will. He was a dry old stick, by all accounts but at least there was a kind of justice around here then. Now..."

She shrugged.

One morning they were making ready to leave a nomadic settlement when a young man galloped into the circle of yurts, raising dust and shouting. Immediately there was pandemonium. Men and women ran in all directions. Within a few minutes, a group of men mounted their ponies, cut out a large number of sheep, goats and ponies and herded them off until they disappeared in a fold in the ground. Behind them three young boys rode, dragging sheets of yurt material to remove the tracks.

There was a period of peace as the Uyghurs ostentatiously went about their normal business. The headman came across to Xiang Li and Te Zhu.

"Taxmen," he said. "Best you set out before they come."

Te Zhu looked at Xiang Li who was lost in thought.

"No," he said at length. "No, we will stay. But tell me, why do you hide half of your herd?"

The headman snorted. "The level of taxes is clear, has been for years. This man," he jerked his thumb towards the east, "will take twice his due and keep half for himself. So we hide half the herd. He'll still take half of the rest but at least we'll keep our best bloodstock. Otherwise he'll take all the best."

Half an hour later a dust cloud appeared on the eastern horizon. Within minutes it resolved itself into a half-squadron of cavalry, approaching at the trot. As they arrived at the village, the squadron split into two wings which enveloped the yurts. A small man in an ornate robe rode forward with a clerk, escorted by ten soldiers. The headman went to meet him. Xiang Li moved forward so that he could see and hear. Te Zhu followed.

The headman gave the name of the nomadic sub-tribe. The taxman clicked his fingers at the clerk who handed him a bamboo slip. The taxman perused it.

"Twelve sheep, sixteen head of goats and five pairs of ponies or their equivalent in gold," he said then looked over at the depleted herd in their rough pen to one side of the yurts. "Where are the rest of them, old man?"

The headman explained that, as the Gōng would be aware, it had been a poor season. The rains had come late and the wasting sickness...

The Taxman cut him off. "Equivalent in gold?"

"We are a poor tribe, Gōng..."

"Sergeant, take twelve sheep, sixteen head of goats and six pairs of horses." He turned back to the headman. "The extra pair of horses is a penalty for your attitude."

The Headman began to protest. Xiang Li stepped forward.

"May I know at what percentage you are levying tax?" he asked.

The taxman looked down his nose. Before him he saw a ragged, travel-stained man with a straggly beard.

"And who are you?" he asked.

"I am the Gōng Xiang Li, Governor of this province," he said quietly.

For a moment the taxman was taken aback but then he looked more closely at the man, the old woman and the mule.

"And I," he said, "am the Emperor of The Land."

Then he laughed and his escort laughed with him.

"Sergeant," he said, "have a man check those panniers for contraband."

"Gōng!" barked the sergeant. A cavalryman dismounted, went to the mule, unstrapped the panniers and turned them upside down. All their food, their water skins, Te Zhu's pharmacy and their poor belongings fell into the dust. The cavalryman stirred them with his boot until that which was not squashed, was covered in dust.

"No, sergeant," he said when he had finished. "No contraband. Mind you, these are nice panniers."

He offered them up to the sergeant who took them and handed them to another of the men.

Xiang Li, who had watched the proceedings with a lack of passion, turned to the taxman and said in an even voice, "May I know your name?"

The taxman raised his chin. "You may. I am Hwang Ming-Tun and you will address me as Gōng."

Xiang Li folded his arms.

"No, Hwang Ming-Tun," he said, "I will not address you as Gōng. What you have just done makes you an accessory to vandalism and theft. Please return my panniers, otherwise you will be answerable."

"How dare you? How *dare* you, you miserable nobody," said Hwang. "Sergeant, give this man a thrashing."

He turned his horse and walked it out of the circle of yurts.

The sergeant didn't hold any brief for the taxman. He considered him a puffed up little toad. Nor did he hold any ill-will towards the man he had been told to thrash. Indeed, he thought the way the man had stood up to the taxman was the best entertainment he'd had the whole of this never-ending trip. He walked his horse over to Xiang Li, uncoiling a whip from his saddle. He glanced over at the taxman who was busy picking out the best of the flock. He leant down to Xiang Li.

"Right. Let's get this over with. Just make a lot of noise. He won't notice."

He raised his whip and brought it down with a crack, just to the right of Xiang Li.

"Go on, shout," said the sergeant.

It was clear to Te Zhu that the Gōng was not going to co-operate so as the whip descended a second time, she cried "Ow!" in her best baritone. The sergeant smiled at her and went on punishing the dust. After a minute he stopped, coiled his whip and shouted, "Let that be a lesson to you. Don't never cheek the Gōng again."

He winked at Te Zhu and rode off. Shortly afterwards, the tax-gathering party rode away with neither another word nor a backward look. The headman walked over to Xiang Li.

"Thank you for trying but that was very dangerous, you know? He might have had you killed. It has happened before."

Xiang Li smiled. "It was small thanks for your hospitality but it seems to me that it is high time that the Governor returned."

The headman gave them an old set of panniers and they collected such of their belongings as were still usable, then set out again. In later years, at the annual gathering of the Uyghur tribes, the headman would often retell this story.

Chapter Fifty-eight

Korla

On they tramped and on across the never-ending steppes. Occasionally it rained and there were wind storms but mostly they travelled under a peerless blue sky as summer slowly aged. Sometimes Te Zhu thought she was carrying the sky on her back. It felt as if they had been travelling for ever. There was no extreme of heat, cold or danger they had not experienced and so their journey was marked by a serenity which penetrated deep into their bones.

The highway they followed was a wide mesh of tracks, all heading slightly to the south of east. This marked the route of the ubiquitous caravans, transiting from The Land to the great trade route that carried silk and other precious commodities to the markets beyond the mountains. They passed caravans heading west and occasionally shared their camps at night. The closer they came to inhabited lands, the more rumours and gossip they picked up.

"Nay, it was the fat one, I tell you," said one camel puller to another, both of them lit by the dancing flames of the cooking fire.

"It was not," said another. "The fat one was in prison then. It was the ratty one allowed the barbarians through the passes."

"Well, anyway," said the first, waving his hand dismissively, "it is the fat one who is back in power now and, by all accounts, feathering his nest like a … like a … very fat thing with feathers."

"He's holed up in the Summer Palace," said the other. "They say he's too scared for his own safety to go to Korla. Reckon he's holding the Governor's wife there. Kidnapped," he finished darkly.

After many weeks, with summer sliding into autumn, they

came upon the first cultivated land. The looping track narrowed and became one dry, earthen road, slowly losing height as it approached the fertile plains. The harvest was almost in, the fields dusty with chaff. Peasants laboured to load stooks of cereals onto carts. In the orchards, apples and stone fruit were gathered. And yet to Xiang Li's eye, all was not well. It was difficult to tell but yields did not look good and it was essential to the weal of the Province that an abundant harvest should be put away for the winter.

They came to the first of the wind mills which Xiang Li had designed and it stood, unmoving. The Gōng went over to it and laid his hand on the lattice tower, peering upwards.

"Gearing uncoupled," he muttered to himself. "The bearing seized, no doubt. Sheer inefficiency!" he said to the mule.

After this episode, their pace quickened. As ever, Xiang Li said nothing to Te Zhu, but it was evident that his desire to be home was even greater than before. That night there was the first hint of frost.

And so, on an autumn evening, with the first star awake and a chill in the air, they came to the Summer Palace on the Black Lake and found the gates closed for the night. Xiang Li led the mule up to the gates and knocked. After some time a small grille slid open.

"What do you want?" said a hairy mouth.

"I would like to come in," said Xiang Li.

"Well you can't," said the mouth. "Gates open at sunrise."

And the grille slid shut.

The erstwhile ruler of a million subjects sighed, turned and led the mule a few yards away to a grassy spot, sheltered by some large rocks. He removed the panniers then, with a little coaxing, he persuaded the mule to lie down. He wrapped his cloak tight and made himself comfortable within the warm curve of the mule's flank, as he had done a hundred times before.

Te Zhu waited to see him settled then set off, following the wall of the palace. After nearly a quarter of a mile, she came to a small gate. She poked around in the dark for a moment then came up with a large, iron key. With this she opened the door, went within and locked it again. She stood for a few moments, breathing in the night scents of her garden.

She identified blue-flowered onions and lavender, underscored by a pleasing odour of fresh mulch and wood smoke. Then there were dahlias. They must be the last of this year's, on the point of going over. She hoped the gardeners were not leaving it too late to lift the tubers but she had faith in them and, as far as her nose could tell, they had been performing their duties well.

She made her way by winding stone paths to the far corner where there was a hut built against the southern wall of the palace. It was here that herbs were cured and she knew that there would be a charcoal fire banked up to keep everything warm overnight. She also knew, unless there had been any major changes, that there was a small cot where she had often spent summer nights.

She opened the door and saw by the glow of the charcoal that the cot was indeed there and was made up with fresh blankets. She also noted the net bag hanging from the rafters where mice could not get to it. Inside she found fresh bread, cheese and two apples. She smiled and blessed her gardeners. After nearly two years they had not given up on her. She ate a light meal then, making a mental note to wake early, lay down and was quickly asleep.

Chapter Fifty-nine

Awakening

"Mei Su. Wake up, Mei Su."

Mei Su came awake and knuckled her eyes. Who was calling her at this hour? Why? She looked at the window; it was still dark.

"You must get up, Mei Su, and go to the main gates."

She gasped and sat up.

"Te Zhu! Mother! Is that you?"

"Yes, child, it is I and you must get up," said a shadowy figure.

"But, how, why...?"

"No time for questions, child. Arise. Dress warmly then go to the main gates. They will be opening shortly. I will be in the garden such time as you want me."

The figure was gone. Only later did it occur to Mei Su to wonder how it had got past the guard at her door. Or perhaps it had been a sending. In any case, Mei Su threw aside her bed clothes with a feeling of hope which had not been hers for a very long time. She dressed, wrapped herself in furs, then opened the door to her chamber. The sleepy guard came to attention.

"I have been summoned," she said vaguely and swept past the guard before he could object.

Along dim corridors she hurried, past guttering torches and down several flights of stairs. Then she was outside in the street, walking quickly down the slope that led to the gates. Dawn was well-advanced. The eastern towers were outlined in pinky grey but the gates were still closed. She turned aside into the guard house. A sleepy sergeant recognised her and came to his feet.

"My Lady," he said.

"Open the gates," said Mei Su.

"But, my Lady, my orders are..."

"Open the gates, now!" Mei Su stamped her foot.

The sergeant considered his options. They were not extensive. He turned to a pair of guardsmen, standing uncertainly in the shadows.

"You two; open the gates."

The guardsmen hurried outside, followed by the sergeant and Mei Su.

"Stand to the guard!" shouted the sergeant. He had no intention of being found wanting if the Uyghur hordes were waiting outside. With commendable speed, half a dozen guards tumbled out of the guardhouse on the opposite side of the gates and took up a ragged defence line facing the gates, spears at the ready.

The first two guards had removed the massive locking bar and, at a nod from the sergeant, grasped the handles of the right-hand gate and began to haul it open. Before the sergeant knew what was happening, Mei Su had slipped past him and through the widening gap.

"My Lady," he shouted, but she was gone. Cursing, he turned to his defence line.

"Outside, you lot, and make sure you don't spear the Lady."

Mei Su stopped and looked about her, not sure what she was looking for. At first she could see nothing in the grey half-light. Then she made out a dark shape which moved. It gave a whinnying hee-haw. There was a scuffling noise then a dry voice saying, "That time already, mule? Perhaps they will open the gates shortly and we can find you a dry stable and some oats."

She knew that voice although it was slightly hoarse.

"Xiang Li?" she said. "Gōng?"

She took a couple of steps forward and in the growing light saw a man's figure, sitting against the flank of a mule.

"Ah, Mei Su. I see you have prevailed upon them to open the gates at last," it said.

"Xiang Li!" she shrieked and hurried to kneel beside her husband, taking him in her arms.

Oh gods, thought the sergeant, *now we're for it*. "Form honour guard," he ordered. It couldn't do any harm. His bemused squad separated into two short ranks, facing inward, either side of the gates, spears at the carry.

Governor and wife separated, holding each other at arms' length.

"But husband, what have they done to you? You are filthy and that beard..."

"Yes," said the ruler of a million subjects, sniffing his arm, "I suppose I do smell rather badly but it is strange how one ceases to notice these things."

"Well, *I* notice them," said Mei Su. "Come, we must get you to a bath as soon as possible."

She helped him to his feet as though he were an invalid (although, indeed, he was probably fitter and healthier than he had been in his entire life). Timing his order to perfection the sergeant called the honour guard to attention as the Governor, his wife and the mule entered the gates. The sergeant saluted, his whole figure redolent of martial zeal.

"Ah, very good, sergeant," said the Gōng, handing him the mule's bridle. "Would you see that the mule is well-cared for and given some oats. I shall visit her later."

With that, the Gōng Xiang Li, Mandarin of the Ruby Hat-pin, Governor, under the Emperor, of Xinjiang Province, passed within the gates he had left two years before.

Chapter Sixty

Chief Eunuch Ping (5)

Chief Eunuch Ping was awakened by a banging on the door of his chamber. He floundered around amongst his bed clothes and hauled himself upright.

"Yes, what is it?" he shouted, testily. It was surely barely daylight.

The door opened a crack. A pale face inserted itself through the gap.

"The Gōng. It's the Gōng, Master."

Ping ran a hand down his jowls. *The Gōng? Surely not!* Nevertheless, a pang of uneasiness suffused his body. He threw aside the bed clothes and pointed at the frightened clerk.

"Come here and explain yourself."

The clerk pushed himself through the gap and stood trembling just inside.

"Master, the Gōng Xiang Li has returned. The guard sergeant has just sent word. Isn't it wonderful..."

He didn't complete the sentence. The Chief Eunuch had blanched and begun gasping, clutching his chest. The clerk wondered if he was about to witness a heart attack.

"Master..." he began.

"Get out, fool," gasped Ping. "Get *out!*"

The clerk fled.

Ping staggered to his feet. This was a considerably reduced Chief Eunuch. During his year in prison, he had lost much weight and had not regained it in the subsequent six months. His skin hung in folds around his lower torso. Much of his hair had fallen out. Truth be told, his nerves were in a bad way.

He began dressing, his mind in a whirl. Since the overthrow and regrettable death of the usurper, Weng Liang, Ping's cupidity had been much reduced, however, there were still a number of practices and transactions which would not bear the light of day. His mind ran in circles like a squirrel in a cage. It didn't help that he no longer trusted anybody and could thus not call upon a subordinate to help him.

Nevertheless, as he tightened his sash, he squared his shoulders, set his features in an unctuous frown, and set out for the Governor's quarters. As he arrived at the door, it opened and a newly-bathed Governor came out, followed by his wife.

"But you must eat, Gōng," she was saying.

"All in good time, Su. We must look after our beasts, our weapons, our men and last of all, ourselves. I shall return shortly."

Then he caught sight of the Chief Eunuch.

"Ah, Ping, how good it is to see you. You have lost weight."

Ping bowed deeply.

"Most noble Gōng, it is with the deepest pleasure that I, and indeed, the whole population of Korla welcome your august person..."

"Quite, Ping," said Xiang Li. "Come with me. I am going to see my mule."

Ping dared a look at Mei Su but saw only puzzled exasperation. He fell in step with the Governor then found that he was almost running to keep up. After ten steps he was gasping. Xiang Li turned to him.

"Ah, forgive me, Ping. Tramping the steppes does tend to increase one's pace. There, is that better?"

"Gōng," gasped Ping, slowing to a dog trot.

"And how have things been, Ping?" asked Xiang Li.

Ping's mind span. *Where to start?*

"The matter of the Golden Dragon Regiment can be easily explained, Gōng," he began.

"Yes, yes, Ping, but how are you? Have the years treated you well?"

"Well enough Gōng. If I may just explain about the imprest account for minor building works..."

Xiang Li waved his hand.

"Ping, I have been remiss, leaving you with all these cares of government. You must learn to enjoy the beauty of each day. See the way the sun back-lights the peaks to the east? Is it not beautiful?"

They turned into the stables. A loud haw-ing noise echoed down the alleyway. Xiang Li made his way to a box stall where a groom was shining the mule's coat with a handful of straw. The mule, her ears pricked, met him at the gate of the stall. Ping watched in silent amazement as the Governor hugged the mule round its neck while the animal licked his hair with a long pink tongue.

"There, mule, are they looking after you well?"

The mule haw-ed again.

"A handful of oats at each meal," he said to the groom. "She has been on a grass diet and will need feeding up but slowly, slowly."

The groom bowed. "Gōng," he said.

"And apples," said the Gōng. "She is partial to apples."

The groom bowed again.

"I will see you later, my dear," said the Governor to the mule.

He set off back down the alleyway, Ping puffing at his elbow.

"Well," said Xiang Li. "I must have some breakfast. You should have some too, Ping. You need feeding up."

"Gōng," puffed Ping.

The Governor suddenly stopped. Ping cannoned into him. Xiang Li grasped his arm and held him upright.

"Steady, there, Ping. Tell me, do you know of a tax collector named Hwang Ming-Tun?"

He did indeed. Hwang Ming-Tun was involved in one of Ping's wealth-creation schemes. The Chief Eunuch cringed within.

"Aaah, I believe I do, Gōng."

"Well, would you find him for me, please. If he is here, bring him to me after I have breakfasted. If he is out about his duties, send for him." Xiang Li sped off up the street.

"Gōng," said Ping, wearily.

Chapter Sixty-one

The Uyghurs Gain a Champion

An hour later, Hwang Ming-Tun was ushered into the Governor's office. In a spirit of casual spite, Ping had told Hwang that he was to be commended by the Gōng and thus the tax official entered the room only slightly nervous and with his pigeon chest thrust out.

"So, Hwang Ming-Tun, we meet again," said Xiang Li, as the man rose from his deep bow.

"Gōng?" said Hwang. "I … Perhaps there has been a mistake, Gōng. I do not think I have met your august person before."

"But yes, Hwang Ming-Tun. You had me thrashed not two weeks past."

Hwang Ming-Tun goggled, turned white and fainted. His consciousness returned as the Gōng heaved him into a sitting position and pushed his head down.

"Deep breaths," said Xiang Li. "Now, let us help you to a chair. Guard!" he called.

Oh no, thought Hwang. *This is where the beating starts.* The guard crashed to attention.

"Some water please and a cup," said the Gōng.

With the tax collector installed in a chair, clutching a cup, Xiang Li returned behind his desk. He sat and steepled his hands.

"I have had ample time to think on my travels, Hwang Ming-Tun. One thing that seems clear to me is that, as an administration, we have been ignoring the welfare of those of our subjects who follow a nomadic life style.

"I wish, therefore, to appoint an experienced official who will make it his business to liaise between the tribes and the administration. He will, in effect, spend his life travelling the steppes, living with the tribes and reporting back, say, at quarterly intervals. It seems to me that you, with your established knowledge of the tribes, would be an ideal candidate. Your comments, please."

Hwang's mind reeled. He knew himself to be hated by the steppe tribes, for what he was: a corrupt official who preyed upon their wealth. He had only survived under the protection of the Imperial Cavalry. He gulped.

"Would I be given a detachment of cavalry, Gōng?" His voice was barely above a whisper. The Governor appeared to consider for a moment.

"I think not, Hwang Ming-Tun. They would act as a barrier between you and the people. No, you would travel on your own with maybe a clerk and a servant."

Hwang hung his head.

"Gōng," he said, "the tribes hate me. They hate all tax officials. I will, of course, do as you order but I fear you will be sending me to my death."

Xiang Li chuckled.

"Come, come, Hwang Ming-Tun, I'm sure you over-dramatize the situation but I would not send you without some thought and preparation. It seems to me that the thing that the tribes value most is their wealth which is a function of their livestock. Now, how would it be if you were to make a gift of livestock (the best bloodlines, of course) to each tribe? And if it should be that there were not enough beasts to go round, then, shall we say, their equivalent in gold?"

Hwang began to breathe more easily.

"And would I indent on the Provincial Treasury in the usual way for the beasts and gold?" he asked.

"Ah," said Xiang Li, raising his hands. "I'm afraid that will not be possible. As I'm sure you are aware, it has been a poor season. The rains came late and then there was the wasting sickness. The treasury coffers are lamentably low. No, no. Try to think of another source, will you? You have two days."

Xiang Li lifted a bamboo slip and began to read. Realizing he was dismissed, Hwang Ming-Tun rose, bowed and began to back towards the door.

"Oh, and Hwang Ming-Tun: that estimable sergeant, the one who thrashed me? What is his name?"

"It is Sergeant Kwan, Gōng, a most reprehensible ruffian," said Hwang.

"Have the ... reprehensible sergeant sent to me, will you? That will be all."

Half an hour later, having been appraised by Hwang Ming-Tun of the fate that probably awaited him, Sergeant Kwan entered the Governor's office. He was a brave man who had faced the Uyghur hordes in his time, but he didn't give much for his chances of surviving this. He crashed to attention and saluted.

"Gōng!" he shouted.

"Ah, Sergeant Kwan. Stand easy, do. Take a seat." The Gōng gestured to the chair with his stylus.

The soldier eased himself into the chair. It creaked.

"Now sergeant, I should probably chastise you for not flogging me when ordered to do so by your superior so consider yourself chastised. For myself I am grateful for the wisdom and compassion you exercised."

Xiang Li leaned back in his chair.

"Tax Collector Hwang Ming-Tun has agreed to take up a new appointment as a liaison official between the administration and the nomadic tribes of the steppes. It seems to me that he would probably benefit from the company of an experienced body guard, one who can help ease him into what will be a challenging position."

'Challenging' isn't the word I'd use, thought Kwan. *They'll murder the little bugger.*

"This will be a diplomatic position, as much as anything,"

continued the Governor. "Military might will not be appropriate. There are, let us say, certain aspects of the official's manner against which he may need protection. The job will carry with it the rank of Master Sergeant and appropriate allowances. I would like you to take it on. Questions?"

Master Sergeant Kwan had many questions but he also knew when to be silent.

"No? Well, that will be all, Master Sergeant."

Master Sergeant Kwan rose. "Gōng!" he shouted.

Governor Xiang Li came from behind his desk. He held out his hand to the soldier. Kwan looked at it for a moment, then grasped it.

"Thank you, Master Sergeant," said the Governor.

The introduction of the Secretary for Nomadic Tribes to his constituency went roughly as Master Sergeant Kwan had expected. It took all of his tact and strength of character to limit the damage to buffeting and insolence. When it was known that the Secretary was paving his way with highly desirable blood-stock or equivalent in gold, he was merely shunned.

However, thanks to Kwan's obstinacy and a recognition on Hwang's part that he had nowhere else to go, their mission slowly blossomed. In the fullness of time, each man married a Uyghur woman. Tax collection became a good-natured game with unwritten rules which led to hours of scheming and counter-plot.

Hwang Ming-Tun never did develop a head for kumis, but this was not held against him.

Chapter Sixty-two

The Women's Mysteries

Te Zhu parted the curtains which hung across the entrance of the High Priestess' robing room. She took in the rich hangings, the lacquered furniture and the several gold-encrusted statues of the Goddess. She fingered the hem of one of the tapestries. Cloth of gold, no less.

"Te Zhu, I have only just been told."

Te Zhu turned and smiled at the tall woman who had held the office of Fragrant Blossom until two years ago. Te Zhu had thought carefully about who should replace her during her absence. It had not been an easy decision. The post was best filled by someone who combined wisdom with a level of insight into their own weaknesses. Such did exist among the initiates but she knew that by promoting one of them over others, she risked setting up tensions which would cause trouble.

In the end she had appointed Fragrant Blossom, the next most senior, in her place. There was little harm in the woman except perhaps a sense of entitlement which arose from her aristocratic origins.

"Greetings, Du Qianru," she said. She gestured at the rich interior of the little cell. "You have made the place very comfortable."

There was a long moment of silence. Du Qianru had become very used to leading the rituals of the Mysteries. Indeed, she was quite clear that she had been born to the position of High Priestess. Such a post required certain characteristics to which one was born. The corollary – (not characteristics normally found in domestic staff) – she repressed but it was there. Now the moment had come. She could stare down this little woman. She could retain the position which was rightfully hers. She could raise the standard of ritual to a level more according to the solemnity of the task.

All this passed quickly across her mind only to be dispelled by the beauty of Te Zhu's smile. Du Qianru broke into a smile herself.

"It is *so* good to see you, Mother," she said and the two women embraced.

"I will remove my belongings," said Du Qianru.

"Thank you, child," said the High Priestess.

Te Zhu had returned.

* * *

Later, Mei Su sought out Te Zhu in the gardens. She found her deep in discussion with the Head Gardener. They were kneeling before a rose bush, discussing aphids, their habits and natural predators.

"My Lady!" said Te Zhu, rising and dusting off her robe.

"Mother!" said Mei Su and she clung to the little woman, sobbing. The Head Gardener removed himself.

"Hush, child," said Te Zhu, holding Mei Su at arms' length. "You have lost too much weight."

"I was so worried, Te Zhu. We received word that you were alive a year ago but then nothing. I have been so worried. But tell me, what of my husband? He seems so … changed."

Te Zhu led Su to a bench in a spot sheltered from the autumn winds. They sat.

"In what way do you find him changed?" she asked.

Mei Su paused, thinking.

"He seems … softer, maybe? And … distracted, as if he is only half here. Yes, that is it. It seems as though he were hearing messages from somewhere far away, messages that I cannot hear."

Te Zhu took her hand in both of hers.

"Mei Su, your husband has suffered much and been exposed to matters which have challenged his very concept of existence. Yet it is not for me to explain any of this, even if I could, for much is hidden, even from me. What he needs beyond all else, my dear, is your love and patience. For you have a great part to play in his coming to terms with what has happened to him. In the fullness of time he will confide in you as he begins to understand. Do you see?"

Mei Su shook her head, scattering small tear drops from her lashes.

"No, Mother. No I don't understand any more than I understand the Mysteries. But I trust you. You stayed with him through everything and you brought him back to me. For that I shall be forever grateful."

"As to that," said the old woman, smiling and patting Mei Su's hand, "nothing would have stopped him returning to you. He forged across the mountains and steppes like a fiery star with me riding in his wake. But come, child, enough of this. Show me the apricots. Have you looked after them? And did they fruit well this year?"

And the two women stood and wandered deeper into the garden and the gardeners heard their laughter and looked at one another and nodded. All was right with the world again.

Chapter Sixty-three

Administration

"The quota of Kirghiz irregular levées has again fallen short of the treaty requirements."

Chief Eunuch Ping ran his stylus down the list. It was a long list and the Gōng was staring out of the window again.

"Gōng?" he said.

"Hmm? Sorry, Ping. I was ... miles away."

"The Kirghiz irregulars, Gōng?"

"Ah yes. Fine fighters I'm told. Do you know, Ping, we saw a company of them in the far north-west, below the foothills of the mountains, mounted on sturdy ponies. Their alignment was perfect and as we watched they changed direction as one – no evidence of a signal or order – rather like a flock of starlings at twilight. In that setting, the sun sinking behind the far peaks, turning the snow to carmine, it was ... magical."

Xiang Li turned back towards the window, resting his arm along the sill. Ping curbed his impatience. He thought back to those halcyon days when he had been answerable only to himself. He knew what needed to be done and did it. And if a little money was involved and if it found its way into his pocket, why, no-one was the loser.

"Ping." The Gōng had turned from the window and was looking at him.

"Gōng?" said Ping.

"Come. Sit. Drink some wine with me."

The Chief Eunuch felt ill at ease. His relationship with the Governor had always been businesslike and unsentimental. He would not wish to foster anything closer. It would be bad for business. Nevertheless he sat on the cushions indicated. Xiang Li rang a small bell and a servant entered with a tray. Drinks were served, sweetmeats provided and the servant withdrew.

"Are you happy, Ping?"

Oh no, thought Ping but "Why, very happy, Gōng," was what he said.

Xiang Li took a sip of wine then placed his cup carefully on the table in front of him.

"When I was away, Ping, did you find it easy to manage affairs?"

Ping sought for the coming trap but, as yet not perceiving it, answered truthfully.

"On the whole, Gōng, yes but largely because of what I had learnt from you during the years of my service."

Xiang Li nodded. "And did you find ... satisfaction in that management?"

Again, Ping answered truthfully. "I did, Gōng. There is a great satisfaction to be had from setting policies in train and seeing them come to fruition. Although," he went on hastily, "there was ever worry in my mind that I was not arranging matters as well as you would have done, Gōng."

"I doubt that, Ping," said Xiang Li smiling gently. "But, you see, it is in my mind, Ping, that you have proved yourself and I can imagine that it is a matter of some frustration for you to move into a subordinate role again."

He took another sip of wine and selected a locust baked in honey. He bit its head off and chewed for a moment.

"Thus I have a proposition for you."

Ping tensed.

"Continue to run affairs. Simply report to me what you are doing. Refer to me anything about which you are uncertain or which you feel I should decide. Apart from that, you will have a free hand. And as far as the outside world is concerned, matters between us will continue as they ever were. Your comments?"

Thoughts flew around Ping's fertile mind. He could still not see the trap, if one existed, but he could see the ramifications, the opportunities for accruing power and wealth. He bowed his head.

"Gōng, you do me too much honour but, yes, I would be very happy to do as you say."

"Good," said Xiang Li, raising his glass. Ping raised his too and had just taken a large mouthful of wine when Xiang Li said, "But Ping, there is one condition. This. Just this. You will please put away all thoughts of corruption and favouritism. I quite understand that such things are endemic in this our Empire, but I wish them to cease in Xinjiang Province, is that clear?"

Ping swallowed hastily, fearful that he would choke.

"Abundantly, Gōng," he wheezed, busily thinking of what he would do and how he would hide it from the Gōng.

But the curious thing is that, on the whole, he did none of these things. Certainly, in the early stages, he tried but in a strange way, corruption had lost its savour. And if he reported to the Gōng, knowing that he was hiding something, Xiang Li simply looked at him gravely, a small smile playing around his lips. The first time this happened, Ping found himself stuttering to a halt while beads of perspiration stood out on his forehead.

Yet it was not chiefly fear that made an (almost) honest man of Chief Eunuch Ping. It was the discovery that exercising clear, just decisions, without fear or favour, was actually far more challenging than the murky deals to which he was accustomed. Above all he discovered that his mind needed continual stimulation. Corruption, veniality, were easy. Honest government ... ah, now there *was* a challenge.

* * *

Xiang Li meditated upon the journey he had made and its outcome. He sent for skilled artificers from the Imperial City and they built a scale model of the country over which he had travelled, in as exact detail as they could manage. He spent much time in the room given over to the model. Often he would take Mei Su there and show her where he had gone and recount his adventures.

She did her best to show interest as Te Zhu had bade her but, although she could understand how important his memories were to him, she had never journeyed anywhere very much so the exercise became a burden. Sometimes she tried to tell him how she had been waiting for him – how her cat had had kittens, how the frosts had nearly killed the gardenias. He too tried to show an interest but soon his eyes would drift back to the model.

That is not to say that any distance had come between man and wife – quite the contrary. Mei Su found him an attentive husband, much more approachable than before. For his part Xiang Li understood, at least in part, how precious was this woman who loved him and how fragile was life.

* * *

And so the Province of Xinjiang entered a golden age which was talked about for years. Never before were the granaries so full or the orchard trees so heavy with fruit. Brigands who once raided outlying villages melted back into the hills. Many bonny babies were born in those years and they grew up knowing no war; although they nearly did. One situation for which Ping did seek guidance from the Governor was when a large Xiongnu army overran the defences on the mountain border and threatened ArAqmi.

"I have ordered General Zhan north with ten regiments of foot, eight squadrons of cavalry and supporting arms. They will be in position within two days. It is not yet clear what the Xiongnus want or where they will attack. I would be grateful for you wisdom, Gōng."

They were in Xiang Li's turret room. The Governor pulled something from a white-hot bed of charcoal using tongs. He held it close to his smoked goggles and scrutinised it for a moment, before laying it aside. He removed the goggles and wiped sweat from his brow with a rag.

"General Zhan? He's a level-headed man, on the whole. A good tactician, if a little stolid. You are wondering, Ping, if there is some way of avoiding the ravages of a major war?"

"Indeed, Gōng," said Ping.

Xiang Li thought for a moment.

"They will be at the mouth of the Zhuangzi Re-entrant, where the ArAqmi River comes out of the mountains?"

"That is correct, Gōng."

"Hmm," said Xiang Li. "I believe there are examples of the Brown Owl butterfly to be seen on the slopes of the ArAqmi gorge. I shall ride north, Ping. Have my mule made ready."

* * *

"No, Gōng! I forbid it!"

General Zhan's face was suffused with blood. He stood beside Governor Xiang Li on the summit of a rounded ridge, looking across a shallow valley at the Xiongnu array.

"Fortunately, General, you are not in a position to forbid it," said Xiang Li. "Be so good as to provide me with an intelligent, unarmed junior officer who speaks the Xiongnu tongue, one who will not be missed if he fails to return."

For two heartbeats it looked as though General Zhan would explode. Abruptly, he turned to his chief of staff and rattled out some orders. Fifteen minutes later he watched as two men, one mounted on a mule, the other on a horse, approached the front line of the Xiongnu force. The ranks opened and swallowed them.

"How do you think they will do it?" asked the General of his chief of staff.

"I would load the body parts on the beasts and send them back across the valley at the gallop," said the chief of staff.

This didn't answer the question the General thought he had asked, but privately he agreed.

Some hours later an aide shouted. The General emerged from his tent, wiping egg from his mouth. The aide pointed. A man on a horse was cantering towards them across the valley floor.

"Stand the men to," said General Zhan, "but quietly, quietly."

The horse arrived. The subaltern dismounted and saluted.

"The Xiongnus have agreed to withdraw sir," said the officer. He seemed surprised at his own words.

The General looked across the valley. Indeed, the rear Xiongnu regiments were falling out and loading wagons. *Still left a solid rear guard,* he thought, but, then, he would have done the same, given the circumstances.

"How did he do it?" asked the General. "And where is he?"

"As far as I could tell," said the subaltern, "he explained that we would probably beat them although there would be a great slaughter, benefiting nobody but if, by chance, they won, there would always be another army because The Land is very, very strong. He suggested that they pack up and return home, thus saving everyone a lot of time and trouble."

"And that was *it*!" said the General.

"Well, sir, I think they saw the force of the argument but weren't going to back down but then the Gōng said, 'Besides, I wish to explore the slopes of the gorge for Brown Owl butterflies, and you are standing in my way'."

The subaltern's imitation of the Gōng's dry tones had been rather too perfect and the General made a note to take it up with him later.

"They laughed," continued the officer. "When they had quietened down, they called for kumis and insisted that the Gōng drank with them. Do you know, sir," he said, scratching himself reflectively, "they all got very drunk but it seemed to have no effect on the Gōng. In the end he got up, thanked them, asked me to help him onto his mule and set off into the gorge.

Told me to come back and report, sir."

* * *

In the late spring, Mei Su, her cheeks aglow, found Te Zhu in the garden. Te Zhu straightened up with a groan. She looked at her protégé.

"So, it has happened," she said.

Mei Su frowned, then dimpled.

"You *knew*!" she said. "But I should have guessed."

They made their way to the bench in the sheltered corner and calculated.

"Early autumn, then," said Te Zhu. "I am so glad for you, my dear."

Mei Su hugged the old woman.

"But why now?" she asked. "Why after all these years?"

Te Zhu shook her head.

"Some things we are not meant to know, Mei Su, but, look around you. Do you see how fresh the colours look this year? Have you noted the buds ready to burst? Have you ever known the Province so abundant and peaceful?"

Mei Su frowned.

"It all comes from him, doesn't it, Mother?"

"Well, to be precise, I think it would be more correct to say that it comes *through* him, but yes."

Mei Su went into labour as the year waned and was delivered of a baby girl. They called her Ruan. Xiang Li was transfixed by the perfection of his daughter and spent much of his time carrying her around the palace, talking to her.

A son was born the following year. He was named Ming-hua. Xiang Li was overjoyed and made plans for the tutors and instructors who would start his son on the path of the Ruby Hat-pin.

In the third year, despite everything Te Zhu could do, Mei Su died giving birth to a second daughter. After the funeral rites, Xiang Li hid himself away in the model room, alone with his grief and refused to have anything to do with the child who had killed his beloved wife. It was Te Zhu who, after two weeks, took the baby from its wet nurse and marched past the guards into the Gōng's chamber.

"Your daughter," she said, thrusting the child into his arms. "She needs a name and the love of a parent."

The little woman swept open the shutters. Sunlight streamed into the room. The baby stared up at the face hovering above her and belched. Without thinking, Xiang Li lifted her to his shoulder and patted her back. The baby was sick. Xiang Li brought her back into his lap.

"She shall be called Yubi," he said.

Te Zhu went to the door of the chamber and beckoned. Servants entered, bringing with them a cradle, a wet nurse, a large supply of linen napkins and a substantial meal. Gently, Te Zhu took the babe from her father and gave her to the wet nurse who retired to a corner and continued the interrupted feed. The meal was placed before Xiang Li.

"Eat," said Te Zhu to the Gōng, as she had on the journey when his spirits had been low. And Xiang Li found that he was ravenous.

* * *

Xiang Li was bereft. He had been unable properly to share his thoughts with Mei Su but he missed the possibility that one day he might.

Zhiqiang Qiu, the Inspector for the North-western Sector visited at Ping's suggestion and sat with him but even he, subtle mandarin that he was, could make little of the Governor's musings. They seemed to centre around birth and death, their similarities and the prospect of redemption. To a man brought up in the worldly certainties of Confucian philosophy such themes were, at best, ephemeral. He was embarrassed for his friend whose mind had once cut like a diamond and so he visited less and less.

Xiang Li sent messengers in an attempt to make contact with Prince Tareqe and Firenze Zariwalla but only one returned and he was crippled with frost-bite from an attempt to cross the great southern mountains.

So the Governor of Xinjiang Province talked to his children and because they were very young and uncritical, they grew up half-understanding a mystery which was very deep and which would stay with them all their lives. Indeed, it would be true to say that in the years that followed, they would come to understand much more than their father.

* * *

Death comes even to Chief Eunuchs. Ping was found one summer's morning having suffered a massive heart attack in the night. Xiang Li mourned his old colleague and wondered how many years he would outlive him. The Cadre of Eunuchs went into conclave and another Chief was elected by means understood by none but they. Chief Eunuch Tseng was competent and scholarly. Ping had groomed him and two others for the post, especially in the aspects of clean, just government. Tseng understood the complex relationship that had existed between his predecessor and the Governor and so the administration glided on with scarce a pause.

For his part, Xiang Li spent more and more time in his turret room, trying, through alchemy, astrology and other arcane arts, to find some sense of order in existence. When his venerable servant, Kwon Ru, passed away, Te Zhu took it upon herself to become the keeper of the turret room. No-one had asked her to but the damp pain dug deep into her knuckles on winter days in the garden and, anyway, the post appealed to her inquisitive nature. If Xiang Li noticed the change, he said nothing.

And so the years passed. The children grew up. Ruan married and moved far away. Ming-hua passed his provincial examinations for the civil service and moved to the Imperial City. Yubi? Well, Yubi was a special child who lived only half in this world. Perhaps it was Te Zhu who understood where she spent the other half of her life. But Xiang Li caught echoes of it and they loved each other dearly. Te Zhu introduced her at an early age to the palace garden and that was where Yubi spent much of her time. It is given to each of us to find our own successor. Te Zhu also introduced her to the Mysteries and, in the fullness of time, she filled the role of Dark Root, as her mother had before her.

* * *

Few know the scholarly, aesthetic Governor well. He is seldom seen outside the palace yet he is revered far and wide in Xinjiang for reasons which no-one clearly understands. The Imperial Administration has put in train his replacement on several occasions, for he is grown very old, but every time it is pointed out that of all the myriad provinces and districts, Xinjiang is by far the most peaceful and well-governed and so they leave well alone.

And now he sits before the water filled globe. It has been a long vigil. The candle gutters. The globe begins to darken.

The hour grows late and his eyelids, heavy. His head begins to nod. Suddenly he jerks awake. Far away but very distinctly he has heard a cock crow three times. Te Zhu hears it too. She clasps her hands tightly beneath her bosom and closes her eyes.

"The poor, poor Babe," she breathes.

Xiang Li gazes towards the west. It seemed to come from there. But at this hour of the night? How strange. How very strange.

The candle dies. The globe becomes dark.

The Gōng sighs. "Birth or death," he murmurs then nods and nodding, sleeps.

Te Zhu banks up the fires, sweeps away ash and turns down all but one of the lamps. Finally she stands before her master. Gently she tucks a fur around him then stands and smiles.

"Sleep, child," she says, laying a hand briefly on his embroidered cap.

She turns down the remaining lamp and leaves the turret room in darkness.

Historical fiction that lives.

We publish fiction that captures the contrasts, the achievements, the optimism and the radicalism of ordinary and extraordinary times across the world.

We're open to all time periods and we strive to go beyond the narrow, foggy slums of Victorian London. Where are the tales of the people of fifteenth century Australasia? The stories of eighth century India? The voices from Africa, Arabia, cities and forests, deserts and towns? Our books thrill, excite, delight and inspire.

The genres will be broad but clear. Whether we're publishing romance, thrillers, crime, or something else entirely, the unifying themes are timescale and enthusiasm. These books will be a celebration of the chaotic power of the human spirit in difficult times. The reader, when they finish, will snap the book closed with a satisfied smile.